Deborah Franklin stretched out her arm sleepily, moving luxuriously in the bed, a small smile curling her mouth. Last night had been so good. Her body still ached gently from their lovemaking; when she touched her skin, it felt sensually alive and femininely soft. She and Mark had always been good together in bed. Good together in every way. She was so lucky...she had worked hard to achieve her luck, though.

'And Ryan said that he was very pleased with what I'd done. He hinted that there could be more in it for me than just an extra bonus, Mark... He didn't say so outright, but I'm almost sure I'm going to get a promotion out of it.'

'Good for you,' Mark had grunted.

She had laughed good-naturedly. Men never really wanted to talk after sex and she couldn't really blame Mark for being tired.

She'd been on a real high, buoyed up by her boss's praise and the tantalising hints he'd thrown about the possible consequences of her hard work. She'd never been coy about expressing her sexual needs; why should she be? Mark and she were equals in all respects. Admittedly, he was that little bit ahead of her up the career ladder, but then he had joined the partnership before her. In fact, he had been the one to suggest that she leave her previous firm and apply for her present post.

'Why don't *you* put in for it if it's so good?' she had asked him then. He had shaken his head.

'Receivership and insolvency work isn't in my field. I prefer creation, not destruction...'

'A good receiver can keep a company going...' she had protested.

'A receiver, yes...a liquidator, no.'

Deborah had smiled. They had met at university, both of them headed for the fast track. Even then she had set her sights ultimately on a partnership within a large firm of accountants while Mark had wanted a life out of London, finance director on the board of some prosperous Midlands company, perhaps.

As he walked back into the bedroom, she smiled invitingly up at him, patting the empty space next to her in bed.

'Oh, no... not again,' he protested.

Deborah laughed, but Mark wasn't laughing with her, she recognised. He was frowning, turning away from the bed and opening a drawer, extracting clean underwear.

'Mark...'

'I'm sorry, Deborah, but I promised Peter I'd be in early this morning...'

'Are you sure I can't persuade you to change your mind?' she teased him, flirting her fingertips against his stomach and then withdrawing slightly as she felt his body tense.

'What is it, what's wrong?' she asked him quietly.

'Nothing... Look, I'm sorry I have to go but...'

'I know, you promised Peter, but since when has your department been so busy that you need to go in early?' she asked him wryly. 'As I understand it, that side of the business has been hit pretty badly by the recession. You said yourself——'

'Look, Deborah, I know you're feeling pretty pleased with yourself, and I'm pleased for you, but just give the gloating a break for a little while, will you?'

Open-mouthed, Deborah stared after his retreating back. What did he mean, gloating? She hadn't been gloating... she had simply wanted him to share her excitement, her pleasure... her pride in what she had achieved. Gloating... That was the kind of language men used to put women down, but Mark had never been like that. That was one of the reasons she loved him so much. He had always accepted her equality. He had always praised and encouraged her.

He came back into the bedroom, his thick fair hair neatly brushed into shape, and removed a clean shirt from the wardrobe. He then bent to switch on the radio, turning the sound up so that she would have had to raise her voice to speak to him above it.

What was wrong with him this morning?

As she watched him, the newsreader was announcing a suicide, a man found dead in his car. Deborah heard the item without paying it too much attention. It was a depressingly common event these days, and besides, she was much more concerned about Mark's comment to her than she was about the death of an unknown man.

'Bad night?' Elizabeth Humphries asked her husband sympathetically as he let himself into the kitchen. He had been called out on an emergency at two o'clock, a bad accident on the bypass, a young boy on a motorbike with serious injuries.

'With luck he'll make it . . . just, although for a time it was touch and go . . . His left arm was severed and some ribs were broken, causing internal injuries. Luckily someone had had the forethought to pack the arm in ice. Twenty years ago, ten years ago even, it would have been impossible for us to reattach it. Surgery's come a hell of a long way since I first started practising. Not that there's any way I could have done an intricate operation like that.'

'Micro-surgery is not your speciality,' she reminded him. 'But without all the hard work you put in fund-raising, the hospital wouldn't have a micro-surgery unit.'

'I know, I know, but sometimes it makes me feel old, watching these youngsters.'

'You're not old,' she protested. He was three months away from his fifty-fifth birthday. She was five years younger.

They had been married for twenty-eight years and she still loved him as much now as she had done then, albeit in a different way.

'You should be in bed,' he told her. 'Isn't today one of your days at the Citizens Advice Bureau . . . ?'

'Yes.'

No matter how busy he was, how overworked, he always seemed to find time to remember what she was doing. He had been the one who'd encouraged her to do voluntary work when their daughter had first left home.

She had been afraid then, convinced that her services wouldn't be wanted. Now, with the problems caused by the recession, they were busier than they had ever been, so busy, in fact...

She frowned as she heard him saying tiredly, 'We had another emergency tonight... not one we were able to do anything about, unfortunately. A suicide.'

'Oh, poor man!' she exclaimed, putting down the teapot.

'You spoil me, you know,' he told her as she poured him a second cup of tea.

She laughed at him. 'I enjoy doing it. Sara rang. She thinks Katie has chickenpox.'

'Oh, lord. Well, a few spots won't hurt her.'

'No, but Ian is already panicking. You know what doctors are like about their own families.'

'I should do... after all, I am one.'

They both laughed.

'Do you remember the time Sara fell off the swing and broke her arm? You were in a worse state than she was. "It's broken, Daddy," she said. "You'll have to set it."'

'Yes, I remember... I was shaking so much I didn't dare touch her and you had to splint it in the end. Some surgeon. Some father.'

'The best,' she told him lovingly, rubbing her face against his head.

'I hope that young lad survives,' he told her more seriously. 'It's always such a damn waste when we lose a young life like that. Sometimes I think I'm getting too old for this job, too emotional. A surgeon shouldn't have emotions.'

'If you didn't care so much you wouldn't be such a good surgeon,' she told him fiercely. 'People trust you, Richard. And with good reason.'

'I wonder what made him do it?'

'What? Oh—speeding... the usual thing...'

'No, not him, the man who killed himself. Such a dreadful thing to do, to end one's life...'

'Mmm, it's ended for him, but for those closest to him... for his family it's just beginning, poor devils.'

*   *   *

Philippa opened her eyes warily. Andrew's side of the bed was empty and cold. She shivered slightly, although not because she missed his presence beside her; that side of their marriage had soured into dull habit ages ago, after Daniel was born.

No, it wasn't his sexual presence in their bed that she missed.

He had been acting so oddly lately. He had never been easy to talk to at the best of times, hating any hint that she might be questioning his decisions... his dictates, as Rory had rebelliously begun to call them. She had hated it when he had insisted on the boys going to boarding-school, but perhaps it had been for the best. When they were at home it was obvious that they were aware of the atmosphere in the house... the tension... Andrew's irritation.

At half-term he had really lost his temper with Rory. What the hell did he do with his clothes? he had demanded. Didn't he realise how much things cost? And what about her...? Why didn't she see to it that the boys had a more responsible attitude towards their possessions, and why the hell couldn't she stop them from making so much damned noise? Wasn't it enough that he provided her and them with every luxury they could want, breaking his back, working damn near twenty-four hours a day? All he wanted when he came home, all he asked in return was a bit of peace and quiet, a home where he could bring his colleagues and clients without feeling ashamed.

Other wives, he had told her bitterly, managed far better than she did. She had stopped herself from pointing out that other wives probably also knew exactly when their husbands were due home... but over the years she had learned the uselessness of trying to argue with him when he lost his temper.

Wasn't it enough, he had raged, that he worked his bollocks off to provide her with one of the most expensive and impressive houses in the area, a new car every year, and a lifestyle that all their friends envied?

'He doesn't provide them for us...he does it for himself,' Rory had said bitterly when Andrew had slammed out of the house.

Philippa knew it was true, but she had shushed her elder son all the same. Their friends...what friends? she had wondered later. They had no real friends, only people he thought were useful...people he either wanted to impress or who impressed him. Her one and only real local friend he dismissed contemptuously, claiming that she and her husband were simply not their financial equals.

Status was something that was very important to Andrew. It was, for instance, no secret to her that, despite the fact that he never lost an opportunity to criticise her brother Robert and his wife, Lydia, secretly he was eaten up with jealousy of Robert; eaten up with jealousy and bitterly resentful of the fact that Robert's marriage to Lydia had allowed him to enter a world which remained closed to him.

Robert had married Lydia because of who she was, because of her family connections and their money, he had declared.

Philippa had said nothing. How could she? After all, hadn't Andrew married her for exactly the same reasons? And hadn't she, deep down inside herself, known it...known it and refused to listen to the small, desperate inner voice which had begged her to reconsider what she was doing?

She had been too angry to do so...too angry...too proud and too hurt. Since it was obvious that she had no worth, no value as herself, as the person she knew herself to be, since it seemed she was not even to be allowed to define the kind of person she was, then she might as well be the daughter her parents, and most especially her father, wished her to be. That person was the kind of person who would automatically marry someone like Andrew...the other Philippa. Her Philippa...her Philippa no longer existed, had been destroyed a long time ago; she had not been strong enough to fight for survival...not without love to sustain her.

Love. There was certainly no love in the relationship between her and Andrew.

Andrew and Robert had been at school together, Robert the son of the area's most successful and respected businessman, Andrew the son of elderly parents who had produced him late in life. Both of them, Philippa suspected—Andrew's elderly, scholarly father whose main interests were his books and his fossil collection, and Andrew's mother, a timid, quiet woman who had been much in awe of her own mother—had never quite got over the shock of producing a child who was so different in outlook and ambition from themselves.

It was typical of Andrew that when Robert had been appointed chairman of the family company Lydia's uncle owned Andrew had immediately started lobbying for promotion to the board of his own employers.

When that had proved unsuccessful, the last thing Philippa had expected was that he would suddenly decide to resign from his job and buy his own company, his own chairmanship.

She could still remember her feeling of dismay when he had told her what he was doing. His mouth had started to twist with bitterness and, recognising what was coming, her heart had dropped even further.

'Of course if that stupid old bag hadn't gone and left what should have been mine to someone else, I wouldn't need to work at all.'

Philippa had said nothing. There was no point in reminding him that his great-aunt Maud had had every right to leave her money to whomever she chose, even if that someone had turned out to be a six-foot-odd itinerant, a New Zealander who had knocked on her door one summer asking for casual work and who had stayed on over the winter to nurse her when she fell ill and broke her hip—facts of which they had known nothing until after her death, until Andrew, in his rage and disbelief, had virtually accused Tom Forster, twenty-nine to Maud Knighton's eighty-odd, of being his great-aunt's lover and of having seduced his, Andrew's, inheritance away from him.

'How could she do this to me...to our sons?' Andrew had demanded, after he and Philippa had left the solicitor's office.

'Perhaps if we had visited her more...' Philippa had suggested hesitantly.

'What, go traipsing up to Northumberland? How the hell could we have done? You know how impossible it is for me to take time off work.'

Andrew had, of course, typically, threatened to take the matter to court, to have his aunt declared insane and the New Zealander guilty of forcing or threatening her into dispossessing him, but to Philippa's surprise and relief Tom Forster had quietly and calmly offered to share his inheritance with Andrew on a fifty-fifty basis.

Andrew hadn't wanted to accept. He had insisted that the very fact that he had made the offer proved that he knew Andrew would win any court case, but Philippa's father and Robert had put pressure on Andrew to accept.

Robert's emerging political ambitions made it imperative that his background, his family and their histories were all squeaky-clean; the last thing he wanted was the full distasteful story of Andrew's quarrel with Tom Forster splashed all over the less savoury tabloids.

Philippa, sensitive to her father's reactions, had been aware of the way he had distanced himself from Andrew afterwards, but Andrew, she suspected, had not. He was not that sort of man; other people's feelings and reactions had always been things outside his understanding.

The last thing Philippa had expected, after all his complaints about how difficult life was going to be for them now that his expectations of what he would inherit had been so drastically diminished, was that he would actually part with some of the money. Not some of it, she reminded herself now, but all of it and more beside: money he had borrowed from the bank, boasting to her about the size of the loan the bank had given him, saying that showed how highly they regarded him and his business ability. She on the other hand had felt sick at the thought of their owing so much money.

'How on earth will you ever be able to repay it?' she had asked him.

He had laughed at her, telling her she knew nothing whatsoever about business, reminding her scornfully that she had no aptitude for it. 'Your father was right; all the brains in the family went to your brothers.'

Philippa had winced. She had borne the burden of knowing she was a disappointment to her parents all her life. Ideally, they would have preferred another boy, not a girl, and then, when they had discovered that their third child could in no way compete intellectually with their elder two, they had turned away from her, concentrating instead on her brothers. She felt that they had been relieved when Andrew had asked her to marry him. She had only been nineteen, inexperienced and confused about what to make of her life.

'I don't want my wife working,' Andrew had told her importantly once they were married, and she had resigned herself to giving up ideas of a career.

All he wanted her to do was to be a good wife and mother, Andrew had told her. He was the breadwinner, the wage earner. He didn't like these strident modern women who seemed so out of touch with their femininity.

On their first wedding anniversary he had given her a diamond bracelet.

'For my good, pretty girl,' he had told her and then he had made love to her with the thing glittering on her arm. He had spent himself quickly and fiercely, leaving her slightly sore inside and unsatisfied. She remembered that when she had opened her eyes he had not been looking at her but at the bracelet.

She had worn it for the birthday meal he had insisted she invite her parents to. She had felt sick and headachy; she had just been pregnant with Rory, although she hadn't known it at the time.

Andrew had lost his temper with her because the soufflé he had told her to make hadn't risen, his mouth thinning into an angry, tight line.

He had never been a violent husband, but he had always resented anything that challenged his authority in even the smallest way. Her inability to make a perfect soufflé had been a challenge to that authority. His authority over her. His desire that she at all times reflect his success...his power...his massive ego.

When the children had been born it was just the same. They had to be a credit to him...always.

No, he had never been an easy man to live with, although no one else seemed to be aware of it. She was lucky to be married to him, other people told her. He was a good husband, her family said...adding approvingly that he had done well.

Just lately, though, he had seemed increasingly on edge, his temper flaring over the smallest thing. One moment he would be complaining about the amount she had spent on housekeeping, or protesting furiously about money she had spent on plants for the garden, the next he was announcing that he was buying a new car...that they were going on an expensive holiday.

When she had protested bewilderedly at his attitude, he had told her harshly that it was important to keep up appearances.

Appearances... Appearances were all-important to Andrew. She might not have much intelligence but at least she was pretty, her father had once said disparagingly.

Pretty...

'Why do I want to marry you? Because I love you, pretty little thing,' Andrew had told her when he proposed, then, 'I can't wait to show you off to everyone,' he had told her when they got engaged, and, looking back, it seemed to her now that he had enjoyed her company in public far more than he had ever done in private.

Pretty... How she had grown to dislike that word.

She could hear a car coming up the drive. She got up, sliding out of bed and pulling on her housecoat. It was silk...a Christmas present from Andrew, 'To wear when we stay with the Ronaldsons,' he had told her with a smile.

'I feel so sorry for him. That wife of his isn't just plain, she's downright ugly.'

'He loves her,' she had told him quietly.

'Don't be a fool. No man would love a woman who looks like that. He married her for her money; everyone knows that.'

The car had stopped. She frowned as she opened the bedroom door. The engine had sounded different from Andrew's new Jaguar.

At first when he had started coming home later and later, she had assumed he was having an affair, and she had been surprised at how little she had minded, but then she had discovered that what he had actually been doing was working.

She had begun to worry then, but when she had tried to talk to him he had told her not to pester him.

'For God's sake, I've got enough on my mind without you nagging me,' he had told her. 'Just leave me alone, will you? This damned recession...'

'If things are that bad, perhaps we should sell the house,' she had suggested, 'take the boys out of private school.'

'Do what...? You stupid fool, we might as well take out an advertisement in *The Times* to announce that we're going bust as do that... have you no sense? The last thing I need right now is to have people losing confidence in us, and that's exactly what will happen if we sell this place.'

Last weekend they had gone to see her brother and Robert and Andrew had played golf, leaving Philippa and Lydia to a rather disjointed afternoon of talk. When the men had got back there was a strained atmosphere between them and Andrew had announced that they had to leave.

Philippa hadn't been sorry to go. She and Robert had never been close. She had always been much closer to her other brother, Michael, and Lydia she had never liked at all. Andrew still hadn't come in. She went downstairs, thinking he must have forgotten his keys. When she opened the door and saw the police car outside, she tensed.

'Mrs Ryecart?'

The policeman came towards her. There was a police-woman with him. Both of them had grave faces.

'If we might just come in...'

She knew, of course...had known straight away that Andrew was dead, but she had thought it must be an accident...not this...not a deliberate taking of his own life. They had tried to break it to her gently. Found in his car...the engine running...unfortunately reached the hospital too late.

Suicide.

WPC Lewis would stay with her, the policeman was saying quietly. 'Is there anyone else you'd like us to inform...your husband's parents...?'

Philippa shook her head.

'I'll make you a cup of tea,' the WPC was saying. 'You've had a shock.'

Suicide...

She started to tremble violently.

CHAPTER ONE

'MUM, Paul's still in the bathroom and he won't let me in.'

Sally paused on the landing, grimacing as she stooped down to pick up the sock she had dropped on her last trip downstairs with the dirty washing. Her back still ached from working yesterday.

'Paul, hurry up,' she commanded as she rapped on the bathroom door.

'He *knows* I'm going to Jane's and I'm going to be late now,' Cathy wailed.

'No, you won't,' Sally soothed her daughter. 'He'll be out in a minute.'

'He's doing it deliberately. I hate him,' Cathy announced passionately.

Sally had just finished loading the washing machine when Paul came into the kitchen. Was he never going to stop growing? she wondered. Those new jeans she had bought for him last month were already too short.

'Where's Dad?' he demanded.

'He's not back yet,' she told him.

Joel had been irritable and difficult to live with ever since they had heard the news that Andrew Ryecart had committed suicide. Sally knew that he was worried about his job, but there was no need to take it out on them—it wasn't their fault!

'He said he was going to come home early,' Paul grumbled. 'He was going to take me fishing.'

Sally's face tightened. This wouldn't be the first time recently that Joel had done something like this. Only last week they'd had a row about the fact that he'd forgotten that she'd arranged for them to go round to her sister's and had arranged to play snooker instead.

'You were the one who arranged to see them,' he had countered when she had complained.

'Well, someone had to,' she had told him. 'If it was left to you we'd never see anyone from one blue moon to another.'

'I forgot,' he'd told her, shrugging the matter aside as though it weren't important. Unwilling to continue arguing with him in front of the children, Sally had gritted her teeth and said nothing, but inwardly she had been seething.

She had still been angry with him about it later that night when he had come in from his snooker match, walking away from him when he started telling her about it and later turning her back on him in bed, freezing her body into rejecting immobility when he had reached out and touched her breast.

They had argued about that as well. In hushed, angry whispers so as not to wake the children. They were getting older now and Cathy in particular was becoming sharply aware. Only a couple of months ago she had come home from school asking if Sally and Joel still had sex.

'Well, you shouldn't have had much problem answering that one,' Joel had grunted when she'd told him.

She frowned again, remembering the conversation which had followed.

'I suppose that's going to be another excuse, is it?' Joel had demanded aggressively. 'You don't want the kids overhearing us. Not that there is very much to overhear these days.'

'Sex—you're obsessed with it,' she had countered. 'We can't discuss anything these days without your turning it into an argument about sex.'

'Perhaps that's because arguing about it is just about all we do,' he had told her angrily.

It hadn't always been like this between them—far from it. When they had first married...when they had first met...

She had been a shy, awkward girl of fourteen, her shyness made worse by the fact that she and her parents had only recently moved into the area. At school she had felt isolated and friendless. Her sister, seven years her senior, was already adult, and it was probably inevitable that the others should have picked up on her loneliness and started bullying her.

It had been Joel who had come to her rescue; two years older than her, a tall, dark-haired, broad-shouldered boy with an air of solid self-confidence about him on which she had instinctively and gratefully leaned.

He was the middle child in a family of five, with two older sisters and a pair of younger, twin brothers. The chaotic and unruly household absent-mindedly presided over by his mother had been in such direct contrast to her own orderly home lifestyle that it had fascinated her. Joel's father was a loud, boisterous bear of a man who made his living in a variety of different ways, from running a market stall to working in a friend's pub.

He had something of the gypsy in him, both in his looks and his way of life. Joel's mother had, so local gossip went, married down when she'd married him. Vague and fragile, and completely unworldly, she treated her children as though she was still not quite convinced that she had actually produced them.

Her elder daughter was more a mother to her siblings than a sister, and Joel at sixteen, already mature beyond his years, had been someone for Sally's fourteen-year-old self to look up to with shy adoration.

They had grown apart after they left school, Joel to begin his apprenticeship and she to begin nursing, and had only met again later through a mutual friend.

There had been sexual attraction enough between them then and more than enough to spare, although Joel had not rushed her into bed.

She had liked that in him. It showed restraint—and respect.

Initially, her parents hadn't been too keen on their marrying. Her mother had cherished hopes of her marrying a doctor, and Sally had had to suffer listening to her mother's praises of her sister Daphne's marriage to a teacher, a white-collar worker.

Both her parents and Joel's were dead now, and Joel's brothers and sisters had moved right away from the Lincolnshire town where they had been born and raised. The only family close by now was Sally's sister Daphne, and Daphne always managed to make Sally feel inferior, second-rate. She and Joel had never liked one another and she knew that Joel disliked her visiting her sister.

'What's wrong with you now?' Joel had demanded after Daphne had summoned her so that she could show off her new kitchen.

'Nothing,' she had retorted, but later that night, looking round her own kitchen, she had suddenly started to contrast it and the rest of her home with Daphne's much larger house. When Joel had seen the kitchen brochures she had brought home, his mouth had compressed immediately.

'A new kitchen?' he had stormed. 'Are you crazy, Sal— have you seen the price of this stuff?'

The quarrel that had followed had been one of the worst they had ever had.

'We could take out a loan for it,' Sally had told Joel stubbornly. 'That's what Daphne and Clifford did. I could work extra hours to pay for it and——'

'No,' Joel had interrupted her. 'We can't afford it and I don't want——'

'We couldn't afford for you to have a new car or a garage to keep it in,' Sally had pointed out bitterly. 'But you still got them.'

She had known from the white look round his lips that she had gone too far, but stubbornly she had refused to take the words back. Instead she had continued recklessly, 'If I'm going to have to work to pay for your car, Joel, I might as well do a bit extra and pay for something *I* want as well.'

Joel hadn't made any response, but the look on his face, in his eyes, had made her catch her bottom lip between her teeth.

Joel was a very proud man—too proud, she sometimes thought—but then her guilt had changed to irritation. Why should *she* be the one to feel bad just because *she* wanted a new kitchen? Was it really so much to ask? The trouble with Joel was that his precious pride was more important to him than she was, or so she was beginning to think.

In the end, Joel had given way and she had got her kitchen. The units weren't the same as her sister's expensive hand-painted ones, of course. Joel had installed theirs himself, working in the evenings and at weekends, and the day he had finished them she had come home from night duty to find that he had worked all through the night to get them finished.

He had grinned at her like a boy as he'd invited her to admire his handiwork, sweeping her up into his arms and kissing her.

He had smelled of wood and paint and sweat, his exuberance reminding her of the boy he had been when they first met.

The kitchen had been perfect...just what she had wanted, and she hadn't resisted when he had whispered suggestively to her that they play out a certain sexy scene from the film *Fatal Attraction* to celebrate its completion...

Paul had put on his coat and was opening the back door.

'Where are you going?' Sally asked him sharply.

'Round to Jack's,' he told her. 'Dad still isn't back and it's going to be too late now.'

She let him go, feeling her irritation against Joel grow. It wasn't fair, the way he always put himself first and refused to pull his weight, leaving her to do everything.

It had been all right, expecting her to run the house and take care of all the kids' needs when she was at home, but now that she was working...

'So stop working,' he had told her last week when she had come home to find the house in a mess and him sitting in front of the television.

'You know I can't,' she had protested. 'We *need* the money.'

'I'm ready, Mum...'

She forced herself to smile at Cathy as she came into the kitchen.

'OK, love, I'll take you now. Don't forget, your dad's picking you up.'

'Huh...if he remembers. Mum, can we go to Florida next year? Nearly everyone in the class has been except for me.'

'Florida's very expensive, Cathy...'

Sally hadn't told Joel, but she had already decided that she was going to try and put something aside from her wages into a special holiday account. She'd love to take the kids to Disneyland. Another few years or so and they would be too old to really enjoy it. It would be worth making a few sacrifices, and if she and Joel both put the same amount away each month...

'Don't forget,' she reminded Cathy as she dropped her off outside her friend's home, 'you're not to leave until your dad comes to pick you up.'

'All right, all right. I'm not a baby, you know,' Cathy told her as she rolled her eyes and tossed her hair.

Physically, Cathy took after Joel's mother, being small, blonde and far too pretty. She had none of Sally's thick dark hair and, thankfully, seldom revealed any of the tension that often clouded Sally's deep brown eyes.

Temperamentally Cathy was far stronger than Joel's mother and, if neither of their children had shown any signs of the superior intelligence Daphne claimed for her son, Edward, they were both doing well enough at school for Sally to feel secretly very proud of them.

It was nice to have the house to herself, she acknowledged when she got back; not that she was likely to have any time to appreciate her solitude. Unlike Joel, she could not sit down in front of the television set oblivious to the chaos around her.

Upstairs the bathroom floor was covered in wet towels and someone had left the shower gel open on the shower floor, so that its contents was oozing wastefully away.

'You should make the children contribute more to the household work,' Daphne had remonstrated with her when she had called round unexpectedly one day and found her sister up to her eyes in domestic chores.

'The way you do with Edward?' Sally had commented wryly.

'Edward is a very special child. With his level of intelligence he needs a constant input of intellectual stimuli to prevent him getting bored. Besides, he's naturally a very tidy boy. Your two need the discipline of taking responsibility for certain domestic chores. But then, of course, I suppose it is difficult for you. If Joel were a different kind of man... Clifford is marvellous in the house. He wouldn't dream of sitting down and expecting me to do everything... but then of course it's all down to background, isn't it?' she had added. 'And with Joel's family background...'

Daphne hadn't meant to be unkind. It was just that, as the older sister, she had always seemed to think it her role to have the freedom to comment on and criticise Sally's family and way of life.

'She's a snob,' Joel had once commented blatantly, and a part of Sally agreed with him, but naturally, since Daphne was her sister, she had felt duty-bound to defend her. She looked at her watch.

She had another half hour before she needed to leave for work.

She finished cleaning the bathroom, emptied the washing machine and refilled it. Both Cathy's and Paul's bedrooms were fearsomely untidy, but she hardened her heart. They both knew that they were supposed to tidy their own rooms.

Where was Joel? Irritably she scribbled him a note, reminding him that he had to pick Cathy up and that he had forgotten his promise to Paul.

It must be nice to be a man, and not have to worry about domestic routine and arrangements, safe in the knowledge that there was someone else there to cope. Well, she reflected, she didn't have that luxury, and if she didn't leave in five minutes flat Sister was going to be reminding her that every minute she was late meant that either someone else had to cover for her or the ward went unstaffed... Sister was a stickler for punctuality, and who could blame her? If only she could impose the same awareness of responsibility on Joel that Sister imposed on her ward nurses.

As she finally locked the back door behind her, she breathed a small sigh of relief.

Wearily Joel opened the back door. The kitchen smelled cold and empty, unlike the kitchen of his childhood where his brothers and sisters had always played. But his mother hadn't always been there, too caught up in doing other things, just like...

He dismissed the thought irritably. No one could ever accuse Sally of not being a good mother—far from it. She doted on Paul and Cathy. Spoiled them, made it obvious that their needs came first in her life—well before his.

He frowned as he caught sight of the note on the kitchen table.

Pick up Cathy. All he wanted to do was to sit down and unwind, to think about what was happening at work.

They had all known that Andrew's suicide had to be bad news for the company. It had been obvious for months that things weren't going well. No one seemed to know exactly what was going to happen, but everyone was afraid that it would mean more job losses, more redundancies.

The other men had turned to him, as foreman, for reassurance and explanations, but he hadn't been able to give them, and on top of his own feelings of anxiety and uncertainty he had felt as though he was somehow failing them, letting them down in not being able to supply the answers to their questions.

He had tried to see the works manager, but the pale, thin girl who was his secretary had simply shaken her head. The last thing he needed was to come home to an empty house and a terse note from Sally complaining because he had forgotten he had promised to take Paul fishing. Didn't she realise how serious the situation was?

He had tried to ring to explain that he was going to be late, but the phone had been engaged.

He hadn't eaten anything all day and his stomach felt empty, but the last thing he wanted was food. He looked at the note again and then checked his watch. He might as well go straight round for Cathy.

Jane's mother gave him an amused look as she opened the door.

'I've come to collect Cathy,' he told her.

She was a plump, slightly over-made-up blonde, the smile she gave him just a little bit too suggestive as she told him, 'Lucky Cathy,' and added, 'Look, why don't you come in and have a drink? And I dare say we could find you something to eat,' she added as they both heard his empty stomach growl protestingly.

'Thanks but I'd better not. Sally's got supper on,' he lied.

'Oh...I thought she was working tonight.' The blonde was pouting slightly now, the pale blue eyes narrowing.

He'd never been a man who enjoyed the dangers of flirting, but her obvious availability and sexuality were making him sharply aware of the contrast between her attitude towards him and Sally's.

His body hungered for the comfort of sexual contact with Sally, but these days she just didn't want to know. Sometimes he felt the only reason she stayed with him was out of habit and because he provided a home for her and the children plus a steady income to support them all. It certainly wasn't because she wanted to be with him.

The children were more important to her than he was. Much more important.

Cathy chattered excitedly all the way home.

'Lindsay Roberts went to Disneyland for her summer holiday,' she told him. 'She was telling everyone about it. When can we go, Dad? Everyone else in my class has been.'

'Stop exaggerating, Cathy,' he told her sharply. Too sharply, he realised when she suddenly fell silent and he saw the sullen pout of her mouth and the tears shining in her eyes.

'Why are you so mean?' she demanded angrily. 'Mum wants us to go.'

'I'm not being mean, Cathy...I...'

He stopped. How did you tell a fifteen-year-old that the way things were right now you were lucky to be able to pay the mortgage, never mind pay for expensive American holidays?

'You're mean,' Cathy told him. '*And* you forgot that you promised to take Paul fishing.

'I wish I lived in a big house like Lindsay's with a garden all the way round it.'

Joel' s mouth tightened. It wasn't Cathy's fault, he told himself. Kids *were* more materialistic these days; the whole world was more materialistic.

'Aunt Daphne's having an extension built on to her house, with a new bathroom. I heard her telling Mum.'

Paul was in the kitchen when they got back. Tiredly, Joel apologised to him and started to explain, but Paul wasn't listening.

'It's OK... I didn't want to go fishing anyway,' he told him curtly.

Joel had never found it easy to get on with his son. He had always felt that Sally over-indulged him, much more so than he had ever been indulged as a boy. He could scarcely even remember his mother spending much time with him. She had not been the maternal type, despite giving birth to five children. Sally, on the other hand, had cosseted and protected Paul to the point where Joel had sometimes felt when he was a baby that he wasn't even allowed to touch him.

'You're too hard on him. He's a child, that's all,' Sally would protest whenever he attempted to discipline him.

'Mum said to tell you that there's cottage pie in the fridge for supper,' Cathy informed him. 'But I don't want any.'

'Neither do I,' Paul announced.

Joel paused in the act of opening the fridge door and then closed it again. The phone rang and he went to answer it. It was the foreman in charge of one of the other production lines at the factory.

'Fancy a pint?' he asked.

Joel sighed under his breath.

'I can't,' he told him flatly. 'Sally's at work and I've got to stay in with the kids.'

'When I grow up I'm *never* going to get married,' Cathy announced when he had replaced the receiver. 'And I'm going to have lots and lots of money and go to America as often as I like.'

'Cathy...' Joel began, and then stopped. What was the point? How could he explain to her?

Later, when both children had gone to bed, he prowled restlessly round the living-room, too on edge to sit down and watch the television. No one knew yet exactly what was going to happen with the factory, but, whatever it was, he already had a gut feeling that it wasn't going to be good.

As a boy he had felt the effects of his father's careless attitude towards a settled existence and regular, reliable work; his mother hadn't seemed to care that some weeks there wasn't any food in the house.

'Make sure you ask for seconds at dinnertime,' Beth, one of his older sisters, had instructed him when he first started school.

He had promised himself even before he and Sally married that his kids would never know the indignity of that kind of poverty; that they would never suffer the effects of that kind of parental irresponsibility.

Three years ago, when Sally had tentatively suggested trying for another baby, he had shaken his head and tried to explain to her how he felt.

Six months later, he had had a vasectomy. Was he imagining it, or was it after that that she had started to lose interest in him sexually, as though she no longer wanted him now that he could not provide her with a child...now that he could no longer fulfil his biological role in her life?

And if he lost his job and he could no longer fulfil his role as breadwinner either, would she reject him even more?

He went into the kitchen and made himself a cup of tea, absent-mindedly leaving the empty unrinsed milk bottle on the worktop.

One of the other men had said to him this afternoon, 'What the hell are we going to do if this place does close down? There's nowhere else for us to go. Not in this town.'

'No,' he had agreed. 'Nor anywhere else locally either. The engineering industry's been hit badly by the recession.'

What he really wanted was to have Sally here at home listening to him while he told her how worried he was, he admitted as he switched on the television and then switched it off again.

She never seemed to have time to listen to him any more, and then she complained that *he* never talked to her.

Increasingly recently at Kilcoyne's he had worked hard in his role as foreman to mediate between the men and the management, and as overtime had stopped and the men had felt the effects in their wage packets he had had them coming to him complaining that they were finding it difficult to manage.

He was in exactly the same boat, but because he was their foreman he had felt unable to point this out to them and tell them that he had his own problems.

He had never really wanted Sally to go out to work, and she wouldn't have had to either if he hadn't been fool enough to take out that extra loan to buy a new car, and then she had wanted a new kitchen—like her sister.

None of them had known then just how high interest rates were going to rise, and, even though now the payments were easier, they were still heavily in debt to the bank. At the time it had seemed worth taking the risk, he had told himself it had been worth it, and that night when Sally had walked in just as he was finishing the kitchen ... It had been a long time since they had made love like that, since he had felt her body clench with excitement and need when he touched her. He had felt really good that night. Happy... secure... a king in command of his own small personal world. And then six weeks later the company had gone on to short time, and Sally had announced that, since he was making such a fuss about the cost of the kitchen, she'd pay off the loan herself.

It had been too late then to take back the angry words he had uttered in the panic of realising just what the drop in his weekly wage was going to be.

And besides, Sally had been proved right. They couldn't have managed without the money she was bringing in.

Knowing that hurt him more than he wanted to admit. He had tried to tell Sally that, to explain, but she just didn't seem to want to listen.

She had changed since she'd started working, even though she herself refused to admit it, grown away from him, made him feel he was no longer important to her.

'You're lucky,' one of the men had said to him today. 'At least your *wife's* in work.'

Lucky. If only they knew.

Sally hummed to herself as she walked down the ward. She always enjoyed her work on Men's Surgical. She paused by Kenneth Drummond's bedside, responding to his warm smile. The forty-five-year-old university lecturer had been very badly injured in a serious road accident several months earlier, and she had got to know him quite well during his lengthy stay in hospital.

She had been on night duty during his first critical weeks under special care and a deep rapport invariably developed between such patients and the staff who nursed them. At times she had felt as though she had almost been willing him to live, reluctant to go off duty in case without her there he might give up and let go of his precarious hold on life.

It was a feeling no one outside the nursing profession could really be expected to understand. Joel certainly hadn't done so.

'You'll have heard my news, I expect,' Kenneth commented as she smiled back at him.

'Yes, Wednesday, isn't it? You'll be glad to get away from here, I expect.'

'Not really.' His smile disappeared. 'To be honest with you, I'm feeling rather apprehensive about it. Not because of any lack of faith in your surgeon's hard work,' he told her. 'He's assured me that he's put enough pins and bolts in me to hold up the Eiffel Tower. No, it's not that.'

'Still, you are bound to feel a bit anxious,' Sally comforted him. 'It's only natural.'

'Mmm. But it's not so much that. To be honest with you, it's the loneliness I'm dreading.' He pulled a wry face. 'I don't suppose I should admit to that, should I? Very unmacho of me. We men are supposed to be tough guys who don't admit to any kind of emotional vulnerability...until we're somewhere like this. I don't know how you nurses manage to put up with us. You can't be left with a very high opinion of the male sex after you've heard us crying into our pillows.'

'It isn't always easy,' Sally admitted. 'It hurts seeing that someone's in pain and that you know you can't always do anything about it. Mind you, it's nothing to what you hear down on the labour ward,' she told him, trying to lighten his mood. 'Of course it's the men who get the worst of it down there. Woe betide any male nurse who tries to tell a woman in the middle of her contractions just to remember how to breathe and everything will be all right...'

'Yes. I've always thought that, when it comes to bearing pain, women are far braver than men and far more stoical.'

'Not necessarily,' Sally told him with a grin. 'I cursed Joel, my husband, to hell and back when I was having Cathy. I swore afterwards that nothing would ever make me go through anything like that again.' She smiled reminiscently.

'You've got two children, haven't you?' Kenneth asked her.

'Yes. I would have liked another, but...'

She stopped, frowning. It wasn't like her to confide so easily in anyone, especially a patient.

'Have you any children?' she asked him directly.

Although he had talked to her a lot during the months he had been in hospital, he had never mentioned any family.

'Yes and no. My wife and I are divorced. She remarried and lives in Australia now.' His expression changed. 'I'm afraid I wasn't either a good husband or a good father. We married very young, straight out of university. Rebecca was pregnant at the time and she blamed me, quite rightly, I suppose, for the fact that her career was over before it had even started. A termination wasn't an option in those days and neither really was single motherhood. James, our second son, was born following an ill-timed attempt at marital reconciliation. We separated before he was born. They—my sons—are adults now, and anyway they look on their stepfather as their father, and quite rightly, so it's ridiculous of me to lie here feeling sorry for myself because I'm going home to an empty house when, in truth, it is empty through my own choice.'

'Have you no one...no family or friend...who could come in and help you out for a few days?' Sally asked him, concerned. He was making a good recovery from his injuries, much better in fact than anyone had believed when he had first been brought in, but it would still be several months before he was able to move about easily on his repaired leg, despite what the surgeon might have to say about his handiwork.

'Not really...' He shrugged his shoulders, powerfully muscled from the exercises the physio had been giving him. 'My colleagues at the university have done more than enough already. I can hardly expect them to do any more. I suppose I'm lucky that I'm in a profession where this——' he touched his injured leg '—hasn't meant that I've lost my job. Lucky in fact still to have the leg,' he added, his face suddenly grave.

'Yes,' Sally agreed simply.

When he had first been brought in there had been a danger that his left leg might have to be amputated, his injuries had been so severe.

'You know, lying here these last few weeks has proved something of a double-edged sword. Once the immediate danger is over and you know you're going to live, you find that you have time on your hands to think about all those things you've pushed into the deepest cupboards of your mind, all hidden safely out of sight and then avoided on the grounds that there simply isn't time to deal with them,' he told her sombrely. 'Having a busy life is a wonderful excuse for not dealing with one's deeper emotional problems, as I've discovered.

'When my wife used to accuse me of being selfish, of living in my own world, I always felt she was being unfair. After all, I had stood by her, hadn't I? I married her, provided a home for her and the family. It's only while I've been lying here that I've come to realise what she meant ... I *was* selfish.' He paused, watching the effect his words were having on Sally, but her expression reassured him, the sympathy in her eyes encouraging him to go on.

'I'm a very orderly man,' he told her. 'I like neatness and tidiness. It comes, I suspect, of being an only child. She was just the opposite, and when I complained about coming home to the disorder of a household containing a small child she would point out, quite rightly, that she simply didn't have the time to do everything.

'I suspect that part of my irritation stemmed from resentment of the fact that she put the baby's needs before mine. I've always believed that she was the one who abandoned our marriage, who broke faith with it by having an affair with another man.' He paused and gave Sally a painful look. 'Oh, yes, she managed to find time for that. No doubt the appeal of spending time in bed with her lover was far greater than that of doing the housework ...

'I shouldn't be criticising her though,' he added, shaking his head. 'I realise now that in many ways I had never properly committed myself to our marriage. The family was a duty, a responsibility I shouldered because it was the right thing to do and then, having been seen to do the right thing in the eyes of the world and publicly, I privately turned my back on them by giving to my work, and consequently to myself, my self-esteem, my ego, the time and attention I should have given them.

'Will you think very badly of me if I tell you that there were many many nights when I deliberately made extra work for myself rather than go home; that I preferred the quiet calm of my work to the noisy, untidy chaos of our home?'

'No,' Sally told him honestly, shaking her head. How could she say anything else, when she too knew what it was like to dread returning home, even if it was for different reasons?

'We should never have married, of course. We weren't suited; we didn't even really like one another. I was never the kind of man she wanted, as she proved when she left me. Her lover was all the things I wasn't and am not...'

Sally made a soft, sympathetic sound that made him stop and smile ruefully at her.

'Oh, I don't envy him...in any way. His type of competitive macho sexuality has never been something I've wanted to emulate. There, now I really have revealed my inner self to you,' he told her.

Sally flushed a little as she looked away from him. He was so very different from Joel—in every way. Joel would never talk to her as openly as Kenneth was doing, never discuss his innermost feelings with *anyone*, never reveal any aspect of himself which might show him in a bad light. Like the man Kenneth's wife had left him for, Joel too possessed a competitive male sexuality.

Kenneth's nature was kinder...warmer. A small shadow touched her face, and, seeing it, Kenneth told her gently, '*You* are all the things a woman should be, Sally. All the things any man could possibly want in a woman...'

Sally made a small protesting sound beneath her breath, but he heard it and shook his head.

'No, it's true. And so is something else.' He turned his head and looked at her. 'I'm going to miss you and our conversations very, very much indeed...'

'All patients miss their nurses when they first go home,' Sally told him huskily.

'Ah...I suppose that's a tactful way of telling me that all male patients fall a little in love with their nurses,' he retaliated. 'Very true. Although in my case I suspect it's rather more than a little. You must be very glad that you're happily married, and that you've got a wisely protective husband to stand between you and the endless stream of smitten male patients who would probably make your life a misery with their protests of undying love.'

He was smiling at her with his mouth, but his eyes were unsmiling. His eyes... She caught her breath.

It was just as well he *was* going home, she told herself severely half an hour later when she went for her break.

Sally grimaced disgustedly as she walked into the kitchen and caught sight of the empty, unwashed milk bottle. Joel had left three used teabags in the sink and they had made a dirty brown stain on the surface she had left clean and shining when she went to work. His mug was on the worktop, unwashed. She scooped up the teabags with one hand and turned on the hot tap with the other, her mouth compressing. She could hear Joel coming downstairs, but she didn't turn round.

'Do you *have* to leave the place in such a mess, Joel?' she demanded as he came into the kitchen.

She could tell from the sound of his feet that he was wearing his slippers, which meant that he wasn't dressed...which meant... She could feel her stomach muscles tightening protestingly, resentfully, her whole body tensing when he came up behind her and slid his arms round her, trying to nuzzle his face into her neck as he told her, 'It's Saturday morning. Leave all that and come to bed. You must be worn out.'

'Too worn out for what you've got in mind,' she told him shortly, edging away from him, relieved when he abruptly let go of her.

'For goodness' sake, aren't I allowed even to touch you now? What's the matter with you?'

'*Nothing's* the matter with *me*,' she denied, turning round. 'And as for touching me...all you ever want these days is sex, sex, sex. Why don't you think about what I might want for a change? Like not coming home to find the place looking like a tip...'

'It's an empty milk bottle, Sal, that's all,' Joel told her wearily. 'OK, so I should have rinsed it out, but to be honest with you I had other things on my mind——'

'Just as you had other things on your mind when you were supposed to come home early and take Paul fishing, I suppose,' she interrupted him angrily. 'You're always accusing me of spending too much time with the kids, Joel, but whose fault is that? If you spent a bit more time with them yourself...'

'They don't want me...they...'

He stopped when he saw the stubborn look on her face.

'I tried to ring, but the phone was engaged. Probably that sister of yours boasting about her new extension...'

Sally stared at him. 'How do you know about that?'

'Cathy told me. It seems this house isn't good enough for her any more. She wants to live somewhere with a garden all the way round it. When you're complaining to her, perhaps you ought to try explaining to her that if you'd got yourself a husband like your sister's she might have been in with a chance,' he added bitterly.

'Oh for goodness' sake, Joel, stop feeling so sorry for yourself,' Sally protested. 'If you could see some of the patients from the wards...' She stopped abruptly, tensing inwardly as she recognised what she was doing. It was unfair of her to compare Joel to Kenneth Drummond. Unfair and unwise? 'Look, it's been a long night and I'm tired. If you go up and get dressed now you could do the supermarket shopping while it's still quiet and then——'

'Yeah...and pushing the trolley will give me something else to think about instead of sex, sex, sex—is that it?'

Sally flinched as she saw the bitterness in his eyes, but she was not going to give way and be bullied into making love with him. If he wanted to sulk like a spoiled child, well, then, let him.

'Sally...'

Gritting her teeth, she ignored him, keeping her back turned until she heard him leave the kitchen. Upstairs in the bathroom, Joel showered angrily, turning the water to its fullest force, welcoming the savage pounding on his skin as a release of his tension. He hadn't wanted to have sex with Sally, he had simply wanted to touch her...to hold her, to make her focus her attention on him and listen to him while he tried to explain. To explain what? That he was afraid... Oh, she would love that. The last thing she had time to do these days was to listen to his problems.

She ought not to have been so uptight with Joel, Sally admitted tiredly as she pulled the duvet over herself. She'd make it up to him later... cook him a special supper, bribe the kids to stay out of the way, try to get him to listen while she tried to explain what she wanted from him, *needed* from him now that she was working.

Yes, they could talk later.

CHAPTER TWO

'GOODNESS, I'd forgotten how bad London traffic is, hadn't you?' Deborah exclaimed. 'Emma said it was eight for dinner at eight-thirty. Will we make it in time, do you think?'

Without waiting for Mark to reply, she added, 'I can't believe it's over eighteen months since we last saw them. Their moving down to London has made the distance too great between us for frequent visits.'

She gave Mark a quick, amused look as he stamped hard on the brakes and cursed as someone cut in front of him.

'I told you you should have let me drive the London stretch of the journey,' she reminded him cheerfully. 'You know I'm a much better driver than you.'

'You mean a much more aggressive one,' he retorted.

'My driving is not aggressive, it's simply self-assured,' Deborah corrected him. 'I think we have to take a left here, Mark... Oh, no, you missed it. Now we'll have to go all the way round again. You really should...' She saw the muscle starting to twitch in his jaw and bit back the comment she had been about to make, saying instead, 'Ryan told us on Friday that we're going to be appointed as liquidators for Kilcoyne's. No official announcement has been made as yet. They're going to wait until after the funeral for that. Apart from the bank there are quite a lot of trade creditors outstanding. Not that they're likely to recover very much. The bank seems to have all the security pretty well tied up——'

'Where did you say we had to turn?' he interrupted her tersely. Mark had never enjoyed city driving or heavy traffic. Unlike her. She positively revelled in the cut and thrust of it, the tussle of wills with other drivers, the challenge of outwitting them.

'Wow...do you think we've got the right place?' Deborah asked when they finally reached the address Emma had given her. It was a quiet, elegant square, and, while it might not compare in size or grandeur with some of London's more famous squares, it was nevertheless very obviously an exclusive and expensive address.

'Toby must be doing well if they can afford somewhere like this,' she added as they left the car. 'Emma said he'd recently bought into an accountancy practice. Quite an upmarket one too, apparently.'

'Well, that should please her,' Mark commented sourly. 'She always was a bit of a social climber.'

Deborah eyed him in surprise. 'She's ambitious, that's all—she wants Toby to succeed.'

'Of course she does, she wants him to succeed so that she can boast about how well he's done to her friends. What happened to *her* career, by the way? As I remember it, she'd got it all planned that she was going to make a big name for herself in the media.'

'Well, she was doing very well until the TV station she was with lost its franchise. It was a case of last in first out. Since then she's been doing some part-time PR work for a friend.'

'Part-time PR work—well, they certainly haven't bought this place with what she's earning from that,' Mark announced as he eyed the elegant façade of the building in front of them.

Deborah watched him thoughtfully as she pressed the intercom buzzer. He had been so scratchy and grouchy lately, so unlike his normal placid, calm self.

Emma came down herself to let them in. Small and vivacious, her tiny frame and delicate features hid a personality that was extremely strong-willed and tenacious. She was not a woman's woman, and unlike Deborah she had made few friends at university. Deborah had found her competitiveness more amusing than threatening and had often teased her about the streak of conventionality which had made her insist almost as soon as they had left university that she and Toby marry instead of opting to live together as Deborah and Mark had chosen to do.

She and Mark had been invited to the wedding. A lavish affair held at a small, carefully chosen village where Emma just happened to have an ancient relative living. It had been a fairy-tale occasion, and a tribute to Emma's talents as a master tactician and planner.

'Mmm...this is really something,' Deborah enthused generously as Emma ushered them into the apartment. 'You could virtually fit the whole of our place into your living-room and have space to spare, couldn't you, Mark?' she commented as she admired the expensive silk curtains and the specially woven off-white carpet that covered the floor. 'You must be doing very well, Toby,' she added when Emma's husband brought her her drink.

'Oh, it's nothing to do with me,' he told her without smiling. 'Emma bought this place herself—with her own money.'

Deborah felt her scalp prickle slightly as she picked up on the highly charged atmosphere which had suddenly developed. She looked helplessly at Mark, who was standing looking out of one of the long Georgian sash windows.

'Don't pay any attention to Toby,' Emma advised brittly as she flashed her husband a quelling look. 'I've already told him, if he wants to make a fool of himself by behaving like a spoilt child then that's his choice.'

Despite the elegant comfort of the antique-furnished traditional dining-room and the excellence of the meal Emma served, Deborah was relieved when it was finally over. Emma and Toby had barely talked to one another all evening other than to make sniping remarks at one another. Toby made constant references to Emma's money, in between sneeringly putting her down and being irritatingly sorry for himself.

After dinner, while Toby took Mark off to his study to show him his new state-of-the-art computerised set-up, Deborah helped Emma to clear the table and wash the expensive antique dinner service she had used for the meal.

'This is lovely,' she commented appreciatively as she carefully dried one of the plates.

'It's Sèvres,' Emma told her. 'I only bought it a month ago and Toby's already broken one of the plates—deliberately, of course. I never imagined he would ever behave like this, Deborah—he's so childish, so resentful; but, after all, why shouldn't I enjoy the money and spend it on what I want? My grandmother left it to me, not to me and Toby. He seems to think that just because we're a couple...just because he's the man, he should be the one to make the financial decisions within our relationship and to have the financial power. That's what it's all about, of course. He was quite happy when he was the one earning more than me, making me feel I should be grateful to him when he insisted on buying me something, paying when we went out—not that that happened very often,' she added darkly. 'That's another thing I've discovered about him recently: he can be unbearably mean. Take this dinner service, for instance...he wouldn't speak to me for three days after I'd bought it and I don't know what he's complaining about really; after all, I did give him the money to buy into the partnership, and, all right, so I haven't had this place put in joint names, but after all that's only common sense, isn't it, with the divorce rate as high as it is?

'He seems to think I'm deliberately trying to humiliate him by letting people know that I'm the one with the money. You wouldn't believe how unpleasant he's being...mind you, you could see for yourself the way he is tonight, couldn't you, embarrassing us all with his childishness? I've told him he must either accept things the way they are and live with them or——' She gave a small shrug.

'You mean you'd leave him, end your marriage?' Deborah asked her, shocked.

'Why shouldn't I? No woman needs to stay in a relationship that isn't working for her any more, does she, especially not one with the financial assets that I've got? I've warned him, if he doesn't like what's on offer there are plenty more men who would.'

'You're not wearing your engagement ring,' Deborah commented as she dried the last plate.

'No...' Emma gave a small shrug. 'I was never very keen on it in the first place. My grandmother left me a lovely antique ring which I'm having cleaned and re-sized. I'll probably wear that instead.'

Deborah frowned, remembering the excitement and triumph with which Emma had flaunted the small diamond Toby had given her the day they got engaged, but she had to agree with her that Toby did seem to be behaving unreasonably and unfairly. He had made it more than plain over dinner how much he resented Emma's inheritance.

'Take it from me, Deborah,' Emma warned her as she dried her hands and smoothed on hand cream, 'when a man tells you that he sees you as an equal, don't believe him. What he means is that he's perfectly prepared to pretend that he does, just so long as he remains more equal than you.'

Some men might be like that, Deborah reflected as she rejoined Toby and Mark, but Mark certainly wasn't one of them. One of the reasons she had been drawn to him in the first place was his quiet air of calmness, his lack of the kind of keen competitive edge that sometimes drove her; she was wise enough to recognise that, no matter how challenging a relationship with a kindred spirit might be, in the end its sheer intensity and ferocity would burn itself out.

She loved Mark and she admired him for all the qualities he possessed which she did not. She applauded his intelligence and diligence, and the very lack of the ruthless drive to gather and hold power, which the others had teased him for at university, was among the qualities she admired most in him. Mark, with his steadfast, quiet strength, counterbalanced her own impetuosity and impatience. She valued his judgement and, although she would never have admitted it to anyone, least of all him, for fear of ridicule, a small, secret part of her was still semi-inclined to set him apart from the other men she knew, to place him, if not on a pedestal, then certainly far above men such as Ryan Bridges, her immediate boss, whose Machiavellian nature and love of intrigue and power had taken him in ten years with the practice from a newly qualified lackey to a partnership and control over the receivership and liquidation section of the business—via, it had to be admitted, an astute marriage to the daughter of one of the most senior partners who had died only a couple of years after his retirement.

It was a well-known fact within the company that Ryan was not above breaking his marriage vows when it suited him, but his affairs were invariably brief and always ended should the recipient of his attentions begin to interpret them as anything other than the brief satisfaction of his sexual needs and ego.

Even while a part of her unwillingly admired him for his sheer drive and determination, Deborah knew that she could never be happy with a man like that. He might pay lip-service to the ideas of female equality, but lip service was all it was, even if his department did have a far larger proportion of qualified female staff than any of the others. There was a reason for that, and it had nothing to do with the superiority of the girls' accountancy qualifications.

No one spending any length of time in the department could miss the fact that Ryan had a taste for tall, long-legged young women, nor that he enjoyed overwhelming their intelligence and common sense with his sexuality.

He had tried it on with her when she'd first joined the firm, but she had made it more than plain that she just wasn't interested. Since then he had treated her with amusement and knowingness. He was a very sexually overpowering man, in every sense of the word. At six feet two, he had the physique and the handsomely battered face of an ex-rugby player, and at thirty-five he possessed such strong sexuality that sometimes Deborah felt as though you could almost smell it on the air after he had left the room.

She was constantly torn between admiration and loathing of him. As an accountant, a fellow professional, she admired him and all that he had achieved; as a woman . . . She gave a small shiver, redirecting her thoughts to the couple they had just left as Mark unlocked the car.

'What a dreadful evening,' she commented as he started the engine. 'Poor Emma, I felt so sorry for her. I never imagined that Toby could ever behave so badly...'

Mark was frowning.

'What exactly do you mean, Toby is behaving badly? Quite frankly I thought he showed remarkable restraint. If I'd been him I think I'd have throttled her well before we reached the main course, and smashed every bit of her damned dinner service into the bargain. God, I don't know how he stands it. It must be like selling your soul to the devil. She's certainly got the whiphand in that relationship, and you can see that she intends to use it.'

'What do you mean?' Deborah asked him, frowning. 'It is her money; it's only natural that she should feel she has a right to decide how it's spent...'

'Oh, yeah, it's her money all right; she made sure we all knew that, didn't she? I've never seen a man so humiliated and emasculated. Poor sod, he told me that when they go to bed now he feels like a stud being paid for sex. He says it's totally changed her, and that——'

'A stud—Toby?' Deborah started to laugh.

'What's so funny?' Mark asked her curtly.

'Well, it's just that Toby... and you... well, you're just not the stud type, are you... not like...?'

She winced as Mark crashed through the gears, realising too late that she had offended him. 'Mark, I didn't mean that as a complaint... I like you the way you are,' she told him gently, reaching out and touching his knee lightly. 'As far as I'm concerned, over-sexed, pushy men are a complete turn-off. All they can think about is their own satisfaction. They never see past their own egos or even think about what a woman might want.'

'Whereas poor unsexy sods like me have to make sure we know all about how to make our partners happy if we're ever going to be lucky enough to get a decent lay... is that what you're saying?'

Deborah gave him a surprised look. What on earth had got into him? He was reacting as though she had been criticising him personally and not merely passing comment on the evening and the relationship between Emma and Toby.

'Well, at least having too much money is never likely to be a problem we'll have to face,' she told him with a grin. 'I don't have any rich old grandmother wanting to leave me her all...'

'It isn't the money, it's the way Emma's using it as a weapon to bludgeon the life out of Toby that's the problem,' Mark told her. 'And the way she's enjoying doing it. That's what really sickens me...'

'Mark, that isn't true!'

'Isn't it?' he asked her grimly. 'Would you admit it, even if you thought it was, or would you just close ranks in female solidarity?'

'That's unfair,' Deborah protested. 'I'd never support another woman simply because she was a woman. You know me better than that, surely.'

'Yes, I'm sorry,' he agreed. 'It's just that I'm feeling a bit edgy at the moment. Peter said there were comments made at last week's partnership meeting about the fact that the income from our section is down—again—and guess who got a real kick out of pointing it out?'

'Ryan?' Deborah hazarded. 'Well, you can't blame him for feeling pleased that we're doing so well. Splitting the receivership and liquidation side of things off into a separate department was his idea. I know he can be a bit over the top at times.'

'He's a clever bastard, I'll give him that.'

'Yes, you have to admire him for what he's achieved,' Deborah agreed.

'But not for the way he's achieved it.' Mark pointed out.

'No,' she agreed, stifling a yawn. 'I still can't believe how much Emma and Toby have changed. She always seemed to lean on him so much...'

'A real clinging vine, and now that she's outgrown his support she's threatening to strangle him. She's one of the most manipulative women I've ever met. I wouldn't be surprised if she'd staged the whole thing tonight, just to give her grounds to divorce him.'

'Oh, Mark, that's not fair.'

'Isn't it? You know you can be very naïve when it comes to human motivations.'

'Mmm...perhaps, but not naïve enough not to know how lucky I am to have you,' she told him lovingly as he stopped for some traffic lights and she leaned across to kiss him lightly. 'Seeing Toby with Emma tonight made me realise all over again how lucky I am to have you. He was so obviously jealous of her, Mark, it was horrible, so demeaning for both of them. I could never imagine you behaving like that. You've always encouraged me to stretch myself and grow...you were the one who talked me into applying for this job and persuaded me I could do it... You've always been so generous both personally and professionally.'

'Ah, perhaps that's because I enjoy the superior role of mentor,' he told her teasingly.

'Superior...we'll see about that,' Deborah challenged back, laughing at him as he bent his head to kiss her and then cursed as the lights changed to green and the car behind made a noisy protest at his slowness.

'Mmm...that was lovely,' Deborah commented drowsily as she smoothed her fingertip lovingly down Mark's back. It was still slightly damp with perspiration from their lovemaking and she bent her head to breathe in the scent of him and kiss the indentation of his spine.

'Hey, I thought you said you wanted to leave early in the morning...'

'Mmm...so I did, but it isn't morning yet, is it?' she teased him as she stroked her hand over his hipbone and the vulnerable flesh of his stomach.

Mark had a lovely body, wholesomely, perfectly male in a way that never failed to delight her senses. Unlike Ryan, who was so obviously and overpoweringly sexual that the fastidious side of her nature automatically retreated from such potency.

Mark's sexuality was far more subtle than that, and, to her, far, far more erotic. He was a generous lover, experi-

enced enough to know how to please her but not so arrogant as to resent her showing him how he could increase
that pleasure.

She herself was an uninhibited lover, her sexuality both
voluptuous and yet at the same time unexpectedly refined,
so that she always carried with her an air of somehow being
slightly set apart from the rest of her sex.

Some men...men like Ryan...seemed to find that a
challenge that irked and irritated them. Mark was not like
that, though. He accepted that, no matter how sensually
voluptuous she might be in bed, when they were not in bed
the other side of her nature was repulsed by the kind of
man who had to make constant sexual comments and
innuendo.

She laughed herself at the odd marriage within her of
sensualist and prude, but no one else other than Mark was
allowed to laugh about it with her. While she was quite
happy not to be married, she believed totally in a monog-
amous relationship and in fidelity within that relationship.
She would never dream of being unfaithful to Mark, and
if she ever did it would mean that their relationship was
over. And if he was unfaithful to her? Her fingers ceased
their erotic journey as she stared into the darkness.

Mark would never do that to her; he knew how much
he meant to her. He knew how much she needed and depended on him, even if others did not. It wasn't just love
and desire that kept them together, it was trust as well,
trust and respect; shared goals and ambitions and a shared
belief in one another; a shared support for one another.

As a child she had been teased for being too much of an
idealist, and so she had learned to conceal that vulnerability within her, but Mark knew it was there.

'How do I look?' she asked him a short while later when
they had torn themselves out of bed.

'Fine,' Mark replied absently without turning round.

'Oh, Mark,' she protested.

'What is it?' He put down his razor and turned round.

'You can't have forgotten,' Deborah protested.

'Forgotten what?'

'That Ryan's taking me out to lunch.'

Mark grunted. 'Oh, that—probably wants to proposition you—again.'

'No, it isn't that...he's been dropping hints all week about how pleased he's been with my work and how much the department is expanding. I think this is it, Mark...I think he's actually going to put me in charge of my own section...give me something to really get my teeth into...'

'Some poor bankrupt to savage, you mean...wow, won't that be great?'

Deborah gave him a startled look. There was a thread of acid bitterness in his voice that she had never heard before. 'Look, I know you don't like that side of things...'

'Save it until tonight, will you, Deborah? I've got a hell of a lot on my mind right now. Somehow I don't think your department's the only one in for a reshuffle, only we're on the down side of the seesaw.'

Deborah frowned. 'What do you mean, Mark—what's...?'

'Forget it,' he told her. 'I'm just a bit on edge, that's all. Good luck at lunchtime, and a fiver on it that he will proposition you.'

Deborah laughed. 'The way you did the first time we went to bed. Remember?'

'As I remember it, you were the one who did the propositioning on that occasion.'

'I was drunk...It was Dutch courage...'

'Not the next day when you rang up to ask me if it was still on for dinner, it wasn't,' he reminded her with a grin.

'All right, so I finally got tired of waiting for you to do the asking, but I don't recall ever hearing you say no.'

They were both laughing as he leaned over to kiss her. Last night had been good between them, Deborah reflected happily as she finished getting dressed. Very good! She loved it that their sexual relationship was so harmonious; it made her feel complete, wholly, fully alive and fully a woman. She would hate to have the kind of lover who bullied or domineered her...the kind of lover that a man like Ryan would be, or the kind Emma complained that Toby had become.

'So...you're looking very pleased with yourself today... good night last night?'

Deborah smiled vaguely, tucking a strand of her sleekly bobbed chestnut hair behind her ear. 'Yes, as a matter of fact it was; we had dinner with some old friends.'

She knew what Ryan was trying to do, but she wasn't going to be tricked into playing that game.

He had brought her to one of the area's most exclusive and expensive restaurants for lunch and it hadn't escaped her notice that the majority of the other lunchers there were very obviously couples.

'Nice place, this, isn't it?' he asked her. 'You should see the bedrooms, all four-poster beds and the fabrics all silk and velvet...very sensual...very tactile...very romantic.'

Deborah refused to respond. She knew from experience that sooner rather than later he would lose interest and stop baiting her. And halfway through their main course he did.

'I like you, Deborah,' he told her, 'and I like the way you work. You're intelligent and ambitious and you know how to get the best out of people...how to handle them, and that's something that's very important in our line of work. We're dealing with people at their most vulnerable and volatile and therefore at their most dangerous... It's just as well Andrew Ryecart committed suicide before we were appointed and not after. It wouldn't do the firm's reputation a lot of good to have that kind of thing splashed all over the papers. You'll know that we've been appointed to handle the liquidation?'

'Yes.'

'It's going to be a tricky one; there are no assets to speak of, and there is some suggestion of misuse of company funds before he killed himself. The bank are reasonably securely covered; there's a fairly large equity in the house, plus the value of the site—we'll never be able to find a buyer for the business as a going concern, of course, and the trade creditors won't get much.'

'And the workforce?'

'Preferred creditors.' He gave a small shrug. 'That will be the first thing you'll have to do, of course: issue them all with redundancy notices. Then it will be a matter of going through the books and...'

Deborah's heart had started to thump heavily with excitement but she fought to control it, asking carefully, 'Does that mean that you're putting me in charge of the liquidation?'

Ryan put down his cutlery. 'Is that what you want?' he asked her quizzically. Deborah laughed. Even now he still could not resist flirting with her.

'It's certainly a step in the right direction,' she agreed demurely.

'Mmm...' he agreed softly. 'I thought it might be.'

Careful, Deb, Deborah warned herself as she caught the undertone in his voice, but before she could make any comment he had started outlining what he planned to do, the staff he intended to put under her authority.

'This one might seem easy, but that doesn't mean it *will* be,' he warned her. 'There's going to be a lot of bad feeling stirred up locally; the widow doesn't have a clue about what's going on or the fact that she's virtually going to be out on the street. Luckily there's family money there.'

They discussed the procedures involved over the rest of their lunch and when they finally got up to leave Deborah's heart was singing with excitement. She couldn't wait to get home and tell Mark her good news. They had made a rule not to have any contact with one another at work of a personal nature, and she knew what he would say if she broke it, even for something as important as this. Unlike Ryan's, Mark's ethics were fixed and wholly reliable.

'There will be an increase in salary, of course,' Ryan told her as they left the restaurant. 'Oh, and a new company car. What's Mark got?' he asked casually. Absently

Deborah told him, cars were not something that interested her very much.

'Ah, well, yours will be the more upmarket model, but I'm sure you'll be able to find a way of soothing any hurt male pride.'

Deborah looked at him. What on earth was he talking about? Mark simply wasn't that kind of man. No, Mark would be as thrilled for her as she would have been for him if their positions had been reversed. She and Mark had a totally equal and loving relationship in which neither of them competed with the other, but supported and protected one another instead.

Mark...Mark. Oh, she couldn't wait for tonight... They would really celebrate...not at some expensive restaurant, but at home, together...in bed. She hugged the anticipatory pleasure of what she was thinking to herself as Ryan drove them back into town.

CHAPTER THREE

'IF DAD'S really dead does that mean that we can come home and live with you and go to school there?' Daniel said to her.

Philippa closed her eyes as she felt the weakening rush of relief surge inside her. All the way on the drive up here to their school she had been worrying about the boys' reaction to Andrew's death, but now as she stood with her arms around both of them, her face resting protectively against Daniel's head, she was forced to recognise that the distance and uninterest with which Andrew had always treated his sons was reciprocated in their calm acceptance of his death.

She had gently urged Andrew repeatedly to spend more time with them, to involve himself more in their lives, but he had dismissed her fears about the gulf she could see between them as typical feminine over-reaction.

'Boarding-school will be good for them,' he had insisted. 'It will teach them how to be men. You're too soft with them. Always kissing and cuddling them.' The rest of the family had supported his decision.

'Boys need discipline,' her elder brother had told her, adding disapprovingly, 'You're far too over-indulgent with your two, Philippa. If you're not careful you're going to turn them into a pair of——'

'Of what?' she had challenged him quietly. 'A pair of caring, compassionate human beings?'

She had regretted her outburst later, especially when she had walked past the open study door and heard Robert telling her husband, 'That's the trouble with Philippa; she's always been inclined to be over-emotional; but then that's women for you, bless 'em.'

The condescension in her brother's voice had made her grit her teeth, but years of being told as a child that girls

did not argue or lose their tempers, and that pretty girls
like her should be grateful for the fact that they were pretty
and not go spoiling themselves by being aggressive and
argumentative, had had their effect.

She often wondered what her parents would have said if
she had ever turned round and told them that she would
cheerfully have traded in her prettiness for the opportunity
to be allowed all the privileges of self-expression and self-
determination that her brothers possessed. That her blonde
hair and blue eyes, her small heart-shaped face with its full-
lipped soft mouth, her slender feminine figure and the fact
that by some alchemic fusing and mixing of genes she had
been given a set of features that combined to make her
look both youthful and yet at the same time alluring were
not in fact assets which she prized but a burden to her.
People reacted to the way she looked, not the person she
was, and she found this just as distressing; it made her feel
just as vulnerable and undervalued as it would have done
a girl who was her complete physical opposite. People only
saw her prettiness; they did not see her; they did not, she
suspected, want to see her. It had been her father who had
been the strictest at forcing on her the role model of pretty,
compliant daughter, praising her when friends and family
commented on the way she looked and curtly reprimanding
her when her behaviour did not conform to that visual image
of sweet docility.

'Oxford... are they out of their minds?' her father had
demanded when the head of the small all-girls' school she
had attended had written to him suggesting that she felt
that it might be worth while, that with a little extra coaching
she believed that Philippa could win a place there.

And after that Philippa had found that the precious time
she had needed for that extra study was somehow whittled
away with family duties she wasn't allowed to evade.

There were other limitations imposed on her as well. Her
father did not approve of girls or women who were self-
confident and noisy, women who held opinions and freely
voiced them, women who took charge of their own lives.

Philippa had felt very angry sometimes when she was growing up, not just with her father but with her mother as well, who stood by her husband and agreed with everything he said.

Philippa had realised even before her younger son's birth that her marriage had been a mistake, an escape from her family which inevitably had been no escape at all, but simply a deeper entrenchment in the role her father had already cast for her. But by then it had been too late to do anything about it. She had her sons to consider and she was determined that somehow she would provide them with the happy, secure, enriching childhood she herself had been denied. And for boys especially a father was an important, an essential part of that childhood.

Now, as she realised how little emotional effect the news of their father's death was actually having on them, she wondered if perhaps after all she might have been wrong, and that maybe if she had been strong enough to brave the avalanche of family disapproval a separation from Andrew would have caused she might have found that not just she, but the boys as well would have had easier, happier lives.

Because there was no getting away from it: life with Andrew had *not* been easy. Materially comfortable, yes; easy, no, and happy—never.

And yet she had married him willingly enough.

Yes, willingly, but lovingly... She flinched a little. She had believed she loved him at the time... had wanted to love him, had looked upon marriage to him as a secure haven after the pain, the agonising misery of...

'Can we come home with you now, today, Mum?'

Philippa pushed aside her own painful thoughts and smiled at her elder son. 'No, I'm afraid not, Rory.'

Much as she would have loved to have the comfort of them at home with her, she did not want them exposed to all the gossip and speculation that Andrew's suicide had caused locally. Their fees were paid until the end of the current year and she had already decided that it would be best if they remain here until then. That would give her time to sort things out at home.

She had rung Robert almost immediately after the police had left that fateful morning. He had been in a meeting, his secretary had informed her, but she had rung back later to say that Robert would ring her that evening.

He was going to the factory today, but had already complained to her that he was a very busy man, with his own business to run and that he could ill afford to take time off to sort out the mess his brother-in-law had made of his life.

'You realise, of course, that the company's virtually bankrupt,' he had told her angrily when he had called round after the visit to Kilcoyne's.

She hadn't, although she had wondered, worried especially about the money Andrew had borrowed, but years of conditioning, of being subservient to the men in her life, had programmed her into not exposing emotions they did not want to handle, and so she had simply sat silently while Robert told her.

'This whole mess really is most inconvenient. It couldn't have happened at a worse time for me—you do know that, don't you? I'm putting myself forward for selection as our local parliamentary candidate and this whole unsavoury business is bound to reflect badly on me.

'Of course it's typical of Andrew; he always was a trifle melodramatic for my taste. He should never have bought Kilcoyne's in the first place. I did try to warn him. You might have told me he was likely to do something like this.'

Philippa had stared at her brother, willing back the angry tears she could feel prickling her eyes as she swallowed down the huge swell of anger threatening to overwhelm her.

'I didn't *know*,' she told him quietly.

'Don't be ridiculous. You *must* have had some inkling. You were his wife. An intelligent woman, or so you've always claimed. You *must* have guessed . . .'

'I knew he was having financial problems, but he wouldn't discuss them with me,' she had told him woodenly.

'The whole world and his wife knew he was having financial problems. I told him months ago that there was no point in panicking the way he was doing, letting everyone know that he couldn't hold the business together. I warned you at the time against marrying him, Philippa,' he had added critically, while Philippa had gritted her teeth and then said as slowly and quietly as she could,

'No, you didn't, Robert. You *wanted* me to marry him. You said he would be a good husband for me.'

'Rubbish... I never said any such thing.' He'd given her an angry look. 'Not that it matters now. What's past is past, and what we have to do now is to get this whole mess cleaned up as quickly and quietly as possible.'

'How?' she had asked him.

He had shrugged impatiently and turned his back on her, walking over to look out of the French windows. 'Well, the bank will have to be informed, of course, if they don't know already, and after that it's their problem...'

'*Their* problem...'

He had swung round then, eyeing her irritably. 'Oh, come on—you *must* have realised for yourself that the reason he killed himself was because of the business. I don't know what the exact financial situation is, of course, and in my position I obviously can't afford to get involved—not now. No, your best bet is to leave everything in the hands of the bank. They'll do everything that's necessary. Look, Philippa, there's nothing I can do...'

Nothing you can do, or nothing you *will* do? she had asked herself after he had gone and she was mentally reviewing her brother's assets: the huge house he and Lydia owned, the château in France they had bought three years ago which he constantly boasted had now practically trebled its value, not to mention the rental money it brought in from carefully vetted holidaymakers.

What would he have said if she had told him that it wasn't his financial help she had actually wanted, but the help, the support, the sturdy male shoulder to lean femininely and weakly on as she had been conditioned to do since birth?

She had grimaced at herself as she passed the hall mirror.

What good were a pretty face and even prettier manners going to do her now?

And from the past, an echo of a pain she had long ago told herself she had never, ever felt, never mind forgotten, had come the taunting words to haunt her.

'Yes, you're pretty, Philippa, as pretty and prettily packaged as a little doll and just as insipid and lifeless. What I want is a real woman, a woman who laughs and cries, who sweats and screams when she makes love, who is a woman who thinks and feels...a woman who isn't afraid to be a woman, who cares more about what goes on inside her head than on her face, a woman who thinks it's more important to nourish her intellect than her skin—in plain fact, a woman full stop, and not a pretty cut-out cardboard doll.'

A woman who didn't need a man to lean on and turn to... A woman who could stand alone... A woman such as she could never be... Had never been allowed to be.

'So you'll stay here at school until the end of term and then we'll decide what we're going to do,' she told the boys now. She had already made up her mind that they would not attend the funeral. It was a farce to dress them up in black as her family would expect her to do, and to grieve for a father they had never really known, never mind loved.

They were *her* sons, she decided fiercely, her responsibility, and she would bring them up as she thought best; if that was not the way in which her family approved...

She saw the headmaster before she left, pleased to discover that he supported her decisions.

She was a very pretty woman, Henry Carter reflected as he watched her go. The first time he had met her she had been with her husband and the older man had completely overshadowed her. He had thought her pretty then, but docile and slightly boring. Today she had looked different—sharper, more alert, the substance of the woman she obviously was rather than merely a shadow of her husband.

He had never particularly liked the man and had wondered wryly if he had ever realised how much of his real personality and insecurity he betrayed to others with his hectoring manner and his need to ensure that others knew of and envied his material success.

Small wonder that he had felt unable to face life without the support and protection of that success. Henry Carter sighed slightly to himself, he might not have particularly liked him but he would nevertheless not have wished such a fate on him.

The recession was biting deeply into the lives of the boys and the school, with fees unpaid and pupils leaving at the end of one term and not returning at the beginning of another without any explanation. So far Andrew had been their only suicide, but there were other tragedies that went just as deep even if they were far less public.

It occurred to him as he ushered Philippa to the door that almost as strong as his pity for her was his contempt for her late husband.

When she reached home Philippa parked the car and climbed out tiredly. Her body ached almost as though she had flu. It was probably delayed shock, she decided distantly; the doctor had warned her to expect it, even offering to prescribe medication to help her overcome it.

She had felt a fraud then, seeing herself through his eyes, a shocked, distraught wife abruptly made a widow by her husband's own hand, her grief too heavy a burden for her to bear.

She had been shocked, yes, but her grief . . . where was that?

So far her emotions had been a mixture of disbelief and confusion, the woolliness with which they had clouded her brain occasionally splintered by lightning flashes of an anger so intense that she instinctively suppressed it.

The house felt cold. She had turned off the heating this morning when she'd left, economising. She had very little idea what personal financial assets Andrew had had.

Robert had seemed to think that she would be reasonably well provided for, but that did not allay her guilt and concern about what might happen to Andrew's employees. According to Robert the company was virtually bankrupt.

That was something else she would have to do: see the bank. Robert had offered to go with her but after his refusal to help her with the far more worrying problems of the company she had curtly refused his offer.

In the kitchen she filled the kettle and plugged it in.

The hand-built waxed and limed wooden units and the gleaming scarlet Aga had cost the earth; the large square room with its sunny aspect and solid square table should have been the perfect family environment, the heart of their home, but in reality it was simply a showpiece for Andrew's wealth. The only time the kitchen, the house, really felt like a home was when the boys were back from school.

She frowned as she made herself a mug of coffee. She had given up trying to change Andrew years ago, accepting that she would never have with him the kind of emotionally close and loving relationship she had dreamed of as a girl; she had in fact come to realise that such relationships were extremely rare.

And when she looked around her it seemed that very few of her female acquaintances had fared much better. Love, even the strongest and most passionate love, it seemed, eventually became tainted with familiarity and its accompanying disillusions.

She knew women who complained that their husbands bullied them, and women who complained that theirs were guilty of neglect. Women whose men wanted too much sex and those whose men wanted too little. Women whose men were unfaithful, sometimes with another woman, sometimes with a hobby or sport far more dearly loved than their marriage partner.

She had her sons and the life she had built up for herself and for them; the tepid sexual relationship she had had with Andrew had been infrequent and unexciting enough to cause her neither resentment nor pleasure—and besides she had not married him for sex.

Sex ... No, she certainly hadn't married him for that. Nor he her.

She had married him because ...

Edgily she put down her coffee-cup and walked over to the answering machine, running back the tape and then playing it. There was a message from the funeral parlour and as she listened to it she wondered idly how long it had taken the speaker to develop that deeply sepulchral note to his voice. Which had come first, the voice or the job?

As she allowed her thoughts to wander she acknowledged that she was using them as a means of evading pursuing what she had been thinking earlier.

The second message was from the bank manager asking her to make an appointment to call and see him, to discuss her own private affairs and those of the company. She frowned as she listened to it. Why would he want to see her about the company's financial affairs? She knew nothing about them.

Perhaps it was just a formality.

The tape came to an end. She switched it off and almost immediately the phone rang. She picked up the receiver.

'Philippa... it's Mummy...'

Mummy. How falsely affectionate that small word was, making it sound as though the bond between them was close and loving. In reality Philippa doubted that her mother had ever *allowed* herself to love her. Like her father, her mother's attitude had been that love was something which had to be earned. Love and approval had not been things which had been given freely or from the heart in her childhood home, and Philippa was bitterly conscious of this now as she caught the thread of disapproval running beneath the soft sweetness of her mother's voice.

When Philippa had been growing up she had never been punished by smacks or harsh words as other children had been; that was not her parents' way. An icy look, the quelling words, 'Philippa, Daddy is very disappointed in you,' and the withdrawal of her mother which accompanied the criticism had always been enough... More than enough to a child as sensitive as she had been, Philippa recognised, and her reactions to them were so deeply entrenched within her that just hearing that cold disapproval in her mother's voice now was enough to make her clench her stomach muscles and grip the receiver as she fought to control the answering anger and pain churning resentfully inside her.

'Robert has been telling us how foolish Andrew was. Your father and I had no idea he was behaving so recklessly. Your father's very upset about it. No one here seems to have heard anything about it yet, but it's bound to get out, and you know that he's captain this year of the golf club——'

Philippa was trembling again. 'I doubt that any of his golfing cronies are likely to hear about Andrew,' she interrupted, trying to keep her voice as level and light as she could, but unable to resist the irony of adding, 'And of course Andrew wasn't Daddy's son...'

'No, of course there is that,' her mother allowed patiently, oblivious to Philippa's sarcasm; so oblivious in fact that she made Philippa feel both childishly petty and furiously angry. 'But he *was* your husband and in the circumstances Daddy feels that it might be a good idea if you didn't come over to see us for a while. Poor, dear Robert is terribly upset about the whole thing, you know. I mean, you do live almost on his doorstep and he's held in such high esteem... Have you made any arrangements yet for the...?' Delicately her mother let the sentence hang in the air.

'For the cremation, you mean?' Philippa asked her grimly. 'Yes. It will be on Friday, but don't worry, Mother; I shall quite understand if you don't feel you want to be there.'

'It isn't a question of wanting...' her mother told her, obviously shocked. 'One has a duty, and Andrew was after all our son-in-law, although I must say, Philippa, I could never really understand why you married him, nor could Daddy. We did try to warn you...'

Did you... did you really, Mother? Philippa wanted to demand. And when was that... when did you warn me? Was it after you told me what a good husband Andrew would make me, or before you pointed out that I would be lucky to find another man so suited to me... or rather so suited to the kind of wife you had raised me to be? If you really didn't want me to marry him, why wouldn't you allow me to go on to university; why did you insist on keeping me at home, as dependent on you as a pet dog and just as carefully leashed?

'But then you always were such a very impetuous and stubborn girl,' her mother sighed. 'Robert was saying only this morning how much both Daddy and I spoiled you and I'm afraid he was right.

'Have you made any plans yet for after...?'

'Not yet,' Philippa told her brusquely. 'But don't worry, Mummy; whatever plans I do make I shall make sure that they don't cause either you or Daddy any problems.'

Philippa replaced the receiver before her mother could make any response.

Her palms felt damp and sticky, her body perspiring with the heat of her suppressed anger, but what, after all, was the point in blaming her parents for what they were, or what they had tried to make her? Hadn't they, after all, been victims of their upbringing just as much as she was of hers? This was the way she had taught herself to think over the years. It was a panacea, an anaesthetic to all the pain she could not allow herself to feel.

CHAPTER FOUR

'The trouble with long weekends is that they just don't last long enough,' Richard grumbled as he drained his teacup and reached for the pot to refill it. Elizabeth laughed.

'Fraud,' she teased him affectionately. 'You know as well as I do that you can't wait to get back to your patients. I heard you on the phone to Jenny earlier.'

Jenny Wisden was Richard's junior registrar and as dedicated to her work as Richard was to his. She had married the previous year, a fellow medic working in a busy local practice.

'Poor Jenny,' Elizabeth had commented at the time.

Richard had raised his eyebrows as he'd asked her, 'Why poor? The girl's deliriously in love; anyone can see that.'

'Yes, she is, and so is he. She's also a young woman on the bottom rungs of a notoriously demanding career ladder. What's going to happen when she and Tony decide they want children?'

'She'll take maternity leave,' Richard had informed her, plainly not following the drift of her argument.

'Yes, and then what? Spend the next eighteen years constantly torn between conflicting demands and loyalties, knowing that she's got to sacrifice either her feelings as a mother or her desire to reach the top of her profession.'

Richard had frowned then.

'What are you trying to say? I thought you were all for female equality...women fulfilling their professional potential. You've lectured me about it often enough...'

'I am all for it, but, once a woman has children, biologically and materially the scales are weighted against her. You know it's true, Rick: once Jenny has children she won't be able to go as far in her career as she would if she were a man. She'll be the one who has to take time off to attend the school concert and the children's sports day. She'll be the one who takes them to the dentist and who worries about them when they're ill, feeling guilty because she can't be with them.

'No amount of paid substitute care, no matter how professional or good it is, can ever assuage a woman's in-built biological guilt on that score.'

'Mmm—damn waste it will be too. Jenny is one of the best, if not *the* best junior registrar I've ever had.'

'Well, perhaps in future you should remember that and when you're lecturing your students you should remind them all, but especially the male students, what sexual equality really should mean—and I'm not referring to a token filling up and emptying of the dishwasher now and then.

'Do you realise, Rick, that, despite all this media hooha about the "New Man", women are *still* responsible for the major part of all domestic chores? Sorry,' she'd apologised, with a wry smile. 'I didn't mean to start lecturing you, but...'

'I know.' Richard had smiled, standing up and leaning towards her to kiss her.

'I saw Sir Arthur yesterday,' Elizabeth told him now.

Sir Arthur Lawrence was the chairman of the hospital board, an ex-army major, rigidly old-fashioned in his views and outlook, with whom Richard had had so many clashes over the years.

'Oh, did you? What did he have to say for himself? More complaints about overspending on budgets, I suppose,' Richard grunted.

Elizabeth laughed. 'No, as a matter of fact he was very complimentary, praising you for all the work you've done to help raise money for the new Fast Response Accident Unit.'

Richard grunted again. 'You should have told him not to count his chickens. We need government funding if we're to go ahead with it, and we haven't heard that we're going to get it yet. The Northern is putting up a pretty good counter-claim to ours. They maintain that they're closer to a wider range of motorway systems than we are...'

'And we're closer to the centre of the region and we have better access to the motorway,' Elizabeth reminded him. 'And you've got a much better recovery record.'

'Mmm...well, that's no thanks to Sir Arthur; you should have heard the objections he raised when we opened our recovery ward...'

'Admit it, you enjoy fighting with him.' Elizabeth laughed.

Richard pulled a face. 'He's twenty years behind the times...more... Hell, is that the time? I've got to go. You're at home today, aren't you?'

'Yes. I thought I might drive over and see Sara. She sounded a bit down when I spoke to her yesterday.'

'Yes, it's no picnic being a GP's wife—nor being a GP, either.' Richard kissed her, smiling at her as he suggested, 'Why don't we go out for dinner together tonight... Mario's? Just the two of us,' he added.

'Just the two of us,' Elizabeth responded, emphasising the 'just'. 'Mmm...that would be lovely.'

'I'll get Kelly to book us a table,' he promised her as he picked up his briefcase and headed for the door.

After he had gone, Elizabeth made herself a fresh cup of coffee and picked up a buff folder from the dresser. The dresser had been an antiques fair find, which she and Richard had stripped of its old paint, a long and laborious job which she suspected had cost far more in terms of their time and paint-stripper than had she bought the ready-stripped, polished version from an antique shop.

There was a sense of satisfaction in having done the work themselves, though, and she had enjoyed those hours in Richard's company. They had reminded her of the early days of their marriage, when it hadn't seemed so unusual to see him wearing old clothes and getting dirty. 'You're so lucky, you and Richard,' her friends often told her enviously. But their marriage had suffered its ups and downs just like any other. Where they had been lucky perhaps had been in that both of them shared the same deep commitment to their relationship, so that, at times when both of them might have viewed their individual roles within it from opposing and conflicting viewpoints, their joint desire to keep their marriage alive and functioning had continued to survive.

She had not always experienced the same contentment in their relationship, the same pleasure in being herself as she did now, Elizabeth admitted. There had been times, when Sara was young, when she had felt Richard growing away from her... when she had felt threatened by and resentful of not just the claims of his work but his evident involvement with it.

It had been an article in the local newspaper absently flicked through in the hairdressers which had initially sparked off her interest in community work. With a twenty-year-old degree and no professional skills whatsoever, she had humbly approached the local community liaison officer, explaining that she would like to give her services and that she had time on her hands with her daughter living away from home, but that she had no skills she could put to use.

'No skills?' the other woman had queried. 'You run a home, you've brought up a family, you drive a car. Don't worry, we'll soon find something for you to do!' And so they had.

Elizabeth smiled to herself now, remembering how terrified she had been that first day, manning the reception desk at the Citizens Advice Bureau, and then six months later when she had been asked if she would like to train as a counsellor. She had protested that she was not experienced enough to give advice to others, that her life, her relationships were very far from perfect, and certainly did not justify her handing out advice to others.

'The more problems our counsellors have faced in their own lives, the better they are at listening compassionately to the problems of others,' she had been told crisply.

She sat down and opened the folder.

She had recently attended a national conference on the effects of long-term unemployment and redundancy on people. She frowned as she read through the notes she had made. They were certainly getting an increased number of people coming to them for advice on how to cope with their unemployment—women in the main, anxious not just about the loss of income but the effects of their husband's redundancy and consequent loss of self-esteem on the men emotionally, and on the family as well.

If the gossip going round following Andrew Ryecart's suicide was correct in suggesting that it had been caused by financial problems with Kilcoyne's, it seemed likely that the town would soon have more men out of work. The company was one of the town's main employers, one of the last light engineering companies left in the area. There would be no alternative jobs for people to go to.

Elizabeth nibbled the end of her pen. She had suggested at last week's general staff meeting that it might be an idea to put together a special package formulated specifically to help such cases. People were individuals, of course, with individual problems, but . . .

'It's a good idea,' her boss had agreed. 'But we simply can't spare anyone to work on it at the moment, unless . . .'

'Unless I do it at home in my spare time,' Elizabeth had offered wryly.

'I'm sorry, Elizabeth,' her boss had apologised. 'But you know how things are: we're all suffering cutbacks and underfunding, just like everyone else.'

That was true enough. Richard had been complaining that the hospital now seemed to employ more accountants to watch over its budgets than they did nurses to watch over its patients.

'Richard, have you got a minute?'

Richard paused, frowning as he glanced at his watch.

'Barely,' he told the hospital's chief executive. 'My clinic starts in half an hour and I've got a couple of phone calls I need to make first.'

'I really do need to talk to you, Richard,' the other man insisted. 'We've got a committee meeting coming up soon and we still have to go through your budgets.'

Richard grimaced, suppressing his instinctive response, which was to say that he was a surgeon, not an accountant. It was pointless losing his temper with Brian; he was just as much a victim of the financial cuts being imposed on them as he himself was.

'Look, let's go into my office,' Brian suggested, taking advantage of his silence.

Irritably Richard followed him, shaking his head when Brian offered him coffee. 'No, I forgot for a moment— you're a tea man, aren't you?'

'I drank too much coffee when I was a student and a young intern,' Richard told him. 'They talk about working long hours now, but when I first qualified... Still, we didn't have the same pressures on us then that they do now, nor the huge diversity of skills and facts to learn. These days there seems to be a new drug on the market every day and a new set of complications to go with it, never mind all the new operating techniques, and then of course there's the paperwork...'

Brian Simmonds watched him sympathetically. He had remarked at last month's meeting to the new area health chief administrator that it was perhaps unfair to expect some of their senior and older medical staff to be able to absorb the intricacies of the new technology and the tighter control of finances as speedily as the younger ones.

'If that's the case, then perhaps you ought to be thinking about pensioning a few of them off,' had been David Howarth's cold response. 'It appals me to see how much money we're wasting paying top salaries to people who could quite easily be replaced by someone younger—and cheaper.

'The whole area health system needs reorganising and rationalising. We've got far too many small specialist units competing with one another. It would make much more sense to nominate specific hospitals to deal with specific areas of expertise. Out of the eighteen hospitals in this area, a good number of them have specialist heart units, and both your hospital and the Northern have specialised micro-surgery units. Older surgeons like Richard Humphries...'

'Richard Humphries was the first local surgeon to specialise in his field,' Brian had protested defensively. 'He really pioneered the treatment in his area...'

'But Richard Humphries is a man not far off sixty who, no matter how excellent a surgeon he might be, has made it plain that he just isn't equipped to deal with the financial implications of working in an independent hospital. Christopher Jeffries at the Northern, in contrast, has already shown that he has an excellent grasp of the way we're going to need to operate in future to make sure we're financially viable, and he's twenty years younger than Richard.'

Brian hadn't repeated their conversation to Richard. Richard and David had taken a dislike to one another virtually at first sight, and Brian already knew from past experience that Richard was simply not a man to compromise on what he believed were the best interests of his patients for any mere financial reasons.

Richard epitomised all that was best in the Health Service, its principles and its goals, while David on the other hand represented the new financial cutting edge that was being imposed on it to try to counteract the burden of a growing population and the rapid advances made in medical technology.

He sighed to himself, knowing that the problem was one thing, but finding the answers to it was something else again, and while David and his like believed that the answer was a far more hard-nosed response to the provision of health services, and while publicly Brian might feel it was politic to agree with him, privately he couldn't help but sympathise with Richard's totally opposite point of view.

Sympathising with him was one thing, failing to get across to him the message that if financial restraints were not self imposed then they would be imposed from outside was another matter, and one that could potentially prejudice the whole hospital's future.

'Our accountant was on the phone yesterday,' he told Richard now. 'It seems that she still hasn't received your budget forecasts for the next quarter...'

'What exactly is the hospital paying me for?' Richard countered irritably. 'Filling in forms or operating on patients?'

Brian sighed again. 'Richard, I know how you feel, but try not to make too much of an enemy of people like David.' He moved uncomfortably in his seat. 'There *are* areas where savings can be made. The Northern——'

'The Northern has a far lower post-operation recovery-rate than we do here,' Richard interrupted, and added bluntly, 'And you already know my opinion on the reasons for that...'

'You're getting too old and too idealistic, Richard,' his GP son-in-law had told him drily the last time they had met. 'And if you think you've got problems you should sit at my desk for a couple of days.' Too idealistic he might be, but too old...Richard frowned, wondering why the thought should make him feel so edgy and defensive. He wasn't even sixty yet. No age for a surgeon. Heavens, he could remember when he'd got his first internship: the senior surgeon had been close to seventy and everyone apart from the matron had gone in awe of him. It hadn't mattered that you had to shout to make yourself heard because he was going deaf; watching him operate had been a privilege. In those days age and experience had been things to honour and respect—not like today, when the moment you got past forty-five you were considered to be past your best.

Back in his office, he found that his secretary, Kelly, had already sorted his mail into urgent and non-urgent piles. On the top of the urgent pile was a GP's report on one of her female patients. As he studied it he pushed aside his conversation with Brian, frowning as he read the doctor's findings.

A lump had been detected in the patient's breast and an immediate operation would be necessary to perform a biopsy and removal if the lump was found to be malignant. She was a relatively young woman, only in her mid-thirties, and he knew from experience the trauma she would experience over the potential loss of a breast, but given the choice between that and losing her life...

His frown deepened as he reached into his jacket pocket for his diary, flicking it open until he found what he was looking for.

'Kelly, how much emergency space have I got left on Thursday?' he asked his secretary.

'Thursday,' she repeated, studying his lists. 'None...'

'Well, then, we'll have to make some; Mrs Jacobs needs surgical attention straight away.'

'But Thursday's just two days away; you could afford to hold on until early next week.'

'No, it has to be Thursday the tenth; the date is crucial,' he told her. 'Let me see the list, will you?'

When she handed it to him he studied it thoughtfully.

'We'll cancel Sophie Jennings' non-urgent operation and put that in the beginning of next month,' he announced.

Kelly pulled a small face. 'We've had to cancel it once already due to another emergency, and you know how much she complained then...'

'It can't be helped,' Richard told her. 'Get her file out, will you, and I'll write to her? Oh, and get me Mrs Jacobs' file as well; I'd better phone her and speak to her personally.'

'Problems?' Elizabeth asked later that evening as they sat at their table in Mario's and she watched Richard pushing his food unenthusiastically round his plate.

'No more than usual,' he told her drily. 'All I ever seem to hear from Brian these days is money and budgets. What the hell is happening to the world today, Liz, that we judge the success of a hospital not on how many lives it saves, or on how much it improves the quality of its patients' lives, but on how much money it can save?'

Elizabeth shook her head sympathetically. It was a familiar argument and very much a sore point with him at the moment.

'The Health Service is under a great deal of financial pressure,' she reminded him gently. 'Look at the way you've had to go to the public to raise money to help fund this new Fast Response Accident Unit. At least that's one cause that you and Sir Arthur are united on.' She smiled. 'He's every bit as keen and determined to get the unit for the General as you are.'

'Yes,' Richard growled. 'Someone ought to tell him that he'd be doing everyone a better service if he concentrated more on his fund-raising and less on finding fault with everything we do... Everything's changing, Liz—good men being pensioned off for no better reason than the fact that...' He paused, shaking his head. 'I feel so out of step somehow. Am I wrong to believe that we should put our patients first?'

'No, you're not wrong,' Elizabeth assured him. She put down her knife and fork, feeling her way as tactfully as she could. 'But knowing you're right isn't always...you can be very stubborn,' she told him gently. 'There are circumstances when it's sometimes easier to get your point of view across by being a little more flexible.'

She knew what was really bothering him; she and Sara and been discussing it earlier.

'How's Dad going to feel if the General amalgamates with the Northern and they offer him early retirement?'

'Offer him early retirement?' Elizabeth had queried ruefully. 'Your father is far more likely to see it as being pensioned off; he won't like it at all.'

'No, and it won't help that your working and your career is just beginning to take off...'

'Oh, Sara, you're not being fair,' she had protested. 'Your father has always encouraged me in my work...'

'Mmm...but his career has always taken priority, hasn't it? Oh, I know how pleased he is for you, how proud he is of you, but if he was sitting at home all day while you——'

'It won't come to that,' Elizabeth had interrupted her firmly.

'No? Ian was saying the other day that two or three of the older, more senior men at the Northern have already been approached with a view to getting them to go, and Dad is only a few years off sixty...'

Now, as she watched him, Elizabeth's heart sank a little. She knew how much his work meant to him and she knew what a blow it would be to his pride, his sense of self-worth if he was asked to retire before he was ready.

Perhaps if she subtly tried to underline the advantages of his not having to work as hard, just as a precautionary measure. Her mouth curled into a rueful smile. Burgeoning career woman she might be, but in many ways she was still very much caught up in the traditional role of the support-ive wife. That was how her generation had been brought up.

'Oh, did you manage to get over to see Sara?' Richard asked her, changing the subject.

'Yes,' she told him. 'She's feeling a bit frazzled. I offered to have Katie for a few days to give her a break; I've still quite a lot of holiday leave to take.'

'You always were a soft touch,' Richard told her. 'For all of us...'

'I'm glad you're honest enough to include yourself in that comment,' she teased him.

'How do you feel about getting out of here and going home?' Richard asked her urgently, leaning across the table so that the hovering waiter could not overhear what he was saying.

Elizabeth looked at him quickly to confirm that she hadn't misunderstood the subtle message he was giving her. In the early days of their marriage, when their passion for one another had still been new and exciting, it had been no strange thing for them to leave early from dinner parties and other social events, Richard claiming quite untruth-fully that he was on call, when in fact what he had wanted, what they had both wanted, was to go home and make love.

Laughing together, they had hurried back to their small flat, their urgent eagerness for one another as intoxicating as a heady wine, but these days their lovemaking, although still pleasurable, tended to be a far more leisurely and considered affair, its spontaneity tempered originally by the demands of a growing family and more latterly by their individual career demands and a certain natural lessening of the intensity of their desire.

'Does that mean what I think it means?' she asked him in amusement, and then laughed as she saw the way he was looking at her.

'We are not teenagers any more!' she told him ten minutes later when he took hold of her in the street, kissing her firmly before hurrying her towards their car.

'Who says we need to be?' he whispered as he paused to kiss her a second time. 'Just because we aren't under thirty, it doesn't mean that we automatically stop functioning properly, that we aren't just as capable as our juniors. There are, after all, times when experience and knowledge count for a lot more than youth and enthusiasm...'

Elizabeth touched his face gently.

'Oh, Richard.' There's no shame in growing older, she wanted to tell him, but how could she, when all around them was the irrefutable evidence that there was? Being old and ill and dependent—these were now the taboo subjects that sex and birth had once been.

Richard wasn't alone in dreading retirement as an acknowledgement of the beginning of his own old age.

CHAPTER FIVE

PHILIPPA opened her eyes and shut them again quickly as she remembered what day it was.

Outside it was still not properly light, but she knew she would not go back to sleep. She threw back the duvet, shivering as she felt the cool draught from the half-open window.

The cremation was not due to take place until two o'clock—plenty of time for her to do all the things she had to do...

'You'll be having everyone back to the house afterwards, of course,' her mother had announced when she had rung to discuss what arrangements Philippa had made for Andrew's cremation. 'It would look so odd if you didn't.'

'I don't think that's a good idea,' Philippa had protested. 'Especially in the circumstances.' Death was a difficult reality for people to handle at the best of times, but when it came through suicide...

'You'll have to do it, Philippa,' her mother had insisted. 'People will expect it.'

What people? Philippa had wanted to ask her. She supposed she ought not to have been surprised by the number of people—their so-called 'friends'—who had rung ostensibly to commiserate with her and offer their sympathy, but in reality to dissociate themselves from Andrew and the taint of his failure just as quickly as they could.

Oh, they would want to be seen to be doing the right thing: they would send flowers, expensive, sterile displays of wealth and patronage. They would talk in public in low voices about how shocked they had been... how sorry they felt for her, and of course letting it be known how tenuous their acquaintance with Andrew had actually been, but she

76

doubted that many of them would be seen at the crematorium.

And after all, who could blame them? Not Andrew, who would have behaved in exactly the same way had he been in their shoes.

Her black suit hung on the wardrobe door. She eyed it rebelliously. It wasn't new and certainly had not been bought for an occasion such as this. She liked black, and it suited her fair paleness.

The fine black crêpe fabric clung flatteringly to her body, or at least it had done; with the weight she had lost since Andrew's death she doubted that it would do so any longer. The black velvet reveres of the jacket added a softening richness to its simple classic design.

It was really far too elegant an outfit to wear for such an occasion.

A woman...a widow who wasn't really grieving for the loss of her husband would not have cared what she wore; there could not be any colour that could truly portray to the world what she was feeling.

A surge of contempt and bitterness swamped her. The contempt she knew was for herself; and the bitterness?

She walked into the bathroom adjacent to the bedroom. The bitterness... That was for Andrew, she admitted as she cleaned her teeth.

As she straightened up, she stared at her reflection in the mirror. Her face, wiped clean of make-up, showed beneath the harsh lighting of the bathroom exactly what effect the last few days had had on her. Pitilessly she stared at it, noting the fine lines touching the skin around her eyes, the pale skin and the tension in the underlying bones and muscles.

There, she was admitting it at last: it was not grief she felt at Andrew's death, not the sorrow and pain of a woman who had lost the man who was her life's partner, her lover, her friend, the father of her children.

What she felt was anger, bitterness, resentment.

Andrew had known what lay ahead of him...of them...and, unable to confront the situation he had brought upon himself, he had simply turned his back on it...evaded it, leaving her...

Her body started to shake as she tried to suppress her feelings, her hands gripping the edge of the basin.

Anger, bitterness, resentment; these were not emotions she should be feeling...but the guilt, the guilt that went hand in hand with them, that underlined them and seeped poisonously into her thoughts—yes, that was an emotion she could allow herself to feel.

Andrew had been her husband and, yes, she had married him willingly, caught up in a rebounding tide of pride, determined to prove that she was fully adult, fully a woman...and a woman capable of being loved by a man who would treat her as a woman and not a stupid child.

She closed her eyes. She had tried her best to be the wife Andrew wanted, to keep the bargain she had made with fate; she had tried to do it, to infuse into their relationship, their marriage, the warmth and sharing which Andrew could not or would not put into it; but nothing she had been able to do had ever really been able to disguise the poverty of the emotional bond between them, and in her worst moments since Andrew's death she had even begun to wonder if this was his way of punishing her, if by leaving her in the manner he had... But then common sense had reasserted itself and she was forced to acknowledge that their marriage had come so far down the list of Andrew's priorities that it would have been the last thing he would have taken into account in making his decision...that *she* would have been the last thing he would have taken into account?

Oddly, that knowledge, instead of freeing her from the burden of her guilt, only served to increase it. Yes, she had tried, but had she really tried hard enough?

'You can't be serious. You didn't even *know* the man; why the hell should you want to see him cremated? It's ridiculous...disgusting...'

'Ryan thinks it's the right thing to do.' Deborah stared angrily across their bedroom at Mark.

The violence of his objections to the discovery that she intended to attend Andrew Ryecart's cremation had caught her off guard, and touched a nerve which she herself had not wanted to acknowledge.

She dismissed the thought, reminding herself that she couldn't afford to damage her professionalism with inappropriate feminine behaviour.

'It's a token of respect, that's all,' she told Mark, turning away from him so that he couldn't see her face.

'What? Don't give me that... It's blatant voyeurism and if you really believe anything else... You've changed ever since Ryan gave you this commission.'

'No, I haven't,' she denied. 'If anyone's changed, it's you. What's the matter with you? You're behaving almost as though you're jealous.'

'Jealous... who the hell of?' he challenged her.

It had been on the tip of her tongue to say, 'Me', but suddenly, for no real logical reason, her heart started to beat too fast and she found she could not actually say the word.

'I suppose you mean Ryan,' he told her, answering his own question. 'My God, that only underlines what I was just saying. If you really think I could ever be jealous of a creep like that...'

As he studied her downbent head and the way her dark hair swung over her face, concealing her expression from him, Mark knew that he had over-reacted. The bright morning sunshine highlighted the chestnut shine on her hair and the lissom softness of her body.

His own ached abruptly in a sharp spasm of sexual response. He wanted to pick her up and carry her over to their bed, spread the soft, warm femaleness of her underneath him and make love to her with such passion that she would not be able to suppress her sharp cries of pleasure, her body's response to him, her need and desire for him. He wanted, he recognised, her recognition of him as a man... as a source of power and strength. That knowledge shook him, disturbing him, making him reject the sexual message his body was giving him.

What he wanted, a cold black corner of his mind told him, was her acknowledgement of his power over her, her subservience to him.

But no, that could not be true. He was not that kind of man; he never had been; that kind of egotistical need was a male trait he despised. Their relationship was one of mutuality and respect.

Or at least it had been. Deborah seemed to have more respect for Ryan these days than she did for him.

Test her, a small inner voice urged him. Let her prove to you that you're wrong.

'If you'll take my advice you won't go,' he heard himself saying.

Deborah lifted her head and frowned as she looked at him. 'I don't have any option. I have to go,' she told him. 'Ryan...' When she saw the expression on his face, she reminded him quietly, 'He is my boss, Mark.'

'Yes,' Mark agreed equally quietly.

It was only later, when she was actually in her own office, that Deborah asked herself why she had not pushed Mark to explain more rationally why he felt she should not attend the cremation.

Admittedly Philippa Ryecart was not involved with the company in any official capacity and until she had had her first meeting with the bank, who were the company's main creditors, she would not know to what extent Andrew's personal assets were involved. It was not unknown in such cases where a man knew his business was failing for him to withdraw as many of its assets as he could, converting them into funds for his private use, and it would be part of her job to discover if this had happened.

Scavenging among the rotting carcasses of the dead, Mark had called it, and she supposed to some extent he was right.

It all depended, though, on what attitude you took. 'The company's creditors have every right to try to recover their money,' she had pointed out to him defensively.

'Every right,' Mark had agreed and had then added, 'How will you feel, Deborah, telling people that they're going to lose their jobs; that their redundancy money and very probably their pension as well has gone?'

'I'm not responsible for the company's failure,' Deborah had defended.

'No, but you're the one who's going to have to stand there and tell them . . . you're the one who's going to have to look at their faces and see the fear in them.'

'Stop it,' she had told him fiercely, asking, 'Why are you doing this to me, Mark? It's my job, you know that . . .'

'Yes, I'm sorry,' he had apologised, his face softening as he'd recognised her distress.

They had made it up and she had told herself that it was silly to feel so hurt, but now they were quarrelling again.

It had been tempting this morning to admit to him that she didn't want to go to the cremation, but Ryan had warned her against letting her emotions get in the way of doing her job properly. He had also let it slip that some of the other partners felt he was taking a risk in allowing her so much responsibility and that they had felt he should have appointed a man to head the team, with her as second in command.

She now felt honour-bound to prove to them that she was up to the job, not just for her own sake but for Ryan's as well.

She had wanted to explain all this to Mark but his attitude had made it impossible for her to confide in him. It hurt her that he couldn't be a little more understanding, that he couldn't seem to see how important it was to her that she prove herself, and how much she needed his support and approval.

Ryan came into her office just as she had finished making arrangements to see the bank. He smiled at her as she replaced the receiver and said softly, 'I like the suit. Black looks good on you.'

As his glance flickered over her, Deborah suspected that it wasn't only her smartly cut black business suit that he was envisaging her in. Ryan would definitely be the black underwear, stockings and suspender type, she acknowledged, but she let his slow, sensual appraisal of her pass without comment, saying meekly, 'I'm due at the crematorium at two; it seemed the right thing to wear.'

'Ah, yes... pity... I was going to suggest you join me for lunch. I'm seeing Harry Turner, the bank's regional director, and I thought it would give you an opportunity to do a bit of networking.'

Deborah shook her head with genuine regret, half hoping he would suggest that she give the crematorium a miss, but he didn't. If he had done, would she have told Mark the truth or would she have let him assume that she had not gone because he had not wanted her to? She frowned. Why should she need to employ such deceit? She and Mark had always been totally honest with one another.

Mark saw Ryan leaving Deborah's office. He had been on his way there himself to apologise for his surliness this morning, but now he abruptly changed his mind.

He had never liked Ryan; he admitted that freely. There was something about the man, about his attitude to life and to other people, that irked him. Ryan, while paying lip-service to the views and opinions of others, nevertheless still managed to betray an arrogance and lack of consideration for any viewpoint but his own which left Mark breathless... and envious?

No, of course not. But he was aware that in the eyes of the world, in the eyes of his peers here at work, according to the ancient code of male approval he would be judged inferior to Ryan.

Ryan was a swaggering, macho buccaneer of a man who, despite the fact that modern conditioning demanded that his male peers disapprove of him for those traits, still, because of those very characteristics, secretly appealed to a part of the male instinct.

And the female? Did Deborah perhaps secretly despise him and wish he were more like Ryan?

Mark frowned. Was it really Deborah's contempt that he feared, or his own? Was it in her eyes that he feared comparison with Ryan, or his?

His thoughts were too uncomfortable to pursue; they opened up a vein of insecurity and weakness within himself from which he instinctively retreated.

As he walked back into his own office he almost bumped into the girl coming out. He frowned as she dimpled a smile at him, wondering who she was. She had a small, curvy figure and the confidence to show it off, amusement lightening her eyes as she saw him studying her.

'Sorry,' he apologised wryly.

'Don't be,' she responded unexpectedly. 'I was enjoying it.'

She had gone before he could make any further retort, the scent of her perfume lingering behind her.

'A computer? And just how the hell are we supposed to afford that?'

Sally gave an exasperated sigh as she heard the anger in Joel's voice, intervening, 'Don't bother your dad with that now, love. We'll talk about it later.'

She waited until Paul had left the kitchen before turning to Joel and asserting, 'There was no need to be like that with him. He was only asking. Have you heard anything yet about the factory?'

'If I had, don't you think I'd have told you?' he responded irritably.

Sally gritted her teeth. She knew how worried he was, but didn't he realise how difficult he was making it for her...for all of them...with his moodiness and bad temper? It wasn't their fault that he might be going to lose his job.

Guiltily she looked away from him. She had tried to be sympathetic, but she had her own problems. Sister was pressuring her to work more hours on a regular basis but she was already overstretched, trying to keep things organised at home and working as well. And Joel didn't help.

'Do you have to leave your things all over the place?' she demanded crossly now as she glared at the jacket he had dropped carelessly on the table.

'It wouldn't be there if Paul hadn't stopped me to pester me about his damned computer,' Joel growled back. 'It would be on my back and I'd have been out from under your feet. It's really good to know how much I'm wanted in my own home.'

'Well, it's your own fault,' Sally responded defensively. 'If you weren't so bad-tempered all the time, snapping at the kids for no reason, behaving like...'

'Like what?' he challenged her. 'Like a man who's about to lose his job and doesn't know where the hell his next wage packet is coming from or if there's going to be one?'

'You don't know yet that you will be made redundant,' Sally protested, 'and besides...'

'Besides what?'

She took a deep breath. She hadn't meant to tell him like this; she knew how he felt about her working even part-time.

'Sister wants me to work full-time... It would mean a lot more money, Joel,' she told him quickly before he could say anything. 'Not enough to cover your wages, I know, but if we cut back on things...'

'Cut back? I've got a better idea,' Joel told her, white-faced. 'Why don't I just get myself out of here completely, then you could make a real saving? It isn't as though you need me any more, is it? Not now that *Sister* wants you to work full-time. Not if I'm not in work.'

Sally felt irritation explode inside her. She hadn't got time for this, for listening to Joel felling sorry for himself, she had the washing to do, and the ironing from the last load, and she wanted to do the supermarket shopping before she went to work; the last thing she needed was Joel having a tantrum. She hadn't got time to quarrel with him about it either. Not the time, nor the inclination, and certainly not the energy.

'You're going to be late for work,' she told him grimly instead.

She turned her back on him as he reached for his jacket, tensing as she felt him move towards her. A part of her wanted to turn round and lift her face for his goodbye kiss, but another part of her, the angry, resentful part, wouldn't let her. She was tired of being the one to compromise, who always gave way for the sake for peace. She knew he was worried about his job—she was worried too—but taking it out on the kids wasn't fair on them.

As he saw the rigidity of her back, Joel's own face hardened. It seemed that no matter what he did these days he was always in the wrong, in the way, his presence not wanted or needed in bed or out of it.

Paul came into the kitchen after Joel had gone.

'Everyone else at school's got a computer,' he began to grumble as he followed Sally round the kitchen. 'What's wrong with Dad, anyway?'

Sally put down the plates she was carrying to the sink and walked over to him. At thirteen he considered himself too big for hugs and kisses these days but right now he looked so forlorn, so young and vulnerable that she reacted instinctively, hugging him to her and ruffling the top of his hair.

He no longer had that baby, milky smell which had once been so familiar to her, so loved; now he smelled of trainers and school mingled with other strange, alien, youthful male scents which showed how quickly he was growing up and away from her.

She felt him wriggle protestingly in her arms. 'Aw, Mum...'

'Don't worry about your dad,' she told him. 'He's got a lot on his mind at the moment.'

Joel stopped the car three doors down from his own house and then reversed abruptly. He couldn't go to work leaving things like that with Sally. Perhaps he had over-reacted, snapping at her like that and then quarrelling with her, but he couldn't sleep properly for worrying about what would happen if he was made redundant. It was his role, his responsibility, his life function to support and protect his family, and if he couldn't do that, then...

As he walked past the kitchen window he looked inside and saw Sally hugging Paul. He could see her love for their son in the soft curve of her mouth, its tenderness and warmth. How long was it since she had held *him* like that... since she had looked at *him* with love?

As he turned away from the door and headed back to his car he felt the angry pain burning inside him like bile.

Jealous of his own son. Sally had accused him of it often enough in the past. He had denied it, of course—he loved the children—but seeing her holding Paul like that had made him sharply aware of the contrast in the way she treated him and the way she opened to them.

Deborah had timed her arrival at the crematorium to coincide with that of the last of the mourners, so that she could slip inside and sit at the back of the room without attracting any attention.

The first thing she noticed was how few people were actually there.

A small, very pretty blonde woman in black who was presumably the widow, an older couple beside her—her parents perhaps. Another couple, the tall man with a rather imposing and self-important manner, the woman at his side signalling by her body language that she considered herself above the proceedings, as she held herself slightly aloof from the others. She was dressed in a way that proclaimed her county origins; the Hermès scarf was plainly not a copy and neither were the immaculately polished loafers she was wearing. She looked the type to have sons at one of the better boarding schools and daughters who rode in gymkhanas and did a season working in Val d'Isère for a friend of a friend at one of the most exclusive chalets before marrying men who were something in the city with the right kind of county connections.

Without knowing why, Deborah instinctively disliked both of them.

There were a handful of other mourners, their numbers barely filling the front two rows of seats, and suddenly she felt not just out of place but guilty almost of the kind of tactless and distasteful rubbernecking she had always despised. Mark had been right. She should not be here.

Quickly she turned round and hurried towards the door, slipping silently outside.

Ryan would laugh at her when he knew what she had done, mock her for her squeamishness, but as she looked at Andrew's pale, fragile blonde widow she hadn't been able to stop herself imagining how she would have felt in her shoes... the pain and anguish the woman must be experiencing... Had she known what her husband had intended to do? She could not have done, of course. How much greater then must be her pain and despair, her sense not just of loss, but also of having somehow failed him.

She got into her car, switching on the ignition. Suddenly all she wanted was to be at home with Mark. Just the two of them together, safe in their own private world where no one else, nothing else could intrude.

'Just the local paper, thanks,' Joel told the girl behind the counter in the newsagent's as he handed over his money.

It was all over the factory that there was to be a big meeting with the bank and some firm of accountants on Monday morning. And then what? The spectre of redundancy hung heavily over him as he left the shop. He didn't really know why he had bought the local rag—he already knew what he would find in the 'situations vacant' column, or rather what he would not find. This area, this town which had originally grown prosperous from the profits of the small local engineering firms which had supplied the car industry, now had no jobs for men like himself. The apprenticeship he had been so proud to get, the skills he had worked so hard to learn—what use were they to him now? A piece of machinery programmed by a computer had virtually made his skill obsolete.

As he paused in the street, turning to the 'situations vacant' page, the print blurred in front of his eyes. Part-time check-out girls for the local supermarket, newspaper-delivery boys and girls, auxiliary nursing aides at the hospital.

He grimaced as he read this last entry. Sally complained fiercely that he objected to her working, calling him old-fashioned and unfair, but it wasn't her working that he minded but the fact that it was necessary. It hurt his pride that he no longer earned enough to support his own family, and it hurt him even more sensing that Sally found an enjoyment and pleasure in her work that she no longer seemed to find with him.

He folded the papers, his attention caught by the slow progression of a funeral cortège. His mouth twisted as he watched it.

They were cremating Andrew Ryecart today—that pale, fragile-looking little blonde in the front car must be his wife. She looked younger than he had expected. He felt the anger and bitterness swelling inside him as he stared at the car. It was all right for her. She would be financially secure; that sort always were. She would not be scanning the papers praying desperately for another job... any job just so long as it was a job. He was forty-four years old and the shadow of his father and the way he had lived his life, earning a few pounds here and there through a variety of casual jobs, not seeming to care about the contempt others held him in or how it might affect his family, hovered over him.

Joel had sworn that that would never happen to him; that his kids would always be able to hold their heads up high, that they would never know the humiliation he had known as a child, or the deprivations.

When his teacher had suggested putting him forward for the qualifying examination for a free place at a local independent school, his father had laughed out loud. A son of his, go to some posh private school?

'You can forget it,' he'd told Joel. 'That's not for the likes of us. Come sixteen you'll want to be out earning, not wasting your time getting some fancy education.'

Joel seldom thought about that these days. What was the point? And besides, he had been happy... happy and content with his life until they had started having all these money problems, until Sally had started making him feel inferior to that brother-in-law of hers, with his posh job and his detached house.

Well, there was no way he would ever be able to give Sally anything like that. Not now... They'd be lucky to keep their existing roof over their heads if he was made redundant, even with Sally working full-time.

Philippa glanced idly out of the car window. There was a man standing on the side of the road, staring fiercely at her, his black hair ruffled by the sharp breeze. He had a hard, sharp-boned face, his body tall and lean, and just for a moment, although really there was no physical resemblance between them at all apart from the dark hair and the fact that they were both male, there was something so hard and angry in the way he was looking at her that her heart jerked in angry panic and she was momentarily thrown back into the past to another man and his anger.

Quickly she looked away, biting down hard on her bottom lip to stop it from trembling.

Michael, her second brother, lived in Edinburgh and couldn't make it for the cremation. He had telephoned her the night before to apologise, explaining that he was committed to giving a presentation to the clients of the design company he worked for.

Philippa had reassured him that she understood. She had always been closer to Michael than she had to Robert. Three years younger than Robert and three years older than herself, Michael had been the ideal older brother, offering her comfort and sanctuary when the criticism of her parents and Robert had been too much for her.

She had missed him when he had left home to go to university and now that he was working quite a distance away, but, although they had always kept in touch, he and Andrew had never really hit it off.

Elizabeth saw the funeral cortège on her way back to the office after lunch.

She paused automatically and quietly by the side of the road, noting as she did so how few of the other pedestrians trudging down the street even glanced at the slow procession, never mind paid it the old traditional mark of motionless respect. Those who did were in the main like herself, offspring of a generation to whom strict observance of society's conventions had been important.

As the cortège passed, leaving her free to cross the road, she gave a small shiver. Such sad things, funerals. Both she and Richard were fit and healthy and not old by any means at all, but not young any more either. She had her daughter and a grandchild, her work and some very good friends, but none of them could ever fill the space, the emptiness in her life that would come if she lost Richard. Physically he looked much closer to fifty than sixty, with a full head of hair and a lean, athletic body.

She smiled a little to herself, recalling just how athletic that body could be and just how much pleasure she still got from touching him and being touched by him in turn, but then he had always been a particularly tactile man, hugging and kissing his daughter and showing her physical affection, which had not been common at the time among their peers.

She remembered once seeing him reach out and fiercely hug one of his young male students when the boy had finally passed his examinations after two daunting failures. The boy had looked surprised and slightly embarrassed at first, but Elizabeth would never forget the look of pride and joy which had quickly followed. It had brought home how severe and hard the pressure was on boys to conform to their sexual stereotyping from a very young age. For a moment that young man had looked again like a small boy, thrilled by the acknowledgement and acclaim, the approval of a male parent.

She had often wondered if it was this side of his nature that made Richard such a skilled and almost intuitive surgeon. Although he was in every single way a very vigorously male man, there was also, she thought, a softening, warming mixture of some feminine instincts and emotions in his genes which in her eyes only served to underline and increase the effect of his masculinity.

*   *   *

Robert was making a speech. His voice was full-bodied and measured, grave, as befitted a person speaking of the dead. He was asking them to ignore Andrew's weaknesses in the final months of his life and to think instead of the man he had been before he fell victim to the unfortunate circumstances which had led to his taking his own life. To listen to him, one would have thought he felt nothing but sympathy and compassion for Andrew, Philippa reflected as she watched him.

Was this really the same man who had told her that he couldn't help her, that he couldn't afford to be tainted by the relationship between them, who had betrayed so conclusively his own weakness of character; his own selfishness and instinct for self-preservation?

It surprised her a little how distant and divorced from the proceedings she actually felt, more as though she was merely a casual observer rather than Andrew's widow, her feelings, her emotions numb and frozen. Would they, like thawed fingers and toes, start to ache with violent pain when that numbness wore off?

Robert had stopped speaking. People shuffled politely, waiting for her to make the first move. Silently she did so, pausing as she emerged into the cold rawness outside the crematorium, her body stiff as she thanked people for coming and accepted their expressions of sympathy.

There had been few mourners there, few brave enough to admit that they knew the dead man. Was it that they feared that they might be contaminated by the failure which had destroyed him? Philippa smiled bitterly to herself.

'Come along, my dear,' her father urged her, taking hold of her arm. 'We all understand how you must be feeling.'

Did they? She doubted it, Philippa thought savagely as she pulled away from him, ignoring his irritated frown and her mother's displeased tutting.

Oh, she knew how they expected her to feel, the conventional emotion she was expected to betray. The shock, the tears, the grief.

But it was none of these she felt as she walked back to the car.

If she wept now it would not be for Andrew, it would be for herself, and they would not be tears of grief but tears of anger and resentment. Tears of admission of a helplessness she could not afford to feel—neither for her sons nor for herself.

CHAPTER SIX

PHILIPPA dressed apprehensively for her appointment with the bank manager. What did one wear for such an interview? Her black suit was probably the most appropriate and businesslike thing she had in her wardrobe, but she shrank from putting it on again so soon.

The only other formal outfits she possessed were the pretty silk dresses and matching jackets, the expensive silk and cashmere pastel-coloured separates which Andrew had always insisted on her wearing; the kind of clothes which looked fragile and luxurious. School open days and private garden and house party clothes, Philippa had always privately thought of them. Pretty clothes for a pretty woman; expensive and impractical clothes to show off and underline Andrew's wealth and achievements.

And totally unsuitable for her to wear now; they would make her feel like a modern Marie Antoinette, flaunting her luxuries while others went without.

Now that she was over the initial shock of Andrew's death, now that she had forced herself to admit the anger and resentment she felt at what he had done, she had started to broaden the scope of her thoughts and anxieties. She might not be responsible in any way for the fate of the factory, of those who worked in it, but that did not stop her feeling concerned, anxious, guilty almost, mentally comparing their fate with her own.

In the end she wore the black suit, crushing down her feelings of distaste as she put it on.

She had driven up to the school yesterday, Sunday, to see the boys, and her car would now need filling with petrol, she reminded herself as she left the house.

Both Rory and Daniel seemed to be coping well with their father's death, but she suspected that the reality of it would

not really touch them until they returned home for the
Easter holidays.

Her appointment at the bank was not until ten o'clock
and she had plenty of time, she assured herself as she pulled
in at the garage where she always got her petrol. Andrew
had an account there; it was one of those domineering male
traits which she often resented in him that, while he always
insisted on her having the best of everything, he did not
like handing actual cash over to her. The bills for all her
credit cards were sent to him; her car, her clothes, even
their food were all paid for via these cards and the small
amount of actual cash he allowed her carefully monitored
by him. Not because he didn't trust her, but, she suspected,
because he enjoyed and needed to feel he was in control of
her and of her life.

She filled her tank with petrol and then walked into the
shop.

The woman behind the till was the wife of the garage
manager. Philippa smiled at her as she asked her if she
would put the cost of her petrol on their account.

The woman flushed uncomfortably and glanced uncertainly over her shoulder towards an open door that led into
what Philippa presumed was an office. Then, even though
there was no one else in the shop, she lowered her voice
slightly as she leaned towards Philippa and asked awkwardly, 'I'm sorry, Mrs Ryecart, but could you possibly
pay cash?'

Taken aback and flushing slightly herself in response to
the woman's embarrassment, Philippa reached automatically into her handbag, fumbling for her purse.

'It's the rules, you see,' the woman was explaining uncomfortably. 'The account was in your husband's name
and . . .'

'Yes, yes, of course. I understand,' Philippa assured her.
She could feel her face starting to burn with embarrassed
heat as she opened her purse. How much money did she
have? Please God, let it be enough to pay for her petrol.
Why on earth hadn't she had the sense to realise for herself
that this would happen? Andrew had always countersigned

the petrol bill at the end of the month when he'd paid it and she ought to have recognised that with him dead problems might arise. The garage obviously had done.

Even as she felt the relief of discovering that she had enough cash with her to cover the bill, she was still furiously angry with herself and dismayingly aware of how dismally lacking in common sense and ordinary everyday awareness she must be not to have anticipated what might happen.

She could sign cheques on the joint account, a concession it had taken her many months to win, but only for amounts of fifty pounds at a time and never more than two hundred pounds in one month.

No doubt this was one of the reasons why the bank manager wanted to see her, she acknowledged as she left the garage and got back into her car.

Neville Wilson was a pleasant enough man, very much the archetypal bank manager type, worthy and perhaps a little on the dull side, addicted to his golf, and the type of man who enjoyed observing the conventions of small-town life and who would, in Philippa's estimation, feel uneasy and out of his depth without them.

Andrew had often boasted to her that he was the bank's biggest customer and that because of his flair and initiative, because of the way he had expanded the company, Neville's stock had been increased with his head office.

'It's no wonder they've never promoted him,' Andrew had told her after they had left one of the Wilsons' dinner parties. Andrew had been in a good mood that night, boasting at the dinner-table about the new contract he expected to win.

'He's too cautious . . . too stuck in his ways. I keep telling him that these days to make money you have to spend it. His own boss agrees with me. In fact I'm beginning to think I should deal with the regional office direct and bypass Neville. I'd get much faster results that way. They understand how important speed is these days.'

Andrew had also been in an unusually expansive mood that night. He had made love to her when they went to bed, a sure sign that he was in good temper.

Made love... Philippa grimaced to herself at how very much her parents' daughter she was at times. She and Andrew had not 'made love' at all—they hadn't really even had sex; they had simply been physically intimate, physically but not mentally and certainly not emotionally.

She hadn't seen Neville socially for several months after that, not until they had both been guests at a mutual acquaintance's dinner party.

'I'm sorry to hear that Andrew didn't get that Japanese contract after all,' he had said quietly to Philippa after dinner. 'It must have been a disappointment to him. I know how much he was counting on it.'

Philippa hadn't said anything. How could she have done? She had had no knowledge of the contract he was discussing and so she had simply smiled and changed the subject, asking him if he had managed to take time off to visit Wentworth to watch the golf—a special pro-am match which she knew would have appealed to him.

Now, as she remembered that conversation, her mouth twisted bitterly.

Had Neville perhaps been trying to warn her even then that things were going badly wrong for Andrew? But even if he had, what could she have done? She was the last person Andrew would have listened to or confided in.

Face it, she told herself as she walked into the bank. Andrew would not have listened to anyone who tried to tell him something he might not want to hear. He was simply not that kind of man.

She was several minutes early for her appointment and, bearing in mind the fact that she had used virtually all her spare cash to pay for her petrol, Philippa was just about to draw some cash from their account when she remembered the humiliating situation at the garage and decided to wait until she had spoken to Neville and sorted out whatever paperwork was necessary to enable her to take over their accounts.

At one minute to ten a young woman walked into the banking hall, tall and dressed in a smartly discreet, soft caramel-coloured business suit and a toning cream silk shirt. She gave off an aura which Philippa immediately envied. Although physically she was extremely attractive it was immediately obvious to Philippa as she observed her that it was not her looks that gave her her enviable air of self-confidence and assurance, her unmistakable and enviable professionalism.

This young woman was all that she herself had never been, Philippa acknowledged as she watched her; there were perhaps eight years, maybe even less between them but Philippa felt that they were divided by a gulf not of time but of life's experience.

She saw Neville coming out of his office, and stood up, but it was the girl whom he greeted first, before turning to Philippa and making an apology that he hadn't been able to join the other mourners at the crematorium.

As he showed them both into his office, it was the girl again whom he showed to the more prominent of the two chairs, quickly introducing her to Philippa as the representative of the firm of accountants the bank had called in to handle the firm's liquidation.

Thanks to Robert, she had been semi-prepared for such an announcement, but the gravity of Neville's voice and the way he was frowning down at the papers on his desk still heightened her anxiety, the shock of hearing what she dreaded sliding coldly through her stomach, her body tensing.

Habit and training cautioned her simply to sit and listen, to retreat into the protection of a semi-frozen silence, but older instincts urged her to accept reality, warned her that it wasn't just herself she had to protect and defend but her sons as well.

Neville was still frowning. He coughed and cleared his throat.

'I realise this has come as a shock to you,' he told her. 'But it has to be discussed, I'm afraid.'

'Yes...yes. I appreciate that,' Philippa told him huskily. 'It's just...' She could feel her throat beginning to close up, weak tears of fear and panic threatening to flood her eyes.

She couldn't cry...she mustn't cry...she was not going to cry, she told herself fiercely. Out of the corner of her eye she could see the expression on Deborah's face and momentarily envied her.

She was young, so obviously self-confident and in control of her life, that faint hint of pity Philippa could see in her eyes making her feel worse rather than better.

Gritting her teeth, she lifted her head and looked directly at Neville.

'Could you explain the exact situation to me, Neville?' she asked him quietly. 'I...Andrew didn't discuss his business affairs with me. He wasn't that sort of man and I——'

She broke off, her face hot, aware of how stupid she must sound and aware too of the covert message within her words, the in-built need to apologise for herself and ask forgiveness.

Neville Wilson watched her. She was still in shock, poor woman, and no wonder. This wasn't the first time he had been in this situation and it wouldn't be the last. He had warned Andrew about the risk he was taking, but Andrew had refused to listen and it was no surprise to Neville to hear that he had kept Philippa in the dark about his business affairs.

'A lot of men are like Andrew,' he told Philippa. 'I sometimes suspect that it's partly the excitement of the secrecy of keeping everything to themselves, of being totally in control that drives them on and makes them successful. Unfortunately, it's the same need for secrecy and control that works so dangerously in reverse when things go wrong.

'I tried to warn Andrew on several occasions about what he was doing but...'

'But the bank still loaned him money,' Philippa intervened quietly.

Neville gave a small shrug. 'Things were different then. It was a time of expansion; head office wanted us to lend and Andrew had the collateral, or at least...'

'Your husband's business isn't the only one to suffer,' Deborah told Philippa. 'One of the problems a lot of small businesses have had to face is that the value of their collateral, the means by which they secure the money they borrow, has sharply depreciated. Bankruptcies are very much on the increase at the moment...'

'And suicide?' Philippa asked sharply before biting her lip and apologising huskily. 'I'm sorry... It's just...'

She was here, after all, to listen to what Neville and this young woman had to say, not to give way to her own emotions or express the anger and resentment she felt at what had happened to her.

Deborah watched her. There was no mistaking the other woman's shocked distress. Deborah actually felt sorry for her, her plight reaching out to her in a way she hadn't expected. Would she have felt a similar empathy had Philippa been a man? She didn't know, but then a man would not have been in such a situation, would he?

In the office and at home reading the bank's file on the company and its owner, it had been easy to criticise and condemn, to be distanced from the effect that Andrew Ryecart's financial ineptitude and arrogance had had on other people's lives, but here, facing one of, if not the prime victim of Andrew's overweening pride, Deborah suddenly realised exactly what Mark had meant when he had said that it was a side of their work he simply had no stomach for.

But it was her job to find the stomach for it, as Ryan would no doubt point out mockingly to her when she tried to express her present feelings to him.

Silently she listened as Neville Wilson explained the position to Philippa.

'Andrew fell into the same trap as many other people during the eighties,' he told her. 'He bought the company when interest rates were low and then borrowed heavily to re-equip it, bringing in new plants and taking on extra men, secure in the knowledge that there was an increasing market for his goods. Over-trading is the term we bankers use for it,' Neville told her drily. 'But, unfortunately, men like Andrew very rarely listen to our words of caution. Additionally, matters were made worse in Andrew's case by the fact that not only did interest rates rise steeply, but he had also gambled on winning an extremely large new contract and had expanded, borrowing extra money to spend on the plant and new buildings on the assumption that he would get this contract. At that time the value of his assets merited such a loan but, of course, now...'

'I suspect that your husband's accountants, like the bank, would have cautioned him to think very carefully about what he was doing,' Deborah intervened. 'We always counsel companies not to put too many of their eggs in the one basket, so to speak. Several small contracts are always much wiser and safer than one large one. Several small ones to provide the bread and butter and one large one for the jam are, of course, even better. Even if your husband had obtained this large contract he could still have been facing severe problems. What a lot of these large companies do is use their contracts as bait, and once they have their fish well and truly hooked and dependent on their contracts to stay in the business they use that power to force down the price of the goods or services they're buying. It's standard market practice but often, in the euphoria of obtaining a good new contract, even the most sensible of businessmen can forget that fact.

'In your husband's case, unfortunately, he was already over-committed financially before he expanded to take on this contract. Once he realised he wasn't going to get it, the only way the business could have survived would have been via a very large injection of cash. He couldn't borrow any more money. He had already borrowed up to the full extent of his assets and as it is the bank will be very lucky to recoup all of its money.'

'So there's no way the company could be kept going?' Philippa asked her.

Deborah shook her head. 'No, I'm sorry, there isn't. If there were, the bank, or more likely your husband's accountants, would have recommended appointing receivers; they would have taken over the running of the company and tried to keep it working as a going concern until they could find a buyer...'

'And there's no way that still could be done?' Philippa asked her eagerly. Perhaps if she talked to Robert, stressed to him how many people would be put out of work if the company closed down, played a little upon his pomposity... his public image and the acclaim he would receive locally if he 'saved' Kilcoyne's... 'If there were someone who could invest...'

Deborah shook her head again. Why was it that she felt so much pity and compassion for this woman? She was the antithesis of everything she was herself, pitifully defenceless and unaware, the kind of woman who probably never worried about anything other than what to serve at her next dinner party, whose knowledge of world affairs was probably limited to the name of Hillary Clinton's dress designer and who was probably more familiar with the current cost of a Chanel suit than with the current state of the share index.

The kind of woman who almost exactly mirrored the type personified by her own mother.

Deborah frowned abruptly. Where had that thought come from?

'Not unless this someone could come up with two million pounds,' she told Philippa briskly.

Philippa could feel the colour leaving her skin, her blood felt as though it was being sucked back through her veins by some giant vacuum pump, leaving her physically shaking... physically nauseous.

'Two million pounds! B-but that's impossible...' she started to stammer. 'Andrew would never borrow so much money... He couldn't!'

Deborah said nothing, pausing for a few seconds before removing a sheaf of papers from the file in front of her and saying quietly, 'It's our job as liquidators appointed by the bank, who are the main creditors—that is to say your late husband's biggest debts are with them—to recoup as much of this money as we can, and this process is normally done by liquidating the company's assets ... hence the term liquidation.

'What I have here is a list of those assets over which the bank has a charge; that is to say that when your husband borrowed this money from the bank he secured it by signing over to the bank those assets.'

Philippa tried to listen but she was still in shock, still stunned by the extent of Andrew's debt. Two million pounds ... how could he have borrowed so much money?

Deborah looked up at Neville Wilson. It was his job to explain to Philippa Ryecart the extent of her husband's debts and the consequences of them.

Silently she started to replace her papers in the file.

'And the people who work for the company?' she heard Philippa asking her urgently as she stood up. 'What will happen to them?'

'They'll be served with redundancy notices,' Deborah told her. 'There'll be a formal meeting this afternoon informing them officially of what's happened and ...'

'Redundancy!' Philippa shivered as she looked across at Neville.

'There isn't any alternative, I'm afraid,' he told her. 'It's standard procedure in such cases. Every extra day the company is in operation merely adds to its debt. I just wish I'd been able to persuade Andrew to listen to me when I tried to warn him about the risks he was running, but——'

He broke off as Deborah interrupted him to say quietly, 'I'll be in touch tomorrow morning as arranged.' She turned to Philippa. 'I'm sorry all this has to come as such a shock to you,' she told her.

As she left the office she was thanking her lucky stars that she was not the sort of woman who could ever fall into the kind of trap that Philippa had been caught in. To be so dependent on a man and so unaware of his financial affairs.

It crossed her mind that Ryan was very much the same kind of man as Andrew Ryecart had been.

In Neville's office Philippa stood up, preparing to leave, but Neville waved her back into her seat, saying, 'Not yet, Philippa—we still have one or two things to discuss...about Andrew's personal affairs.'

Andrew's personal affairs. Philippa stared numbly at him. She was still in shock. She had gone beyond her own personal anger and bitterness now, totally overwhelmed by her awareness of how many lives Andrew's egomania had destroyed.

All those people soon to lose their jobs; and in a town where all too probably they would not be able to find new ones.

'How could he have done it, Neville?' she asked shakily. 'How could he have taken such a risk?'

'He was that kind of man, Philippa,' Neville told her. 'He thrived on the excitement of taking that kind of gamble. He enjoyed taking risks.'

'With other people's lives...other people's welfare?' Philippa asked him bitterly. At the back of her mind was the thought that Andrew had not merely been a gambler addicted to the dangerous thrill of taking a risk, he had also been a coward, happy to gamble recklessly with the futures and livelihoods of others, but totally unable to face up to the consequences of losing that gamble when it affected him personally.

'You wanted to talk to me about Andrew's personal affairs,' she said wearily instead. 'The house was in Andrew's name but I suppose it will only be a formality having it transferred into mine as his widow...like the bank accounts.' She pulled a wry face. 'To be honest I haven't given much thought to that side of things and I should have done. It was a bit awkward at the garage this morning when I went to get petrol. They've stopped Andrew's account and I had to use the last of my cash. I'll need to draw some more from the joint account.'

Neville cleared his throat and looked down at his desk. 'I'm afraid it's not quite as simple as that, Philippa.'

As she looked into his face and saw his expression Philippa felt her stomach drop with all the speed and sickening effect of a high-speed lift. She knew even before he spoke that there was something seriously wrong, but her throat had gone so dry she couldn't even begin to ask what it was.

'Let's take the house first, shall we?' Neville was saying. 'When Andrew approached the bank for an additional loan we could only grant it against some sort of security. The company's assets were already tied up to secure the existing loans he had and so the only security Andrew had to offer was the equity in the house, and of course his insurance policies. If the house had been in joint names the bank would, of course, have been obliged to inform you of this and to get your signature to a document agreeing to it; however, as it was in Andrew's sole name...'

Philippa was shivering and yet it wasn't cold in the room.

'What are you trying to tell me, Neville?' she asked him through chattering teeth.

'The bank now owns the house, Philippa, along with all of Andrew's other assets.'

Philippa could see how much he was hating telling her this; she could see it in his eyes, and in the nervous betraying movements of his fingers as he fiddled with the file on his desk.

'And, like the company's assets, these will have to be sold and the money utilised to pay off the bank's borrowing.'

'And how long...how long will that take?' Philippa asked him.

What she meant was, how long would it be before she no longer had a roof over her head?

'I don't know. That will be head office's decision, not mine, since they sanctioned the extra borrowing.'

'And the bank accounts?' Philippa asked him, drymouthed. 'The money in them?'

Surely there must be something for her... If not, how on earth was she going to manage...how on earth would she live?

Neville shook his head.

'They're all well over the overdraft limits, I'm afraid, Philippa.'

The overdraft limits. She swallowed, swamped by shock and despair.

'I truly am sorry about all this,' Neville commiserated with her.

It was a far more common situation than many people realised. He could name half a dozen small business sole traders whose partners were living in blissful ignorance of the fact that the bank now owned their homes and that all that stood between them and repossession was the size of the current month's or in some cases the week's takings.

Philippa stood up, the room felt so claustrophobic she could hardly breathe.

'I'll be in touch with you just as soon as I've heard from head office,' Neville was saying, adding awkwardly, 'In the meantime, try not to worry too much. At least the boys' school fees are paid until the end of the year. The local Citizens Advice Bureau run a debt counselling service, Philippa. Why don't you go along and see them?'

What for? Philippa wanted to ask him. Are they going to give me the two million pounds to repay Andrew's debts? But she was so close to tears she dared not risk saying anything. It wasn't Neville's fault that Andrew had behaved so recklessly...so...so dangerously.

Had Robert known about any of this? she wondered as she stumbled into the fresh air. Was that why he had been so anxious to dissociate himself from things? And her parents? How would they react once they learned that she was going to be homeless?

She could feel the hot, weak tears of panic and self pity buried in the back of her eyes as she hurried towards her car, head bent not so much against the sharp buffeting wind as against the potentially curious and pitying glances of any passers-by.

She had parked her car in the town square, empty on a Monday of its market stalls. The square was dominated by the commanding façade of the town hall, built at the height of the Victorian age and far too large and domineering for its surroundings.

As she unlocked her car and removed her ticket, Philippa suddenly realised that the pound coin she had used to buy parking time had been virtually all the change she had got from paying for her petrol, and those notes with which she had paid for it had been all the money she had had.

The panic that hit her as she stood clinging on to the half-open door of her car was like nothing she had ever experienced in her life. It rolled over her, swamping her, reducing her to such a shocked and humiliated state that she could feel the shame of what had happened as though it were a fire that physically scorched her body.

For how long had they virtually been living on credit ... owing money to the bank? For how long had she been spending the bank's, other people's money, totally unaware ...? Why hadn't she realised ... questioned ... guessed ...?

But no matter how hard she tried to lash herself into a self-anger strong enough to obliterate her fear, it just wouldn't go away.

Somehow she managed to get herself into her car and get the engine started, her body trembling violently as she tried to come to terms with what she had learned.

When she got home and saw her brother Robert's car parked outside the house and Robert himself standing beside it looking anxiously down the drive, her relief was almost as strong as her earlier panic. Robert would know what she ought to do, she comforted herself as she got out of the car. She was his sister, her sons his nephews; they were a family and he was far more experienced and knowledge-able about financial affairs than she was.

'What is it?' he asked her as soon as he saw her face. 'What's wrong?'

Philippa shook her head. 'Let's go inside,' she told him, and then she realised that he wasn't on his own and that his wife was in the car.

She got out and gave Philippa a cool look. 'Duty' was a word she was frequently heard to utter and, looking at her, Philippa could see that it was 'duty' which had brought her here now.

'You've seen the bank?' was Robert's first question once they were inside.

'Yes,' Philippa confirmed. She swallowed hard as she told him, 'The bank has called in a firm of accountants to act as liquidators, and...'

'Never mind the company—what about Andrew's personal assets?' Robert asked her.

Philippa led them both into the sitting-room before turning round and saying quietly, 'What assets? Apparently this house and all Andrew's other assets, including his insurance policies, have been signed over to the bank as security for the money Andrew borrowed.'

It shocked her to realise that this did not surprise Robert as much as it had done her, and she could see from the way Lydia's mouth thinned what she thought of her announcement.

'Neville is going to let me know what will happen once he has heard from his head office,' she told Robert numbly, like a child repeating a carefully learned lesson.

Lydia gave a small snort of derision. 'There is only one thing that can happen. They'll put the house on the market and sell it. You really should have refused to allow Andrew to take such a risk, Philippa...'

'Not now, Lydia,' she heard Robert saying uncomfortably before he turned to her and suggested with false cheerfulness, 'It's a cold day, Philippa... How about a cup of tea?'

'Yes, of course; I'll go and make one.'

It was only when she was in the kitchen that she realised that she had run out of teabags and that in all the shock of Andrew's suicide she had forgotten to buy any more.

She went back to the sitting-room, to ask if they would have coffee instead, and stopped outside the door as she heard her sister-in-law's voice raised in sharp exasperation.

'Oh, really, Robert,' she was saying. 'You must admit that Philippa's brought this whole thing on herself. She ought to have had a far tighter grip on things. If she'd spent a bit more time watching Andrew and a little less spoiling those wretched boys, she probably wouldn't be in this mess now. How could she be stupid enough to allow him to sign away the house? I know she isn't exactly the most intelligent of women…but quite honestly I don't think we should be here…or getting involved. It won't do you any good at all to be connected with such an appalling mess. I respect the fact that she's your sister but really, what can we do?'

'If she loses the house——' she heard Robert saying uncomfortably.

'*If* she loses it?' Philippa could hear the derision in Lydia's voice. 'Of course she'll lose it, and as to what she'll do, then I expect she'll have to go and live with your parents. We can't have her living with us. Think of how embarrassing it would be, a constant reminder to people of what's happened, and that is the last thing you need. And it's not just her but those two boys as well. We'd probably end up having to pay their school fees as well as Sebastian's.

'And that's another thing. I can't pretend to approve of the way those boys are being brought up. They'd only be a bad influence on Sebastian and of course there would be other difficulties. Obviously Sebastian will ultimately have a very different adult life, and much better prospects than they will be able to expect. Daddy was saying the other day, by the way, that this year we really must consider letting Sebastian go out with the guns. Daddy first went out with them when he was seven and Sebastian is coming up for ten now.'

'Where is that tea?'

Shaking with anger, Philippa went back to the kitchen, rebelliously making the coffee in the thickest pottery mugs she could find, knowing how Lydia would react to them.

She wasn't disappointed. After one look at the tray she was carrying her sister-in-law gave her the briefest of chilly smiles and shook her head.

'Coffee? Oh, no, I never touch it. Not at this time of the day. Silly of me, but I still think of it as something one only drinks after a dinner party.

'Robert and I were just saying, Philippa, that perhaps the only fortunate aspect of this whole sorry affair is that at least your parents will be able to offer you a home. Although I must say,' she added disapprovingly when Philippa remained silent, 'I still cannot understand how you could have allowed Andrew to behave so foolishly. You must have realised what was happening.'

'Must I?' She turned away from her sister-in-law and looked directly at her brother, asking him, 'When did you realise, Robert?'

He cleared his throat and flushed uncomfortably, but before he could say anything Lydia was answering for him, her voice ice-cold with disdain as she informed Philippa, 'Well, of course we knew something must be wrong when Andrew came to see us and asked Robert to lend him some money. I mean, one simply doesn't do that sort of thing. It was all extremely embarrassing. I was very cross with him for putting Robert in such an awkward position. No family member should ever ask to borrow money from another. It always leads to problems.'

'Yes, I'm sure you're right,' Philippa agreed, somehow overcoming her shock to find her voice. Turning her back on Lydia, she looked at her brother and told him frankly, 'Well, you can rest assured that I shall never ask you to lend me money, Robert—and as for my sons,' she added, turning back to Lydia and giving her a fierce, betraying bright-eyed look, 'Sebastian is the one I feel sorry for, not them.'

She barely registered Lydia's outraged, 'Well, really!' as her sister-in-law stood up, her face flushed as she bridled at Philippa's comment. 'I think it's time we left, Robert. Your sister is obviously overwrought,' she announced.

Philippa went with them to the front door, waiting until Lydia had passed through it before touching Robert lightly on the arm and saying with quiet irony, 'Thank you for your help and support, Robert.'

She watched him flush without feeling the slightest bit of remorse, still so angry about Lydia's criticism of her sons that she didn't care how recklessly she was behaving.

CHAPTER SEVEN

JOEL could feel the tension the moment he walked in through the factory gates; smell it on the air almost like an animal scenting death.

As a child he had often heard his father boast that he was descended from Romany folk; tinkers more like, Joel had heard others sneer behind his back when he made his claim, but there were occasions when he was aware of this inheritance, felt it in the odd prickle of his skin, the unfamiliar intensity of his awareness of the emotions of others, felt it in the certainty of the way he knew odd things, even while he struggled to deny the experience.

He hung back slightly, watching the other men; some of them, the older ones, walked with their shoulders hunched and their heads down, showing their defeat, avoiding looking at anyone else or speaking to them, while the younger ones adopted a much more aggressive and don't-care swagger, hard, bright eyes challenging anyone who looked their way; but all of them shared the same emotion that was gutting him.

Fear. He could taste it in his mouth, dull, flat and metallic.

As he crossed the visitors' car park—just one of the many fancy and very expensive changes Andrew had made to the place when he'd taken it over—he paused to study the small group of business-suited men and women huddled together by one of the cars.

They were all that was left of the company's management team; the ones who had not been able to scramble off the sinking ship in time, he reflected bitterly as he watched them, the ones who had been either too stupid or too scared to recognise what was happening and leave before it was too late.

As he watched them Joel felt all the anger and fear he had been feeling since Andrew's suicide boiling up inside him.

It was because of them, because of their greed and mismanagement, that he was in the position he was today, but what did they care about what he felt, about his life, his fears, his needs? All they cared about was having a flash office and fancy company car. His face darkened as he recalled the problems his buying a new car had caused.

He clocked on automatically and then went to hang up his jacket. When he came back he saw that instead of working most of the other men were hanging about in small groups talking. The meeting with the management was scheduled for one o'clock.

Only one of the young apprentices was making any attempt to work, and Joel frowned as he heard Jim Gibbons, one of the older men, telling him to stop.

'What's the point?' he challenged Joel when Joel went over to tell him to leave the lad alone. 'None of us will be in work by the end of the week—not the way things are looking.'

'We don't know that,' Joel told him.

'Oh, come off it. Why the hell else did Ryecart top himself if it wasn't because he was going bust? This place is finished and we'll be lucky if we come out of it with our last week's wages, never mind our redundancy money. It's always the same: the bank will get some fancy firm of accountants in to make sure they get their pound of flesh, but when it comes to us getting what's rightfully ours...who the hell gives a toss about us? Course, it's all right for you. You've got your missus in work. A nurse, isn't she, down at the hospital? Smart pieces, those nurses, and not behind the door in bed either, if you know what I mean, or so they say... Does she keep her uniform on in bed for you, Joel?'

Joel forced himself to ignore the others' laughter. It was just their way of letting off steam, of coping with their fear; there was nothing personal or malicious in it.

'I hate it when Mum isn't here in the morning,' Cathy had grumbled earlier as she'd played with her cereal, and Joel had immediately felt both guilty and irritated as he heard the resentment in her voice; guilty because of his inability as a husband, a father and a provider to earn enough to support them all and irritated because of the way his children distanced themselves from him. It was Sally they wanted, not him, Sally they always turned to, her more than him.

Right from being a toddler of no more than two, his son had fiercely rejected any attempt Joel made to touch or hold him.

'He's a real mummy's boy,' Sally had said then, laughing softly as she'd taken over and held him. And, watching the way his son had clung to her, it hadn't just been the pain of rejection Joel had felt, but an actual physical jealousy as well.

Sally claimed that he was far harder on Paul than he was on Cathy.

'He's a boy,' he had told her in mitigation of his own behaviour.

Sally had just shaken her head, pursing her mouth in that way she had of showing her disapproval of what he said and did.

Sometimes these days it was hard to remember that that same mouth had once curved with joy and love for him ... had softened into helpless passion beneath his, had widened in shared laughter with his.

Yes, things had changed. She hadn't even cared enough to wake him this morning before she'd left to wish him luck, to tell him that she understood how he felt; to tell him that, in work or out of it, he was still the man she loved; it made no difference to her.

He put down the mug of coffee the apprentice had brought him, its contents untasted.

The boy was only sixteen, red-haired and pale-skinned, tall and gangly with a prominent Adam's apple and a voice which had still not broken properly.

He had attached himself to Joel, following him about everywhere, reminding Joel of the crossbred whippet pups his father had bred and sold. This boy had the same un-gainliness and clumsiness. His parents were divorced, his father remarried with a second family, and Joel was aware of a responsiveness to the boy's unexpressed need within himself that he had never been able to express with Paul.

Duncan needed his approval, shyly semi-hero-worship-ping him in a way that Paul had never done.

'I put sugar in it,' Duncan told him now, watching him put down his untouched coffee.

'Yeah, it's fine,' Joel assured him as he looked at his watch. Ten to one.

'Joel, what's going to happen...to us...?' Duncan blurted out, his pale skin flushing as not just Joel but several of the other men turned to look at him.

Before Joel could say anything, the door opened and the works manager walked in. He had aged years in the last few weeks, and no wonder, Joel reflected. He was in his fifties with one son at university and a daughter injured at birth who needed constant care.

'The council offered them a place for her at a special home,' Sally had told him. 'But Peggy Hatcher wouldn't hear of it.'

Joel watched as Keith Hatcher held open the door for the rest of the management team and the woman left to walk in.

She was a girl really still, not a woman, Joel reflected as Keith introduced her, her skin glowing with health and youth and good food. She looked glossy and polished as shiny and bright as a newly minted coin, so plainly un-touched by any of the disillusion and pain that life could hold that Joel felt a surge of anger against her.

What did *she* know of the lives of people like him...their problems, their hopes?

She had started to speak, her voice clear and firm. She was talking about the large amount of money Andrew had borrowed from the bank, explaining that it was because of his inability to repay this debt that the bank were now forced to put the company into liquidation in order to sell off its assets in an attempt to recoup what they could of their money.

The bank regretted the necessity of having to do this but they must understand that they really had no alternative; the company had been operating at a loss for some considerable time. They would all be issued with formal redundancy notices, she told them, making it sound as though in doing so the bank was doing them some sort of favour, Joel reflected mirthlessly as he watched her eyelids flutter betrayingly while she made this last statement.

So she wasn't totally unaware of what she was doing, then. He saw the way she suddenly found it impossible to look directly at them, dipping her head instead.

'What about our redundancy payments, and our pensions?' Joel asked her as she finished speaking, raising his voice so that she couldn't avoid hearing him.

'Ay...what about them?' someone else echoed, others taking up the cry, while she shuffled her papers and tried to look calm.

'Your normal statutory rights will naturally be honoured,' she informed them. 'You will be put on a list of preferred creditors and paid out once the liquidation is complete.'

When? Joel reflected bitterly. Their normal statutory rights fell a long way short of what they might have expected to receive had those of them with long service records been made redundant in the normal way of things.

'When does this redundancy take effect?' Joel asked her.

'Immediately,' she told him steadily.

'Immediately.' Joel stared at her. He had expected her to say that it would be a few weeks...a month or so. He knew his shock must be registered on his face, just as it was on the faces of the men around him; he knew it because he could see the pity in the woman's eyes as she dipped her head again and looked away from him.

Some of the men were turning to the union rep., demanding that he do something, but the man was just as helpless as they were themselves.

'The factory will be closed as from tonight,' the woman was saying in that cool, elegant, distant voice which belonged more surely to some posh dinner party than here on the factory floor. 'The accountants' office will remain open as there will be certain formalities to be completed.'

The company accountant didn't look too pleased at that prospect, Joel noticed. Personally he wouldn't have put it past Ryecart to have been up to all sorts of financial tricks.

No doubt he had feathered his nest warmly and safely enough. His wife wouldn't need to go out to work full-time to pay the mortgage and put food on the table, he reflected savagely.

'What will we do now, Joel?' Duncan asked him timidly an hour later.

'Do? Why, we get ourselves down to the social services and get ourselves on the dole just like the three million or so other poor sods who can't find themselves a job,' Joel told him savagely.

The dole... the scrap heap more like, because that was what it amounted to and that was all they were to the likes of Ryecart and his kind... so much human scrap... and not worth a single damn.

He could feel the anger and despair pounding through him like an inferno, a volcano of panic and fear which he couldn't allow to spill over and betray him.

He had known that this was likely to happen and he had thought he had prepared himself for it, but now that it *had* happened it was like being caught up in one of the frightening nightmares of his childhood when he was suddenly left alone and afraid in an alien landscape with no one to turn to.

He had prided himself always on being in control, on managing his life so that he never fell into the same trap as his father, so that he never had to live from day to day, dependent on the whim of others; but now all that was gone and along with his anger he felt a choking, killing sense of fear and aloneness.

All he wanted was to go home to Sally, to hold her and be held by her, to take comfort in her body and the security of her love, to know that she still saw him as a man . . . still valued him and his maleness and did not, as he did, feel that it was diminished by what had happened.

But these were feelings that he sensed rather than understood and analysed, knowing more that he needed the comfort of her body and warmth, her reassurance and her love than understanding why he needed them.

'I don't know how Mum's going to manage now. She relies on me and my wages,' Duncan was saying miserably.

'You'll soon get another job, son,' Joel told him automatically, reaching out to reassure him even though he knew his reassurance was as worthless as the promises that Ryecart had made them about the success of the company and the security of their jobs.

'Have you thought any more about what I said about working full-time?'

Sally paused, shifting her weight from one foot to the other.

'I'm sorry, Sister, but I haven't had the time to talk it over properly with Joel yet.'

'Well, don't leave it too long; there are quite a few others here who would jump at the chance of the extra money. You're a good nurse, Sally, and it's a pity you never went on to specialise further. Still, it's not too late.'

Sally stared at her. Sister O'Reilly was one of the old-fashioned sort, in her fifties, single and possessed of a lofty disdain for all members of the male sex above the age of twelve, excepting the Pope but including every male member of the medical profession.

'She ought to have been a nun,' one of the younger nurses had commented crossly when Sister had ticked her off for flirting with one of the interns on the ward, but Sally, who had shared night duty with her and knew a little more about her background than most, had told the girl not to be dismissive.

'She's forgotten more about nursing than you'll ever learn; and she started learning by nursing her mother and taking charge of her family when she was ten years old.'

That family were all scattered over the world now, some married with their own children, others in the church, and it had been Sister O'Reilly who had taken unpaid leave from her job to go home and nurse the father she had never loved—who could love a man who gave a woman a child every year, even though he could see it was slowly killing her?—through his last illness.

She was one of the old-school nurses and any kind of praise or sign of approval from her was so rare that Sally could only stare at her.

Her, take specialised training, even expect to become a Sister? Just wait until she told Joel that. Joel . . . today was the day he would learn what was happening at the factory.

She knew that he was expecting the worst, but at least they wouldn't be as badly off as some others. Why couldn't Joel see that and be glad about it instead of . . . ?

When they had first been married he had wanted to help her with the chores, sliding his arms round her waist while they were washing up, kissing the side of her throat, insisting when she was pregnant with Cathy on carrying the vacuum upstairs for her, refusing to let her do any heavy lifting or moving.

And then, when she had first brought Paul home from the hospital and discovered how difficult it was to cope with an energetic toddler and a new baby, he had taken charge of not just the washing-up and the vacuuming but the washing and ironing as well.

She remembered how it had reduced her to silly emotional tears to see his big hands gently trying to smooth out Cathy's little dresses and Paul's tiny baby clothes as he'd struggled to iron them, the frustration and helplessness in his eyes as the fiddliness of the task had threatened to defeat him. But he hadn't given up, and if his ironing had not been up to the standard of her own it had still moved her unbearably to witness his love and care for her and their children.

It had been after that that the first threads of tension had started to pull and then snarl up their relationship.

Paul had been a difficult baby, colicky and demanding, clinging to her and refusing to go to anyone else. He had even gone through a stage when he was two when he had actually screamed every time Joel went near him.

He had grown out of it, of course, but Joel had never been as relaxed or loving towards him as he was with Cathy, and that had hurt her.

Sometimes it was almost as though he actually resented Paul and his demands on her time and attention, seeming not to understand that Paul was a child and that there were times when his needs had to come first.

She knew Joel was worrying about his job and what was going to happen to them if he was made redundant, but why take it out on her and the kids? It wasn't their fault.

At two o'clock, when her shift ended, her feet and back ached. The last thing she felt like doing was going home to tackle the housework and the ironing. No doubt Joel and the kids would have left the kitchen in its usual mess this morning. Wistfully she imagined how wonderful it would be to go home and find the kitchen spotless, not a dirty plate or cup in sight, the sink cleaned, the floor swept and washed, everywhere smelling fresh and looking polished.

Like her sister's home? Only Daphne had a cleaner three mornings a week, a small, nervous woman whom Daphne bullied unmercifully and whom Sally privately felt sorry for.

'I don't know why I have her; she never does anything properly,' Daphne had once complained within the woman's hearing. 'I'm constantly having to check up on her.'

Sally remembered that she had been as embarrassed for her sister and her lack of good manners and consideration as she had been for poor Mrs Irving, her cleaner.

Not that Daphne would have understood how she felt. It amazed Sally sometimes that her sister wanted to remain in such close contact with her; after all, they had little in common these days other than the fact that they were sisters, and Daphne made such a thing of their upmarket lifestyle and their posh friends that Sally was surprised that she didn't drop her and Joel completely.

'What, and lose out on having someone to show off to?' had been Joel's acid comment when she had remarked on this to him. 'Don't be daft. I'll bet not many of her posh friends would let her get away with putting them down the way she does you.'

'She doesn't put me down,' Sally had defended her sister. 'And it's only natural that she should be proud of their success and...'

'And what?' Joel had demanded bitterly. 'Get a real kick out of rubbing your nose in it and making it plain that she doesn't think you've got much to be proud of? Oh, I've seen the way you look round this place when you come home from there.'

'Joel, it isn't true. I love our home,' Sally had protested, but it was true that sometimes she did feel slightly envious of Daphne. She only had to think of the benefits Daphne could give Edward that she and Joel could never give their two, especially not now.

Tiredly she pulled on her coat. Joel had bought it for her last winter, just before the company had cut all overtime. She had protested at the time that it was far too expensive, but she had loved it so much she hadn't been able to resist it.

They had seen it in the window of a small exclusive shop in the city, marked down in price to make way for the early spring stock. It was a clear, soft red that suited Sally's dark colouring, three-quarter-length, in a style that would never be outdated.

She didn't normally wear it for work, but she had forgotten to collect her mac from the cleaners, and because it had been a cold morning she had decided to wear it.

Her six-year-old basic-model car had gone in for a service and it was cold standing at the bus stop so early in the morning.

She was on her way out through Casualty when someone called her name. She stopped automatically, her face breaking into a smile as she saw Kenneth Drummond coming towards her on his crutches.

'Kenneth...Mr Drummond,' she corrected herself. 'What are you doing here? I thought Wednesday was your day for seeing Mr Scott.'

'It was, but there was some emergency and so they asked me to attend Mr Meadows' clinic this week instead, lucky for me. Oh, and by the way,' he added as he smiled down at her, 'you got it right the first time.'

When Sally looked puzzled, he said softly, 'Kenneth, not Mr Drummond.'

Oh, heavens, she wasn't really going to start blushing, was she? Sally wondered shakily. She hadn't missed, either, the significance of that deliberate 'lucky for me', nor the way he had looked at her when he'd asked her to call him Kenneth.

She had always liked him, of course, laughing with him and teasing him, listening to him and talking to him, but somehow it was different now that he was no longer one of her patients and instead of her looking down at him he was the one now looking down at her. He was a big man, nearly as tall as Joel but not quite as broad across the chest. As he touched her arm lightly she noticed that his hand felt smooth, not like Joel's, whose skin was rough.

'Are you just off?' he asked her now.

Sally nodded. 'Yes,' she agreed ruefully. 'I'm on my way home to the housework and the ironing.'

'I was just going to have a spot of lunch; I had hoped I might be able to persuade you to join me. I still haven't totally got full control of these things,' he told her wryly, gesturing towards his crutches.

Sally frowned hesitantly. 'Dressed like this?' Sally gestured to the uniform she was wearing beneath her coat. 'We aren't supposed...'

'We'll ask them to find us a quiet corner and you can keep your coat on. Please...' he wheedled.

Sally laughed, she couldn't help it.

'You don't fool me,' she told him, laughing. 'I know exactly what you're up to.'

His face sharpened, his voice deepening slightly as he gave her a look that for no reason at all caused her heart suddenly to beat a little faster.

'You do?'

'Yes, you just want me with you because of these,' she told him, gesturing towards his crutches.

She really shouldn't be doing this. She had a pile of ironing waiting for her at home, a hundred and one small jobs she needed to do, but why should she always be the one to do them? she decided rebelliously.

'Come on,' Kenneth instructed her, taking charge so easily and adeptly that they were out in the car park and heading towards his car almost before she knew what was happening. When he stopped next to a huge BMW saloon car and unlocked it Sally stared at him in consternation.

'Is this yours? How on earth do you drive it?'

'It's automatic and I've still got one good leg,' Kenneth told her, laughing. 'Come on, get in. I promise you I'm perfectly safe...as a driver...'

He couldn't really be flirting with her, could he? Sally wondered feverishly as she got into the front passenger seat. No, he was just being polite, friendly. The trouble with her was that she was so out of touch, so unused to being in the company of an attractive, communicative man that she didn't know how to respond any more, or how to read the subtle messages her senses were picking up from him.

She was being ridiculous, he just wanted someone to talk to, she told herself quickly as he started the car and then turned to smile at her.

'I know a pub where the bar meals are reasonably good and with a bit of luck midweek it should be fairly empty.'

As he watched her, Kenneth wondered how long it would be before she guessed how deliberately contrived this meeting had actually been. He had missed her like hell since he'd returned home, and it had only taken a chance discovery that there was an alternative clinic he could attend, plus a bit of time spent working out her shift pattern, to have him altering his appointment and then hanging about in Outpatients trying to make himself as unnoticeable as possible until she came off duty.

He had earned himself one or two sharp looks from a couple of nurses and one of the porters, but it had paid off.

Kenneth had no illusions about his situation. His feelings for Sally were far stronger than hers for him, if indeed she had any, but she was not totally unaware of him; that pretty little flush and sideways look had told him that.

For a man who claimed to need help with them he was remarkably adept at managing his crutches, Sally reflected as Kenneth parked his car and ushered her into the pub.

He had been right about its being quiet, and its setting out in the country, away from the town, meant that she was unlikely to bump into anyone who knew her.

She frowned. What had put that thought into her head? Why should it matter if anyone saw her? She wasn't doing anything wrong. She was just having lunch with an ex-patient, that was all.

Kenneth found them a table tucked away in a small natural alcove and then gestured to the menu blackboard behind the bar, asking her what she would like to eat.

When Sally saw the prices she hesitated, force of habit making her run down the list for the cheapest item.

'What's wrong . . . don't tell me you're dieting?' Kenneth teased her.

She laughed. 'No, it's just . . .'

'Just what? Nothing there that you fancy?'

'No, it's not that.' She could feel herself starting to flush slightly. 'It's all so expensive,' she whispered to him, watching as he frowned as he too studied the board, his voice gentle as he told her,

'Order whatever you want, Sally, and let me enjoy spoiling you a little bit . . . you deserve it.'

Sally had to look away from him. She could feel her face burning again, but this time not because she was embarrassed.

How long had it been since Joel had said anything to her like that . . . had made her feel valued and precious . . . had made her feel that it was a privilege and a pleasure to be with her?

In the end she ordered a lasagne and Kenneth did the same.

'Now,' he commanded when they had both been served, 'tell me what's wrong.'

'Wrong?' Sally stared at him, too surprised by his astuteness to question the intimacy of his demand. 'It's nothing...' she started to deny, and then when she saw his face she shook her head and admitted, 'It's Joel. He should hear today about his job. The factory he works for could be closed down and all the men made redundant. He's taking it very badly...' She bit her bottom lip. 'Worse than he needs to, really. It won't be easy but we could manage. I could go back to work full-time... Sister even said to me today that she thought I should take more training to help my career.' Sally laughed.

'I'm sure she's right,' Kenneth interrupted her. 'You're a very bright girl, Sally,' he told her before she could say anything. 'And it's a pity that...'

He stopped speaking abruptly.

'That what?' Sally challenged him.

'Nothing,' he told her quietly, and then admitted, 'I was going to say that it's a pity that your family didn't see to it that you had the chance to fulfil the potential you've so obviously got, but I didn't want you to think I was being critical of... of anyone.'

He meant of Joel, Sally recognised swiftly.

'Oh, you mustn't feel sorry for me,' she told him lightly. 'I was quite happy to give up work and stay home with the children.'

'Yes, but you're not happy now.'

Sally almost choked on the mouthful of food she had taken. She put down her knife and fork and looked at him.

'What makes you say that?' she asked him unsteadily.

'I can see it in your eyes,' he told her.

She looked across uncertainly at him, a tiny inner voice of caution warning her that what she was contemplating doing was dangerous, but the temptation to unburden herself to someone, to him, was too strong to resist.

'Tell me,' Kenneth insisted softly.

'I can't,' Sally protested. 'It's not...you're not...'

'Yes, you can. I'm not your patient any more, Sally, and I want to hear...to help.'

She shook her head as though trying to clear her thoughts.

'It's things at home,' she told him helplessly. 'Joel doesn't seem to realise how difficult it is for me, trying to work and doing everything there as well. He used to be so different but now it's almost as though he wants to make things as hard for me as he can...and not just for me. It's the kids as well. He's always finding fault with them, snapping at them. I *know* how worried he is about his job, but that's all the more reason why he should...'

'Perhaps he doesn't like the idea of your working, being independent, meeting new people,' Kenneth ventured.

Sally looked at him.

'But he *knows* we need the money. I can't believe he's behaving so childishly. I mean, what would it cost him to clear the table in the morning and rinse a few plates? And if he would just offer to do something to help out instead of me always having to ask, to nag... He went to the supermarket the other day and came back without any washing powder. Can you believe that? When I asked him why he said they hadn't got the brand I'd put on my list. I mean, he *knew* I was waiting to do the washing.' Sally, lost in the relief of being able to unburden herself to someone, didn't hear the frustration and anger in her voice, but Kenneth did.

He had been attracted to her almost as soon as he was well enough to be aware of her; there was a quietness about her, an orderliness, a neatness that appealed very strongly to the aesthetic streak in his nature.

He liked the simple, natural way she wore her thick, dark hair, her lack of artifice and flirtatiousness. Other men might consider her sexuality to be covert, muted, but he liked that in her. The obvious had never appealed very strongly to him; he found it irritating, offensive almost.

He had seen the look in Sally's eyes when they talked; had recognised how unused she was to the stimulation of informed discussion, of good conversation, and how, unlike many of those he tutored, she had a humbleness, a modesty, a vulnerability that touched him. She would be a pleasure to teach, to nurture. It was obvious to him that her present way of life and in particular her husband were not truly fulfilling her.

It had shocked him at first to discover how much he missed her now that he was back at home, the strength of his feelings for her catching him a little off guard. Lying in his hospital bed, flirting with her, he had in many ways simply been playing a game, but now it wasn't a game any longer.

He wanted Sally in his life and he wanted her there badly.

It was obvious to him that her husband did not appreciate her, not as he would have done...not as he would do. He grimaced slightly as he glanced at her coat.

'You should be wearing cream,' he told her. 'That's what I would have bought you. Cream cashmere; you have the colouring for it. So few women do. Something plain and elegant with a skirt to match and a silk shirt to go with it.'

'Cream cashmere?' Sally flushed and laughed at the same time. 'I could never wear anything like that,' she denied, shaking her head slightly. 'Even if we could afford it, it would be far too impractical.'

'It would suit you,' Kenneth insisted. 'You deserve it,' he added. 'You deserve so much more out of life than you're getting, Sally. So very, very much more. I just wish that I——' He broke off and she flushed even harder, guessing what he had been about to say.

It both alarmed and excited her that he should make his feelings for her so obvious; that he should talk to her so intensely and with such emotion. Joel had never been very good at expressing his emotions verbally. Oh, he had told her he loved her, but he had looked so awkward with the words, so uncomfortable...he wasn't at ease with them in the way that Kenneth was.

Being with Kenneth was the complete opposite of being with Joel. With Kenneth she felt relaxed, happy, warmed by his appreciation of her. With Kenneth there was no tension, no inner dread, no anxiety. And no guilt?

She moved uncomfortably in her seat. Already she had told Kenneth far more about herself, about her personal life than she should, certainly more than she had intended telling him.

Normally she was far more reserved, but Kenneth had a way of drawing her out, making her feel that her thoughts, her feelings were important to him.

Kenneth saw the small betraying movement she made and, correctly reading her thoughts, knew better than to risk pressing her any further. He had sown the seeds; now he would just have to wait patiently for them to grow, for her to realise how much he could give her.

There was one question he could not resist asking her, though.

'But you do still love him...your husband, despite everything?'

'Yes, of course I do,' Sally responded quickly. Too quickly? she wondered uneasily; her heart jumped shakily in her chest as she acknowledged that it was almost as though she dared not allow herself to consider Kenneth's question just in case...

Just in case what? Of course she loved Joel; of course she did.

'I must go,' she told Kenneth. 'The kids will be back from school soon.'

'Yes, of course. It won't take long to run you back,' Kenneth assured her.

Immediately Sally tensed. 'No, I'd rather you dropped me at the bus stop, if you don't mind.'

She could feel herself flushing again as he looked at her. It wasn't that she felt she had done anything wrong she assured herself defensively, but her neighbours were the sort who wouldn't waste time in coming round to find out how she had come to arrive home in such state.

It would be easy enough to explain to them, of course, to tell them that an ex-patient had offered her a lift, and, even as she heard Kenneth agreeing pleasantly that if that was what she wanted then that was what he would do, she felt both angry and flustered with herself for the way she had over-reacted. Like someone guilty...someone who had something to hide.

Nevertheless, it was a shock to see Joel's car in the drive as she walked up to the house, and as her heart started to thump uncomfortably against her ribcage and her stomach tensed with anxiety at the shock of seeing his car there at such an unexpected time of the day her footsteps slowed slightly.

He was in the kitchen when she walked in, his back turned towards her as he filled the kettle. The breakfast things had been removed from the table, she noticed absently as she hurried over to him, but the surface was smeared and there were coffee-mug rings where Joel hadn't thought to wipe it clean.

'Why aren't you at work?' she asked him anxiously as she took her coat off, but the moment he turned round she knew the answer. She could see it in his face, in the defeated look in his eyes.

'What work?' he asked tonelessly. 'There is no work. No work, no wages, and no damned redundancy either by the looks of it.'

'Oh, but that's not possible! You've worked there since leaving school.'

'Yes, well, it seems that doesn't count for anything. According to what we were told this afternoon, we're only getting our current week's wages because the bank didn't want it all over the newspapers that they weren't going to pay us. As far as our redundancy money goes, we won't know if or what we're going to get until everything's been sold off.'

Sally could see from his face, hear in his voice just how much this extra blow had affected him. He looked and sounded not frightened exactly... more beaten and vulnerable, stripped of his confidence, his head, his whole body bowed.

'Oh, Joel.' She walked up to him, instinctively moving towards him, gripping hold of his upper arms. 'Don't look like that, love,' she begged him. 'It will be all right; we'll manage.' Instinctively she adopted the soothing, reassuring voice she used to her patients and small children; the look in his eyes frightened her. She had never seen him looking so vulnerable and defeated. 'It isn't as though we weren't expecting it.' She felt him move and then take hold of her, wrapping his arms around her, holding her almost painfully tightly as he buried his head against her.

'Sally...'

She tensed as the kitchen door opened and over his shoulder she saw Cathy walk in. Joel tensed too and she wasn't sure which one of them moved first, if it was she who pushed him slightly away or he who released her.

'What's wrong with Dad?' asked Cathy as Joel turned his back on them and walked out of the kitchen and towards the stairs without saying anything.

'Nothing,' Sally told her. She wanted to go after Joel and tell him everything would be all right, that they would manage, but Cathy was demanding her attention and she could hear Paul whistling outside. As she hesitated, the phone rang. She went to pick up the receiver, sighing as she heard her sister's voice on the other end of the line.

Daphne wanted to tell her about the new dress Clifford had bought her for a dinner date he was taking her to, and as she listened Sally could feel herself growing not just increasingly irritated with her sister but angry with her as well. How could she go on and on about her dress, boasting about how much it had cost, when she and Joel...? Quickly Sally swallowed down her feelings. It wasn't Daphne's fault that Joel had lost his job.

Upstairs Joel stared out of the bedroom window. His eyes, his throat, his whole body ached. He could hear Sally's voice from the kitchen as she assured Daphne that yes, she was sure that blue was the right colour. Joel's body stiffened in angry resentment. Even her damned sister meant more to her than he did. She'd got more time to talk to her about a dress than she had for him.

Just for a moment there in the kitchen, as he had held her, he had felt the warmth of her against him. It had almost been like the old days when it had been just the two of them, when they'd been so close that sometimes she'd even seemed to read his mind.

Just holding her like that and being held by her had felt so good...it had made him feel so much better. He had even been tempted to tell her how afraid he felt, how alone, but then Cathy had walked in and all at once *he* didn't matter any more.

Some of the men had been talking about picketing the factory, staging a sit-in. They had asked him to join them, but what was the point? It wouldn't bring their jobs back. Besides, he doubted that they'd actually go through with it. They were just a group of hot-heads who couldn't accept that there was nothing they could do; that they just weren't important enough, just didn't count enough to be able to do anything. That girl had made that much plain when she had talked about their redundancy money.

'Preferred creditors', she had called them, along with the tax people and the VAT people and God alone knew who else, and Joel could guess just who would come first when it came to getting their money and it wouldn't be them.

Was this what he had done his apprenticeship for...worked for? Today had underlined for him as nothing else had ever done just how little he mattered and just how little value he had as a human being.

He had wanted to share with Sally the pain and hurt of knowing that...had needed to share it with her. But she had more important things to do, like talk to her sister about a dress!

CHAPTER EIGHT

DEBORAH paused outside the elegant building which housed the practice's office.

She had been surprised at first when Mark had told her that he wanted to leave London for somewhere quieter and more rural, but once she had been with him to the pretty cathedral city of Lincoln she had fallen in love with it as quickly and easily as she had done with Mark himself. She remembered now how it had crossed her mind when she'd come up here for her own first interview with the practice that it would be a good place to bring up children, and how astonished she had been to have had such a thought.

Children were not something which were on her current agenda; once she was past her thirtieth birthday, with her career firmly established, then she might think seriously about the issue.

Mark agreed with her; she could not envisage and did not want to envisage their relationship ending, but neither at the moment could she imagine herself settling into cosy domestic motherhood.

It had surprised her at first that the city should boast such a busy, thriving accountancy practice, but Mark had explained to her that the business had originally sprung up to service those clerics attached to the cathedral who had independent means, growing steadily from that to embrace the engineering industries developing in the nearby towns. As the industries had prospered, so too had the practice.

The neat lines and pretty demureness of the building gave Deborah pleasure. Not for the world would she have admitted this to anyone else; that almost sentimental romantic streak in her nature was a part of herself she preferred to keep private.

She could just imagine Ryan's reaction, for instance, if he ever caught her gazing dreamily at the building. He had been complaining only the previous month about how difficult it was to house modern technology inside such an old-fashioned shell.

It was no secret that he had tried to persuade the other partners to sell and move to a modern purpose-built office block on the outskirts of the city. They had not been of a mind to move, however, and Deborah suspected that Ryan's wife, Alice, had influenced their decision. She might not be an active partner in the business, but her father was still held in such great respect that her views were always listened to.

Ryan had been furious about it, virtually flaunting his relationship with his current lover in front of everyone in retaliation for his wife's refusal to do as he wished.

She had to know about his affairs, Deborah reflected, so why did she stay with him? Was it because she simply didn't care what he did? Some women were like that, but not her; if she ever discovered that Mark had been unfaithful to her...

It wouldn't be her pride that drove her to leave him if she did, nor even her self-respect; it would simply be the knowledge that something was broken... destroyed... that he... that their relationship was not, after all, all that she had thought.

The meeting at the factory had been far more difficult than she had envisaged—not because of the technical questions she had been asked, but because of the awareness of what her announcement was going to mean to the men who heard it.

She had already been unsettled by her interview with the widow, she admitted to herself as she walked into the building. She wondered what kind of man Andrew had been, to have left his wife so ill-prepared for the problems she was going to have to face.

She had heard one of the men at the factory commenting bitterly that he bet that Andrew had secreted enough money away so that his family wouldn't have to worry, and for a second her sympathy for Philippa Ryecart had almost overwhelmed her professionalism and she had been tempted to tell him how wrong he was.

She had done no such thing, of course.

She grimaced to herself, imagining Ryan's reaction to the news that she had allowed her emotions to get in the way of her professionalism. Mark would have understood, though. Mark! As she got into the lift she glanced at her watch, wondering if she had time to see him before her meeting with Ryan.

'Don't you trust me?' she had challenged Ryan when he had told her that he wanted her to report back to him after she had visited the factory.

'I do,' he had assured her. 'But you know how it is with some of the old brigade here.'

'You mean they don't think I'm up to handling this on my own?'

'They're an old-fashioned bunch. Some of them don't think that liquidation and receivership is a woman's field. How does Mark feel about your imminent promotion, by the way?' he added conversationally.

'He's very pleased for me,' Deborah had told him.

'Mmm, well, it takes all sorts, I suppose,' Ryan had told her, adding outrageously, 'Personally, I don't think I'd care too much for the thought of my woman overtaking me professionally. I like to be on top... Out of bed, although not necessarily in it.'

Deborah had known that she ought to make at least some sort of protest against his remark, even if it was only to point out to him that she was not Mark's 'woman', his possession, but his equal partner in their relationship; but equally she had also known that to do so was to allow herself to be drawn into the sexually flirtatious verbal conflict that Ryan loved and excelled at, and that, once having allowed him to draw her into that arena, she could potentially be leaving the door open for him to try to take things a stage further.

She had no illusions about his motives. Ryan would seduce her if he could and for no better reason than that it would amuse him to do so. She was heartily grateful for the fact that he was quite simply not her type. He was a very, very dangerous man, and, even recognising what he was and what he was doing, she was still aware that there was a tiny perverse and very feminine part of her that was very keenly aware of how easy it would be to fall into the trap of wanting to challenge so much openly chauvinistic masculinity and sexuality, to make him acknowledge the power of her femininity.

'Nothing to say?' he had teased her softly as she'd fought down an irritating inclination to drop her gaze from his.

'Sorry...' she apologised vaguely. 'What were you saying...?'

He had laughed then with one of those mercurial changes of temperament which made him so fascinating and so dangerous, but that night in bed with Mark, when he had switched their positions so that she was kneeling astride him, she had had a momentary and totally unwanted vision of Ryan. Even in allowing a woman the position which was supposed to establish her right of control, he would still demonstrate his need to dominate the situation; his hands, unlike Mark's, would not guide her gently on to his body, giving her the freedom to orchestrate her own pleasure, but would instead hold her captive to the exhibition of his own desire while he pretended to let her take control.

'What's wrong?' Mark had asked when she'd lifted herself away from him.

'Nothing,' she had told him as she'd lowered herself to take him in her mouth—out of guilt for thinking about another man at such an intimate moment, or out of the more prosaic realisation that on this occasion she was simply not likely to reach orgasm?

She wanted to be with Mark now, she admitted as she got out of the lift; she wanted to unburden herself to him, to let down her defences with him in a way she never could with Ryan and admit how much what she had had to do today had upset her.

However, Ryan was already walking down the corridor towards her.

'Good, you're back,' he announced. 'Come into my office and we'll run through everything.'

'A debriefing session?' Deborah asked him drily.

He gave her a quick, sexually challenging smile. 'My dear Deborah, I'd be delighted to debrief you if that's what you want... but not in my office, eh...?'

Just in time Deborah managed to stop herself from grinding her teeth and pointing out that his comment, as well as being unsubtly schoolboyish, was also a form of sexual harassment.

It might be true, but it would also be counterproductive, so instead of making any response she ignored what he had said, simply accompanying him back to his office instead and sitting down in the chair he waved her into.

'So let's start with the bank and the widow,' Ryan instructed.

'As we already know the bank holds a charge over both the company assets, such as they are, and all the personal assets as well.'

'Which are?' he asked.

'Not very much: the equity in the house, and a handful of insurance policies, which of course are worth nothing since he committed suicide.'

'Mmm... and any private, hidden resources?'

'I don't think so,' Deborah told him. 'Or at least, if there were, his wife... widow... isn't aware of them.'

Her expression changed slightly as she remembered how shocked Philippa had looked when she had learned the full extent of her husband's debts.

'Are you sure about that? After all, she's got every reason to try to hang on to anything he might have managed to put aside, hasn't she? And it certainly isn't unknown for men in Andrew's position to resort to a little bit of company fraud and hive off company assets for the benefit of his family.'

Deborah shook her head. 'He wasn't the type,' she told Ryan.

His eyebrows rose. 'Too honest? Oh, come on, Deborah...'

'Not too honest ... too arrogant and too egotistical,' she corrected him. 'I don't think it ever occurred to him even to think about his wife and sons. I don't think he was even prepared to accept that the business had failed.'

'Mmm ... well, we'll let that one ride for the time being, but it might be a good idea to keep an eye on our widow ... just in case she decides to take an unexpected holiday abroad or suddenly discovers an inheritance from a long-lost relative!'

Deborah put down the file she was holding. Ryan's sexual manipulation she was prepared to tolerate, but when it came to her professionalism ...

'Either you're prepared to trust my judgement, Ryan, or you aren't. And if you aren't ...'

'Yes?' he invited when she paused.

She took a deep breath and told him levelly, 'If you aren't, I'd rather you found someone else to handle the liquidation. I can understand that having backed my promotion you're anxious that I don't foul up, but if you can't trust me to make a basic character judgement ...'

'It isn't that I don't trust you,' Ryan told her smoothly. 'It's simply that I suspect that because of your own nature you aren't always aware of quite how devious others can be. Your honesty and openness are traits I greatly admire in you, Deborah, but when it comes to judging other people ...'

'You think I'm too naïve to know when I'm being lied to ...'

'Well, let's say that I think you could be inclined to err on the side of compassion.'

'Because we're both members of the same sex?'

'Well, there is that, although in my experience your sex is more inclined to be enemies than allies ... Have you arranged another meeting with the widow?'

Deborah shook her head. He hadn't taken her up on her challenge, but he hadn't backed down either. Typical Ryan, and unless she wanted to be branded as 'emotional' she suspected she would have to let the matter drop.

'Well, it might be an idea if you did.'

'If you think I should. Perhaps you'd like to be included in the meeting so that you can make your own assessment of her?'

'If you feel that you need me there, then of course I'd be delighted to help.'

This time Deborah did grind her teeth.

'What about the factory? How did you get on there?' Ryan asked her, deftly changing the subject.

'I explained the situation to the workforce and advised them that they'd all be issued with redundancy notices. I also explained to them their position as preferred creditors.'

'Mmm... Did you tell them that we're only expecting a low dividend and that they'll be lucky to get as much as fifty pence in the pound of what they're owed?'

'No, I didn't,' Deborah told him evenly. 'After all, we don't know yet that that will be the case.'

'Mmm—I forgot to warn you this morning: it might be an idea to get a security firm in to guard the place. We don't want anyone taking it into their head to stage a sit-in. We want to get everything sold off and the liquidation completed as quickly as possible.'

He frowned as his intercom buzzed and his secretary announced that a client was waiting to see him. 'Look, I haven't got any more time now, but there are still a few points I need to go over with you. This client is going to take up the rest of the afternoon, but we can take care of what's left after he's gone. We'll go to the wine bar at six.'

He was already standing up, dismissing her, not allowing her to refuse the suggestion.

Irritably Deborah went back to her own office. She should have thought about that point he'd raised about security for the factory herself and it galled her that she hadn't done. She could do it now, though.

'Sorry,' the office manager told her when she got through to the firm they always used. 'But we can't get anyone there until Wednesday now. Would you believe we're short-staffed?'

When she had put the receiver down she picked it up again, punching in Mark's extension number, but it was one of his colleagues who answered the phone, telling her that Mark was having a case meeting with their head of department.

She would have to get hold of him later to warn him that she was going to be working late. Briefly she wondered what his meeting was about, and hoped that it might be some new business.

He had become very reticent recently about discussing his work with her. She frowned, reflecting on this. It wasn't like him to be so edgy and irritable, and she had felt hurt by the way he seemed to be shutting her out of his professional life, as well as by the attitude he had taken to her promotion.

His obvious disapproval had taken the edge off her pleasure and sense of achievement, and today's events had underlined the fact that her promotion had come about through another person's downfall. She didn't feel particularly sorry for Andrew—in her opinion he had been a weak and very egotistical man—but his wife, his family, and those who had been unfortunate enough to be employed by him... She tensed a little, wondering how she would feel if Mark had been one of those men who would be going home today to break the news to their partners that they were out of work.

Of course she and Mark were in a very different situation; they were both professionals with separate careers, neither of them financially dependent on the other.

How many other lives besides his own had Andrew ruined with his reckless refusal to listen to anyone else's advice, his egotistical belief that he was immune to the dangers and risks inherent in his narrow-viewed way of running a business?

She wished now that she hadn't agreed to meet Ryan after work. In her present mood it was Mark she wanted to talk to, to confide in and share her emotions with.

Mark waited tensely as Peter Biddulph, his boss, finished studying the list he had in front of him.

Peter was about ten years older than Ryan, but a very, very different type of man. He was quiet, solid and not the type to put himself at risk in any way, but the clients trusted him and felt that their business affairs were safe with him. He was a calm, pragmatic man who seldom became irritated no matter what the provocation; a man whom others, including Mark, liked and admired.

Mark knew from the office grapevine that over the years there had been several attempts to entice him away from the practice, but he was not ambitious in the sense of wanting the prestige of a high-profile lifestyle or the material benefits that went with it.

The good name of the practice, though, meant a good deal to him, as did the success of his side of the business, and it was no secret within the firm that beneath his outward calm he was becoming increasingly concerned about the way in which the liquidation and receivership side of the practice's business was beginning to overtake their own.

'Ah, Mark,' he said now as he put down the list he was studying, steepling his fingers together and frowning as he studied them. 'I've got a list here of the accounts you took over when you joined us.' His frown deepened. 'Originally there were fifty names on that list. Now there are under forty.'

Mark could feel his tension increasing, his skin growing tight and hot across his facial bones as he fought down his instinctive need to defend himself and let Peter finish speaking.

'We all know, of course, that these are difficult times for industry. The recession and its aftermath are going to be felt for some years to come. Any business portfolio containing, as yours does, so many small industrial concerns is bound to mirror those effects. It isn't, after all, mere coincidence that the liquidation and receivership side of the practice is increasing in almost exactly the same numbers as ours is decreasing, no matter how much Ryan might choose to pretend that such an increase is hard-won and the result of energetic personal endeavour. The senior partners are not, of course, oblivious to the effect of market forces, but Ryan does tend...' He paused, frowning, and Mark knew that it was a sign of how disturbed he was by their falling business that he was actually discussing Ryan in such terms with him.

It was obvious there was no love lost between the two men; they were complete opposites in every way after all, and there was even some gossip—never substantiated—that before Ryan had come on the scene Peter had been dating Alice. If it was true Mark wondered if she ever regretted having married Ryan instead. Peter was a devoted and faithful husband and a doting father to his three daughters, while Ryan...

'When you originally came to us, Mark, the expectation was that with projected business growth you would ultimately become head of your own department, overseeing our industrial accounts, with your own qualified staff beneath you. However, obviously now...'

He looked up at Mark and told him quietly, 'At our last board meeting Ryan suggested that, in view of the loss of business in the industrial sector, instead of being expanded it be combined with our shop-business accounts, which have also been heavily depleted because of the recession.

'Needless to say I pointed out to the senior partners that all the signs are that the worst of the recession is over, and that history indicates that in its aftermath new businesses will flourish and that again, historically, such new businesses will in their early stages have to make heavy calls on our expertise and time, something we shall not be able to give them if our own staff resources have been depleted.'

He was frowning again, and Mark wondered bitterly what else Ryan had had to say; the man was a chancer, an aggressor, a privateer who fed off the weakness of others. He wouldn't just enjoy the opportunity to boost his side of the business and rate its importance over theirs, he would also have great personal satisfaction in putting Peter himself down... Peter or any other man. Ryan wasn't the sort who could ever accept anyone else as his equal, and he could certainly never be subservient to anyone.

'The partners saw my point, of course,' Peter was saying, 'but nevertheless . . .'

Mark guessed what was coming. He had sensed weeks ago now that the promotion he had originally been promised when he'd joined the practice was not going to be forthcoming.

'I'm sorry, Mark, but it won't be for very long. Charles will be retiring at the end of next year, and then of course naturally you will be in charge of the two combined sections, and in the meantime with both sections under his overall supervision that at least will free you to have more time to search actively for new business . . .'

Mark stared at him. His heart was pounding heavily and sickly; he could feel the pressure building up inside his stomach, the nausea and tension. His skin felt hot and cold at the same time, burning one second and then clammy with the ice-cold sweat of dread the next.

'Are you saying that my section is going to be amalgamated with Charles Sawyer's?' he managed to ask.

Peter was avoiding looking directly at him. 'The senior partners felt it would be for the best. As I said, it will at least free you to——'

'I'm an accountant, not a salesman!' Mark exploded.

This was far, far worse than he'd expected. He had come into Peter's office prepared to hear that the promotion he had been promised would not be forthcoming, but to learn as well that he was effectively being demoted, control of his own section taken away from him, and to be told that he had to go out and get new business . . . He could feel his face, his whole body burning with the humiliation of it. No wonder Peter couldn't look him in the eye. He felt like a pariah . . . a leper . . . a failure . . . and it was all Ryan's doing. Ryan, who . . . He had to get out of Peter's office. If he stayed any longer he would only say something he might later regret.

Like telling him to tell Ryan what he could do with his job? Was that perhaps what they . . . Peter, Ryan, the senior partners . . . actually wanted? Did they—were they deliberately trying to humiliate him so much professionally that he did leave? After all, with his section combined with Charles's, what real need did they have of him?

More time to get new business... and just how the hell was he supposed to do that?

'I really am sorry, Mark,' Peter was saying. 'But, as I said, Charles will be retiring soon, and of course there's no question of your having to take any reduction in salary... It's just as well Deborah didn't join you on this side of the business. I believe she's doing very well, by the way. Ryan was singing her praises to the senior partners. They weren't too happy about his intended promotion of her to take charge of this liquidation, but he assured them that she's up to handling it.'

It was five o'clock when Mark left Peter's office. The room he shared with the others was empty; after all, what need was there for any of them to work late? He frowned as he read the message on his desk. 'Deborah rang 4:00.'

He picked up his telephone receiver and then put it down again. It would be just as easy to walk over to her office.

The door was open and she was speaking to someone on the phone when he walked in. As he waited for her to finish he mentally compared the office she shared with her colleagues with his: it seemed lighter, brighter; the very air seemed to breathe energy and enthusiasm. There were flowers on her desk and half a dozen fat files.

He could feel something painful and bitter twist in his stomach. It wasn't jealousy, he told himself as she replaced the receiver and smiled at him. How could he be jealous of Debs? He loved her...

'Mark...'

She stopped speaking, her attention switching from him to Ryan as he strode into the room, pushing back the door with arrogant disregard for anyone standing close to it.

'Sorry, Mark,' he apologised insincerely. 'Didn't see you standing there.'

'I just came to see if you were ready to leave yet,' Mark told Deborah curtly, ignoring Ryan.

'Sorry, Mark,' Ryan repeated before Deborah could speak. 'You're too late; Debbie already has a date at the wine bar—with me...'

Debbie...since when had Ryan been calling her Debbie? She hated anyone calling her that. Mark could feel his hackles rising and his face starting to flush with anger and resentment. He knew that Ryan was deliberately trying to rile him and make him feel small and that the last thing he should do was to let him see that he was getting to him, but, coming on top of the humiliation of his interview with Peter, it was too much for his self-control.

'Ryan wants to go over a few points with me about this liquidation,' he could hear Deborah saying, but he wasn't really listening to her or focusing on her; instead he was watching Ryan, watching the wolfish pleased-with-himself smile curling on the other man's face. He was enjoying this, Mark knew; enjoying putting him down, making him look small, and Deborah was helping him do it... Couldn't she *see* that? Couldn't she *see* what Ryan was doing? Was she totally blind?

Abruptly his emotions changed shape, anger suddenly dominating them—anger against Deborah for the way she was letting Ryan manipulate her...use her...to get to him.

'Don't keep her up too late, will you?' he heard Ryan laughing as he turned to leave the office. 'She's going to have a very busy day ahead of her with this case.'

As he turned into the corridor Deborah followed him.

'Mark, I'm sorry...'

'Sorry for what?' he demanded bitterly. 'Making me look a fool in front of Ryan? Well, so am I, and——'

'What...what are you talking about? I was just going to say I was sorry I hadn't managed to let you know I'd be working late... How did your meeting with Peter go?'

'Working...in the wine bar? Come off it—you know as well as I do what he's up to...and he must think he's in with a damned good chance otherwise he wouldn't bother wasting his time, would he?' Mark accused her angrily.

He caught her fiercely indrawn breath and knew he had gone too far, knew that his accusation was baseless and unfounded, but his own emotions were too raw for him to be able to draw back from it and admit that he was wrong, too raw for him to explain. Any minute now and Ryan would come striding into the corridor flashing that wolfish grin of his, throwing his weight around.

'Haven't you got to go?' he asked Deborah tensely, adding sarcastically, 'After all, we mustn't keep your date waiting, must we...?'

'Problems?' Ryan asked Deborah when she walked back into the office.

'No,' she denied.

'Mmm...I just thought poor old Mark didn't look too pleased.'

'I'd forgotten that we'd arranged to go for a meal,' Deborah lied.

'Ah, I see... Well, then, since you're missing out on a meal as well as his company, perhaps I'd better feed you as compensation.'

He knew damn well she was lying about the reason for Mark's bad temper, Deborah was sure of it, and now she was trapped into having a meal with him, which was the last thing she wanted.

Why on earth had Mark behaved like that? Why hadn't he listened to her...let her explain?

From longing to be with him to talk over her day and her feelings about the liquidation, she was now almost dreading going home.

Dreading going home to Mark? But that was impossible. Unthinkable!

CHAPTER NINE

'ANOTHER drink?'

Deborah shook her head, starting to tense as Ryan leaned across the table and asked her, 'What's wrong? Not still worrying about the boyfriend having a sulk, are you?'

'Mark *wasn't* sulking,' Deborah denied quickly. 'He isn't that kind of person.' But she suspected that her body language was betraying her as she moved uncomfortably in her seat and saw the knowing look in Ryan's eyes.

'You can't afford to give this job anything less than one-hundred-and-twenty-per-cent commitment. Let Mark do his own worrying. You can't solve his problems for him.' He gave a brief dismissive shrug. 'He made the wrong choice and now he's paying for it... tough. OK, so no one likes being demoted, but he must have seen what was coming, and in his shoes...'

'Demoted...?' Deborah stared at him.

'Ah, he hasn't told you yet...' He gave another small shrug. 'Look, let me get you that drink and we can——'

'No...no, I really can't stay.'

If what Ryan was saying was true, then no wonder Mark had seemed so on edge and touchy. But *why* hadn't he *said* something to her...why hadn't he *shared* his feelings with her the way she had always done with him? As Ryan had just said, Mark must have had some inkling of what was going to happen.

Now pride battled against anxiety as she fought down the temptation to ask Ryan exactly what was going to happen.

Mark would hate the thought of her discussing him with Ryan, she knew that, and yet surely he must have realised that Ryan was likely to say something to her. Hadn't it occurred to him how hurtful it would be for her to hear something like that from someone else?

'It bothers you, doesn't it?' Ryan asked softly now, causing her to focus unhappily on him and be betrayed into insisting otherwise.

'No...I...'

'Yes, it does,' Ryan insisted. 'After all, if he can keep something like that hidden from you, just think of the other things he might not have told you.'

As she gritted her teeth Deborah tried to remind herself that Ryan was being deliberately manipulative; that situations such as this were meat and drink to him; that he loved pitting people against one another, that he loved confrontation.

'He only saw Peter this afternoon,' she pointed out, trying to remain calm. 'He hasn't *had* much opportunity to tell me.'

Ryan laughed. 'Nice try, but it won't work. Think about it, Deborah. Either the man's so much of a fool that he didn't know what was coming, or he knew and chose not to tell you; either way... You're a very intelligent woman, Deborah, and a very beautiful one. You need a man who can match you...help you...teach you...not a boy still crying for his mother.'

Deborah could hear his contempt for Mark in his voice and she could hear something else as well. Up until now she had always put Ryan's sexual flirtations towards her down to a simple, meaningless flexing of his male muscles, an automatic showing off of his sexuality, and she had accordingly distanced herself from it and ignored it, treating it as a facet of her working life which was irritating rather than dangerous.

Now she wondered a little uneasily if she had been too sanguine. There had been a very definite sexual warning in the way Ryan had just looked at her, the way he had spoken to her, and the way she herself for a moment had felt that small dangerous awareness of coming close to being flattered by his interest in her. Ryan was a very experienced seducer, she reminded herself, who well knew a woman's vulnerabilities and how to play on them.

He was also her boss and a married man, and, even if all her love and her loyalty had not been given to Mark, that combination was surely so notoriously explosive that no woman who valued either her emotional or financial security would ever risk getting involved.

Ninety per cent of her appeal to Ryan was the fact that she was unavailable, and almost all of the remaining ten per cent was probably caused by the fact that he enjoyed putting one over on another man... in this case Mark, she told herself wryly. The fact that Mark had not discussed his work problems with her was a personal issue to be discussed between the two of them, and she was no gullible girl, to fall into the tempting trap Ryan was setting for her.

'It's kind of you to offer me a fatherly shoulder to cry on, Ryan,' she said firmly now. 'But I know you didn't bring me here to discuss my personal affairs.' She gave him a wide, disingenuous smile, concealing her amusement as she watched his brief tell-tale reaction to her description of him as fatherly.

'I appreciate the help and advice you've given me professionally. I really have to leave now, though...'

'Running away...?' Ryan taunted her softly, quickly rallying.

Deborah ignored him. 'I've got some reading up I want to do.'

He didn't make any further attempt to persuade her to stay but, as they left the wine bar, he turned to her and told her, 'Sooner or later you're going to have to make a decision—you know that, don't you? He can't keep pace with you, Deborah, and you're either going to have to accept that or risk losing everything you've worked for. You're not doing either yourself or him any favours by letting him cling to you. A real man wouldn't do it. He'd want to sink or swim by his own endeavours...'

'Mark is a real man,' Deborah told him, suddenly very, very angry with him, 'and he's all the man that I need and want...'

'Then you're a fool,' Ryan told her brutally.

Her temper was still up when she let herself into the flat.

Mark was lying on the sofa, an empty glass on the floor beside him next to the foil dishes which had obviously contained a takeaway meal. The smell of it hung in the air. The sight of it, the message of solitude and defeat both it and he were screaming quietly and accusingly at her, darkened her anger to guilt.

Mark had neither spoken to her nor looked at her; he was leaning back in his chair, eyes closed as he focused on the music being fed to him through the earphones he was wearing. Was he sulking? Or punishing her?

She frowned, pushing the thought away, forcing herself to smile and sound cheerful as she stood in front of him and touched his arm. He opened his eyes but did not remove the earphones.

'Chinese...mmm...I'm starving too...'

'Didn't he offer to feed you? Perhaps he thought he wouldn't be able to push it through on his expenses...'

'I did say we were only going for a quick drink,' Deborah pointed out mildly as she bent down to pick up the detritus of his meal.

When she walked back into the sitting-room he was still lying on the sofa. She walked over to him, removing the earphones despite his protest, and demanded quietly, 'Mark, why didn't you tell me?'

'Tell you what?' he demanded truculently.

'About your...' she hesitated over using the word demotion and substituted instead 'your...job...'

'My job...' His mouth twisted bitterly as he sat up. 'What job?' he asked her. 'I don't have a job any more...just a share in someone else's... My God, when I think of what I gave up to come here... If I'd stayed on in London...' He got up, pacing the floor. 'No need to ask who told you, and I bet he enjoyed it as well. Smug bastard——'

'You could always have told me yourself,' Deborah interrupted him pointedly. 'Why *didn't* you tell me?' she asked him, her emotions getting the better of her as she pushed her hair back off of her face and sat down opposite him.

'When?' he asked her harshly. 'You've been far too busy to listen to anything I might have wanted to say recently.'

Deborah stared at him in disbelief as she heard the petulance in his voice, saw it in his face. She couldn't believe he was behaving so childishly. He had always seemed so mature, so secure.

'After all, why the hell should you listen to me?' he added bitterly. 'You've got far more important things to think about. My God, it's ironic, isn't it? When we first came here I was the one with the glowing future . . . the promised promotion . . .

'Do you know what Peter told me today? He said it wasn't good enough just to be an accountant; I had to be a salesman as well. A salesman . . . I can guess where that came from . . . your boss knows all about selling, doesn't he? After all, he sold himself when he married into the partnership. Well, if that's what it takes to succeed, I'd rather be a loser and——'

'Mark, you aren't a loser!' Deborah protested, interrupting him. 'It's the recession that's responsible for the loss of business, not . . .'

'Not me personally. Thanks, yes, I do know that . . . Pity I didn't follow your example, isn't it? Then I might be able to brag about my promotion and my new company car.'

Deborah stared at him, her face starting to flush with anger.

'That's not fair . . . I can understand how you must be feeling, but——'

'Can you . . . *can* you . . . ?' Mark interrupted her. '*Can you* understand how it feels when a shit like Ryan stands there smirking at you, gloating . . . ?'

Deborah didn't know what to say. His behaviour was so out of character and unfamiliar to her. She could understand his being upset—anyone would have been—but his comments about her . . . about Ryan . . . they were not what she had expected to hear from him.

'It's only a temporary set-back,' she told him. 'Things are bound to pick up, and when they do...'

'Oh, for God's sake... Don't you understand anything? This isn't just about the recession... It's...' He stopped abruptly.

'It's about what?' Deborah pressed him.

Mark shook his head. 'It doesn't matter. I'm tired...I'm going to bed...'

Deborah watched him unhappily. His behaviour was childish and unfair.

'No,' she contradicted him quietly. 'You can't leave it like that, Mark, and you know it. I am sorry about what's happened and I felt very hurt this evening hearing about it from Ryan and not from you. I know I've been wrapped up in this liquidation, but...'

'Why shouldn't you be? After all, you've always made it plain enough how important your career is to you.'

Deborah caught her breath at the thinly veiled accusation behind his words. Now her compassion was being overtaken by anger.

'Yes, it is,' she agreed firmly. 'Just as yours is to you. We've both of us always known that—and always accepted it until now...'

Mark looked at her. What she had said was true. Until now they had both accepted the importance of the other's career; until now... until hers had suddenly and unexpectedly overtaken his. He pushed the thought aside quickly. His takeaway meal tasted sour in his mouth—or was it the mean bitterness of his thoughts that was turning his stomach over? How could he admit to her that it was jealousy that was fuelling his fear and sense of failure? How could he admit it to her when he dared not even admit it to himself?

'I'm sorry,' he told her wearily. 'I suppose I am over-reacting. Even though I had guessed what might be coming, it was still a bit of a shock...'

'The recession won't last forever,' Deborah comforted him.

He gave her a twisted smile. 'Don't tell Ryan that,' he advised her.

'What exactly did Peter have to say?' she pressed him, ignoring his comment.

He told her, while she listened carefully.

'You'll only be working in tandem for a year,' she consoled him when he had finished 'and by then——'

'The recession will be over?' he interrupted her wryly. 'Stop trying to play Pollyanna, Debs. As a career move it's hardly likely to show up as a highlight on my c.v., is it, unlike your promotion? Ryan stopped me in the corridor this morning to commiserate with me because I wouldn't be getting a new company car this time round. He laughed when he told me I could always pretend to people that I'd been allocated yours. A top-of-the-range job, so I hear. Clever girl... What colour have you chosen?'

Deborah stared at him.

'I haven't...' Ryan had mentioned to her that she'd be getting a new company car, but other than register the information she hadn't given it another thought. She'd been far too busy thinking and worrying about how she was going to handle all the complications of the liquidation...

'Why don't you choose one?' she suggested, trying to lighten his mood.'

'There's no need to humour me,' Mark told her. 'I'm not a child, Debs...'

No... but you're coming dangerously close to behaving like one... The words hovered dangerously on her tongue, but she suppressed them. It was natural that he should be feeling upset, and Ryan hadn't helped, needling him like that. Why did men always have to take such things personally? If their positions had been reversed she knew she would have been just as disappointed as Mark at having her promised promotion withdrawn, but...

She frowned over that mental 'but', shying away from the implications of it, the questions it raised.

'I was looking forward to our having dinner together tonight,' she said instead, dismissing the thought that she was deliberately trying to placate him, to smooth away his bad feelings in the same way her mother used to take on the responsibility of smoothing away her father's bad moods.

As though she had somehow been responsible for them…as though…

'I felt awful when I was at the factory today, telling them that they were out of work.'

'I hope you didn't tell Ryan that?'

'No, I didn't. My work is something I discuss with him, but when it comes to my emotions…' She gave him a direct look and got up and went over to him. 'When it comes to those, you are the only person I want to share them with.'

Guilt touched Mark's heart. She was so open and honest, shaming him with her generosity and her love.

He reached out and pulled her down on to his knee, tucking her head into his shoulder and smoothing her hair back off her face. She moved against him, rubbing her skin sensuously against him, her movements as soft and pliant as a cat's.

'I'm sorry I've been such a pig,' he told her gruffly. 'I wanted to tell you about my job, but I didn't want to spoil your pleasure in your promotion.'

He knew as he said it that it wasn't strictly the truth; and that he was not only editing his real thoughts, but upgrading them as well, washing them clean of his real and much less admirable feelings.

As she listened to him Deborah expelled her breath on a small sigh of relief. Earlier, listening to him, she had come perilously close to suspecting that he actually resented her promotion. Now she was glad that she had resisted the temptation to say as much. She was beginning to let Ryan influence her judgement too much, she told herself; in future she must guard against letting his little digs at Mark get to her.

She and Mark were equals, playing their own individual roles in their relationship. There was no question of either of them wanting to be superior to the other in any way.

'I suppose Ryan made a pass at you this evening?' Mark commented, tugging gently on her hair.

'Only a half-hearted one.' Deborah laughed. 'He knows that he's not my type and the man I'm interested in is you.'

Because he wasn't like Ryan...because he wasn't all the things that Ryan was...because he wasn't as much of a man?

Deborah frowned as Mark got up and moved away from her.

'Mark...'

'Not tonight, Debs...I'm not exactly in the mood. Unlike your superstud of a boss, I can't deliver sex on demand.'

Deborah said nothing, but there was a note in his voice that upset her. Because Mark was unnecessarily comparing himself to Ryan or because he might have been insinuating that she was ignoring his emotional needs in favour of her own sexual ones?

'Still hungry?' she heard Mark asking her. 'You said that Ryan hadn't fed you,' he reminded her.

'No—no, he didn't,' she agreed.

'Right, you stay here and I'll go into the kitchen and make you my famous and incomparable cheese omelette.'

As he went into the small kitchen he wondered if Deborah could hear the false heartiness in his voice as clearly as he could himself. He had never had to pretend with her before, to conceal what he was really feeling.

She was so generous...so warm...so giving and loving. He had seen the look in her eyes when he'd told her he didn't want to make love.

How long was it going to be before in bed was the only place she still actually needed him? Ryan was her professional mentor now, not him... He paused, staring out of the kitchen window into the darkness. His own emotions confused him and made him feel uncomfortable and guilty.

He ignored them, turning his attention to the omelette. When he took it into the sitting-room Deborah smiled at him sleepily.

'Mmm, that smells wonderful,' she told him appreciatively. As he watched her eat it he remembered something he had meant to ask her earlier.

'Who's the new little blonde clerk?'

Deborah frowned thoughtfully. 'Oh, she's taken Myra's place while she's on maternity leave.' She wrinkled her nose. 'I know I'm being prejudiced but she is a bit bimboish, isn't she? Short skirts, dyed hair and that "helpless little me" act...'

'Bimboish... I thought...'

'You thought what?' Deborah prompted him, suppressing a yawn.

'Nothing,' Mark told her, removing her plate. He had thought the little blonde had been very soft and feminine. Her clothes weren't as elegant as Deborah's, of course, but there had been a shy, admiring sexual speculation in the way she had smiled at him that had made his hormone level rise abruptly...

'Don't let Ryan get to you,' he heard Deborah saying gently to him.

She had followed him into the kitchen, and as he turned round she put her arms around his neck and pulled him close to her, nuzzling her face affectionately into his neck.

'Mmm... all right, I won't; I'll let you get to me instead, shall I...?' he suggested as his hand slid over her body, cupping her breast; she felt him harden unmistakably against her.

She lifted her head, giving him a surprised look.

'I thought you didn't want...'

'I've changed my mind,' he told her, taking hold of her and starting to kiss her. After all it didn't really matter, surely, that it was the memory of another and very different woman that had suddenly aroused him? After all, it was Debs he was holding now, her body he was caressing, her mouth he was kissing, her familiar scent filling his nostrils, her soft little moan of pleasure...

CHAPTER TEN

RICHARD frowned, glancing at his watch as he parked his car in his designated spot. It had taken him ten minutes longer than usual to get to the hospital. The traffic on the bypass was becoming increasingly heavy with the closure of a local school and its amalgamation with another.

He was still frowning as he strode towards the hospital entrance. He was due to attend a meeting this morning at the Regional Health Authority's head office, about the siting of the Fast Response Accident Unit.

The suggestion to open such a unit locally had originally been his and he had worked hard to get the scheme off the ground, and, while logically he knew and believed that what really mattered was not where the unit was sited but how well it served its patients, another part of him slightly resented the fact that his idea, once formally adopted by the regional authority, was no longer solely his, and that they were now coming under increasing pressure to compete against another hospital for the unit.

'It's all these endless bloody meetings,' he had complained to Elizabeth at breakfast. 'They waste so much damned time. Committee men, accountants; *they* might have time to spend sitting around empire-building, but I don't. All I ever hear from Brian Simmonds these days is, "Don't forget, we can't afford to antagonise the committee."'

He had never liked the subtle behind-the-scenes manoeuvrings, the back-stabbings, the constant battle for power and control. He was a *surgeon*, that was where his skills lay... his forte did not lie in manipulating people, in being subtly persuasive, in distorting facts so that they showed to his advantage.

Unlike Christopher Jeffries, the consultant at the Northern, who seemed positively to enjoy the cut and thrust and the back-stabbing that went on at their meetings.

The issue should have been clear-cut enough, after all. It was simply a matter of deciding which hospital could best serve the needs of the public as the home of the Fast Response Accident Unit. Only that issue now seemed to have become clouded by others, so that it had become not just a battle to win the allocation of the unit, but a battle to determine which hospital would ultimately be superior to the other.

A morning at the Area Health Authority offices, trying to defend his own hospital's position and at the same time promote it as being superior to its rival, was far more exhausting than a whole week spent in Theatre, or at least it had been. In every operating theatre there was always some degree of tension; there had to be—the use of the word 'theatre' to describe the operation area was almost too appropriate. There, if one had time to observe it as an audience, the full drama of life and death was played out before one's eyes.

But that tension did not affect him negatively. It was a part and parcel of his life. A surgeon who claimed that he did not feel or experience it was, in his opinion, a surgeon who had no awareness of the trust and responsibility that others placed in him.

'Ah, Richard. Good—ready to leave. We might as well both travel in my car; it won't save much for practical purposes, but every little helps. I wanted to have a word with you about the budgets.'

Richard cursed under his breath. He had hoped to have a few minutes to go through his post before leaving for the Authority's headquarters, but Brian was making it plain that he was ready to leave.

The General had been one of the first hospitals to opt to become self-governing under the new government scheme, and, although Brian had been enthusiastic about the changes, Richard was still not wholly convinced. In theory the idea might be a good one, but as a surgeon he had an in-built dislike of equating health with money. It was his job to help people, not to divide them into those who could afford to be helped and those who could not.

'Yes, the budgets,' Brian announced once they were both inside his car and he was driving out of the hospital car park.

'You know what we're doing, don't you, with these budgets and quotas?' said Richard with concern. 'We're forcing some of the GP practices at the bottom end of the social scale to abandon patients who badly need their care. Of course a nice middle-class practice with sensible, healthy patients who take care of their health is going to manage its budget better than one where half its patients are teenage girls with a couple of illegitimate children and the other half pensioners who've never had the opportunity, the luxury, of taking care of their own health.'

'I know what you're saying, Richard, and of course there's no question of our abandoning those practices, those people... All I need for the time being, while we've got this decision hanging over us about the Fast Response Accident Unit, is for you to try to keep within the budgets. The chief administrator is an accountant by profession, and not...'

He stopped as Richard made a brief derogatory noise in his throat.

'That says it all, doesn't it?' he told Brian. 'We're here to promote health but we're run by accountants.'

'It's the way of the world these days,' Brian told him. He could see both sides... Sometimes he envied David Howarth, the chief administrator. He had no idea how difficult it could be here at the sharp end dealing with men like Richard, who, for all their dedication and brilliance when it came to their work, all too often stubbornly refused the need for financial discipline. Sometimes he felt as though he was single-handedly performing a balancing act worthy of Atlas himself.

He glanced at Richard's set face and sighed. He would just have to do what he could to keep Richard and David as far apart today as possible. David was one of the modern breed of administrators, the task of administration and financial control of much greater importance to him than the nature of the 'business' that finance related to. He had been head-hunted by the Authority from industry and it was common knowledge that in his previous position the spectacular improvement in cash flow he had achieved had been via a cost-cutting exercise which had involved a ruthless reduction of staff.

David had already hinted that he considered that the General was top-heavy with senior men, some of whom he would like to see pensioned off to open the door to more effective rationalisation and cost improvement.

'But we don't have anyone even remotely close to retirement age yet,' Brian had protested. 'Richard is in his mid-fifties and Leslie Osbourne is fifty-one.'

'In industry these days it isn't unusual to see men at the top going at fifty,' David had told him smoothly.

Brian frowned uncomfortably, remembering that interview. He was close to fifty himself.

Richard grimaced and flexed his muscles tiredly. Strange how sitting in a chair could make his bones ache so much more than operating.

The atmosphere in the room was tense and slightly dangerous. David enjoyed creating that kind of mental tension and aggression, Richard suspected.

As he glanced round the table he was aware that of the seven men there he was the oldest.

He frowned slightly, not wanting to acknowledge what lay behind that awareness. Leslie Osbourne wasn't that much younger than he—only a handful of years—and Brian was only a few years younger than Leslie, but he still couldn't help being aware that the three representatives present from the Northern were all younger, closer in age to David than to himself.

Leslie Osbourne, their senior anaesthetist, was making some comment to him. Leslie had travelled separately to the meeting, having spent the last couple of days at a conference.

As Richard turned his head to respond to his comment he was aware of David watching him.

David was a thin, tense man, slightly smaller than average height, which perhaps was at least part of the reason he felt such a need to exercise so much control over others and to challenge them to flout his authority, Richard reflected. He had pale blue eyes and a slightly underhung jaw. There was something almost weasly about him, even down to his quick, edgy body movements.

He would never have made a good surgeon; he was too impatient, too quick. It baffled Richard that anyone could ever have thought that such a man was the right person to head a health authority. He might be a brilliant accountant, but he knew nothing about people, their vulnerabilities, their needs.

As their glances engaged, Richard saw the dislike flicker briefly in David's eyes before he looked away.

No, I don't like you either, he acknowledged mentally.

It pleased Richard to see that David was the first to look away and turn towards Brian. It was petty of him to feel that small sense of victory, he knew, but that was the effect that David had on him.

'Yes, Brian, I agree that you're putting forward an excellent case for the accident unit to go to the General,' he heard David saying. 'And you've certainly spoken very emotively about the benefit that would accrue to the public as well as the General. However, in this instance we can't allow ourselves to be governed by our emotions. There are other things to consider. As chief administrator my prime concern is how effectively we can justify the financial outlay for such a service, and I'm afraid that on its present record the General is not proving to be very good at sticking to its financial targets.

'I don't want to start making specific criticisms or allocating specific blame. This meeting, after all, is to discuss the siting of the new unit, not to go over the old ground of budgets, but...' he paused and across the table his eyes met Richard's for a moment '...I cannot stress how important it is that the new unit is run efficiently financially, and I'm worried about the General's present showing, especially on the surgical side. Of course we're all agreed that the essence of a good accident unit is speed and efficiency, value for money, especially as far as the Department of Health is concerned. On paper I admit that your figures look good, but with your surgical budget already disastrously overspent... The public needs to feel confident that such a unit can deliver what it promises... How can either it or I have that confidence when you can't keep your existing departments within their budgets and your operation level up to their quotas?

'I'm sorry to say this, but on your present showing I'm afraid that you're beginning to fall very much behind the Northern's figures.'

Richard had heard enough.

'This unit is about saving lives, not money,' he told David sharply. 'Any good surgeon will tell you about the risks you take with people's lives once you start treating them like conveyor-belt products; they are each and every one of them individuals with individual needs.'

'Yes, I'm sure,' David stopped him angrily. 'But the days of surgeons playing God are, I'm afraid, Richard, gone forever. We are a public service and as such we are financially accountable to the public, a public who have every right to demand to know for instance why one hospital manages to perform almost twice as many hip replacements in a given period as another, and why that same one is somehow managing to reduce its drugs bill in addition to increasing its number of operations...'

'I judge the success-rate of my work not on how many operations I perform or how cheaply I deal with my patients' aftercare, but on providing the best chance of recovery and a good quality of life,' Richard told him quietly.

Inwardly he was seething with anger at the injustice and ignorance of David's criticisms. He might not be an accountant, but when it came to his own field of surgery...

'And I could ask you why, if this other hospital is doing as well as you think, GPs and their patients appear to prefer to come to us...?'

The tense, uncomfortable silence which followed his outburst left Richard wishing he had not allowed David to provoke him.

'Not every patient prefers the General, Richard,' David contradicted him silkily. 'In fact I received a letter only this morning from one of your patients complaining about the fact that you have postponed her operation on two successive occasions and asking that she be referred to another hospital. I didn't mean to bring this up in public, but since you yourself have focused the meeting on more personal issues I feel that in defence of the Northern's surgical unit I owe it to them to mention this complaint.'

The last time he had been humiliated so publicly had been when he was still a raw medical student but his reaction to David's comment was much the same now as it had been then: the sense of shock and discomfort, the awareness of other people's attention being focused on him with varying degrees of pity and amusement, the earburning sense of shame and the immediate and fierce desire to vindicate himself.

Only he wasn't a student any more, and the thought of having to justify himself to David Howarth of all men met with such a wall of resistance from his pride that he was powerless to do anything other than simply sit there.

It was left to Brian to say uncomfortably, 'I'm sure there's some logical explanation for delaying this patient's operation, David... Sometimes these things happen with non-urgent surgery... It's unfortunate, I know, that it should have happened more than once, but...'

'Are you telling me that it's common practice at the General to delay non-urgent operations more than once? You know how the Minister feels about this sort of thing, Brian, and it certainly doesn't augur well for the General's claims that it is the better choice for the new unit... I'm not sure too many accident victims would be happy to be told that their surgery had to be delayed,' he added sarcastically.

'Everyone at the General has worked very hard to help raise the extra cash for this new unit,' Brian began desperately. 'You know that——'

'I'm sorry, Brian,' David interrupted him smoothly, standing up, 'but we really must leave it there. I've got a meeting this afternoon.' He was halfway to the door before he stopped and turned round, the cold pale blue eyes surveying Richard triumphantly.

'Richard, a word in my office before you leave if you please... and I'd like you there as well, Brian...'

'Now, this complaint... the first thing we need to establish is that Mrs Jennings is correct when she claims that her operation has been delayed on two occasions.'

David smiled coldly at Richard, obviously already sure of the answer.

'Yes, it has,' Richard agreed tersely. He was damned if he was going to explain or excuse himself to this jumped-up, undersized accountant, who didn't know the first thing about surgery anyway.

'I'm sure that Richard had a perfectly good reason for delaying the woman's operation, David,' Brian was saying palliatingly next to him.

'Yes, I'm sure he had,' David agreed smoothly. 'And since the surgery is non-urgent there is no question of any lack of surgical judgement... fortunately...'

Richard froze. He knew damned well what David was up to, trying to suggest that he had shown a lack of good judgement, trying to intimate that he was getting too old to stay on top of things.

'However, I'm sure we all have to accept that there was a certain degree of lack of perception, shall we say? Of course, we all know it's easily done,' David continued, steepling his fingers and looking at Richard over the top of them. 'Pressure of work, strain, stress. All of these things build up and tend to lead to such misjudgements... Fortunately, as I've already said, in this case no one's life was put in danger, but I shall have to write and apologise and I suspect from the tone of this letter that we'll be very fortunate if we can keep it out of the local Press—and you know how the Minister feels about that kind of thing. I'm sorry to say this, Richard, but it only takes one mistake like this to prejudice people's minds against the efficiency of an entire hospital.

'As Brian said, I'm sure you had a perfectly good reason for this postponement...'

Angrily Richard stayed silent. He wasn't going to risk saying anything to David. He had already come dangerously, disastrously close to losing his temper with him once today, and there was no disguising the elation in David's manner towards him, now that he believed he had him wrong-footed.

'Can we assure Mrs Jennings that her operation will now receive priority?' he asked Richard. 'And an apology from you personally, Richard, might not be a bad idea.

'Oh, I'd like a word with you in private if you don't mind, Brian,' he continued, giving Richard a dismissive look.

As calmly as he could, Richard left his office.

The Health Authority's area offices, he decided bleakly as he went outside to wait for Brian, had as little to do with the saving of people's lives, with healing them and helping them, as the head offices of a bank. Money—that was what this place was all about. Money...not people...

'Brian, I wonder if you've given any more thought to suggesting to Richard that he take early retirement?'

Even though he had been semi-expecting it, Brian felt his heart sink.

'I doubt that he'd be interested, David. He's a first-rate surgeon. We're lucky to have him.'

'Are we?' David asked him drily. 'Mrs Jennings doesn't appear to think so.'

'We often have to alter operation times to make way for more urgent cases,' Brian appeased uncomfortably.

'This isn't just a matter of placating one angry patient; there's also the problems of the budgets and Richard's refusal even to try to stick to them. Quite honestly, Brian, if he can't move with the times and accept the way things are, then he is just going to have to make way for someone who can.

'I don't like to say this, but I really think you do need to keep a closer eye on him... for the patients' sakes if nothing else. I understand your loyalty to him, but I have to warn you that he could quite easily cost the General the new accident unit.'

'Richard's worked hard to help raise money towards it...'

'Yes... I know. Oh, by the way, your hospital's got someone to take over your psychiatric post. If he accepts you'll be very lucky. He's a first-rate psychiatrist, very highly qualified—over-qualified for the post really, but it seems he's anxious to come back over here for personal reasons... He's been working in the States for the last few years. I shall be writing to him later offering him the position.

'Now, about Richard... remember what I said, Brian. Quite honestly I think that, of all your options, persuading him to take early retirement would be the best... for the hospital's sake...'

The hospital's, or yours? Brian wondered cynically as he left David's office. It was obvious that the young man did not like Richard, but Richard unfortunately didn't seem to realise his own danger and exacerbated the situation instead of easing it.

From his office window David had a clear view of where Richard was standing in the car park waiting for Brian. Tall and broad-shouldered, with a thick head of strong dark hair, touched with distinguished wings of grey at his forehead, he was perhaps the epitome of every woman's fantasies of what a senior surgeon should look like, and the epitome of everything that he, David, most disliked and resented.

He could remember quite clearly the day he'd realised that he was never going to achieve such an enviable height, nor such almost film-star male good looks, and the bitterness that realisation had caused him, the jealousy and resentment.

But the tables were turned now and it was Richard and his type who were outsiders, doomed soon to be as extinct as dinosaurs, unable to adapt to fit into a world which had changed too fast for them.

Uncanny how much of a resemblance Richard bore to that long-ago schoolboy who had taunted him with his small stature and lack of macho maleness. He was smiling as he turned away from the window and went back to his desk to pick up Sophie Jennings' letter of complaint.

CHAPTER ELEVEN

TODAY was the day she had her appointment with the Citizens Advice Bureau, and in preparation for it, and also in an attempt to exert some kind of control and order over the chaos of Andrew's financial affairs, Philippa had spent the previous evening making lists of the positive and practical steps she could take to help herself.

It was a pitifully short list, but she still studied it with fierce concentration as she ate her breakfast. She had made herself a vow that she was no longer going to sit back and let life and other people make her decisions for her as she had done with Andrew; that she was going to grit her teeth and assert herself a little more, something she ought perhaps to have done years ago, she acknowledged self-critically now as she studied the list in front of her.

Her first priorities had to be: a) to find herself a job—any kind of job, just so long as it brought her in some income—and b) to do something about ensuring that both she and more importantly the boys had somewhere to live once the house was sold.

With half-term just over, the boys weren't due any more holidays until Easter. How quickly would the bank want her out of the house and how soon would they be able to sell it?

She wished now that she had questioned Neville Wilson more closely on these points, but at the time she had been too shocked to do so...

If the worst came to the worst she would just have to go cap in hand to her parents and ask if they could stay with them. It was the last thing she wanted to do, especially in view of their attitude, but for the boys' sakes she might finally have to do so. Where previously she had resented Andrew's insistence on sending them away to school, now she was almost grateful for it. At least while they were at school their lives were protected and secure... for the time being.

Next year... but she couldn't think as far ahead as next year at the moment—she dared not even think as far ahead as next week.

She looked at her list again... A job... She smiled wryly to herself. She wasn't so naïve as to imagine she would find work easily.

There were training schemes, though, she told herself. She had spent the last few days studying the local papers and visiting the Job Centre, obtaining as much information as she could on what kind of training schemes might be available to her, and this was one of the things she hoped to discuss with the Citizens Advice Bureau counsellor.

She glanced at the kitchen clock. It was time for her to leave; she had made her appointment as early in the morning as she could, not wanting to spend all day worrying apprehensively about it.

She stood up, smoothing down the skirt of her suit. She had seen an advertisement in the local paper for a second-hand clothes shop; they must buy clothes as well as sell them, and what good was a wardrobe full of expensive clothes to her when she hadn't really got enough money to eat?

Which was her own fault and no one else's, she told herself firmly as she left the house, muttering under her breath, 'I'm *damned* if I'm going to start wallowing in self-pity.'

She had two clear choices ahead of her now, two clearly diverging paths she could take: she could either succumb to the fear, misery and despair she could feel waiting to overwhelm her, to pounce on her like shadows lingering threateningly in the dark, or she could fight the situation just as hard as she could and look upon what had happened as an opportunity to prove to the world, and more importantly to herself, just how strong she could be. A chance to have a fresh start and make her life what she wanted it to be, to be answerable only to herself and her sons.

She had her health, mentally and physically; she had a good brain even if she had lazily allowed it to semi-atrophy, and, perhaps most important of all, she admitted to herself, she also now had the impetus to make use of them; they were after all the only assets she now had, and if when she was younger she had not been able to motivate herself to use them for her own benefit, when it came to protecting and nurturing her sons...

The offices of the Citizens Advice Bureau were housed in a building next to the town hall. As Philippa approached them a young woman came down the steps towards her; she had a baby in a buggy and a toddler by the hand and Philippa automatically hurried up the steps to help her with the buggy.

As she turned to thank her, Philippa saw how very young she was, barely out of her teens. Her face looked pinched and thin, her collarbone sticking out sharply beneath the baggy black clothes she was wearing.

The toddler had a runny nose and the baby was crying; despite the cold wind neither child was wearing mittens and nor was the mother, and as she watched them Philippa felt a surge of angry despair against a world which on the one hand sanctimoniously and sentimentally semi-worshipped the ideal of motherhood—a motherhood that was depicted by an idealistic image of a glowing, perfect young woman clutching an even more perfect, glowing child, the status of both of them enhanced by a wealth of material assets— and yet on the other hand seemed deliberately to ignore the fact that motherhood for so many meant nothing like that. This was the reality of modern motherhood, this young, tired-looking girl.

And she thought she had problems, Philippa acknowledged as she hurried back up the steps.

The girl behind the reception desk gave her a friendly smile and asked her her name. The waiting-room had a shabby and yet somehow comforting air about it, slightly reminiscent of a doctor's surgery, with its faded notices and a pile of ancient out-of-date magazines.

Lost in studying her surroundings, Philippa started slightly when she heard someone saying her name, and focused on the elegant woman speaking to her.

'I'm Elizabeth Humphries,' the counsellor introduced herself as she showed Philippa into her office. 'We spoke briefly on the telephone when you rang to make your appointment.'

How much did she already know about her? Philippa wondered uncomfortably as she took the chair she was offered. The news of Andrew's suicide and the problems with the business had made headlines in the local paper and she suspected it would be naïve of her to think that this woman hadn't guessed who she was.

How did she feel, having to offer the same help and advice to the woman whose husband was responsible for so many other people losing their jobs?

But just in case she hadn't heard, Philippa gritted her teeth and briefly outlined her situation.

Elizabeth heard her out in silence, causing Philippa to grimace slightly and ask, 'You must feel that there are other people who need your help much more than I do. People...'

'Is that what you think?' Elizabeth asked her quietly. 'Or are you really trying to say that you believe that only a certain social class needs to come somewhere like this for advice? You'd be surprised how many professional and apparently financially stable people do come to us for debt counselling.'

'Yes, I understand that,' Philippa acknowledged.

'But you still don't feel that you should be sitting here...?' Elizabeth smiled at her. 'We're here to help and advise you,' she told her gently. 'Not to sit in judgement. Now, have you brought a list of your debts with you?'

Philippa handed the list over to her. 'I have written to them all explaining the position, but...'

'That's good,' Elizabeth told her approvingly. 'You'll find that most of them will be prepared to accept a minimal payment and...'

Philippa shook her head.

'I can't even afford that until I find some kind of work. I don't know what, though. I don't have any qualifications or training. My biggest worry at the moment apart from the debts is going to be finding somewhere to live. My husband bought the house in his own name with a legacy. He signed it over to the bank when he needed money for the company and, of course, the bank now want to call in their security.'

'Do you have family who could perhaps help?' Elizabeth asked her.

Philippa shook her head. 'Not really... my parents... although I had thought if I could get a job I could perhaps rent somewhere...'

'If you get accepted on a government training course, you will be paid a small amount while you're on it,' Elizabeth told her. 'And then, of course, there are other benefits you can claim, but I'm afraid when it comes to rehousing you... The effects of the recession have meant that there's been a tremendous backlog of people needing to be rehoused, many of whom have had to go into bed and breakfast accommodation in the meantime. Have you discussed with the bank when they will expect you to vacate the house?'

Philippa shook her head. Her whole body had gone icy cold when Elizabeth had started talking about her housing problems.

'It might very well be worth your while getting in touch with them, in pre-empting them, in fact, and pointing out to them the advantages of allowing you to remain in the house in a semi-official capacity as their nominated caretaker,' Elizabeth told her.

When Philippa frowned, Elizabeth explained, 'The housing market is still very depressed, especially at the higher end; the bank may very well decide not to sell immediately but to wait until things improve slightly and they can get a better price. If that were to happen it would make sense for them to protect their investment from any risk of being broken into and vandalised. They may very well be

prepared to allow you to stay on in a caretaking capacity
rather than go to the expense of employing someone else
to do so. They might not agree,' she warned Philippa, 'but
in my view it would certainly be worthwhile discussing it
with them. Don't expect them to agree immediately,
though,' she added. 'You may find you have to be persistent and work on them. Some people, especially women and
especially in such circumstances, find it difficult to be
assertive.'

Elizabeth looked speculatively at Philippa as she spoke.
She was a very, very pretty woman; even the stress and
strain she was under couldn't hide that fact. Was she also
the type of woman who had been used to using her prettiness
as a bargaining counter, using it to sway the judgement of
others in her favour, or did that slightly grim look of her
mouth and eyes actually mean that she could be firmer,
more decisive than her pretty-pretty looks seemed to imply?

Elizabeth suspected that it might. She was trained to observe people and their reactions, the unspoken ones as much
as the spoken, and she had noted that beneath her discomfort and embarrassment with her situation Philippa was
obviously quite used to and quite happy relating to her own
sex, and did not, as another woman with the same degree
of physical attractiveness might have done, give any hint
that she would be more comfortable dealing with a man,
with whom she could flirt and use her attractiveness.

'I'll make you an appointment to see the social services
people,' she told Philippa now.

She stopped speaking as Philippa winced.

'I've got two sons at private school; how can I claim
Social Security benefits?' Philippa asked her uncomfortably.

'You can because you must,' Elizabeth replied briskly.
Philippa flushed guiltily as she caught the note of censure
in her voice, but she couldn't bring herself to explain that
it wasn't so much pride she had felt as guilt. Those people
whom Andrew had caused to lose their jobs—they were the
ones who were entitled to state help, not her.

As she listened to Elizabeth explaining to her the various
options open to her under some of the government training

schemes she tried to imagine what her mother's reaction would be when she heard what she was doing. That was something else her father wouldn't want to have mentioned at his golf club... his daughter claiming Social Security.

She left Elizabeth's office with her head buzzing with information and determined to take Elizabeth's advice and approach the bank with a view to their letting her stay on in the house until it was sold. Even if it was only for a few months, it would give her a few months of relative security in which to concentrate on other things.

And the most important of those things had to be getting herself equipped to find a job and earn some money so that she could support herself and the boys.

As she walked across the square, she saw a woman collecting for charity. Automatically she stopped and put her hand in her pocket, freezing with anger and embarrassment as she remembered that the days were gone when she could put her hand in her pocket and give away loose change. What loose change? she derided herself as she hurried past the woman, head down, face flushed.

Elizabeth had been right when she had told her that she couldn't afford not to claim Social Security, whatever benefits she was entitled to, no matter how guilty it made her feel to have to do so.

Philippa rubbed her eyes tiredly. It had been a long day and her telephone call with Neville Wilson had left her feeling physically and mentally drained.

He would put her request to his head office, he had told her, but he had not been able to give her any real idea as to whether or not they would allow her to stay on.

She had sensed from his voice that he was sympathetic to her plight but, as he had pointed out, it would not be his decision. All she could do now, as far as the house was concerned at least, was wait... wait and hope. And she would, she admitted, have preferred the activity of doing something constructive, which in itself was an unexpected change of attitude for someone who had previously sat back and passively let life and others dictate their own terms to her.

At nine o'clock, just as she was about to go upstairs to run a bath before going to bed, she heard a car pulling up outside... She had starting going to bed early as much to keep warm as to sleep. During the day she could find some physical activity to keep herself warm; at night it wasn't quite so easy.

She paused in the hall, watching as the security lights flashed on, and then as she heard male footsteps crunching over the gravel she wondered if Robert had perhaps had a change of heart and come to visit her.

He hadn't. When she opened the door she discovered that her visitor was one of her husband's philandering friends, a man called Frank Jarvis.

She stared at him for a few seconds in confusion. He was carrying a huge bunch of flowers, white lilies, she recognised, blooms she had never really liked.

'Philippa... my poor girl.'

He leaned forward and, recognising that he was about to kiss her, Philippa stepped back.

'I brought you these,' she heard Frank telling her as he walked into the hallway and handed her the flowers. He smelled very strongly of aftershave, Philippa noticed distastefully as she took the lilies.

'I was just on my way to bed, Frank,' she told him coolly.

'Yes, I know I'm calling at a late hour... Look, why don't we make ourselves a little bit more comfortable— unless you'd prefer me to come upstairs with you and tuck you up?'

Philippa didn't bother to make any response, leading the way instead into the cold drawing-room.

He sat down on one of the plain cream sofas and patted the seat next to him, draping his arm along the back of the sofa as he told her, 'Come and sit down here next to me and then we'll talk.'

Talk? What was there to talk about? Philippa wondered, deliberately avoiding the space next to him on the sofa and choosing the security of a chair instead.

'You know how much I've always admired you, Philippa,' he told her as she sat down. 'In fact, if I'm honest, I always envied old Andrew being married to you. You're a very beautiful woman—an intelligent woman as well, I suspect.'

He paused and then smiled at her.

'I don't like to think of such a pretty woman missing out on life's treats. Pretty women should have pretty things... enjoy themselves...'

Philippa started to speak, but he held up his hand, silencing her as he continued, 'When Andrew was alive he provided those things for you, but Andrew's dead now.' He got up off the settee and came towards her while Philippa stiffened in dislike and disbelief.

'I'm a very rich man, Philippa, a very rich man who appreciates pretty things...pretty women. Women like you shouldn't have to worry about money. And there's no reason why you should. I think you know what I'm talking about, my dear. There's a very nice little mews house close by the cathedral in town. You'd be very comfortable there. I'd like to show it to you but, of course, like any sensible man, I'm sure you'll understand that I like to ensure I'm investing my money wisely, that it's buying me...exactly what I want.'

Philippa could feel the anger pouring through her in a red-hot tide. Did he really honestly think that she would actually consider selling herself to him, leasing him the use of her body in return for his little mews house? Her fury was so intense that it literally rendered her speechless.

'Why don't we go upstairs now, and talk the whole thing through?' she heard him saying smoothly as he came towards her.

Another moment and he would be touching her. Philippa's flesh crawled in anticipatory revulsion, galvanising her into action. She stood up, distancing herself from him as she said quietly, 'I've got a much better idea...'

She could see the expectant sexual glisten of his eyes, hear the gloating note in his voice, and her stomach heaved.

'Oh, and what might that be?'

'Why don't I pick up the phone and ring your wife and tell her what you've just said to me?' she suggested levelly, firmly retaining eye-contact with him as the meaning of what she was saying sank in.

He was a man who could, she suspected, be a bully and physically violent, and she could sense now his desire to take hold of her and hurt her.

Without taking her eyes off him, she told him coldly, 'Please leave—*now*!'

'If you think that by doing this you're going to up your price then you've mistaken your man,' she heard him telling her, his voice thickening with anger as he added brutally, 'You might be a pretty woman, Philippa, but I should be careful if I were you. After all, you're not so young any more, and that sharp tongue of yours will drive more men away than it will attract: sexual domination might turn some men on; verbal domination certainly doesn't. If I were you I'd be careful not to place too high a value on myself; you might price yourself out of the market and, when you do, don't bother to come knocking on my door,' he told her sneeringly, adding venomously, 'Come to think of it, you probably wouldn't have been much use in bed anyway. I'll lay odds I'd get a better fuck off a girl on the streets; better and cheaper.'

There was more in the same vein, all of which Philippa heard out in silence.

Later, when he had finally gone and she had bolted the door behind him, she leaned against it, shaking, not so much with fear as with nausea and anger.

Previously she had looked upon Belinda Jarvis with a mixture of irritation and contempt; now she felt profoundly sorry for her.

As she walked past the open drawing-room door she automatically went to close it and then recoiled as she caught the smell of the aftershave which still hung on the cold air.

When she unlocked and pushed open the French windows, the icy breeze brought her skin out in goose-bumps but she scarcely noticed the cold.

Upstairs in the bathroom, she scrubbed her skin so hard with the loofah that it physically burned. No doubt the incident had had its funny side, she acknowledged, but right now she wasn't in the mood to see it.

He had really genuinely believed that she would accept his proposition. Was *that* how people…men…saw her…as a commodity to be bought and sold, a possession? She had heard apocryphal tales of divorced and widowed women being approached by the hitherto irreproachably faithful spouses of their woman friends and their ex-husbands' male friends with offers of sex, but for Frank Jarvis to assume…

Did he and other people really believe she was so weak, had so little going for her, so few options open to her that she would welcome such an offer? Well, she would show them, she decided fiercely; she would show them all: her parents, her brother, Frank Jarvis…Blake Hamilton…

Blake Hamilton. She went very still. Now why on earth had she tagged him on to that list? Her subconscious must have been well and truly disturbed by Frank Jarvis's visit for it to fling such a remote piece of her past at her.

She had put Blake firmly and permanently out of her mind the day she'd agreed to marry Andrew.

And out of her heart? She gave a small angry shrug. Now she was being ridiculous. She had had a crush on Blake, that was all, her feelings for him created by teenage hormones and fuelled by fantasy. They had been no more real than her romanticised, idealised image of him; his treatment of her, his rejection of her had proved that.

She tensed as she heard the phone ringing, tempted to ignore its summons, but common sense told her that it was hardly likely to be Frank Jarvis telephoning to pursue his suit of her.

A wry smile curled her mouth. No, indeed.

When she answered the phone she wasn't sure whether to be relieved or not when she heard the boys' headmaster's voice.

'Both boys are fine,' he assured her, anticipating her anxious question. 'Perhaps because they've got each other and maybe partly because they aren't the only pupils we have here to have suffered some kind of personal trauma. The reason I'm actually calling is the Easter holidays.'

Guiltily Philippa recognised that she had been so concerned with making plans for the future that she had overlooked the present.

'Both boys are down to go to Italy with the school, but I'm afraid that when your husband paid the school fees no extras were included.'

'How much, exactly, is involved?' she asked him unhappily.

When he told her her heart sank even further. The last thing she wanted to do was to cancel the boys' trip at the last moment, but she couldn't see what alternative she had. There was certainly no way she could afford that kind of money.

'You don't have to let me have your decision right now,' she heard the headmaster telling her quietly. 'But perhaps if you could telephone me tomorrow evening...'

'Yes...yes, I'll do that,' Philippa told him.

After she had put the phone down, she stood where she was, staring unseeingly in front of her. What should she do? What *could* she do other than ring the boys and explain to them that she couldn't afford to let them go to Italy?

They would be bound to feel humiliated and embarrassed in front of their friends and schoolmates at having to drop out at the last minute.

The last thing she had ever wanted for them was that they should grow up believing that they should judge themselves and others only by their material assets, but Andrew's death was bound to have made them feel vulnerable and insecure.

And then there were the practicalities to consider. If they came home, she would have to feed and entertain them, and, much as she herself longed for the comfort of having them with her, for their sakes she could not give in to such selfishness.

For their sakes she would have to bite down on her pride and go cap in hand to her parents, she acknowledged tiredly. Not a prospect she relished one tiny little bit. In fact today had been a day filled with so many unpalatable realisations that it was a wonder she wasn't suffering from mental and emotional indigestion, she admitted ruefully.

Half an hour later, as she got into bed wearing her plain cotton nightshirt, she tried to envisage the nightwear Frank Jarvis would have expected her to don had she accepted his offer.

What did his tastes run to? Something in black, and restricting, rendering her a passive object for him to paw over and play with; a physical present he had bought for himself all tied up in silk and ribbons.

That kind of relationship was the total antithesis of what she had once dreamed of having. The one she had once believed she would have... in the days before Blake had taken those dreams and deliberately destroyed them.

Then she had believed that the smiles Blake gave her, the way he watched her, talked to her, treated her meant that the exciting, overwhelming physical and emotional turmoil she was in whenever he was there wasn't just felt by her; that he shared it... But that had been before he had told her the truth, before he had humiliated her, almost destroyed her, cruelly confronting her with the fact of the matter: that she was nothing more to him than the silly, immature, spoiled sister of one of his friends. It had been the shock of discovering how badly she had misjudged the situation, how little he really thought of her, how wrong she had been to believe that he cared about her that had been responsible ultimately for her marriage to

Andrew. Unable to believe any longer that she could trust her own judgement, she had given up trying to fight against her father's control of her life.

But that, in the end, had turned out to be just as much of a mistake as loving Blake. How many more mistakes could she allow herself to make? Not many, and certainly not the one of becoming involved with someone like Frank. No, certainly not that one. Her flesh crawled at the thought.

CHAPTER TWELVE

'PIPPA...'

Startled, Philippa looked up, pushing her hair out of her eyes as she watched her visitor approaching her. She had been so busy digging over the weed-infested vegetable garden that she hadn't even heard her arriving.

If she had ever been asked to name her closest woman friend, it would have been Susie's name that she would have given.

They had met originally when both of them were doing voluntary work and immediately a rapport had developed between them despite their apparent differences.

Andrew had never particularly approved of the friendship; Susie and her husband Jim didn't move in the same social circles as they did. Jim was a self-employed builder who had established a small business for himself dealing mainly in property repairs and extensions; he had a very good reputation but, as Susie had once said ruefully but fondly, he would never become rich. Neither of them was particularly money-conscious or ambitious and their lives revolved mainly around their family. Susie had a warmth and generosity about her that had immediately drawn Philippa to her. They got on well together and Philippa knew that if she had been the type to confide in others Susie would have been the one person she would have felt able to turn to.

Susie had been away staying with her mother when Andrew had died, and Philippa had felt reluctant to get in touch with her. Afraid to put their relationship to the test.

But now, as she looked into her friend's face, she realised how much of an injustice she had done her.

'Pippa,' Susie repeated now as she hurried over to her and gave her a fierce hug, ignoring Philippa's warnings about the soil clinging to her wellington boots and her gloves. 'How are you? I'm so sorry that I haven't been in touch before now. Jim rang me with the news, but Mum was celebrating her seventieth birthday and I couldn't rush away and take the children from their doting grandmother. I got back last night and I was going to call round then, but...'

'Let's go inside,' Philippa suggested.

She could feel emotional tears prickling the back of her throat and stinging her eyes, and as she blew her nose she asked Susie shakily, 'Why is it so much easier to cry over something that makes you feel happy than something that really hurts?'

'Perhaps because it's easier to acknowledge good feelings than bad ones,' Susie suggested as Philippa opened the kitchen door and ushered her inside.

As she made a cup of coffee and they sat down, Philippa felt for the first time since Andrew's death that she could unburden herself and share what she was actually feeling.

'I still can't believe that Andrew could act so recklessly and not tell you...' Susie said angrily when she had related the full story to her. 'I'm sorry, Pip,' she added apologetically. 'I know he was your husband and I...'

Philippa shook her head.

'It's all right,' she told her. Although she had never discussed the specifics of her marriage with Susie, she suspected that it must have been obvious to her friend that she and Andrew did not share the same kind of close, loving relationship that Susie had with Jim.

'Have any of Andrew's friends been round?'

'What friends?' Philippa asked her cynically, and then added, 'Although I have had one offer...'

As Susie waited and watched her she couldn't help contrasting Philippa's life with her own. She felt so sorry for her, not so much because of her financial problems—she and Jim had known some hard times in the past—but because of the paucity of her relationship with Andrew and her family.

'Someone, a supposed friend of Andrew's, called round last night. I must be pretty dim...I didn't realise at first...'

Susie frowned as Philippa told her what happened.

'I can see the funny side of it now,' she told her wryly. 'But at the time...'

Susie watched as her eyes became shadowed.

'It wasn't so much his cold-blooded suggestion that I should become his mistress that hurt as the fact that he so obviously believed that I would be only too grateful to accept. The way he took it for granted that I could be bought, like a...like a new car, or some other inanimate object that had taken his fancy. He said that all I'd ever wanted from Andrew was his money...made me feel that my marriage to Andrew had been a form of prostitution, and it hadn't...I didn't... Is that how people see me, Susie, as a woman quite happy to exchange her pride and self-respect for money?' she said painfully.

'No, of course it isn't,' Susie told her robustly. 'To be honest I've always rather envied the way you not only don't seem to have any vanity where your looks are concerned— and you certainly could have; I've seen the way male heads turn when you walk into a room—but also that you never seem to trade on them. Given the temptation of looking the way you do, I don't know that I'd be strong-minded enough to resist.

'In fact I suspect that very few woman would be. I'm sure I'm not the only woman to wear her husband's favourite outfit or to make that little bit of an extra effort every now and again when I have to break the bad news about a huge fuel bill or when the kids want something...

'Not that Jim doesn't see straight through it. In fact it's become a kind of early warning signal, I suspect, rather than anything else. It must have been horrid for you, though; you should have rung me.'

Philippa shook her head. 'He left quickly enough once I'd threatened to tell his wife. He made me feel so dirty, though, Susie, as though something I'd said or done had somehow made him think that I...' She gave a small shiver. 'How awful it must be to feel that you don't have any option other than to sell your body. How many women have to do that, Susie...? How many women have no other way of feeding their children and themselves...?'

'Too many,' Susie replied soberly.

'No woman should be put in that position——' Philippa began fiercely, and then broke off. 'I'm sorry. It's just that thinking about it...about him and the way he treated me...has made me realise how much worse things could actually be. At least I've got the choice of refusing him. I wish the bank would get in touch, though. If they're not prepared to...if they decide to sell the house immediately and I have to leave——'

'You know you'd always be welcome to come and stay with us,' Susie interrupted her quietly. 'You and the boys. With Rosie starting at university in the autumn we'll have two empty bedrooms and...'

'Oh, Susie...that's the second time you've made me cry,' she accused as she blew her nose. 'Sometimes I feel so angry with Andrew, Susie. Why couldn't he have been satisfied with what we had? Why did he have to take so many risks? I feel now that the boys and I never really meant anything to him at all, and I can't help wondering how much of that was my fault...'

'None of it,' Susie told her firmly. 'You're not responsible for Andrew's faults, Pip, and you've got to stop blaming yourself for them.'

'Pull myself together and get on with sorting my life out, you mean?' Philippa laughed.

'Come back with me for lunch,' Susie urged her.

'I can't,' Philippa told her, shaking her head. 'I've got an appointment with the social services people this afternoon. I'm dreading it,' she admitted ruefully.

'I'll come with you,' Susie offered.

'To hold my hand?' Philippa shook her head and smiled. 'No... It's time I learned to stand on my own two feet. I keep trying to tell myself to look on what happened as a challenge and opportunity, the way they tell you in all the magazines.'

'The power of positive thinking,' Susie said. 'Does it work?'

Philippa grinned at her. 'Let's just say that my personal success-rate is under fifty per cent—well under!'

'Mmm... I read somewhere that what you have to do is to write down a set of affirmations... you know, statements that you make that are positive, and then you repeat them to yourself in front of a mirror and...'

'It sounds like a form of self-hypnosis,' Philippa laughed.

'It's supposed to work,' Susie assured her.

Philippa gave her an amused smile.

'So are diets,' she pointed out and they both laughed.

Susie had been complaining ever since Philippa had known her that she needed to lose at least half a stone, but so far she had never managed to stay on any of the diets she had started for more than a few weeks.

As Philippa walked her to her car, she realised how much better seeing Susie had made her feel... how much less alone and, shocking though it might sound, how good it had felt to laugh and push aside all her problems.

'Thanks for coming,' she told Susie emotionally as she hugged her.

'I meant what I said about you and the boys staying with us,' Susie told her quietly. 'In fact I wish you'd move in with us now...'

'What, after I've just spent a whole morning digging over what's left of the old vegetable patch? I can just see Jim's face if I started digging up his precious roses,' Philippa teased her. 'No,' she told her more soberly. 'I've got to try and see this through by myself... other women manage, bring up their children single-handed, support themselves.'

'Mmm... by choice and without the handicap of a mountain of debt.'

'Not always,' Philippa pointed out. 'I've hidden behind the role that other people have cast for me for too long, Susie. I need to know now whether I'm actually capable of being any different, or if I simply accepted that role because deep down inside I knew that it's true that the only thing of any value about me is my pretty face. Something that is really nothing to do with me, an accident of genes, not a personal achievement at all,' she said bitterly. 'Am I really supposed to be proud of that, Susie? To feel that it's to my credit? Do you think I'm so unintelligent?'

'Of course not,' Susie told her fiercely.

'Thanks... let's just hope that you're right.'

'I am,' Susie assured her. 'Just you wait and see.'

'No... waiting to see isn't any good any more... What I have to do now is *work* and see... starting with my interview with the social services people this afternoon.'

'I'll ring you tonight,' Susie promised as she got into her car. 'You can do it.'

Philippa laughed. 'Is that what I've got to tell myself?'

'Why not?' Susie challenged her. 'It can't do any harm.'

Philippa stepped out into the street, letting the door to the Social Services office swing closed behind her as she breathed in the clean, cold air.

She had had to wait more than half an hour after the official time of her appointment for someone to see her.

'We're running late,' the woman interviewing her had apologised as she'd asked her to sit down.

It had been hard not to let herself be overwhelmed by her guilt and discomfort as she'd answered the other woman's questions. Despite what Elizabeth had told her, it had still felt wrong that she should be sitting there claiming state benefit, and she suspected that the other woman had thought so as well, although she'd been far too professional to show it. Her briskness hadn't quite hidden her tiredness and Philippa had tried to answer her questions as quickly and concisely as she could.

The ordeal of her interview had dissipated her earlier more optimistic mood and she was glad to leave the office, with its depressing smell of despair and defeat, behind her.

Joel saw her emerging from the Social Services office from the other side of the street. He had seen her inside the building earlier and had recognised her immediately.

Even without knowing who she was she would still have drawn his attention. The way she was dressed would have made her stand out like a sore thumb even if her face hadn't. Initially it had angered him that she should be there—what the hell did someone like her need state benefits for?—and then as she'd turned her head he had seen the look in her eyes, had remembered what Sally had said about hearing that she had been left with nothing other than a mountain of debts.

As she'd felt him watching her she had lifted her chin and stared back at him, and, although there had been nothing remotely sexual in the way she'd looked at him, just for a heartbeat of time he had felt his body respond to her with such unexpected force that it had taken him completely off guard.

He was not a man who had ever allowed his sexuality to rule him. In his view a man's sexual response to a woman was his responsibility and not hers, and a man who couldn't take that responsibility wasn't much of a man.

As he'd turned away from her he'd told himself that that was what happened when you had a wife who no longer wanted you in bed, but deep down inside himself he'd known that his reaction had been more than a mere transfer of sexual frustration from one woman to another.

She'd looked oddly vulnerable standing there despite her fancy clothes and the air of aloofness she was trying to project.

Now, as he watched her step out into the street, he saw the youth darting out of the side-street beside her and running up behind her, reaching out for her bag.

He called out a warning at the same moment as the would-be thief made a grab for her bag.

Philippa swung round, her body tensing as she heard Joel call and felt the hand on her shoulder-strap, hanging on to her bag as the youth tried to take it from her, pushing her to the ground as Joel raced across the road to help her.

As soon as her attacker saw Joel he let go of her bag and ran off. Shakily Philippa got to her feet. The shock of what had happened had brought her dangerously close to the edge of bursting into tears...her whole body had started to shake and she felt physically sick. A small group of people had gathered to see what was going on, adding to her discomfort and embarrassment.

'Are you all right...?'

Joel's hand was on her arm, his body protectively shielding her from the onlookers. He was a tall man, broad-shouldered and dark-haired, and for some reason the warm male scent of his body felt so comforting that she was actually tempted to lean closer to him.

It was a totally unfamiliar sensation to her, this instinctive feminine awareness of male comfort and strength, this knowledge that if she did act on her impulses and lean closer to him his arm would curl protectively around her, holding her safe; she could almost hear the steady, comforting thud of his heartbeat, feel the protective warmth of his body.

Shockingly, tears suddenly filled her eyes, an inexplicable sense of loss filling her with pain as she recognised how different a man like this was from the men in her life.

For the first time in years she was aware of feelings she had thought she had successfully dismissed: a sharp, aching sense of deprivation and loss; an awareness of all that her marriage had denied her.

Angrily she pulled away from Joel, irritated by her own weakness, thanking him tersely for his help.

There was no way he could let her walk away on her own, Joel acknowledged as he watched her; for one thing he didn't think she was physically capable of doing it. She looked as weak as a kitten and when he had held her he had actually been able to feel the shape of her ribs beneath her clothes. Sally was a slim woman but her body was nicely covered with flesh as a woman's body should be. This woman felt as though she hadn't eaten a decent meal in weeks. He was surprised she'd had the strength to hold on to that bag of hers.

'I'll walk you to your car,' he told her gruffly.

Philippa shook her head.

'No. No, I'm fine...honestly...' But when she turned to look at Joel she saw from his face that he wasn't going to be deterred and she was forced to tell him, 'I don't have my car with me...I...I walked...'

'From Larchmount Avenue; that's almost two miles away.' Joel was frowning, standing in front of her so that she couldn't really walk past him.

Philippa eyed him uneasily. How did he know where she lived?

Joel read her mind.

'I recognised you in the social services office,' he told her. 'I used to work for your husband.'

Philippa flushed uncomfortably. 'I...I'm sorry——' she began, but Joel interrupted her, shaking his head as he told her gruffly,

'It's not your fault, and besides, he seems to have left you as badly off as the rest of us.'

Philippa didn't try to deny it.

She still felt slightly sick and shaky and she wanted to get home. As she moved to walk past Joel he fell into step beside her. When she hesitated and looked at him, he told her lightly, 'I could do with the exercise; my wife complains that I spend far too much time sitting around making the place look untidy.'

Despite his smile Philippa could hear the bitterness in his voice. 'Why aren't you using your car? Walking around isn't the safest thing for a woman to do these days...'

'It wouldn't start,' Philippa told him, adding drily, 'And besides, walking's cheaper.'

They both stopped walking and looked at one another.

'Yeah,' Joel agreed. 'It helps to fill the time as well. Did Social Services give you a hard time?'

'Not really, but I feel so bad about being there.'

'Tell me about it,' Joel derided.

'You...you haven't been able to find another job?' Philippa ventured.

'No, and there isn't much chance that I will find one either,' Joel told her. 'Not round here.'

He paused as he saw the look in Philippa's eyes, his voice softening slightly as he told her, 'It isn't your fault.'

'I feel as if I'm to blame,' Philippa said, stopping as she realised how intimately they were talking. They were strangers, she reminded herself, and yet...

'You're not,' Joel told her. 'In many ways we're both in the same boat.'

'Well, if we are, I'd better warn you now that we're not likely to get very far,' Philippa told him humorously. 'Because I'm not much good at rowing...or anything else,' she added more soberly.

'It isn't really that hard,' Joel told her. 'Rowing...all you need is someone to show you how.'

As she listened to the lightly husky timbre of his voice a tiny shiver of awareness ran down Philippa's spine. There was nothing either overtly or covertly sexual about his comment and she could see from his expression that he hadn't intended to make any sexual innuendo, and yet... Did he have the same awareness of her that she had of him?

Philippa was used to men being aware of her, making passes at her, but she certainly wasn't used to being sexually aware of them like this.

'Your wife...' she asked quickly. 'Does she...does she work?'

'Yes...she's a nurse,' Joel told her. He suddenly looked very bleak, Philippa recognised, as though talking, even thinking about his wife was somehow painful for him.

'Have you got children?' she asked, anxious to establish some kind of neutrality between them and to banish that disturbing sensual intimacy she had sensed earlier.

'Two—a girl and a boy. Not that you'd know it. It's their mother they've always turned to, and why not? She's also the one who holds the purse strings now...'

'I've got two boys,' Philippa told him. 'They're both at boarding-school. Andrew...I didn't want...but Andrew insisted. He said I was spoiling them.'

'Sally spoils our two, especially Paul. The minute they want anything she drops everything else...'

Philippa could sense the resentment in his voice. Was he really jealous of his children? she wondered.

'It's a habit mothers fall into,' she said gently. 'You see, when they're little they're so dependent on us that we automatically have to put them first. It doesn't necessarily mean...'

She stopped and Joel looked at her.

'What? That they do come first? No, when I was growing up it certainly didn't then but Sally keeps on telling me it's different now.'

'We all want to give our children the things we feel we didn't have ourselves.'

'Mmm...well, all my two seem to want is the latest piece of electronic rubbish...a new computer is what Paul is after now... I offered to take him fishing the other day but he said fishing bored him...'

He stopped as he saw the small betraying expression flicker across Philippa's face. 'What is it?' he asked her.

'Nothing,' she denied and then added quickly, 'Your children are very lucky to have a father who wants to spend time with them.'

She didn't say any more, and Joel didn't press her to explain.

So she thought his children were lucky to have him as a father? He doubted whether Sally would agree.

As they reached the front gate to her house Philippa stopped. Joel gave a small start of surprise. He hadn't realised they were there. They only seemed to have been walking for a few seconds.

He didn't want to end their conversation, to let her go, he recognised; there was something about her that had a soothing, warming effect upon him, that somehow made him feel good about himself. He couldn't explain exactly what it was, he only knew that during those few seconds while he had held her and felt her body tremble slightly against his he had been intensely aware of her vulnerability.

'It was kind of you to walk me home,' Philippa told him now.

'I enjoyed it,' Joel told her truthfully. 'It was...good to have someone to talk to.'

'Yes,' Philippa agreed, acknowledging all that he had left unspoken.

'I could come round tomorrow and take a look at your car for you if you like,' Joel offered.

Philippa felt her heart give a small betraying flurry of half-beats.

'Oh, I couldn't put you to so much trouble,' she protested.

'It's no trouble,' Joel assured her. 'It will give me something to do...'

'Well, if you're sure you don't mind...'

She shouldn't be doing this, Philippa acknowledged on a small burst of panic.

'I...I can't afford to pay you,' she told him awkwardly. 'I'll...'

'There's no need... As I said, it will give me something to do. Come on,' he added, glancing up the drive. 'I'd better see you inside...'

She ought to have invited him in for a cup of coffee, Philippa acknowledged guiltily when Joel had gone, but she had already nearly consumed her small stock of coffee this morning with Susie's visit, and according to the Social Services, unless she had misunderstood the woman, it might be some time before she actually received any money.

It hadn't helped discovering that, while the owner of the second-hand shop was more than delighted to sell her clothes, she wouldn't actually receive any money for them until a customer came into the shop and bought them.

'I work on a flat commission basis,' the woman had told Philippa briskly, 'and I'll account to you at the end of every month.'

So much for hoping that she could use the money for the boys' school trip... which meant that she now had no option other than to go to her parents... It made no difference knowing that her father could easily afford the relatively modest amount involved; she was a grown woman of thirty-four and, even if her relationship with her parents had been a good one built on mutual love, she still wouldn't have wanted to approach them for money. She was not, despite what others seemed to think, a woman who enjoyed being financially dependent on others; she never had been. Even as a teenager, she would have preferred to be allowed to earn her own pocket money, but there had been no question of her father allowing her to do that.

She remembered how scathing Blake had been about her financial dependence on her parents.

'Can't you see what you're doing? They're buying you, Philippa, and you're letting them. If you really wanted to go to university, to be independent, you'd find a way of financing yourself.'

'How?' she had demanded tearfully.

She had loved him so much . . . worshipped him in dumb, heart-aching silence. He had filled all her teenage dreams with fantasies of how it would feel to have Blake's mouth touching hers, kissing her the way she had seen lovers kissing in films, open mouth pressed to open mouth in hungry, fierce need. Her body had grown hot and achy just thinking about how it would feel to have Blake kiss her like that.

In the privacy of her bedroom she had studied her naked body, shivering as she'd watched her nipples grow into hard, urgent points when she'd imagined Blake touching her, but a fantasy was all it had been, and after that final quarrel between them, when he had made it clear to her what he thought of her, she had been almost feverishly grateful that they had not been lovers, that she had been spared the final humiliation of being used sexually by him in the way that she herself had pitifully and stupidly invited.

But she had no illusions left. That restraint had been for his sake and not for hers.

The pain of loving him and of forcing herself to destroy that love had left her very weak, with no energy to spare for any further battles with her father.

Andrew's intense and determined courtship of her had been a panacea, a means of distracting herself from a pain she could neither suppress nor deny. Her father had approved of him, and at least marriage to Andrew would be some form of escape.

Only by convincing herself that she had found someone else to love would she be able to banish the humiliation of Blake's rejection of her, by convincing herself that she was worthy of being loved.

Sometimes, just occasionally, when she was feeling particularly reckless, she allowed herself to wonder what her life might have been like if she had not visited Blake that evening.

All through the winter and then the spring she had been looking forward to the summer holidays, to what she feared would be Blake's last visit to her home, since Michael would soon have completed his course. She was eighteen now, not a child any longer but a woman, a woman who was determined to put to the test what all her feminine senses were telling her. It wasn't enough any more to watch Blake smile, to listen to him talk and to dream her dreams of him alone in bed at night. The kisses she wanted from him now were no longer merely the fantasy ones she conjured up for herself.

All her burgeoning femininity told her that Blake was aware of her, that when he smiled at her and watched her he was well aware of the effect he was having on her and that the burning look she sometimes saw in his eyes meant that he too wanted more...

Frustratingly, though, once he had arrived, she never seemed to get the chance to be alone with him; someone else, normally her father or Robert, would appear and the opportunity to show him how she felt, to encourage him to recognise that she was no longer a child, would be lost.

Once or twice they had been alone, but on both occasions she had been stricken by such a paralysing shyness that she hadn't been able to say what was in her heart.

The first time had been when she had seen him emerging from the guest bathroom one evening, his legs bare beneath his robe, bare and soft-furred. Her stomach had contracted on a sudden surge of shocked excitement, hot shivers burning her skin like fine needles. She had taken a step towards him but he had stepped back, leaving her feeling self-conscious and confused.

The second occasion had been when she had gone in search of Michael to fasten her pearls and had found Blake in her brother's room waiting for him.

'Perhaps you could fasten them for me,' she had suggested shyly, her throat so constricted with her awareness of him that her voice had sounded unfamiliarly husky. She had turned her back to him as she spoke, lifting the weight of her hair off her shoulders, her body trembling even before she'd felt the heart-stopping cool touch of his fingertips against her hot skin.

She had been standing in front of the bedroom mirror and had watched as Blake fastened her pearls, greedily drinking in the sight of his dark head bent over her fair one, achingly aware of the proximity of their bodies, of the heat she could feel coming off his, of its strength and maleness. All she had to do was to close her eyes and lean back against him...

But, even as the thought had formed, Blake was placing his hands on her shoulders and turning her round, his eyes sombre as he'd begun, 'Philippa, I...'

She never learned what he had been about to say because Michael had walked in, apologising to Blake for keeping him waiting, teasing Philippa and grimacing as he saw the pearls she was wearing.

'Daddy likes me wearing these,' she had told him, not wanting to explain just why it was so important to her to keep her father in a good mood. She sensed instinctively that her father did not particularly like Blake, but she had no idea why. It was true that Blake's family did not have money or position but Blake was very clever, much more so than either Robert or Michael.

One day he would be rich and successful. Blake himself had laughed when she'd told him so a couple of summers before, plainly amused by her childish defence of him. She had been only sixteen then... a girl still...

As she had left her brother's bedroom she'd reminded herself that Blake's visit had barely begun and that there was still plenty of time...

Only there hadn't been...one afternoon she had come in from a game of tennis to find Robert and Blake deep in conversation.

Blake had looked oddly bleak...angry almost, and Robert's face had been unpleasantly flushed. At first Philippa had thought they must be arguing about something but it turned out that she had been wrong and that Robert had simply been giving Blake a telephone message.

When Philippa had learned that Blake was leaving she had barely been able to conceal her disappointment, tears all too ready to fill her eyes. She hadn't even been able to say goodbye to him because her parents had insisted on her accompanying them to a dinner they were attending. When she'd returned, Blake had left. All Michael could tell her was that he had said something had come up that Blake needed to attend to immediately.

Philippa had worried that Blake's mother, who she knew suffered from some incapacitating disease, had taken a turn for the worse.

She knew a lot about Blake's background, information she had gleaned and cherished over the years from both her brother and from Blake himself.

She knew that his father had been killed in an accident when Blake was fifteen and that his mother's illness had developed shortly afterwards. She knew that Blake had had to work to finance his education; and that he had returned to university after a year away working to finish his degree course.

She also knew, but because her brother had told her, that in addition to financing his own education Blake also helped to support his mother.

Tears had closed her throat when Michael had told her this.

Blake had shared a small flat close to the university with her brother; his mother lived several miles away in purpose-built sheltered council-provided accommodation. Philippa had never met her but she'd yearned to do so; she could imagine what she would be like, how much she must love her son and the bond there would be between them.

Philippa had been wretchedly miserable after Blake had gone, her misery compounded by the arrival of her A level results and her father's irritated refusal to even so much as discuss her desire to go on to university.

'Daddy is quite right,' her mother had told her. 'If you had won a place at Oxford, at one of the good women's colleges, Somerville, for instance, things might be different, but those new modern universities... Daddy is only doing what's best for you, Philippa,' she had added. 'And I think you might try to appreciate that fact, to appreciate just how lucky you are instead of being so difficult.'

Unwisely Philippa had continued to argue, even being rash enough to say, 'Blake says that everyone should make use of their intelligence; he says that the only real independence comes from being self-sufficient; he says that everyone, man or woman, should be able to...'

'Philippa, I'm afraid I'm not really interested in what that young man has to say. In fact I believe he has had rather too much to say. That type always do.' She had given Philippa a thin smile.

'This is exactly the sort of thing your father means when he says that university is not the place for you, that it will expose you to the wrong kind of influences... to people... men like Blake...'

'Michael likes Blake,' she had protested. 'They're friends.'

'The acquaintanceships a man may make are entirely different from those suitable for a young girl,' her mother had informed her. 'Your father and I might have tolerated Blake Hamilton's presence here in our home for Michael's sake, but it was obvious right from the start the kind of person he was.'

Philippa had wanted to protest, to object, but she could hear her father's voice in the hall and knew from bitter experience that she would have no chance of winning any argument with the two of them ranged against her.

After all her high hopes, this was turning out to be the worst summer of her life. Misery filled her as she remembered how she had pictured talking to Blake, being with him...discussing her future with him, seeing the pleasure and approval in his eyes, watching the realisation dawn in them that she was now grown-up. She had even visualised exactly where 'it' would happen...in the garden, not the formal, carefully cultivated part, but the tangled wild area beyond the tall yew hedge where field poppies grew in the untidy grass and the stumps of the stricken elms which had been cut down three summers ago provided seats that were close enough together and tilted at such an angle that she would have had to lean very close to Blake when she was talking to him. So close that she might just possibly have slipped off her seat, necessitating Blake's reaching out to catch hold of her...

Her stomach muscles had clenched when she had visualised this particular moment, the way he would look at her, the way his expression would change, the way he would hesitate for a moment, looking deeply into her eyes before brushing her hair off her face and then, as though completely unable to hold back any longer, bend his head to kiss her, gently at first, and then later...

A delicious *frisson* of fear and excitement had run through her at the thought of being kissed by Blake. But now Blake was gone and sometimes, when she tried to conjure up his image, to re-create the intensity and magic of that anticipation, all she could actually feel was a sense of loss and panic. On the morning of her birthday she searched the post, hoping that there might be a card from him, because after all he had sent her one when she had sat her exams, wishing her good luck; but there wasn't one.

Her parents had planned a small dinner party to celebrate the event, inviting those of their friends who had suitably aged children of their own.

Philippa hated every second of it, but most especially when her father stood up and made a brief speech and then handed her the keys to the car he had bought her as a birthday present. She had been taking lessons for the last ten months and had surprised and shamed Robert, who had taken his test three times, by getting her full licence on her first attempt.

Only Philippa knew that the tears filling her eyes at her father's generous present were tears of misery and resentment.

She didn't want a car. She wanted...she wanted her freedom, the right to make her own choices...her own decisions.

As she listened to the envious comments of her peers she was bleakly aware that the money spent on her birthday present could have quite easily put her through university, and just for a second she fantasised about running away, selling the car...defying her parents. But she simply wasn't that kind of person, the habit of obedience too deeply ingrained.

Michael was due home in four weeks; perhaps, she decided, she could arrange to visit him at the flat once he was back at university. Then she could see Blake and...

And then, totally unexpectedly, her parents were invited away for the weekend, by an influential acquaintance of her father's who, like him, was a keen golfer. No invitation had been extended to Philippa; Robert was away visiting Lydia's family and, despite her mother's reservations, Philippa was to be left at home alone.

The decision to visit Blake wasn't made overnight; at first it was nothing more than a tentative, daring but impossible wish, but it grew stronger. Her imagination even subtly provided her with the ideal excuse for such a visit...an excuse that, once it took root, like the original desire, swiftly became a necessity.

Blake, she was sure, would be able to think of some way for her to get around her father... Blake would convince her parents that she should continue her education, she decided, conveniently ignoring the fact that Blake was the last person her father was likely to listen to.

While her mother fussed about what clothes to pack, Philippa mentally planned. Studying maps, making surreptitious notes, firmly ignoring the small, frightened voice

that warned her that no good could come of such deception. Her need to see Blake was paramount, totally
overriding everything else.

At night, once she was in bed, she closed her eyes and
visualised the look in his eyes when he opened his door and
saw her standing there, and her body shivered in anticipatory excitement. He would know, of course, exactly how
she felt, just as she would be able to see from his face how
much he had missed her... how much he wanted her.

And once she had gone to him, given herself to him,
once they had acknowledged their feelings for one another,
there would be no going back... Blake would not allow
her to go back. She would be his then, and nothing her
parents could do would change that.

Her imagination ran on busily; she saw herself rushing
home to the flat from her tutorials to get Blake's supper,
the plain gold band of her wedding-ring adding a new maturity to her status. She saw herself buying flowers for the
flat, while Blake looked on admiringly at the small feminine
changes she had made to it. She saw him pleased and proud
of her the day she got her degree, sweeping her up into his
arms and telling her how much he loved her; she saw him...
In the darkness she blushed furiously at the intense intimacy of her thoughts.

Her parents left home early in the morning but Philippa
waited almost until lunchtime to do the same, still half
afraid that for some reason they might come back.

The journey would only take her a couple of hours, or
so she had estimated... What she had not allowed for,
though, was taking the wrong exit off the motorway and
getting well and truly lost afterwards, so that it was early
evening before she finally turned into the road where Blake
lived.

It was a chilly, wet evening, sullen grey rainclouds darkening the sky. She parked the car outside the flat, running
through the rain to the door and ringing the bell.

A huge drop of rain fell on her face, smudging her
mascara, and she was just trying frantically to rub it away
when the door opened.

'Blake...' Tired and emotional, she would have hurled herself into his arms if he had not fended her off.

'What is it...what's happened?' he demanded. 'Is it Mike—has something happened to him...?'

'Michael?' Philippa stared at him. This wasn't what she had planned...what she had imagined...Blake holding her at arm's length, looking at her so coldly, more concerned, it seemed, with her brother than with her.

Fiercely she tried to banish the small feather of disquiet starting to curl uncomfortably inside her stomach.

'Blake, I had to see you. I need to talk to you...'

He didn't seem to be listening to her.

'How did you get here?' he demanded.

'In my car...' Wearily she gestured to the car parked by the kerb.

'Your car...?'

'Yes...they...Daddy gave it to me for my birthday.'

'Oh, yes, I suppose I should have guessed.' The sardonic tone of his voice made Philippa flinch a little. She shivered, suddenly feeling cold and very unsure of herself. He didn't seem the same Blake somehow.

'Look, you'd better come in and tell me what all this is about,' he told her, frowning as he turned away from her and opened a door off the hall.

The sitting-room that lay beyond it was sparsely furnished and pin-neat; a book lay open on the desk, an anglepoise lamp illuminating it.

'Oh, I'm sorry—were you working?' Philippa apologised awkwardly.

Blake's mouth twisted. 'Typical Philippa,' he commented. 'Showing us all how well she's been brought up, how nice her manners are...how good she is. My God, you aren't real!' he exploded suddenly with such violent intensity that Philippa tensed against it. 'You can't be,' he added as he turned round and stared angrily at her. 'You arrive on my doorstep talking some nonsense about needing my help and then you——'

'I do need your help,' Philippa told him. 'Daddy won't let me go to university...'

'Surprise, surprise,' Blake responded cynically. His mouth curled downwards when he saw her face.

'Oh, come on—you must have known it would happen... The car, I take it, is your reward for toeing the line, for doing what he wants...

'What are you really doing here, Philippa—what is it you really want from me? Or can I guess?'

He was beginning to frighten her now; he wasn't like the Blake she knew at all.

'I—I've already told you,' she stammered. 'I...I wanted to talk to you...to ask for your advice.'

'My *advice*?' The harshness of his laughter hurt her ears. 'So you want my advice, do you? Very well, I'll give it to you. My advice is that you stop trying to deceive yourself and face up to reality, but then *you* don't like reality, do you, Philippa? *You'd* much rather be Daddy's little girl, shielded from all the unpleasant things in life like having to make decisions and having to do without a new dress every week, pearls round your neck and everything else he provides you with. That's what you really want, isn't it, Philippa...?'

'No, of course it isn't,' Philippa denied. His attack shocked and hurt her. She'd had no idea he could be like this, speak to her so brutally...as though...as though he didn't even like her, never mind...

Tears started to fill her eyes but she tried to blink them away.

'I *do* want to go to university, but...'

'But what?'

'But I can't,' she told him shakily. 'Not without my parents' support.'

'Why not?' Blake demanded curtly. 'Other people do...other people work to finance their education, but of course you could never do anything like that, could you, Philippa...?'

He took hold of her hand and examined her pretty french-polished nails, stroking the softness of her skin, but there was nothing loving and tender in his touch, nothing remotely approaching desire.

'No,' he said under his breath, more to himself than to her, or so it seemed to Philippa. 'No, you couldn't——'

'Yes, I could,' Philippa cut in painfully, hating the way he was looking at her, the contempt she could see, hear and almost feel in his attitude towards her. 'I could work... I could...' Her voice died away as she saw the way he was looking at her, saw her dreams being destroyed in front of her, consumed in the ice-cold fire of his anger, crumbling beneath the crushing weight of his rejection of her.

'Blake...'

There was no mistaking the appeal in her voice, even she herself could hear it, and she flinched from it, mortified by what she was revealing but helpless to stop it.

'No...' Blake told her thickly, shaking his head. 'Oh, no...no. No, you don't, Philippa...' And then, with a harsh frown, he took hold of her, crushing her against his body so hard that the impact of his muscles against her body actually hurt, the sensation of the soft dark hair on his bare arms touching her own skin, the maleness of him overwhelming her to such an extent that she immediately panicked, fighting to break free of him, subdued only by the fierce pressure of his mouth as it took hers in a bruising, punishing kiss that was nothing like the tender, almost reverential embrace she had imagined.

The kiss was hot and hard and angry, bruising her lips, forcing their compliance, the thrust of his tongue parting them for his to take marauding possession of her mouth. Her breasts hurt from the pressure of his muscles against them, her legs were shaking, her whole body in a state of semi-shock.

The tears she would not allow herself to cry ran down inside her throat instead, clogging it with their salt taste.

'What is it...what's wrong?' Blake demanded, his lips against her ear. 'This *is* what you came here for, isn't it...? This *is* what you wanted...?'

'No,' Philippa denied desperately, trying to break free of him, but he refused to let her go.

'Don't lie to me,' he taunted her. 'I've seen the way you look at me...the way you watch me...the hunger in your eyes. But then of course you would lie, wouldn't you, just as you're lying about your reason for being here...just as you're lying about not being able to go to university...?'

'I'm not lying,' Philippa protested.

'Yes, you are,' Blake insisted. 'There's only one person stopping you from going to university,' he told her harshly, 'and it isn't your father. It's you. You want it all, Philippa, don't you? You aren't prepared to make any effort, *any* sacrifice...no, others can do that for you while you sit there prettily and accept it as your due.

'Well, shall I tell you something about that prettiness, Philippa—shall I? In reality it isn't prettiness at all, it's ugliness...ugliness, because without intelligence, without character, all it is is just a vapid, empty mask. That's all you are, Philippa...just an empty, pretty mask, not a real woman at all. Yes, you're pretty, Philippa, as pretty and prettily packaged as a little doll and just as insipid and lifeless.' And Blake poured out more painful words in the same vein.

He released her then, pushing her away from him with such force that she almost fell.

The hall door was still open and, reacting instinctively, driven by her desire to escape both from him and from his humiliation of her, she took to her heels and fled.

He ran after her, following her right out to the car, and she thought he might actually open the door and drag her out of it, but to her relief there was a policeman walking down the road towards them and, taking advantage of his presence, she turned the key in the ignition and drove off.

The pain of Blake's rejection of her, of knowing how he felt about her, was so intense that there were times in the following weeks, many, many of them, when she didn't know how she was going to bear it. Only her pride kept her going. Her pride was, after all, all she had left.

She couldn't believe how she had ever been stupid enough to imagine that Blake had wanted her, that he might share her feelings, and whenever she thought of what she had done she writhed inwardly in such self-inflicted torment that she felt as though she was being burned in the fire of her own self-loathing and contempt.

She hated herself so much that she had no energy left for anything else, and certainly not enough to fight with her parents.

Six weeks later, when she met Andrew, she told herself that he was the balm she needed to soothe and heal her wounds, that in view of everything Blake had said about her she was, as her parents were saying, lucky that Andrew so obviously wanted her.

It was easy then to deceive herself that she was doing the right thing; after all, she had deceived herself before, hadn't she? Easier simply to give in to the pressure her parents were putting on her... easier simply to pretend to herself that she had never really loved Blake at all. But the fear he had instilled in her remained, the fear and the self-doubt...

What if he was right...what if in reality there was nothing there behind her prettiness?

He *wasn't* right, she told herself fiercely now, and she was going to prove it. Wasn't she?

Joel hadn't seemed to find her too vacuous to confide in. He hadn't been contemptuous of her looks.

He was a married man, she reminded herself, someone she barely knew, someone with problems enough of his own; but despite those problems there had been concern for her in his eyes, warmth in the way he'd talked to her... touched her.

They were poles apart in almost every way and yet, listening to him, talking to him, she had felt somehow closer to him than any other man she knew.

Closer to him and drawn to him. As a fellow victim of Andrew's actions, or as a man?

The phone rang, releasing her from the necessity of finding an answer.

It was the boys' headmaster, and she still hadn't spoken to her parents. Coward, she derided herself as she acknowledged that she would have to apologise to him and ask him for a little more time, but before she could say anything

she heard him telling her, 'I think I've solved the problem
of the boys' trip. The school has a special fund for cases
like theirs. I've checked with the administrator and he con-
firms that they are eligible, so unless you particularly want
them home for Easter, which I wouldn't recommend at the
moment, they can go on the trip to Italy as originally
planned. By summer, when they've had more time to adjust
to their father's death, things should be different.'

'At least something seems to be going my way,' she told
Susie later when her friend rang.

'Mmm, looks as if you've hit bottom and are on the way
up,' Susie suggested optimistically.

'Right now I'd quite happily settle for on the bottom,'
Philippa told her.

But, even though she discussed quite openly with her
friend the trauma of her visit to the social services office,
she did not mention meeting Joel.

Why should she? she asked herself quickly as she
replaced the telephone receiver. After all, it was not as
though he had any real relevance to her life, or she to his,
was it . . . ?

CHAPTER THIRTEEN

JOEL tensed as he heard Sally open the kitchen door; his ears and his mind, now attuned to her routine, caught the sound of her exasperated indrawn breath.

'Joel, where are you?'

She came into the living-room and demanded, 'Haven't you got anything better to do than watch television all day?'

'Like what?' he asked bitterly.

'Like finding a job.'

The minute the words were out Sally regretted them, but it was too late, they were said. She watched Joel's face close up and his mouth grow bitter.

'What job?' he demanded. 'There are no jobs, Sally.'

She knew that; after all, she had had to listen to him saying it often enough over the last few weeks.

Guiltily she tried to smother her frustration. It wasn't Joel's fault that he was out of work, after all, even if Daphne seemed to think differently.

Thinking about her sister reminded her of something else she had said.

'No jobs, maybe,' she retorted now. 'But there is work. Daphne was saying only the other day that she knows dozens of people looking for someone to do a bit of gardening or decorating and she's right, Joel. Sister was saying only last week that she's been trying to find someone to paint the outside of her house. Surely you could...'

Joel couldn't listen to any more.

'I could what?' he exploded. 'Go cap in hand to the likes of your sister and her posh friends begging for work?' Angry colour flared across his cheekbones. 'She'd love that, wouldn't she? She'd...'

Sally pushed her hand wearily into her hair. She had just come from a ward where a patient whose life they had been fighting for for over a week had just died; she was mentally and physically exhausted with the strain of working full-time and trying to run things at home as well. 'Well, at least it would be work, and there'd be some extra money coming in,' she told him bitterly.

Did he have any idea what a struggle it was for her to manage? She knew how upset and worried he was about losing his job and she'd done her best to cope and not to add to his worries by admitting that her money just wasn't going as far as she'd hoped, but he knew how much she earned compared with what they'd been bringing home; surely he could see for himself how much she was struggling?

She frowned as her attention was caught by the magazines on the floor beside his chair: two angling ones and one of them was an expensive one, she recognised as the tension and anxiety inside her suddenly exploded in a ball of tight, frightened anger.

'Joel, how could you?' she demanded as she picked them up. 'How could you waste money on these when you know...?' Her voice shook as she threw them down on the floor. 'If you think I'm going out to work, half killing myself, so that you can waste money on stuff like this...'

Joel's face went white. 'They cost three pounds eighty, less than you give the kids for spending money,' he told her with quiet venom.

His words struck at her conscience like physical blows, but Sally was too angry to back down.

'They *earn* that money,' she told him sharply.

When Joel came towards her, for one awful heartbeat of time she actually thought he was going to hit her—Joel, who was the least violent human being she knew. Instinctively she shrank back from him, her eyes widening with fear and shock.

Joel looked shocked too. Shocked and something else, something she couldn't put a name to but which brought a lump of painful aching emotion to her throat as her senses suddenly relayed to her what her eyes had refused to see:

the way his shoulders were hunched, the brooding, bitter, defeated look in his eyes.

She wanted to run up to him and fling her arms round him, to tell him that she was sorry...to explain that she was tired and confused and very, very frightened; that she hadn't realised just what it would mean to have the full financial responsibility of their lives resting on her shoulders; that she ached sometimes for him to take hold of her and tell her that she wasn't to worry, that he would sort everything out, even though she knew that wasn't possible.

She felt so alone, so afraid, but Joel just didn't seem to notice or care.

Other people did, though. Daphne had commented the last time she had seen her on how tired she looked.

'You'd think Joel would find some way of earning something,' Daphne had told her. 'After all, it's not as though he couldn't...not with his upbringing.'

Sally had had to avoid looking at her. It would be a betrayal of Joel to tell her sister how he felt about the life he had led as a child, about the fact that his father had never had a regular job and had had to scrape a living where he could.

Joel had once told her that without the allotment he'd worked on with his father they would often have gone without proper food.

'Jack of all trades, master of none, that was him,' Joel had told her bitterly. 'People used to treat him like dirt: he should never have married my mother... He ruined her life as well as his own...and ours...'

Sally had winced as she'd listened to him. As a girl she had thought his background, his gypsy blood romantic, but Joel had shown her a different side of that inheritance when he'd revealed to her the taunts he had suffered as a child, the determination he had developed never, ever to be like his father.

And yet Sally had liked the older man. He had been very like Joel. He had been kind and gentle, patient, and Sally knew how much it had hurt him that Joel had rejected him.

'There aren't the jobs,' she had said quietly, deliberately misunderstanding her sister as she'd added, 'Not for someone with Joel's training...'

Daphne had given an exasperated sigh. 'You're too soft on him,' she had told her. 'And you're letting him take advantage of you. You should be careful, Sally... after all, what's in the blood...'

'What do you mean?' Sally had demanded unwisely.

'Well, it's a well-known fact that gypsy men live off what their women earn,' Daphne had responded self-righteously.

'Oh, Daphne,' Sally had protested. 'That's not fair— Joel's not that sort of man. He would never...' She had stopped, unable to go on.

It wasn't the money he had spent on the magazines, she wanted to tell Joel, not really, but the words were stuck in her throat, the anger she felt refusing to subside. He was walking towards the kitchen... and away from her, ignoring her.

He paused in the doorway and turned round.

'I didn't buy those magazines, Sally, I was given them,' he told her bleakly. His pride wouldn't let him tell her that he didn't have the money in his pocket to buy them.

She never seemed to think, when she was doling out money to the kids and banging on about not wanting them to suffer because he was out of a job and it being important to them not to lose face in front of their friends, that he might feel the same. How did she think it made him feel, having to refuse to go out with his friends because he didn't have any money in his pocket—or any chance of earning any, from what he had learned at the Job Centre this morning?

Sally swallowed guiltily.

'Did you go down to the Job Centre today?' she asked him, avoiding looking at him.

'Yes, and there wasn't anything...not that I thought there would be.'

'Oh, Joel, please stop feeling so sorry for yourself. You *could* find work if you wanted to... I've just told you, Daphne wants some decorating doing. We need the money,' she told him exasperatedly. 'The tyres on my car are practically bald ... I daren't keep on driving with them. We're so lucky that I've got my job ...'

'Are we?' Joel turned on her. 'I don't feel so damn lucky having a wife who can't stop ramming it down my throat that she's the breadwinner and I'm just another useless mouth to feed ... not like the kids. You don't begrudge what you spend on them, do you? What is it you really think, Sally? That you'd be better off without me ... that you don't really want me around any more?'

'No,' Sally protested. 'You *know* that's not true.'

'Isn't it? Well, you've got a funny way of showing it.'

Sally looked away from him. Please don't let him start on about that again. She'd tried to explain to him over and over again that she was just too tired to make love. She had so many other things on her mind, so many other problems, so many other demands on her, draining her, sex was the last thing she wanted.

It angered her that he could be so selfish, so lacking in understanding and awareness. Sometimes, lying there stiff with resentment, feeling his hands on her body, she'd itched to tell him just to get on with it and get it over so that she could go to sleep, but she had held back, remembering how it had been between them when they were first married, when the children were small, when her body had come alive at the smallest touch and their lovemaking had been so urgent that they had very often not even made it upstairs.

Joel watched her broodingly. He could see from Sally's face that she knew what he was getting at and that she didn't want to pursue the subject. Didn't she realise how bad it made him feel when she turned away from him, when her body received his in a cold, unmoving silence, her lack of response filling him with a fear that to him completely demeaned him as a man? He was showing her how vulnerable he was, how much he needed her ... how much he ached for the comfort of this intimacy with her; the knowledge that he was still important to her; that she still wanted and needed him; that, despite the fact that he had broken all the promises he had made to her about always looking

after her and the kids, she understood and still loved him.
Yes, he was showing her how vulnerable he was, and all
she was doing was turning her back on him, telling him
that he was as little use to her as a man as he was as a
provider. That rejection struck deeply to the heart of his
manhood, hurting him far more than her angry, bitter
words. He could feel the ache in his throat, the pain that
filled him.

'You might at least get in touch with Daphne and find
out exactly what it is she wants doing and how much she'll
pay you,' Sally said quickly, anxious to get off the subject
of sex as quickly as she could.

Joel's mouth tightened.

'You find out,' he told her. 'She's your damned sister.'

'But you will do it...?' Sally asked him.

He looked bitterly at her. 'Do I have any bloody choice?'

Shakily Sally went over to the phone and dialled her sister's number. She was working an extra shift today; one of
the other nurses was off sick and Sally had leapt at the
chance to earn some extra overtime, even if it did mean
she'd have to go without sleep.

'You'll have to do the shopping this afternoon. I'm going
back to work,' she told Joel as she waited for her sister to
answer the phone.

'Oh, and don't forget it's Paul's computer club tonight.
I've made out a shopping list and I'll leave you some money.
You'll have to run me to work as well, Joel.'

She started nibbling on her bottom lip, worrying about
how long it would take her to earn enough to pay for those
new tyres.

'Oh, Daphne, it's me... About that decorating you
wanted Joel to do...'

Silently Joel walked out of the room. Didn't Sally realise
what she was doing to him? For God's sake treat me with
a bit of respect, he wanted to say to her, but how could
he? How could he ask for something he no longer had any
right to?

Sally hadn't even mentioned to him, discussed with him
the fact that she was thinking of working an extra shift.

What had happened to the girl who had stood there in the playground looking up at him so adoringly, the girl who had loved him so ardently and passionately?

That Sally was gone, he acknowledged, and in her place was a woman who looked through him rather than at him, who treated him with impatience and irritation, who no longer bothered to include him in any of her plans... her decisions.

He felt like a spare part in his own home, useless, unwanted... a liability.

He had been so proud being Sally's husband... of being loved by her, of knowing that her love for him was stronger than her parents' disapproval of him.

Did she still love him? How could she? He had let her down, failed her.

Later, he drove her to the hospital and watched her get out of the car, quickly avoiding looking at him.

He looked at the petrol gauge on his car. It was almost on empty. There was probably just enough in the tank for him to do the shopping.

Well, there was no way he was going to ask Sally for any money. No way.

Tiredly Sally pulled off her cap and ran her fingers through her hair.

It was only eight o'clock, but all she wanted to do was go home and crawl into bed. She had just left the hospital when she heard a car drawing up alongside her. When she turned her head and saw that its driver was Kenneth Drummond her heart gave a funny little excited jerk.

'No car?' he asked her through the open window.

Sally shook her head, suddenly oddly tongue-tied.

'Get in, then, and I'll give you a lift.'

She shook her head again, but he didn't drive away. Sally hesitated, some inner sixth sense warning her to resist his invitation, but the queue of impatient traffic building up behind him and Kenneth's obvious intention of staying right where he was until she gave in forced her hand.

The air inside the car was warm and smelled faintly and disconcertingly of Kenneth's aftershave. The leather seat enfolded her, the cold, raw night shut outside the expensive luxury of the car.

She saw Kenneth frown as he looked at her.

'You look exhausted,' he said abruptly. 'What on earth have you been doing to yourself?'

For some reason Sally felt tears pricking her eyelids. Not once had Joel noticed the physical effects the strain she was under was having on her body. He was too wrapped up in his own self-pity to notice her, she thought bitterly as she told Kenneth shakily, 'Very flattering, I must say...I've just worked a double shift and...'

'You've done what?'

'We need the money,' Sally protested. 'Joel's still out of work.'

'Then why isn't he here to take you home?' Kenneth asked her with soft anger.

He still wasn't sure what it was about her that aroused such intense feelings inside him, such intense desire; there was, after all, nothing particularly outstanding about her; she was just another pretty and rather ordinary woman who was nowhere near in the same academic class as he was himself, and he could already imagine the eyebrow-raising there would be among his colleagues if they were to find out about her.

Dear Kenneth...trying to play Pygmalion, the older ones would say, while the younger, brasher lecturers would guffaw and tell him, You've been watching *Educating Rita* too often, Kenny boy...

No, he had no illusions about how they would treat her or him. He lived in a highly competitive world, even if that competitiveness was never acknowledged; a world that was intellectually competitive and not materially sound; yet, just as in a much less rarefied atmosphere, a man's worth was still judged on how he and his partner measured up to their peers.

A partner who had trained as a nurse rather than following the path of a degree would leave him open to the delighted mockery of his fellows.

And yet that didn't stop him wanting her. He could still remember how he had felt when he'd opened his eyes in that hospital bed and seen her leaning down looking at him. The realisation that he was alive, that he could think and feel . . . and feel in every part of himself . . . had brought him such an intense flood of emotion . . .

Sally was so perfectly right for him. Of course she would need teaching, moulding, but unlike his first wife she would not argue or try to compete with him. She would respect his judgement, know that he was right.

He felt his body surge with sexual power and desire, but he made no attempt to reach out and take hold of Sally, to show her how he felt.

When they did make love for the first time it would not be quick or hurried, an unplanned, impromptu event. In fact he already knew where and how it would happen. In his mind's eye he could already see them together, smell the fresh, clean scent of the pure white cotton bedlinen that covered his bed, see it half masking the delicacy of Sally's body, see the expression in her eyes—half-awe, half-delight—as she surveyed the cool elegance of his bedroom.

With Sally he would be in control as his wife had never allowed him to be.

He frowned abruptly, not wanting the unpleasant memory of his marriage to mar what he was feeling now. Sally was nothing like his ex-wife—she was a completely different type of woman, a far less sexually aggressive and far more feminine woman—his type of woman, even if she was still clinging to her stubborn and misplaced loyalty to her husband.

Sally tensed, sensing Kenneth's arousal, waiting for him to react as Joel would have done in the same circumstances.

'This isn't the way home,' she told him quickly, her previous pleasure in his company evaporating. No matter how much she might be attracted to Kenneth mentally and emotionally, her body still reacted against the thought of any kind of physical intimacy; sex to her was a chore, something she felt obliged to endure for the sake of peace and quiet.

'No, it isn't,' Kenneth agreed. He turned his head and smiled at her. 'I'm kidnapping you,' he told her softly. 'And there's nothing you can do about it.'

He saw her face and the expression she was unable to control, and his awareness of how right he had been in his judgement of her made his voice intensely tender as he reached out and touched her hand lightly, telling her, 'Oh, Sally...no...what's happening between us goes far, far beyond the narrow confines of sex... How could you think otherwise?

'It isn't the mere sexual gratification of possessing your body I want, Sally. It's you...you...the whole person. I want your smile, your laughter, your conversation, your calm silence. You...'

Sally shook her head. Tears were threatening to blur her vision. A feeling of joy and relief flooded through her, of gratitude and euphoria.

'What did you think?' Kenneth teased her. 'That I was kidnapping you to have my evil way with you?'

When she flushed, he laughed.

'The last thing I would ever do is force myself on any woman, but most especially not one whom I...love... Is that what he does, Sally?' he probed, watching her. 'This husband of yours—does he...?'

Sally shook her head quickly, not wanting him to continue.

'Have you told him about me?' Kenneth asked her.

'No,' she told him quickly—quickly and guiltily. 'I mean...'

'You mean what?' Kenneth asked her softly. 'That I'm not important enough to mention, or that...I'm too important for you to do so?'

His perception took Sally's breath away. She could feel herself flushing.

'I—we... We don't get much chance to talk about anything these days,' she prevaricated hesitantly. 'I...Joel doesn't like me talking about the patients at home. He——'

'The patients?' Kenneth interrupted her. 'Is that all I am to you, Sally, just a patient? I thought we were friends...'

Friends. Her heart bumped uncomfortably.

'Well, yes...' she agreed. 'But Joel...'

'Joel what? Joel doesn't like you having your own friends? You shouldn't let him dictate to you like that, Sally... You're not his possession, you know. You're a human being with your own rights and needs. That is the worst mistake a man can make: to deny a woman the right to be an individual, not to recognise her as an individual...'

That was exactly what Joel was doing to her, Sally reflected bitterly. He was treating her like a possession.

'I nearly rang you last week,' Kenneth was saying to her.

Her heart thumped crazily again.

'I've missed you, Sally. Have you missed me?'

'Kenneth... I can't...'

'We're friends, remember?' he told her soothingly. 'Friends are allowed to miss one another, to spend time together. I like talking to you... I like the way you listen to me...'

And she liked the way *he* listened to *her*, Sally acknowledged. He made her feel valued and appreciated, unlike Joel, who never seemed even to allow her to finish a sentence these days without jumping down her throat.

It was so peaceful here with Kenneth—so peaceful...

'I want to take you out properly,' Kenneth told her softly. 'Take you out somewhere and spoil you a bit... Where would you like to go?'

Sally stared at him. She *couldn't* go anywhere with him. He knew that.

'Kenneth, I can't... I'm... I'm married.' Her voice wobbled slightly, betraying her so much that her face flushed and she couldn't look at him. Would he guess from her voice how much she longed to put aside the burden she was carrying and to be cosseted and cherished for a little while?

'I'd never let a man support me—I like my independence,' one of the younger nurses had said robustly earlier,
but what she had wasn't independence, Sally recognised;
what she had was in its way just as restrictive and imprisoning as being dependent on someone else. Being the
one who *had* to go out to work, who had to pay the bills
did not confer freedom and independence, she was beginning to realise—instead it brought worry and
responsibility.

'And you and I have already established that we are
friends and that you have a right to your own life. There
can't be any objection to friends spending a few hours in
one another's company, Sally... I'm sure that husband of
yours spends time with his friends.'

'Yes, but they're... they're men...'

'So am I,' Kenneth pointed out, laughing.

Sally laughed too—she couldn't help it, and, after all,
wasn't Kenneth right? She *did* deserve something of her
own, some reward for all the hard work she was
doing... some pleasure of her own.

'I... I don't think Joel would like it...' she appeased.
'He...'

'Tell him you're working another double shift,' Kenneth
suggested.

Sally stared at him. His words had stripped what lay between them of any pretence. Her mouth had gone dry. She
touched her tongue-tip to her lips nervously, panic stirring
inside her.

'Kenneth, I can't,' she protested. The clock on the dash-
board showed that it was gone nine. She had been with him
nearly an hour and yet it felt like only five minutes... less.

'Please take me home, Kenneth... the children... they'll
be wondering where I am.'

'The *children*?' Kenneth frowned. 'I thought they were
teenagers.'

'They are, but...'

'Then they're almost adult... almost independent,' he
told her lightly. 'Stop worrying about them and worry about
yourself instead.'

'Don't you worry about your children?' Sally asked him. Beneath the lightness of his voice she had sensed a hardness that disturbed her slightly. 'Don't you miss them?'

'I hardly know them to miss them,' he told her. 'They look on my wife's second husband as their father, not me, and, as I told you, they are already adults.'

As he heard the small distressed sound she made Kenneth acknowledged her naïveté. He did not miss his children simply because he had never really formed any kind of attachment to them, had never really wanted either of them in the first place. His concern for what others would think and the social mores of the times had been what had led him into marrying in the first place. A young man in his position, striving to establish himself in the academic world could not abandon his pregnant girlfriend, especially when that girlfriend was as strong-willed and verbal as Rebecca.

In his haste to cover up his...their error he had not thought as far ahead as the effect the child they had conceived might have on his life; had even convinced himself that as a young lecturer the gravity that a wife and family would add to his life would only make his older and more senior colleagues view him with greater approval.

The actual reality of what having a child, a baby in his life meant had come as an unpleasant shock.

The small house he had bought—and furnished—with an eye to the kind of effect it would create both on his colleagues and his students was totally unsuitable for a baby, so Rebecca had claimed.

The dark, stern, polished wood furniture, the plain white walls, the bare polished floorboards—Rebecca had wanted all of them banished and replaced with hideously jarring modern colours and materials which he had instantly loathed.

The sheer havoc the small screaming bundle of humanity that was his son had brought into the previous calm of his well-ordered life had brought him to the point where he could scarcely bring himself even to look at the child. The noise, the mess, the smell... He gave a small shudder, which Sally totally misinterpreted.

'That must have been so hard for you,' she commented sympathetically. 'Knowing that another man was bringing up your children...'

There was no point in telling her the truth. After all, how could his dislike of small children affect them? That was another plus point about Sally. She was no foolish young girl who would be irrationally tempted to spoil the perfect harmony of their relationship, their closeness, with children.

He made a small non-committal sound while Sally repeated anxiously, 'I really must go home, Kenneth. Joel...'

'It's all right, we're on our way,' Kenneth soothed her, turning the car round and then pausing to look into her face and watch as the soft colour crept over her skin at his scrutiny of her.

'I'm not going to let you go, Sally,' he told her softly. 'You're far too important to me. I respect your loyalty towards your husband but we both know that he just isn't worthy of you. If he were, you wouldn't be here with me like this.'

Sally shivered slightly as she listened to him. She wanted to deny what he was saying but she couldn't. This time she had spent with him was such a solace to her after all she was enduring at home, a bright, warm patch of clear blue in an otherwise dull, heavy grey sky. Kenneth understood her and what she was feeling in a way that Joel didn't... And didn't want to?

'I'll ring you,' Kenneth told her as he turned the car into the main road leading to her home.

Sally panicked. 'No...you mustn't do that,' she protested.

Kenneth stopped the car. 'Then tell me when I can see you again.'

Sally thought frantically; her brain felt like cotton wool, overloaded with confusion and guilt.

She knew she ought to tell Kenneth that it was impossible for her to see him; that she was married; that she loved Joel; but somehow those words wouldn't come and instead she heard herself saying breathlessly, 'I...Sister did say I could work an extra shift on Monday and I haven't said yet whether or not I will.'

Her mouth had gone dry with the enormity of the deception she was...planning. She had never lied to Joel about anything, nor ever dreamed she would want to, and a part of her was already regretting what she had said, urging her to call back the words, but it was too late—Kenneth was already leaning towards her, touching her face softly.

'Monday it is, then,' he whispered to her before he kissed her with gentle tenderness.

Hot tears stung her closed lids. How long was it since Joel had treated her so gently, with such caring restraint?

Shakily she disengaged herself from him. The kiss they had just exchanged made her feel as though she had crossed an invisible boundary, stepped into a frightening no-man's land.

'Don't worry,' Kenneth told her softly, taking hold of her hand and wrapping it inside his own before carefully opening her palm and depositing a kiss there. 'Everything's going to be all right...'

Later, hurrying home on trembling legs, her heart aching with the weight of her guilt, she felt desperately afraid. She knew other women who had affairs, broke their marriage vows, but she had always believed that she could never be one of them, and yet here she was...

She stopped, swallowing hard and blinking back the tears threatening her, fighting to control the conflicting emotions. She was in sight of the house, one half of her wanting to run quickly towards its familiarity and security, to hide herself away inside it, from what had just happened, while the other half...

She closed her eyes, her mouth trembling, appalled by her own awareness of how much the other half of her wanted to turn round and run to Kenneth.

She had never known such confusion, such pain, such a racking mixture of guilt, despair and resentment, all mixed up with a helpless longing for all that Kenneth wanted to give her.

CHAPTER FOURTEEN

PHILIPPA sank back wearily on her heels, pushing her hand into her hair. Her fingers, she noticed, were shaking slightly. Susie had obviously noticed too, because she was watching her with sympathetic compassion.

'It's all right,' she assured her friend huskily. 'I'm OK... It's just that...doing this...' she waved towards the neat piles of men's clothes stacked on the floor and the empty wardrobes beyond them... 'seems so final somehow...you forget just how much... Andrew was such a hoarder. There are clothes here which——' She broke off, biting down hard on her bottom lip.

'I feel as though I shouldn't really be doing this,' she confessed, 'going through his clothes, emptying his pockets. It makes me feel as though...as though I'm breaking some kind of taboo. It would be different if we'd been closer. As it is...' She shook her head and summoned a crooked smile.

'You do realise, don't you, that if you hadn't come round here this morning and insisted on our doing this these things would still probably have been here when the house is sold?'

'Have you heard yet from the bank?' Susie asked her quietly.

Philippa shook her head. 'No, not yet.' She smoothed her hand down over a jumper she had just picked up. Pale yellow with a motif embroidered on the front, the delicate cashmere felt incredibly soft to her touch. She had bought this for Andrew herself, for his birthday last year, saving the money from her family allowance and the house-keeping. He had worn it once; a token gesture, she suspected, because she had never seen him wear it a second time.

'What is it?' Susie asked her softly.

'I was just thinking how little I actually knew Andrew,' Philippa told her tiredly.

'Some men are secretive,' Susie told her. 'They think that it's soft...unmasculine...giving in to a weakness to confide in anyone or betray what they're feeling.'

'It's not just that...I don't just mean...I didn't even really know the little things about him, Susie... Like the kind of clothes he preferred... I didn't try to know him,' she confided, her eyes filling with tears. 'I just turned away and let him drift away from me. I never cared enough to make an effort to stop him. He must have known that, mustn't he? He must...'

'Stop blaming yourself,' Susie told her firmly. 'It takes two to break a relationship as well as make one... If Andrew had wanted to be closer to you and the boys he could have told you...shown you...'

'Maybe, but even these days isn't the onus always on the woman to nurture the emotional side of a relationship? I'm sorry,' she apologised to her friend, shaking her head. 'I am rather wallowing in self-pity this morning, aren't I? Come on, let's get these things packed up and then I can clean out the wardrobes. Are you sure you don't mind taking them down to the refuge for me?'

'Of course not, but I still think you could probably have sold some of them.'

Philippa gave an involuntary shudder. 'No...no, I couldn't do that.' Selling her own clothes was one thing; selling Andrew's was another. 'Besides,' she added wryly, 'I'm not sure if I have any right to sell them; for all I know they probably belong to the bank.'

Susie watched her sympathetically. As she had said to Jim, her own husband, the previous night, she didn't think she would have the courage or strength to cope with such a situation as well as Philippa was doing.

Now, as she and Philippa packed up the clothes into plastic bags and carried them out to her car, she suggested gently, 'Look, why don't you come home with me this afternoon? We could...'

Quickly Philippa shook her head. 'No...no. It's kind of you, but I can't... I...I want to get some more work done on my vegetable bed while the weather's good. I don't know how long I'll be able to stay on here, but maybe I'll have some early vegetables to pick before the bank tells us to go.'

Philippa knew that she was flushing and hoped that Susie would put her increased colour down to the effort of carrying the heavy binliners of clothes. It was true that she did want to work in the garden, but it was also equally true that there was another reason why she wanted to stay at home, and it wasn't one that she wanted to reveal to her friend.

He probably wouldn't come, of course, probably hadn't even really meant it when he'd offered to look at her car, and really, after all, there was no reason why she should want to see him again, was there? Except that she had enjoyed talking to him...except that he was the first person she had really felt able to let down her guard with...except that when he had stood next to her on the street, protecting her, she had felt so...

'Well, that's the last of them!' Susie exclaimed cheerfully as she dumped the last of the binliners in the back of her estate car. 'I'd better get them down to the refuge... Oh, by the way, I nearly forgot...I brought you these. Mother will insist on sending me home with goodness knows what from the local farm. Honestly, you'd think, to listen to her, that decent fresh food isn't something that's available once you leave the boundaries of Yorkshire, but I suppose old habits die hard, and having been a farmer's wife... Heaven knows how long it would take us to get through three dozen free-range eggs and all the rest of the stuff she made me bring back with me.'

She avoided looking at Philippa as she handed over a covered basket.

It felt very heavy, Philippa acknowledged, and it had to contain far more than a dozen or so eggs and a couple of jars of Susie's mother's home-made jam and pickles.

Tears pricked her eyes. Her pride made her want to refuse but as she looked at her friend she saw that there were tears in Susie's eyes as well.

'Please take it, Pippa,' Susie begged her quietly. 'You know if our positions were reversed you would be the first...' She swallowed and shook her head. 'I hate the thought of you staying here on your own, especially after what you told me the other day. I wish you'd think again about what I said about coming to us.'

'Not yet,' Philippa told her huskily, adding, 'Don't make it too easy for me, Susie, otherwise I might be tempted to give in and take the easy way out, and I can't...I mustn't... Don't you see, that's what I've done all my life...taken the easy way out? This time...this time it's going to be different. You know what they say,' she added, with a weak grin. 'No pain, no gain...'

'Huh... I know it's what they say,' Susie agreed. 'But...' She stopped and looked at Philippa. 'OK, OK, I hear you, but just remember...'

'I will,' Philippa assured her softly, smiling as she looked at her friend and said drily, 'Oh, and you will remember to thank your *mother* for her generosity, won't you?'

She waited until Susie's car had disappeared down the drive before picking up the basket and taking it into the kitchen. As she had suspected, it contained far more than what Susie had said; the cheese was farmhouse-fresh and so was the thick slice of pie which Philippa remembered was a delicacy which Jim loved and which Susie always brought back from Yorkshire with her, like the home-cured ham and bacon.

There was probably enough food in the basket to last for two or three weeks, and all of it far more wholesome and appetising than the diet she had grown used to recently.

Tears blurred Philippa's eyes as she unpacked the food and put it away. This, she suspected, was one of the hardest lessons of all to learn, this acceptance of charity...receiving it rather than giving it.

* * *

Sally tensed as she heard the phone ring. Joel got up to answer it and her stomach muscles locked. It was silly to feel like this, she scolded herself. After all, what really had she done wrong? What if Kenneth did ring her? He was an ex-patient who...

Who had what? Kissed her and made her see all the things that were missing from her life?

'It's your sister,' Joel told her abruptly, coming into the kitchen.

The relief that flooded her was dangerously entangled with disappointment as well.

The postman had arrived as she picked up the receiver and her heart sank as she saw the bills in among the circulars.

'Have you spoken to Joel about when he can do my decorating yet?' Daphne wanted to know. 'Only I'd like him to come and make a start on it as soon as possible, Sally. We've got a dinner party next month. It shouldn't take him long, after all, should it? I mean, it's not as though he's got anything else to do...'

Sally sighed under her breath. 'I'll have a word with him about it now,' she promised her sister.

'What did she want?' Joel demanded when Sally walked back into the kitchen.

Sally sighed again. Joel and her sister had never really hit it off and she knew that Daphne could be something of a snob at times, but was it really too much to ask of Joel that he didn't react aggressively to everything Daphne said or did? Couldn't he see how difficult it made things for her?

Sally looked tired, Joel recognised as he looked at her. She had lost weight as well. He started to frown.

As she walked towards the sink she bumped into the corner of the table, stumbling slightly.

Joel reacted instinctively, reaching out to steady her, putting his hand on the hip she had bumped and rubbing it with his fingers.

She smelled of soap and shampoo, the slightness of her body against his reminding him of how protective towards her he had always felt, of how vulnerable she sometimes seemed. It was one of the most basic and deep-rooted aspects of his character, this need he had to protect and secure those weaker than himself, and now suddenly he had an urge to wrap his arms around her, to hold her and tell her how ashamed he felt. He wanted, he acknowledged, not just to hold her, but to be held in turn; to be told that she understood, that she...

'Joel, no...'

The sharp protest in her voice as she pulled away from him felt like a knife slicing into the vulnerable flesh of his emotions, the irritation and rejection he could both hear and see freezing back the words he had wanted to say.

'Can't you think about anything but that?' Sally demanded bitterly.

'Such as?' Joel challenged her.

'Such as these.' Angrily she threw the bills down on the table.

She hadn't received this month's salary yet and already it was almost accounted for. Paul had come in last night saying he would need new football boots and now here were those bills. She felt sick at the thought of opening them, knowing already that she might not be able to pay them, and all Joel could do was grab hold of her and...

Silently Joel watched her. The unopened bills lay between them on the table. Sally reached for one of them, ripping it open, scanning it feverishly. Perhaps with the money her sister paid Joel for the decorating they might just be able to cover it.

She reached for the other but Joel stopped her.

'That's addressed to me,' he told her flatly.

Sally stared at him. Joel had never minded who opened their post, and invariably she was the one to do so because he was at work when it arrived.

Suddenly she just couldn't take any more.

'You open it, then,' she told him angrily. 'And you pay it as well...'

Bitterly Joel watched as she stormed out of the room. He could still vaguely feel the imprint of her hipbone against his fingertips. Once she would never have confused a gesture meant to comfort and solace with one that was sensual and questioning... Once... once a lot of things had been different...

He picked up the unopened bill and opened it.

'You pay it', she had challenged him. He could feel the painful burn of his emotions searing his eyelids.

Once she got upstairs Sally discovered that she was shaking with reaction to their row.

She shouldn't have spoken to Joel like that, she knew, but couldn't he see the strain she was under? Other people could... Like her sister... like Kenneth.

She sighed and got up. In less than an hour she had to be at work, and before that she had to persuade Joel to do her sister's decorating.

Philippa saw Joel walking up the drive from an upstairs window.

'The car's still in the garage... It's round here,' she told him awkwardly as she went outside to meet him. The wind was ruffling his hair, thick and dark and silky. She had an odd urge to reach out and touch it. To touch him...

Uncomfortably she distanced herself from him, hurrying ahead of him as she led the way round the side of the house. What was happening to her? She just didn't feel like this about men... react to them like this.

She looked over her shoulder, suddenly anxious to tell Joel that she had changed her mind. She didn't want him here. It was too...

He was standing looking at the ground she had been clearing.

'I'm working on my vegetable garden,' she heard herself telling him uncertainly. 'I thought...'

Joel bent down and picked up a handful of soil, letting it trickle through his fingers.

'Good soil,' he told her, 'but you'll have to watch that hedge; cut it down a bit otherwise it will take too much light...'

'You obviously know a lot more about it than I do. Are you a keen gardener?'

'No,' Joel told her abruptly and then, realising how curt he had sounded, he added, 'My father had an allotment—it was one of my chores as a boy to work on it...'

There was an expression on his face that told Philippa that his memories of that work weren't good ones.

'That must have been hard work?' she sympathised.

'Hard and dirty,' Joel told her. 'I used to have to scrub my hands with bleach to get them clean, otherwise...'

He shook his head. He had already said more than he wanted to. Not even Sally knew about all of the humiliation he had suffered in his early years at school when one of the teachers had objected to his touching the school books with his dirt-grimed hands. It had, after all, been before he knew her, a painful memory which he had fiercely suppressed because of the shame it had caused him—and yet for a second he almost revealed it to this woman who was not just a stranger to him but who had, he suspected, no idea what it meant to live in the kind of semi-poverty, the uncertainty which he had known as a child.

'The garage is this way,' Philippa told him.

The garage was large enough to house three cars, and hers looked small and forlorn alone in it. The dealer had repossessed Andrew's within days of his death. It had not, apparently, been paid for. Fortunately, hers had.

As Joel went to switch on the light, Philippa flushed guiltily, remembering that the bulb had gone and that she hadn't replaced it.

'It's OK, I'll do it,' Joel told her.

'I *can* change a light bulb,' Philippa told him, adding wryly, 'Just about! I think I'm going to have to find a night-school course of basic house maintenance. It's ridiculous in this day and age not to be able to change a fuse or wire a plug...'

Joel could hear the frustration in her voice.

'It's not that difficult,' he told her quietly. 'I could teach you easily enough.'

For no reason that she could account for, Philippa could feel her skin starting to heat.

'I'd... I'd better go and let you get on...' she told him huskily. 'I—er—would you like a cup of coffee?'

Philippa deliberately didn't linger when she took Joel his coffee. His head was bent over the open bonnet of her car. He had removed his jacket and rolled up his sleeves. His forearms were much broader than Andrew's had been, much more muscular, his skin faintly tanned beneath its covering of dark hair.

A tiny *frisson* of sensation went through her. Guiltily she looked away.

What was wrong with her? She was behaving like some textbook sex-starved widow. Which, given the true state of her married sex life, was absolutely ridiculous.

She was in the kitchen half an hour later when Joel knocked on the door and walked in.

'I think it will be OK now,' he told her. 'The plugs needed a bit of a clean. It probably needs a good run as well...'

Philippa grimaced slightly. Giving it a good run meant filling the tank with petrol...something she couldn't afford. The electricity bill had come this morning. She saw Joel glancing at it.

'Ours came too,' he told her. 'According to Sally it's higher than usual—my fault, of course. I'm sorry,' he apologised. 'It's just...' He stopped.

'It must be a worrying time for both of you,' Philippa sympathised. 'But at least you've got each other to share it with.'

Joel laughed harshly. 'You think so? Sharing isn't something we do much of these days...'

She had obviously touched a raw nerve, Philippa recognised.

'For a man to lose his job is very stressful in a relationship,' she said quietly. 'Sally... your wife is probably very worried about you; she...'

'Is she?' Joel demanded harshly. 'Well, you'd certainly never know it. All I get from her these days is, "Joel, do this, Joel, have you done that? Joel, don't touch me——''

He broke off, tensing as he looked at her. He had said more than he'd intended to say, Philippa recognised, and the old Philippa—the Philippa who preferred to turn aside rather than face up to things—would have pretended the comment had never been made; but she wasn't that Philippa any more, and so she looked back at him and said quietly, 'Lots of women do go off sex when they're under stress... and men as well.'

'What I want from Sally isn't just sex; what I want to share with her is called making love, and it involves a lot more than a handful of seconds of clinical physical thrusting inside her body. A hell of a lot more.'

Philippa couldn't help it—she could feel the hot colour running up under her skin, knew that her face was on fire with it.

'I'm sorry,' Joel apologised, raking his fingers through his hair. 'I shouldn't have said it. I didn't mean to embarrass you, it's just... Why do women always call it sex when they want to make you feel bad about it... when they want to make you feel guilty, as if we're some kind of emotionless animals? To listen to her now you'd never think there was a time when Sally...' He shook his head.

'But you've got enough problems of your own without having to listen to mine. He was your husband, after all.

'Look, is it OK if I wash my hands?' They were covered in oil, Philippa saw, and there was also a smear of it across his cheekbone.

'Yes, I'm sorry... You can use Andrew's bathroom,' she told him as she opened the kitchen door and led the way across the hall. 'There's a shower in it, although I'm not sure how hot the water will be.'

'Andrew's bathroom?' he queried sharply.

Philippa flushed.

'Yes... it's... it's all right... I've removed all his personal things... and...'

'You had separate bathrooms?' Joel questioned, ignoring what she was saying.

'Yes...yes, we did,' Philippa told him uncomfortably. 'It was...it was easier that way. Andrew...he...he was a very private man...he...' She was floundering desperately for words, both angry and alarmed by what she was being forced to reveal.

Joel could sense her discomfort. What kind of relationship had she actually had with her husband? Not, he suspected, a very close one either emotionally or physically. He wondered if they had had separate beds as well as separate bathrooms and then cut himself off from the thought, sensing the danger that lurked behind it.

Philippa waited in the kitchen for him to come back downstairs. When he did his hair was still damp, his shirt clinging slightly to his skin. As he brought her the towels he had used she could smell the scent of soap on his skin and her stomach muscles knotted frantically against the sensation curling through her body.

'I...thank you for looking at my car for me,' she told him huskily as she looked away from him.

She looked so small standing there, with her blonde hair down and parting to show the soft curve of her neck. If he reached out now he could touch that soft skin with his fingertips. If he did, would she push him away as Sally did or would her body quiver in mute acknowledgement of the desire he could feel aching inside him; would she turn her head and look at him, silently acknowledging what was happening between them...accepting...inviting?

'I'm sorry you're having a difficult time at home,' Philippa told him shakily. 'I wish there were something I could do to help. I feel...'

I feel so guilty, she had been about to say, but Joel moved closer to her and suddenly her throat closed up, trapping the words.

'Just being here with you...talking to you helps,' Joel told her, and as he said it he recognised that it was true, that there was something about her that drew him to her, compelled him to confide in her in a way that was totally foreign to his nature.

He felt at home with her...at ease and yet at the same time fiercely buoyed up by the sexual tension he could feel building between them.

He wanted her, he acknowledged...he wanted her very, very much indeed.

'You must go,' Philippa told him quickly as she stepped away from him. 'I hope everything works out...at home for you. I'm sure it will.'

If he bent his head now, he could still kiss her, Joel decided. But if he did...once he did...

Reluctantly he moved away from her. Didn't he have enough problems as it was without...?

Without what? He was a normal man with all the normal male urges, but he had never once been tempted to be unfaithful to Sally before, had never felt this fierce surge of sharp desire for another woman before.

After he had gone, Philippa walked back to the kitchen and picked up the damp towels he had used, lifting them to her face. She could still smell him on them, the scent of his skin, his maleness. With a small shudder she dropped the towels back on the floor.

Thank goodness she wasn't likely to see him again. Just now, standing next to him, she had sensed his awareness of her and his desire, had known that all she had to do was simply to turn towards him.

Joel had almost reached the town centre when he suddenly heard someone calling his name. Stopping, he turned his head and saw Duncan hurrying towards him.

The youth had changed since he had last seen him. His body had begun to fill out and he walked with more confidence, holding his head up instead of shuffling along with it downbent.

'Joel, how are you?'

'I'm OK,' Joel responded. 'And you...?'

'Great, especially since I joined this club they're running down at the leisure centre for people who are out of work... You ought to come along; they...'

'Can't afford it, mate,' Joel told him.

'It's free,' Duncan announced, adding, 'Look, I'm on my way there now—why don't you come along? Quite a few of the lads from the factory do; as well as being able to use the leisure club's facilities, there's all kinds of voluntary work you can do if you want to.'

'Voluntary work?'

'Yeah. They've got me going down to the hospital visiting some of the old folks they've got in there, doing a bit of shopping and the like for them...'

'Oh, that's where you've got those muscles, is it...doing a bit of shopping?' Joel commented drily.

Duncan flushed and then grinned. 'No...I've been working out at the gym... Might as well, since it's free. Helps to pass the time and you get a bit of company.'

He fell into step beside Joel. Grinning, he told him, 'Why don't you give it a go, get a few muscles of your own?'

Joel laughed. 'Watch it...' he warned him.

He opened his mouth to tell Duncan that he couldn't go with him, then closed it again. After all, what had he really to go home for? Sally would still be out at work, the kids would be out with their friends. All that was waiting for him was the television and Sally's list of chores...might as well go with Duncan. That way at least he wouldn't be wasting money on electricity...*Sally's* money.

It was gone six o'clock when Joel left the leisure centre. He glanced guiltily at his watch. He still hadn't been round to see Daphne and Sally would kill him when she got home if he didn't.

He had been surprised to discover how many of his workmates from the factory were making use of the leisure centre's policy of free entry for people who were unemployed. It seemed that it had become something of an unofficial meeting place for quite a large group of them.

Like him, none of them had managed to find a new job, but as he'd listened to them and contrasted their attitudes to his own Joel had discovered that they had something he didn't. They certainly seemed to be a lot more optimistic and to be getting a lot more out of their lives than he was.

On his way past the swimming-pool he'd stopped to look inside.

'You used to be a keen swimmer, didn't you, Joel?' one of the others had commented.

Joel had frowned in surprise.

'You used to swim for the school team,' the other man had reminded him.

'That was a hell of a long time ago,' Joel had pointed out.

'Maybe, but you were good...I remember watching you. They're looking for volunteers to help coach the junior team they've started here and to give swimming lessons to beginners. You'd be good at that. I remember watching you teaching that lad of yours...'

Joel had shrugged uncomfortably. Teaching his own son and daughter was one thing; teaching others... 'They'll be scraping the barrel if they can't find someone better than me to do it,' he'd retorted curtly.

But as he was walking home he remembered how his games teacher at school had told him that he was a natural athlete. He had wanted him to train for the school swimming and diving team, but he had told the teacher that he wasn't interested.

It hadn't been true...he had ached to accept, but what was the point...who would work the allotment if he wasn't there, who would make sure that the others had food on their plates, and how the hell was he supposed to pay for the kit he would need?

No—better to have people think that he wasn't interested than to risk the humiliation of revealing the truth.

A swimming coach...*him*... As he'd said to George Lewis, they'd have to be scraping the barrel to want him... Still, wouldn't do any harm watching the kids practise... It would be something to do to help pass the time, and if young Duncan really thought that he couldn't work his way around a gym any more...

Grinning to himself, Joel headed for home.

CHAPTER FIFTEEN

'It's the bank who are paying our fees, Deborah,' Ryan stressed. 'You might just try remembering that the next time you feel yourself coming all over bleeding hearts.'

Angrily Deborah stood up.

'What are you trying to say, Ryan—that I'm not being professional?'

'No, of course not; if I didn't think you were up to the job I wouldn't have recommended you for it in the first place. I'm just warning you not to get emotionally involved, that's all.'

'Just because I'm aware of and concerned for the problems that redundancy is bound to cause those who've lost their jobs, it doesn't mean that I'm becoming emotionally involved,' Deborah protested.

Any moment now Ryan was going to start accusing her of reacting like a woman—the ultimate put-down that men like him always threw at women when they wanted to bring them to heel and to remind them who was the boss.

'And,' she added firmly, 'making sure that such people are aware of their rights is in my view simply good business practice, especially from the point of view of the firm's reputation.'

'Our reputation with whom, Deborah? Our clients...the ones who pay our fees and consequently your wages, or every down-and-out no-hoper...?'

'They aren't no-hopers,' Deborah protested angrily. 'These people are out of work through no fault of their own; they...'

She stopped abruptly as she saw Ryan's expression. It was a mixture of irritation and boredom, the impatient drumming of his fingers warning her that she had overstepped the boundaries he had drawn for her.

'All I wanted to do was to make sure that the company's ex-employees knew exactly what the situation was with regard to their financial position...'

'And who the hell is going to pay for the extra time you spend doing that: the extra cost of writing individually to them; the——?'

'We had a moral duty...'

'Grow up, Deborah. This is the real world we're living in. We're here to make *money*, plain and simple, and if you can't understand or accept that then you're in the wrong job. I used to wonder what it was you saw in a wimp like Mark; now I think I know.

'I thought you and I were two of a kind...that we'd make a good team. You know how much opposition there's been from the senior partners about my wanting to promote you ahead of people who've been here far longer.'

Yes, she knew it, Deborah admitted. She hadn't thought much at first about what the consequences of her promised promotion might be—she had been far too thrilled and excited—but it was already becoming evident that there was a certain amount of jealousy and resentment among her colleagues.

So far she had managed to ignore it, reminding herself that it was a simple fact of life that when one member of a group was elevated above the others it was bound to cause a certain amount of turbulent negative emotion—for a while. In fact she had optimistically told herself that such a reaction would prove a good learning process for her, that it would enable her to perfect her people-handling skills. But somehow it wasn't working out.

Peer envy she could handle, or at least she had always thought she could, but when it was linked to an ambiguous and somehow elusive-to-pin-down awareness that those peers were putting her promotion down not to her professional skill, but to the fact that Ryan was showing her distinct favouritism, things were not quite so easy.

No one had directly put such a view to her yet, but it was there none the less. However, confronting it was like trying to reach out and grasp a handful of air. To ask outright among her ex-peers if her suspicions were correct would be an admission of insecurity—an admission to herself as well as to others that she did not have the professional skill to separate herself from their opinions. And it would be to admit to them, and to herself, that she did not have the ability to control and command, the ability to earn their respect even if it was given grudgingly.

And now it seemed that Ryan was turning against her as well, criticising the way she was handling the liquidation, undermining her self-confidence.

For a moment she was tempted to challenge him directly and ask him if he wanted her off the account. She had an odd feeling that for some reason Ryan was deliberately trying to unnerve and upset her, by focusing his criticism of her on the one area where women always felt the most vulnerable—her different emotional attitude from that of men.

Deborah had resolved when she'd first qualified that she was not going to allow the established hard core of old-fashioned chauvinistic men who still occupied so many positions of power within every aspect of the business world to trap her into the ultimately demeaning belief that the only way she, a woman, could survive and succeed in such a world was by accepting and adopting their code of behaviour.

She was proud of being a woman; of her femininity.

'Look, perhaps I am going a bit over the top,' she heard Ryan saying more calmly to her. 'But don't go and mess up on me, will you, there's a good girl?'

A good girl; somehow Deborah just managed to swallow down the retort that sprang to her lips as Ryan walked out of her office.

After he had gone, she found her attention wandering from the work in front of her. Was it her imagination, or had Ryan actually been implying something more than the fact that he had selected her to handle the liquidation?

She got up and walked over to stare out of the window. She knew his reputation, of course, but she had made her position plain enough and basically she suspected that she wasn't really his type. He could be good fun when he set his mind to it, but it was very obvious that he was the one who liked to hold centre-stage, who liked and needed to control those around him, and that kind of man, even if he had been available, even if she had been attracted to him, was not for her.

No... she could never become involved with a man like Ryan, not without losing her respect for him... and for herself.

Ryan had already made one or two taunting comments about her relationship with Mark, implying that she was the more dominant partner, but that simply wasn't true. She and Mark respected as well as loved one another.

She had been so lucky to meet Mark. The depth of her love for him was something that sometimes surprised even her. He was quite literally the rock on which she had built the foundations of her life, and it hurt her unbearably when Ryan tried to put him down.

But, much as she longed to jump to his defence, she resisted doing so, knowing how Ryan would interpret such an action. In his view men did not need their woman to champion or protect them; they did that for themselves.

He was archaic really, a dinosaur, Deborah reflected, but these Chinese whispers infiltrating the office that he had promoted her as a means of getting her into his bed didn't really have any truth to them, surely?

She knew, of course, that he wanted to bed her, but to promote her in order to put pressure on her to do so? No, he wouldn't do anything like that. He must know that she would never give in to that kind of sexual blackmail.

It was just as well they had the Easter weekend coming up, Deborah reflected grimly as she focused her attention back on her work. The liquidation was proving rather more drawn-out than any of them had initially imagined, and she suspected that she was going to have to spend at least part of the weekend catching up with her other paperwork.

It worried her that Mark was taking the becalming of his own career so badly. She knew how he must feel, of course, but it was, after all, a logical effect of the recession and one which he surely must have been anticipating.

'Have you any idea what it feels like sitting there at an empty desk three days out of five?' he had demanded angrily two evenings ago. 'No, of course you haven't,' he had gone on, answering his own question, 'because you made the right choice, the clever, wise career decision... Ryan's right—you are better than me, Deborah...'

'I went into liquidation because it was the only avenue open to me,' Deborah reminded him. 'You were the one who made the original decision to move here, Mark. I was quite happy in London. I only switched to liquidation and receivership because that was the only job open to me up here—you know that.'

They had, after all, discussed it thoroughly enough before she'd accepted the job, but then Mark had been the one with the promising career and the promotions ahead of him and, as he had explained to her, she might find that she would simply be treading water if she came north to join him, because of the rather old-fashioned attitude the firm had to female professionals.

'Then I shall have to change that attitude, shan't I?' she had said robustly.

Then they had both laughed; then they had ended up in bed, making love, the serious matter of their careers pushed impatiently to one side in the heat of their urgent need for one another.

'Be careful,' an older, harder woman colleague had warned her. 'Otherwise you're going to fall into the trap of allowing him to believe that his career, his needs have priority over yours.'

'It isn't like that,' Deborah had protested. 'I want to go, and it is a good career move for me.'

'This time, maybe,' the other woman had responded drily.

'Mark isn't the kind of man who would ever expect me to put my career on hold; he knows how important it is to me,' Deborah had told her.

'Yeah... that's what they all say at first.' She was in her late forties with a bad divorce behind her, and sometimes the scars had still showed despite the good camouflage job she had done on them. 'In my day they used to try to get you into bed with them by telling you that of course they'd still respect you in the morning. That was when we were stupid and brainwashed enough to believe that we needed respect from them. Now they tell you that of course they respect your independence, of course they believe in equality; the only difference is that, while my generation knew fine well they were lying, yours believes them.'

Deborah had laughed, as much at the thought of Mark ever needing to deceive her as at the irony in the other woman's voice.

'It might be a hell of a long way from the kitchen to the boardroom and it's certainly a hell of a hard slog, but what real difference does that journey make when emotionally too many of us are still attached by a piece of elastic to some man who we claim loves us? It hurts like hell when they pull on that elastic, which all of them do... Is that love?'

The bitterness of her divorce had made her overly cynical, Deborah had told herself.

Irritably Mark opened his office door. He was tired of spending half his day sitting at his desk shuffling paper around pretending to be busy.

As he stepped out into the corridor he saw that the blonde temporary clerk was walking towards him, her arms full of files.

'Which way?' he asked her with a grin, his irritation lifting as he watched the deliberately provocative sway of her hips.

Perhaps Deborah was right when she claimed that the girl made deliberate use of her sexuality, but there was something about the sensual sway of those curving hips and the pout of the lipsticked mouth that made a man feel good about his sexuality, Mark acknowledged as he went to open the fire-doors for her.

The fact that both of them knew that she could quite easily have pushed them open herself didn't matter. What mattered was the way she looked at Mark as she thanked him, pausing deliberately in the doorway where there was the least room for both of them and where his arm still curved behind her, holding open the door.

'Thanks... I hadn't realised how heavy these things are.'

As she jiggled them in her arms, the fabric of her blouse pulled taut against her breasts, outlining her nipples. They looked pert and hard, as though...

Hurriedly, Mark withdrew his gaze from her body, offering, 'Let me give you a hand with them.'

'I hope it's the files you mean,' she responded coquettishly, and then giggled as she moved closer to him so that he could take some of the files from her.

She was being quite deliberately and openly provocative, Mark recognised, flirting with him quite outrageously, in fact...

'Goodness, aren't you strong?' she murmured as he relieved her of all the files. 'I suppose you spend a lot of time at the gym; you can always tell a man who takes care of his body. Not that I like anyone who's too muscular...' She pulled a pouting face while she watched him archly, and Mark, who knew quite well that when it came to male physique he was simply average, albeit with the advantages of being six feet in height and having the shoulders that came from playing rugby as a youth, turned his head to hide his grin from her.

She was trying very hard, he conceded, and it surprised him how much he was actually enjoying what she was doing.

'Have you made any plans for the Easter holiday weekend?' she asked him.

Mark shook his head.

'No, neither have I... What I'd really like is to spend the whole weekend away somewhere romantic with a gorgeous sexy man.'

She looked mock-coyly up at Mark from beneath her mascaraed lashes.

'Just the two of us...on our own,' she emphasised purringly.

They had reached the corridor's second set of security doors and as Mark paused to open them for her, even though he was now the one carrying most of the files, she leaned closer to him, ostensibly trying to squeeze through the small gap in the half-opened door, but in reality pressing her body so close to Mark's that he could feel the soft, warm weight of her breasts against his arm.

Deborah had neat, firm and very pretty breasts which at work she kept discreetly concealed beneath heavy silk shirts; the temporary clerk's were much fuller, softer, momentarily conjuring up in Mark's memory echoes of the lustful yearnings of his young teenage self.

'Hey…what's going on here…?' Abruptly Mark turned his head as he realised that a couple of the other accountants were walking towards them down the corridor. Younger than Mark and newly qualified, they were working in the general office, and as the clerk drew away from him, all pouting arch confusion as she thanked him for his help and made a great play of smoothing down her blouse before taking the files from him, Mark could see the look in the men's eyes change from one of mockery to that particularly male kind of respect which was grudgingly given to another man seen to be more sexually successful.

As the clerk disappeared they lingered, turning their heads to watch her undulating progress towards her office.

'Nice work,' one of them commented enviously, adding with a grin, 'Come on, tell us the secret. What is it…your aftershave…?'

Mark grinned and shook his head. 'Sorry, boys,' he told them mock-despairingly. 'But it isn't something you can buy in a bottle…you've either got it or you haven't…'

It felt good knowing that they were slightly envious of him, that they couldn't just dismiss him as a professional no-hoper who had to stand aside and watch his lover fast-track past him, even if the way he was behaving, the comments he was making were somewhat out of character for him.

Since he had grown up, become mature, he had put aside his old macho teenage need to flex his sexual muscles and show off in front of his peers, and he knew exactly what Deborah would think of such behaviour.

Deborah didn't flirt; she simply wasn't that sort of woman. She was too honest and straightforward, and abhorred any kind of deceit or pretence within a relationship. The last thing she would ever do would be to indulge him with a bit of harmless massaging of his ego, either in private or in public.

'Come on, don't hold out on us... Tell us your secret...'

'Yeah... you're a dark horse all right... There we were thinking that——'

'What's going on here? Haven't any of you got any work to do?'

Mark tensed as he recognised Ryan's voice coming from behind him.

'What the hell are you two doing?' he demanded of the two juniors. 'And where's that file I asked you for?'

'Sorry... just going to get it...' one of them apologised, shuffling his feet.

Without waiting for them to be out of earshot, Ryan turned to Mark.

'Look, I know you aren't exactly carrying a full workload at the moment, and I appreciate that time must be hanging heavily on your hands, but, if you've got time to waste, try wasting it with someone from your own department and not mine, would you? *We* do have work to do.'

He turned on his heel, striding down the corridor before Mark could make any retort, his comments completely wiping out the good feeling that Mark's brief flirtation with the clerk had given him, leaving him with the bitter taste of anger and resentment souring his mouth.

'Made any plans for the long weekend?' Peter asked him as he walked slowly back into his office and to the empty desk which was beginning to feel like a prison to him. 'The wife and I thought we might take the camper down to the coast.'

'Mmm...what...? No, we're not doing anything,' Mark replied absently, and then frowned.

How long was it since he and Deborah had had time away together, just the two of them? Last year they had holidayed with friends and this year they hadn't as yet made plans for their main holiday. Deborah had been too busy to talk about it... Just as she was too busy to talk about anything that didn't concern her work and her promotion.

'I'm going to take an early lunch-hour,' he told Peter, suddenly coming to a decision.

CHAPTER SIXTEEN

'WHAT do you mean, you've booked a holiday? Mark, how could you? You know I'm up to my eyes with this liquidation. I can't go... I'd planned to spend the break getting up to date with my other work...'

Deborah stopped her angry pacing of their living-room and turned round to face Mark, pushing her fingers into her sleek hair in an irritated gesture of impatience. 'Why didn't you *tell* me first...?'

'I wanted it to be a surprise,' Mark told her stiffly.

'A surprise!' Deborah made a small explosive sound of disbelief. 'You *know* how important this liquidation is to me,' she protested. 'I can't just drop everything and go off with you. You should have consulted me first, before you booked this holiday—surely you can see that?'

She stopped, frowning as she saw the look Mark was giving her.

'I should have consulted *you*?' he repeated grimly. 'Doesn't that go both ways, Deb—does this equality thing you women are so keen on only work in your own favour? Now that you are the major wage-earner, you get to make all the major decisions—is that it...?'

Deborah couldn't believe what she was hearing. 'You're the one who went ahead and booked the holiday,' she reminded him.

'And you're the one who decided that you were going to work—*without* consulting me. Just tell me something, Deborah. What am I supposed to do while you're working?'

Deborah stared at him, baffled.

'It's a bank holiday weekend,' Mark reminded her forcefully. 'A time for people to spend *together*, *relaxing*, *enjoying* themselves. Oh, but I forgot,' he added sarcastically. 'You're already enjoying yourself—with your work. Well,

forgive me if I can't pretend to be getting the same satisfaction out of mine. It may have escaped your notice, since
you're obviously far too busy these days to notice such
things, but it isn't the greatest mental stimulation in the
world sitting in front of an empty desk five days a week.'

'Oh, Mark, for goodness' sake stop exaggerating. Your
desk isn't empty.'

'Damn near—but that isn't the point. Nothing else
matters to you apart from your work, does it, Deborah?
Everything...everyone has to fit in around your precious
career. How the hell do you think I feel, sitting here night
after night while you're working late, being told to turn
down the television so you can work, being treated as
though I'm some kind of sub-standard human being because I don't measure up to you professionally?'

'That's not fair,' Deborah protested. 'I can't believe I'm
hearing any of this,' she added wearily. 'I thought you
understood... I thought we had an *agreement*. I can't believe this is really you I'm listening to, Mark...what is it
exactly that you're trying to say? That you expect me to
back-pedal on my career because yours isn't going well?'

Mark tensed as he caught the angry contempt in her voice.

'No, of course not,' he denied. 'It's just... Look, I know
how much this promotion means to you, but you've got to
admit that it hasn't exactly come at a good time for me...'

'For you?' Deborah's eyes rounded. 'But this is *my* career
we're talking about...what is it you want from me, Mark?
Am I supposed to pretend that I don't want it...that I'm
not thrilled about it...?'

'No, of course not...' Irritation and guilt mingled inside
him. 'It's just that you might try to be a little less self-
obsessed about it, to remember that there are *other* things
in life. Is Ryan planning to work this weekend as well?'

His question caught her off guard, her face flushing even
though she assured herself she had nothing to feel guilty
about.

'I don't know... He may do... He hasn't said so... Just
that he wants to make sure that I'm really on top
of everything.

'The bank is a major client,' she pointed out defensively when she saw the way he was looking at her. 'Mark, you know how important this promotion is to me... Ryan's already beginning to make noises about having to defend his choice of me for the case to the other partners...I don't want to let him down.'

'No? Why not? You sure as hell don't seem to mind letting me down.'

Deborah froze. 'That's unfair,' she told him angrily. 'And I could make the same accusation of you. After all, you've hardly been supportive recently, have you? I'm beginning to wonder if Ryan's right when he says that you're jealous of me——'

She stopped abruptly, cursing herself under her breath as she realised she had said too much.

'Mark,' she protested as she saw his face.

'Forget it,' he told her bitingly as he turned around. 'Forget the whole damned thing. You go and get on with your precious work, Deborah...I'll spend my weekend painting the flat. Who knows—I might get quite a kick out of it...it will certainly be a damn sight better than spending the weekend in a foursome with bloody Ryan and your fucking work. The four of us just wouldn't get in that double bed together...'

He was behaving childishly and he must know it, Deborah told herself. Her own anger was a tight, hard ball of resentment clogging up her throat, her eyes already stinging threateningly with over-emotional tears.

She hated quarrels and arguments—she always had; and she and Mark never normally quarrelled—or at least they never used to.

Mark's bitterness and anger had caught her completely off guard, the accusations which had spilled from him as they'd quarrelled so unlike him that she could hardly believe he had actually voiced them.

Well, one thing was certain now. There was no way she could give her work the concentration it needed with this hanging over her. Perhaps it would do them good to get away for a few days; to sit down and talk things over rationally. She knew how upset Mark was about his job but she had never dreamed that he might actually resent her success.

Listening to him just now, it had almost been as though he was trying to claim that he felt he was in some kind of competition with her with her work and yet the two aspects of her life were completely different and separate issues.

When she walked into their bedroom he was standing in front of the window staring out of it. He didn't turn round until she touched him. He looked pale and tense. His grey eyes were shadowed instead of warm with laughter, she noticed guiltily. How long was it since they had last laughed together? It had been his sense of humour that had first drawn her to him. And, as with his warmth and gentleness, she had felt able to respond to it and to him without fearing that she was in any way putting herself under his control.

'Perhaps a few days away would be a good idea,' she told him quietly. 'We obviously need to talk...'

Beneath her arm she could feel the stiff resistance in his body. What more did he expect from her? she wondered angrily. Not, surely, an apology... For what? She had done nothing that he would not have done and felt he had every right to do had their positions been reversed.

It hurt her that he should reveal this unwanted side of himself to her; she had thought him above that petty need to have his ego nurtured and massaged which she despised in so many other men.

'Aren't you forgetting something?' Mark asked Deborah as he picked up their suitcase.

Deborah followed his glance towards her briefcase. She shook her head and tried not to feel guilty as she saw its bulging outline.

Ryan hadn't been at all pleased when she had told him that she was going away. In fact, he...

'Ready, then?'

Nodding, she picked up her lightweight jacket and followed Mark out of the room.

'Where to?' she asked him once they were in the car. He had insisted on keeping their destination a surprise and she had done her best to enter into the spirit of the thing, even though in reality she was still far too wound up over her work and their quarrel to feel like playing games.

'At least these few days away together will give us time to talk,' she commented as she followed his directions.

'No,' Mark told her shortly, adding less curtly, 'Let's just forget everything else for a few days, Debs, and enjoy being with one another. Guessed where we're going yet...?'

She frowned. What had got into Mark? He didn't normally go in for that kind of escapism.

'No...' she responded absently. 'You'll have to tell me.'

'Rimington,' he announced.

Rimington? She was startled enough to turn her head to look at him. The small Yorkshire village was the place where they had spent their first weekend away as lovers. Their hotel had been quiet and remote, a converted Edwardian house set in its own parkland, with huge bedrooms and the original attached bathrooms.

It had been November then, the moors surrounding them damp and misty, the log fire in their room far too tempting to leave for very long... like their bed.

Mark had been the first man with whom she had felt truly able to express her sexuality. Joyously she had shown him how much she desired him, how intensely sexual he made her feel. That weekend had been the first time in her life she had felt truly able to let go and to allow someone else to enter the private world of her sensuality.

It had also been the first time she had experienced an orgasm with a man without having to work hard for it. And not just one. Her body, once it had made up its mind to accept Mark, had seemed intent on making up for lost time.

'Hey—steady on,' he had teased her at one point when she was urgently trying to re-arouse him with her hands and mouth. 'I don't have your powers of recovery,' he had told her gently as he'd eased her slightly away from him.

She hadn't been put off, though, whispering to him that he could still give her aroused body the satisfaction it wanted.

'Now why didn't I think of that?' he had murmured softly, his mouth at her breast, his hand sliding down between her legs while she'd clung to him and shivered with anticipatory pleasure.

Sexually they were still as good together, even if recently their lovemaking had become less intense and less frequent...much less frequent.

There had been more than one occasion recently when she had gone to bed after working late to find him already asleep...so deeply asleep that neither the touch of her hand on his body nor the warmth of her mouth against his ear as she'd whispered to him that she wanted him had been enough to wake him up.

'Oh, Mark...Rimington——!' she exclaimed now.

'Don't tell me...' he interrupted her grimly. 'You don't want to go there...'

She shook her head.

'Yes—yes, I do,' she told him softly. 'Of course I do.'

Perhaps Mark was right; perhaps she was allowing herself to become engrossed in her work...making him feel that she was shutting him out, even though he ought to know her well enough to realise that she'd never do that.

Rimington. Just the thought of going back there with him was lifting the burden of tension from her shoulders.

'You're right,' she told him huskily. 'We do need some time together...on our own...'

Mark flinched as he heard the sensual promise in her voice. When he had first booked this break for them it had seemed such a good idea; buoyed up with his harmless flirtation with the clerk, he had remembered how good that first weekend away together had been. He had never known such a generous lover as Deborah. There was no coyness about her, no game- or role-playing, no insistence on any pretence of him having to coax her into physical intimacy.

And then he had certainly not wanted or needed to feign sleep to avoid making love with her.

He tensed and moved uncomfortably in his seat. In every relationship there was bound eventually to be a diminution of that early urgent and compulsive sexual desire.

Diminution, yes ... a total cessation ... He had begun to wonder recently if there was something physically wrong with him as he'd struggled to force his body into reluctant arousal, panicking inwardly in case it failed him, but his physical response to the clerk had proved to him that there was nothing wrong with him physically ... far from it.

The problem must lie elsewhere, then ... with Deborah? Or rather with his reaction to her?

It wasn't that he had stopped *loving* her, he knew *that*, and he had hoped originally that this time away together would help to restore the sexual chemistry which had once burned so strongly between them, but Deborah's reaction to what he had done had left him physically numb, his masculinity somehow threatened and under attack.

He didn't want to talk to her and he didn't want to go to bed with her either, he recognised bitterly. If the truth were known, he was sick and tired of the new role in their lives which she seemed to have cast for him, just as he was sick and tired of Ryan's mocking comments and constant allusions to Deborah's controlling position in their relationship.

Couldn't she see how hard things were for him at the moment ... couldn't she understand ... ?

'Oh, Mark, this is going to be such a wonderful weekend ... just the two of us.' Her eyes were shining.

'When you said you wanted to go out for a walk, I didn't realise you meant a full-blown hike,' Deborah laughed protestingly as she caught up with Mark, who was walking with the group's leader.

'*You're* the one who's always complaining that we don't get enough exercise,' Mark reminded her.

They had arrived at the hotel late the previous evening and it had been dark by the time they had unpacked.

Deborah had pulled a face when he had insisted on their having dinner in the dining-room rather than ordering a room-service meal, but she had accepted it tolerantly enough, just as she had when he had spent the rest of the evening in conversation with a fellow guest, leaving Deborah to make what conversation she could with the man's shyly timid wife.

She had frowned a little this morning when he had got up before her and then come back to announce that he had booked them both on to a local organised walk.

'Come back to bed,' she had suggested, smiling invitingly at him; the spring sun had warmed the pale ivory of her skin to soft gold and he'd known that it wasn't the coolness of the air on her naked body that was flushing her nipples into rosy hardness, but he had still shaken his head, telling her,

'We can't; the walk starts in three-quarters of an hour.'

And he had deliberately stayed downstairs, waiting to come up and announce what he had done until he knew that there would not be enough time for them to make love.

Her sunny acceptance of his refusal and her good humour during the walk had only added to his guilt and also, oddly, to his anger against her. It would have been easier for him to justify what he was doing if she had objected or protested.

'Mmm—I can't wait to get back to our room and that lovely big bath,' she whispered in his ear, teasingly nuzzling it while no one was looking.

'Oh . . . that bath felt good, and so do you,' Deborah told Mark as she slipped behind him, pressing her wet body against his, sliding her hands beneath the shirt he was just fastening over his chest.

'Hey, watch it—my shirt's getting wet,' Mark complained.

Deborah laughed. 'Take it off, then,' she suggested as she bit playfully at the warm flesh of his shoulder.

Standing together like this, with her behind him, her fingertips stroking lightly against his skin, it was not after all as difficult as he had dreaded to will his senses into a state of desire and his body into a state of arousal, Mark discovered to his relief.

Deborah was no textbook lover—she was far too sensual and imaginative for that—her slow fingertip-stroking of his skin deliberately tantalising.

'Had enough?' she asked mischievously when he trapped her provocative fingertip flat against his belly and then added as she pressed herself closer to his back, 'Mmm...I do love your body, Mark. It feels so good to touch... Just the way a man's body should feel...'

'Oh...and how exactly is that?' Mark asked her. He felt safer now with the movement of her hand stilled and under his control. 'Or do I already know the answer to that one?' he added mockingly as he glanced wryly at his own erection.

Deborah laughed.

'No...not because of that, you vain creature...not that it isn't a very...tempting sight,' she added judiciously. 'No, what I meant was that *you* feel good to touch—here,' she explained as she lifted her other hand and slowly traced the width of his chest. 'And here,' she added softly as her fingertips ruffled through the fine softness of his body hair.

'And here.' Her voice had taken on a betraying husky note as she outlined the hard curve of his buttock and then traced the edge of the hairline that surrounded his penis.

'You taste good as well,' she mumbled as she bit gently at his shoulder. 'Taste good, smell good, feel good... Oh, Mark.'

He felt her body quiver with sexual tension as she moved urgently against him.

'I want you so much,' she told him.

He could feel the power her need gave him, weakening her, strengthening him; she was vulnerable now, dependent on him...at his mercy.

In his mind's eye he saw again the pouting mouth of the temporary clerk, her lush breasts, and the subtle envy in the eyes of the other men who had watched her flirting with him.

He could feel his erection harden and strengthen.

He released Deborah's hand, turning around and taking hold of her forearms.

'Oh, no, you don't,' he told her as she tried to reach out and caress him. 'You can look but you're not allowed to touch.'

He kissed her before she could give voice to the startled surprise he could see in her eyes, teasing her mouth with small butterfly kisses that made her moan in frustrated protest and demand huskily, 'No...not like that, Mark... Kiss me properly.'

'What's wrong? Don't you like my kisses any more?' Mark teased her, pretending not to understand what she meant. It gave him an odd, unfamiliar thrill of pleasure to hold her to ransom like this, to feel her body quivering in his hold as he withheld from her the stimulation and satisfaction he knew she wanted.

'Mark...' He could hear the tension in her voice but ignored it, bending his head to circle her nipples with his tongue, first one and then the other, drawing slow, delicate, leisurely circles while she tensed and tried to move her body so that he would take her nipple fully into his mouth.

He had discovered very early on in their sexual relationship just how sexually sensitive she was to that particular type of caress—mainly, if he was honest, because she had told him so, whispering to him how she liked to be stroked and sucked, arching her back and moaning with pleasure when he caressed her the way she wanted.

In those early days there had even been occasions when she had actually orgasmed just through that stimulation alone, and she had admitted openly and freely to him that the sight of her own breasts taut and wet from his suckling was something that she found almost as visually arousing as the sight of his erect penis glistening slickly from the intimate caress of her mouth.

No, there were no sexual secrets about her body that she had withheld from him, no inhibitions about her telling and showing him how best to help her towards orgasm. No secrecy or mystique. No coyness about showing him her pleasure—or lack of it.

'Have you ever thought about faking it?' he had asked her wryly one afternoon when she had forthrightly informed him that it just wasn't going to happen and that she was, thank you very much, on this occasion at least, quite happy to forgo her orgasms.

'Fake it?' She had looked at him in open surprise. 'What would be the point?' she had asked him. 'It would be an insult to both of us; it would devalue our sexual relationship completely, and I wouldn't dream of insulting you by doing it. My orgasm isn't something *you* can either give to me or withhold from me,' she had pointed out calmly. 'And since you don't bestow it on me, it isn't your responsibility when I don't have one. It's up to me to tell you what can and can't help me to have one.'

'Oh, I see—and my role in all this is just to follow your instructions, is it?' He had laughed.

Yes, he had laughed then. When had he stopped laughing? Mark wondered as he felt her heartbeat speed up and her breathing become shallow.

'Mark...'

He ignored the protest in her voice and made his way slowly down her body, rimming her navel with his tongue-tip in the same way he had done her nipples. Her stomach quivered, a rash of gooseflesh breaking out beneath the smooth skin as she trembled slightly.

He knew that if he were to release her arm now and slide his hand between her legs, parting the full outer lips of her sex, he would discover that she was moist and eager for his touch, but he didn't do that. Instead he kissed his way back up over her body, this time avoiding her breasts and concentrating instead on the sides of her arms, the pulse-point in her wrists, the inner curve of her elbows.

'Oh, no, you don't,' he told her thickly, catching hold of the arm he had just released as she reached out to touch him. Holding it behind her back, he pulled her fully against him, watching as her eyes dilated in increased arousal at the movement of his body against her own.

Even though he knew that sexually she was ready for him, he could sense her shock when he dropped back into the chair behind him, taking her with him, positioning her against him so that he could enter her immediately. For a moment her body tensed as though it might reject him, but then she shivered and made a familiar little moan of eager arousal, clinging to him as he moved fully into her.

He sensed that he had caught her off guard by entering her so quickly and without any intimate preliminary caresses, but he knew from the speed and urgency with which she climaxed that she was aroused by the unexpectedness of what he had done.

'Not had enough of me already, have you?' he asked her as she lay panting against him.

Deborah opened her eyes and stared at him. She wasn't used to Mark being so sexually aggressive. Normally she would have found such aggression more of a turn-off than a turn-on, but after his recent disinclination to make love it was such a relief to be reassured that he did still desire her that she was ready to overlook his uncharacteristic behaviour.

'Me, tired?' she scoffed. 'Since when...?'

He was, she realised, still hard inside her.

'You want it...then go ahead, help yourself to it,' he told her softly as she lay straddled across his lap.

This time it took her slightly longer to climax, her muscles trembling slightly when she finally relaxed against him.

'Mmm...I think we'd be more comfortable continuing this in bed, don't you?' Mark murmured to her as he eased her slightly away from him.

'Continuing...?' Deborah blinked. 'I know the air up here is *supposed* to be very bracing,' she joked. 'Oh, Mark, it's been so long since we've done anything like this.' She arched shakily towards him as his mouth caressed her breasts. 'It feels so good knowing you still want me. Mmm—you feel so good,' she told him in a muffled voice as she pushed him gently away and slid down his body so that she could take him in her mouth.

They made love twice more before Deborah protested tiredly that she was going to need a sleep before she could even think about getting ready for dinner.

She couldn't remember the last time she had felt so sexually satisfied, so content and replete. Exhausted, she crawled beneath the duvet, holding it up until Mark joined her, her last act before she gave in to the physical exhaustion claiming her to reach out for some tissues to soak up the familiar seepage of Mark's semen from between her legs.

As she did so, she recognised that her brain was trying to tell her something important, but her need to sleep was too intense for her to listen. As she sank into sleep she was smiling happily, moving back to curl her body into the familiar warm spoon-shape of Mark's.

As soon as he knew that Deborah was asleep Mark got out of bed. Had she realised that despite all his frantic attempts to do so he had not actually 'come'? Mark wondered morosely. He could feel his stomach stiffen in rejection of the knowledge.

Beneath his apparent desire for Deborah he was still holding on to his anger for her; he recognised that his pleasure just now had come not from arousing her and wanting her, but from the knowledge of his sexual power over her... his body's physical protest against the way she was emasculating him professionally. Sombre-faced, he turned away.

What was happening to them, to their relationship, that he should feel so bad and that she should not know it?

CHAPTER SEVENTEEN

'HEY, you're looking very pleased with yourself this morning. Good weekend, was it?' one of the men teased Deborah slyly.

'Very pleasant, thanks,' she responded sedately, ignoring the innuendo behind his grin.

It was going to be a long long time before sexual harassment could be eradicated from the workplace when that kind of remark was so instinctively and automatically a part of the male psyche, she reflected wryly, although, to be fair, the male sex wasn't alone in making observations about other people's sex lives; it was just that when they did it...

It *had* been a good weekend, though, and on the drive home she had generously told Mark that he had been right to insist on their going away, apologising for being so tetchy with him beforehand.

Just for a second she gave in to the temptation to close her eyes and blissfully mentally recapture the pleasure of their time away together.

Mark had always been a sensitive and generous lover, but this weekend... She had never known him to be so sexually demanding before, overwhelming her laughing protest that they weren't engaged in some sort of sexual marathon.

She was normally the one who set the pace for their lovemaking.

'Deborah, a word with you, please.'

Guiltily she opened her eyes, her face flushing slightly as she saw Ryan standing in front of her. She hadn't heard him come into the office and her stomach muscles tensed warningly as she saw the look on his face. Something or someone had obviously annoyed him.

257

'We're having a partners' meeting this afternoon and I'd like an up-to-date progress report on the case. If you can have it ready for me by two...'

Deborah stared at his back as he turned his attention from her. Her heart had started to beat a little bit too fast, while her brain tried to come to terms with the obvious irritation and impatience in his voice and the abrupt change of attitude towards her which it seemed to indicate. She had seen Ryan behave like this before—towards other people.

'Ryan, I'm not sure if I'll have time. I have an appointment with——' she began, but he cut her off, turning back to face her and looking cold as he cut in,

'No? But you *did* apparently have time to spend gossiping about your weekend. I warned you when I gave you this case that it would demand one-hundred-and-twenty-per-cent commitment from you, Deborah. When you came here, one of the first things about you that impressed me was your commitment to your career, but now it seems other things are more important. We don't pay you to sit here daydreaming about your love-life like some moronic teenager...!'

Deborah swallowed hard on her chagrin, uncomfortably aware that there was very little she could do to defend herself from his criticism, no matter how much privately she might dispute his allegation that she was not giving her full concentration to her work.

'I want that report,' Ryan repeated curtly.

Hypersensitively she knew that the small knot of men gathered together round the coffee machine outside her office were talking about her. She could feel her ears burning with the injustice. It had not been fair of Ryan to call into question her commitment to her career, and surely he could have given her a little more time to prepare this report?

Luckily she liked to work with a relatively up-to-date progress chart...determinedly she switched on her computer.

Two o'clock, Ryan had said.

* * *

'Oh, nice shot...'

Mark smiled an acknowledgement of his partner's praise as they both watched the ball he had just hit rolling smoothly down the fairway.

'Golf?' Deborah had been teasingly derisive when he had first taken up the sport, scoffing that it was a game for middle-aged men.

Mark, though, enjoyed it; he liked its need for concentration and care; all the things about it which irritated and amused Deborah pleased and soothed him.

It helped, of course, that he also had a distinct flair for it; more than one golf club 'pro' had praised his skill and all his partners were envious of his handicap and expertise.

Golf, of course, was not one of Ryan's sports.

Initially this morning when a client had rung and suggested a game Mark had intended to refuse, but then he had looked at his empty desk and had changed his mind.

Now, out on the course, listening to his partner's envious praise, he realised how much better he felt, how good it was to be away from the office and his awareness of others' contempt for him, of their seemingly never-ending comments about Deborah's promotion.

'Never mind,' one of the more *louche* and unpleasant of the new crop of junior accountants had commented with a wink and a leer. 'If things get really bad on this side you can always use your influence and transfer over. Mind you, you'll probably have to pay for it...' His leer had deepened and Mark had found himself fighting to control not just his dislike and distaste for the younger man's attitude, but his anger with Deborah as well.

Yes, it felt good to get away from the office—and from Deb? He frowned as he waited for his partner to take his shot.

'Yes?' Ryan's secretary looked up over her glasses at Deborah bossily.

Ignoring the older woman's tone, Deborah smiled and handed her the folder she was carrying.

'It's the report Ryan wanted for the partners' meeting this afternoon.'

The secretary's frown deepened. 'Partners' meeting? What partners' meeting?' she demanded, making no attempt to take the file from Deborah. 'There is no partners' meeting.'

Deborah stared at her. 'But Ryan told me this morning that he needed this report for this afternoon.'

The woman stared back at her implacably. 'There is no meeting,' she repeated.

Back at her own desk, Deborah put down the file. She had worked her butt off this morning preparing that report, and working on it had not just caused her a high output of anxiety, it had also cost her time as well.

'Perhaps if I could see Ryan?' Deborah had suggested, holding on to her temper and ignoring the other woman's aggression. She had long held the view that Ryan deliberately used his secretary as a smokescreen and a barrier, and that her aggression towards other members of the firm amused and even pleased him.

'He's out,' she had told Deborah curtly. 'And he isn't due back in again until half-past four,' she'd added for good measure.

Now, as she stared grimly into space, Deborah wondered what kind of game Ryan was playing with her. Mentally she went over their earlier conversation. Yes, he had quite definitely said that he wanted the report today, and he had also quite definitely told her that there was to be a partners' meeting.

Since his secretary wasn't expecting him back until later in the day, he couldn't have organised the meeting without informing her.

Biting her lip, she put a call through to one of the other partners' secretaries, pretending that she couldn't read an entry she had scribbled in her diary.

'A partners' meeting?' the other woman repeated. 'No, I don't think so, not today.'

Thanking her, Deborah replaced the phone.

* * *

She had had to wait until gone six for Ryan to return, and had in fact been on the point of giving up when she had seen him coming in.

Fortunately his secretary had already left, so there was no one to stop her when she followed him into his office.

'Still here...?' He smiled jovially at her, but the smile he gave her was knowing and sly.

'I had to work late to make up for the time I wasted this morning on your report,' Deborah told him evenly.

'What report...? Oh, that—yes, I'm sorry; the meeting was cancelled. I tried to tell you before I went out, but you were...otherwise engaged...'

Otherwise engaged? She hadn't left her desk all morning, not even to go to the loo, and she knew instinctively that he was lying.

As he had been lying about the meeting in the first place.

She knew that there was no point in challenging him with it, and she suspected from the way he was watching her that he was enjoying the fact that he had put one over on her.

'Come on...let's go and have a drink, and you can bring me up to date with what's happening.'

He gave her a winning smile, so plainly confident that she would agree, that he would be forgiven, so assured, so triumphant!

'Sorry, I can't,' she told him quietly.

'Boyfriend waiting at home with the dinner ready, is he?' Ryan taunted.

'I have to work this evening to make up the time I've lost preparing your report,' she told him evenly.

Ryan shrugged dismissively. 'That's life,' he told her carelessly. 'If you can't hack it...'

He was deliberately goading her, Deborah knew it, but why? Because he genuinely felt she *wasn't* up to the job? Because he regretted choosing her?

Tiredly she made her way down to Mark's office. They had travelled in together this morning; her old car had gone and her new one still hadn't arrived.

When she got there his office was empty. Frowning, she turned round as the door opened, but it wasn't Mark who came in; it was the temporary clerk.

'Oh . . .' She seemed surprised to find her there, Deborah recognised.

'I was just looking for Mark,' Deborah told her pleasantly.

'Mark?' The girl was frowning. 'Oh, but he left ages ago. He said he was meeting a client for a game of golf.'

'Golf . . . ?' Mark had said nothing to her, and what was he doing playing golf when only this morning on the way to work he had told her that he couldn't meet her for lunch?

'Haven't you heard? *We* aren't supposed to eat lunch any more; at least not unless we've found a new potential client to pay for it for us.'

'Oh, Mark, for heaven's sake stop being so childish,' she had told him irritably. 'If things are really that bad, instead of complaining about them all the time, why don't you *do* something about it . . . ?'

'Such as what?' he had demanded bitterly.

'Such as transfer over to us,' she had come back.

'No, thanks,' he had told her.

And now he was out playing golf, apparently having forgotten that he was supposed to be giving her a lift home.

She might just as well have gone with Ryan for that drink after all, Deborah reflected tiredly as she closed the file she had been studying and glanced at her watch. She had taken a cab home from the office, expecting to find Mark at the flat, but it was now nine o'clock and Mark still wasn't home, nor had he phoned.

She got up and went to look impatiently out of the window. What had happened today with Ryan had disturbed her. She badly needed to talk it over with Mark. She had thought she was handling her new responsibilities well; she had been pleased with the progress she had been making with the liquidation, confident of her ability . . . but now Ryan's changing attitude towards her was beginning to make her wonder if she had been over-confident.

It was gone ten o'clock when Mark came in.

'Why didn't you tell me you'd changed your plans?' Deborah demanded as he walked into their living-room.

'I tried to, but your line was engaged.'

'You could have left a message,' Deborah pointed out.

'I'm surprised you even missed me,' Mark told her, nodding towards the work on the table.

'Oh, Mark.' Deborah pushed her hand briefly into her hair. 'The last thing I need right now is more hassle.' Briefly she explained to him what had happened with Ryan, adding, 'I'm beginning to feel that Ryan regrets promoting me, that...'

'Since it hasn't got you into his bed, I imagine he does,' Mark agreed cynically.

Deborah stared at him.

Ryan's predilection for brief·affairs was of course no secret and she was well aware that had she given him the slightest encouragement he would have had no hesitation in adding her to his list of conquests, but for Mark to imply...

She was too angry and upset to guard her words.

'What are you trying to say... that the only reason Ryan picked me for this job was to get laid?'

Mark shrugged irritably. 'Oh, come on, Deborah. You know how Ryan operates.'

The angry contempt in his voice made her face burn. 'That's not fair,' she told him fiercely. 'I *earned* that promotion; it had nothing to do with...'

'With what? The fact that he wants you? Oh, come off it!' When he saw her face Mark sighed. 'Look, I'm not saying that you *would* go to bed with him, but you must have known when he offered you the job what the score was...'

'He offered me the job on professional merit,' Deborah insisted, two hot coins of colour still burning her cheeks.

'Did he?' Mark questioned bitterly. She couldn't believe that Mark, Mark of all people, was doing this to her.

'You're not being fair,' she told him angrily now. 'You're deliberately trying to undermine me, Mark, to make me feel bad about taking the promotion because you...'

'Because I what?' Mark demanded. 'Because I'm such a bloody failure that I can't stand the thought of you doing well? Well, if you think I'm lying, Deborah, I suggest you spend a little more time in the general office now and again. Last week the odds were all in favour of Ryan winning out, but it seems that the weekend you spent away with me has lowered his chances.'

'They're just jealous,' Deborah protested. 'It's just a typical male way of putting women down, bullying and demeaning them. Everyone knows that I'm living with you; that Ryan doesn't interest me in that way.'

'*Everyone*...does that include Ryan?'

'Of course it does! Mark, why are you doing this? I'm having a hard enough time trying to cope with the job and Ryan without...'

'You asked for my opinion,' Mark reminded her.

'Nice one,' Ryan complimented as they left the Inland Revenue offices. 'You handled that well.'

'Thanks.'

Initially Deborah had been very wary when Ryan had asked her to accompany him to a meeting with the Revenue to discuss the tax affairs of one of his private clients. The tax authorities were questioning their client's interpretation of a certain grey area which had allowed him to take advantage of a tax loophole, and Deborah had been alarmed when Ryan had initially left her to answer the inspector's questions.

His behaviour towards her had been so erratic these last couple of weeks that she wasn't sure if she was being offered a chance to prove her competence or thrown to the wolves. Even now, as he smiled approvingly at her, she still wasn't.

She had tried to push her quarrel with Mark and the things he had said to the back of her mind, to reassure herself that she had simply caught Mark at a bad time, when he was feeling particularly low about his own work, and that he couldn't possibly have really meant what he had said about the reasons behind her promotion.

Neither of them had referred to their quarrel since, and on the surface Mark seemed to have reverted to his normal calm self.

On the surface?

On the way back to the office Ryan continued to discuss with her the interview with the Inland Revenue, and by the time she was back at her own desk Deborah was feeling more optimistic. Everyone had a bad spell now and again, she told herself firmly, and Mark was entitled to his just like everyone else. But still deep down inside her there was a small sore place that wouldn't quite heal over. Mark knew how much she loved him. And he knew how sensitive she was on the issue of being judged professionally only on merit. It had been a subject they had discussed at great length in the days when they were both still training.

It hurt her to have to acknowledge it, but deep down inside herself she suspected that Mark was jealous of her success.

She had discovered that increasingly recently she was having to monitor her conversations with him, to check to make sure she was not saying anything which would draw attention to the progress of her career and the stagnation of his. And when she did talk about it she could almost feel him withdrawing from her.

She had tried to discuss it with him, but somehow the issue had become too sensitive for her to do so. And that hurt as well.

'Mmm—wake up, sleepyhead.'

Smiling, Deborah teased her fingers along the inside of Mark's naked thigh, her mouth curving sensuously as she bent her head to nuzzle the warm flesh of his throat. The fine silkiness of her hair caught against his overnight stubble and she shivered in anticipatory appreciation of how it would feel when he licked her nipples while that slightly rough abrasiveness of his bearded skin moved deliciously

against the sensitivity of hers. And it was not just her breasts
that would be extra-specially sensitive to that abrasion.

'Mark...'

She had reached the top of his thigh, one fingertip lazily
exploring the thicker, stronger hair that grew there.

'I know you're awake,' she told him, nibbling at his
earlobe.

She moved deliberately against him, pressing her breasts
against his chest. Her nipples were hard, the flesh surrounding them acutely sensitive. She knew that if Mark
were to slide his hand between her thighs he would find her
body already wet and waiting for him.

'Mark.' She was kissing her way towards his mouth, enjoying her body's arousal and desire, already anticipating
the moment when she would feel him inside her.
Luxuriously she moved against him, laughing as she turned
her mouth towards his.

'Oh, for God's sake, not now...'

Irritably Mark pushed her away and sat up in bed,
reaching for the duvet, which had fallen away from his
body, covering himself with it as he shrugged off her hand.

'Mark!' she protested.

'Look, leave it, will you? I'm just not in the mood. For
Christ's sake, Deborah. What is it with you? I mean, I'm
all for women taking the initiative now and again, but
you... Hasn't anyone ever told you that sometimes it's more
polite to wait to be asked?'

Deborah stared at him, anger taking the place of her
earlier desire. This wasn't the first time recently that he had
refused to make love. And he had certainly never said anything to her before about not wanting her to make the first
move. Far from it.

And to speak to her like that! He was making her feel
like a...like a...

Silently she got out of bed and went to shower and get
dressed.

'Look, I'm sorry,' Mark apologised half an hour later.
'I know I went a bit over the top, but——'

'A bit?' she interrupted him angrily. 'Mark...you could have said something before...you could...'

'Like what? Once you get going it's like trying to stop an express train.'

Deborah poured them both a cup of coffee and then she asked him quietly, 'Mark, what did you mean when you said that I ought to wait to be asked? We've always both agreed that women have as much right to express their sexuality as men.'

'Yes, but think about it the other way... I'm not...' He shook his head and changed tack.

'Something's happened to us lately, Deb. I'm not sure what it is, but we're just not the same people that we were. You always used to be sensitive...so aware... Think about it for yourself. God, twelve months ago we wouldn't have even needed to be having this conversation.'

'No, we wouldn't,' Deborah agreed bitterly. 'Twelve months ago you'd have been only too glad to wake up and find me...'

'That's not what I meant, for Christ's sake, but it does underline everything I'm trying to say. Twelve months ago you'd have *known* that I just wasn't in the mood... Now...' He gave a bitter shrug. 'Now all that seems important is what *you* want, how *you* feel... *You* want sex and so I have to provide it whether I feel like it or not... I'm not bloody Ryan, Deborah...I can't fuck to order.

'Look,' he said abruptly, 'why don't we get right away from here? Make a fresh start...go back to London even...?'

Deborah put down her own coffee-cup.

'You want me to give up my job...now, when——'

'There you go again,' Mark accused. '*Your* job... What *I* want is for us to get back to where we used to be. For us——'

'For me to take a step down to accommodate your ego. That's what you really want,' Deborah asserted, her voice dangerously low. 'This isn't about sex...about us at all, is it, Mark? It's about the fact that you just can't cope with...'

She shook her head, not able to bring herself even now to say the words. 'What are you trying to do, Mark? Control me by refusing me sex, punish me because I'm successful and you're not? Well, you've certainly succeeded,' she told him quietly. 'Not because you won't have sex with me any more, though... after all, I can always get sex somewhere else, can't I?'

She saw from his face that she had hit a nerve, but it didn't really bring her any satisfaction. Outwardly she knew she seemed calm and unmoved by what was happening, but inwardly she felt sick with despair and disbelief. Inwardly she felt as though her heart, her emotions were being ripped into a thousand agonising shards of sharp, tight pain.

She had thought Mark loved her, really loved her, but in reality, he loved himself more; his own ego was more important to him than she was.

Mark watched her angrily. First she made him feel like a complete failure as a man, professionally and sexually, and now she was trying to make him feel guilty into the bargain.

'We can't go on like this, Mark,' he heard her saying.

'No,' he agreed, suddenly purposeful and aware of the only option that was now left open to him—the option he had been putting off taking for days, weeks now... but which was, he knew, now inevitable. 'You don't need me any more, Deb, and I don't want you. It's time we both accepted that and went our separate ways.'

CHAPTER EIGHTEEN

'KEEP it clean...sharp...make each stroke count,' Joel shouted as he ran alongside the boy swimming the length of the pool.

'They're coming along nicely, Joel,' the leisure centre's manager praised him as he paused to watch the three boys climbing out of the water. 'You make a good instructor.'

'Thanks...' Joel looked away from him to check on his pupils.

Ian, the youngest of the three, was by far the fastest, but as yet he hadn't got the rhythm of his breathing quite right, and Joel wanted to have a word with him about it.

'Have you ever thought of taking up something like this professionally?' the other man asked him.

Joel grimaced. 'I'm a foreman, Neil, or at least I was...a working man.'

He thought of Sally's sister as he was speaking. She had made very plain over the years the difference that lay between her husband's career as a teacher and Joel's 'job'. 'I don't have the education...the qualifications...'

'Maybe not, but there's nothing to stop you getting them, is there?' Neil Saunders asked him. 'You've got a natural gift for dealing with kids, Joel—for teaching them...'

It had been his pet scheme, this idea to utilise the skills and at the same time hopefully boost the morale of the unemployed people who attended the leisure centre under their special scheme by getting them involved on an unpaid basis with coaching others.

He had had quite a struggle getting it past the committee, who had pointed out all the problems they could have with insurance and injury risks, but in the end he had got his way.

His wife had teased him for being a crusader, but it gave him almost as big a kick to see how much it boosted the flagging self-confidence of the adults who joined the scheme as it did the kids who benefited from their help.

Joel, though, was outstandingly good. He possessed that rare blending of patience and firmness which seemed to bring out the best in those he was coaching.

'Think about it,' he stressed now as Joel turned away from him and started to walk over to his pupils. 'Oh, and by the way...' He caught hold of Joel's arm, detaining him. 'They could do with a bit of help with the adult swimming classes if you're interested?'

'Yeah...anything else you'd like me to do in the rest of my spare time?' Joel joked, but in reality he acknowledged that it felt good being told that he was wanted, that he was contributing something of value. It felt good having a purpose in life again, he admitted...having a reason to get out of bed in the morning. He had even found himself working on extra schedules for the boys when he was at home, going to the library and borrowing books so that he could pick up on any little tips to help him get the best out of them.

At first he had been apprehensive that Tim Feathers, the professional swimming coach employed by the club, might not just resent his presence, but that he might also dismiss his efforts as a waste of time. However, to his relief and surprise, Tim had warmly welcomed his help.

'If you can take over the juniors that will give me more time to spend coaching the seniors. We're hoping to put a team in for a couple of the internationals this year. Of course, we've left it a bit late. The time to really start training them is when they first start to learn to swim.'

It had been Tim who had suggested that he do a bit of reading up on some of the modern teaching methods. Tim's method of teaching *him* had been to offer praise and encouragement rather than criticism, Joel had quickly realised, and it was a tactic he had immediately adopted into his own teaching programme.

The start of the Easter school holidays had meant that the leisure centre was extremely busy, and, looking back, Joel was amazed that it was barely a fortnight since his meeting with Duncan and that first tentative suggestion that he become one of the centre's volunteer workers.

'I'm off for lunch in half an hour,' Neil told him. 'Fancy joining me?'

Joel shook his head. 'I'd like to, but I've got Paul, my son, with me and I promised him a game of snooker when I'd finished here.'

Paul had been truculent and unresponsive at first when Joel had brought him down to the leisure centre with him.

'Why can't you stay here at home with him?' Sally had demanded irritably when Paul had complained that he wanted to stay at home and watch a video instead of going with Joel.

'Because I've already agreed to help them out at the centre, and besides, it will do him good to get a bit of exercise.'

Sally's face had hardened. 'Oh, come off it, Joel,' she had told him. 'The only reason you want him there is because it suits you.'

Unsaid, but there between them, had been the silent criticism that since she had to go out to work to support them it was his responsibility to take charge of the children during the school holidays. Cathy was at an age where she wanted to spend more time with her friends than with her family. Joel frowned, remembering the way Sally had snapped at him when he had commented that he felt that they might be allowing Cathy to grow up too fast.

It had given him a shock to see her by accident in town with her friends, a mini-skirted bunch of alarmingly adult-looking young women, tossing their hair and pouting feigned uninterest in the comments of the boys watching them.

'She's fifteen, Sally,' he had protested, uneasily aware of how very sexual she had looked with her long mane of hair and her make-up.

'Exactly,' Sally had retorted. 'And at fifteen these days girls consider that they are grown-up...perhaps if you'd paid a bit more attention to her recently and a bit less feeling sorry for yourself you might have realised that. She's not a fool, Joel.'

'No, but I don't want...' He had shaken his head. How could he convey to Sally the way he had felt when he had seen...?

At first glance, not recognising his own daughter among the crowd of girls, he had done what any other man would have done, and turned his head to give them a second absently-appraising glance, amused by their studied pretence of uninterest in the boys watching them, aware of the burgeoning sexuality evident in their long hair and even longer legs.

Surely when he was fifteen girls of that age had looked like girls, not...? Did Sally realise how vulnerable Cathy was...? His heart had turned over as he'd watched one of the boys approaching her, all his protective paternal instincts rushing to the fore. He had only just managed to stop himself from going over to her to find out what was going on, who the boy was.

It had, he admitted, shocked and disturbed him to realise that his daughter, his little girl, had somehow suddenly turned into a sexually attractive and vulnerable young woman.

He had wanted to confide his anxiety to Sally, but instead of listening to him Sally had become angry, and she had been angry as well at the way he had reorganised the kitchen cupboards, claiming that it was impossible for her to find anything.

'Instead of doing that, you could have gone round to Daphne's and started on her decorating,' she had complained.

Well, her precious sister's wallpapering was done now, Joel reflected grimly as he went to find Paul.

They had arranged to meet in the leisure centre's restaurant. He was with several other boys when Joel walked in. One of them was one of the boys Joel was coaching.

'Still want to play snooker?' he asked Paul as he reached them.

'Yeah, I suppose I might as well,' Paul agreed carelessly, but there was a slight swagger in his walk as he came over to join him, Joel noticed.

'Are you going to Aunty Daphne's this afternoon?' Paul asked him later.

'No,' Joel told him. 'I finished her wallpapering yesterday.'

His face hardened as he remembered Sally's sister's comment when he had told her that the room was finished.

'Mmm... doesn't look too bad,' she had told him critically. 'Of course it's a pity there wasn't time for us to get a proper decorator in, especially since the wallpaper was so expensive. We had to order it specially, of course, and I particularly wanted the room finished this week. We're having a dinner party; it's our turn to entertain the headmaster and his wife to dinner... I shan't embarrass you by offering you money, Joel. I know how touchy you can be. I'll take Sally out and treat her to a nice lunch instead. She deserves a bit of spoiling, poor girl.' Her mouth had pursed disapprovingly as she looked at Joel.

'She's working far too hard, you know. When I saw her the other day I thought that she looked as though she was the elder of the two of us, she looked so exhausted... but then I don't suppose she has much option, poor girl, with you and the children to support.'

Joel had managed to wait to vent his temper until he had left the house.

'What the hell is she trying to make out, Sally?' he had demanded later. 'That I *like* being out of work... being dependent on you...?'

'Oh, Joel, please... she's my sister... Naturally she...'

'Naturally she what? Naturally she thinks I'm a lazy sod who enjoys living off his wife... and is that what you think as well, Sal?'

'Oh, Joel, please, not another argument,' Sally had begged wearily.

How could he explain to her, make her understand that he didn't want to argue... he just wanted to put his side, to hear her say that she understood, that she knew how bad he felt, that she didn't blame him for what had happened?

Perhaps Neil had a point, he reflected later as he and Paul walked home. Perhaps it might be worth while thinking about taking some kind of course, getting some professional qualification.

He was enjoying the time he spent at the centre; he liked coaching, the work he was doing, enjoyed watching his pupils' confidence and skills improve. It gave him a real buzz, made him feel good... made him feel that there was some purpose in life. He lengthened his stride, suddenly eager to get home. Neil had given him a number to ring— the professional organisation who would be able to tell him about the options open to him if he took his advice and tried to get some professional qualifications.

'Brown bread,' Paul complained when Joel called both his children down for their tea. 'I don't like brown bread. I want white.'

'What's this?' Cathy demanded, poking suspiciously at the lasagne Joel had made. 'It hasn't got any meat in it, has it?'

She was toying with the idea of becoming a vegetarian... when it suited her.

'Nope,' Joel assured her.

The books he had borrowed from the library had all had sections in them on diet and he had been appalled, when he'd read the ingredients listed on the packets of some of the ready-made meals he had been buying, to see just how little nutrition some of them contained.

Robustly ignoring Sally's irritation, he had decided he could do better himself... much better.

'Brown bread's better for you,' he told Paul. 'And besides, it's all there is...'

Paul scowled, but he still ate the meal, Joel noticed, as did Cathy, even if she was picking suspiciously at it.

'What's for pudding?' Paul asked him.

'Fruit salad and yoghurt,' he told him.

He had bought the fruit cheaply from a market stall late on market day and he had felt quite proud of the meal he had produced. There was a lot more to this nutrition business than he had realised. Food was the fuel that powered the body; and just like any engine the body's engine worked more efficiently on the right kind of fuel.

'Uggh...it's not sweet enough,' Cathy complained as she took a spoonful of the fruit salad.

'Yes, it is...too much sugar's bad for you...'

'Yuck, you're worse than Mum,' Cathy grumbled, but again she ate it none the less, Joel noted.

He looked up as he heard Sally opening the back door.

'Lucky you, Mum,' Cathy teased. 'You're just in time to have some of Dad's delicious nutritious fruit salad.'

'Yeah—the reason this stuff's so good for you is that you wouldn't want to have any seconds,' Paul commented, but there was no malice beneath the teasing grumbling, and they had both cleaned their plates.

'Yes, you sit down, Sal,' Joel invited. 'I'll put the kettle on. You'll never guess what Neil suggested today,' he told her. 'He seems to think that——'

'Joel, how could you?' Sally interrupted him angrily, ignoring what he said. 'When Daphne rang me at work to tell me what you did, I could hardly believe it...do you have any idea how much that wallpaper cost?' she demanded, her voice rising. 'Daphne was practically hysterical. If you didn't know which way the design ran, you should have checked with Daphne first...'

She stopped abruptly, her eyes widening as she accused, 'You did know, didn't you...? You did it *deliberately*. You deliberately hung Daphne's wallpaper upside-down.' Her voice had risen slightly with each word. She was trembling with anger. When Paul started giggling she rounded on him furiously, telling him, 'It isn't funny! Joel, what on earth possessed you?' she demanded. 'Daphne is furious and I don't blame her. The whole room will have to be stripped and redecorated. I've had to offer to pay for the wallpaper, of course...have you any idea how much it cost...?' Her voice was rising again.

'Tell her to deduct the cost from the money she's not paying me,' Joel suggested sarcastically.

Sally flushed. 'Is that why you did it?' she demanded. 'Because...'

'Because she wheedled her way round you to get the job done for nothing,' Joel supplied for her. 'No...it wasn't...'

'Then why?' Sally demanded bitterly. 'You *must* have known how upset she would be... She ordered that paper specially, Joel. She saw it in a magazine. Imagine how she must have felt when her neighbour told her that it was on upside-down...how humiliated and mortified...'

Just as he had felt when Sally had practically ordered him to go round and do the work, Joel reflected grimly.

'Your sister's a snob,' he told Sally flatly now. 'All that matters to her is impressing other people, showing off in front of them. She watched me working.' Watched him...she had practically stood over him like a gaoler; at lunchtime there had been a cup of tea and a couple of semi-stale biscuits. 'She could have told me it was on the wrong way...'

Sally's face was flushed and angry.

'I know you've never liked her, Joel, but I never thought you could behave so...so...so badly... You must have known that she'd discover what you'd done.'

Joel shrugged. He had had a bit of trouble deciding which way the paper's pattern should run himself at first, and if Daphne had bothered to treat him half decently he would have told her so, but her arrogant attitude towards him had irritated him to such an extent that, when she had come into the room to complain that he had only hung one piece of paper, instead of telling her that he had not been wasting time as she was implying but had actually been carefully studying the paper, he had said nothing.

It was Daphne herself who had bossily instructed him on how she wanted it to be hung; all he had done was follow her instructions.

'I did what I was told to do,' he told Sally flatly now.

'But you *knew* it was on the wrong way,' she insisted. 'Don't bother denying it, Joel. I can see it in your eyes. You should have told Daphne...'

'Since when did your sister listen to anything *I* might have to say? I'm nothing...no one. I'm not entitled to have an opinion. I'm too thick to have an opinion—that's what she thinks.'

'That's not true,' Sally protested, but her voice lacked conviction. 'You'll have to go back and redo it,' she told Joel.

'I can't,' he responded. 'I'm too busy down at the centre...'

Sally stared at him angrily.

Daphne had rung her up right in the middle of one of the specialists' rounds. She had tried to tell her sister that it wasn't a convenient time to speak to her, but Daphne had ignored her hints as she'd told her furiously what Joel had done, her voice rising so sharply that Sally had suspected that half the ward must be able to hear what she was saying.

In the end she had had to cut her short, apologising and assuring her that Joel would repaper the room.

Fortunately it obviously hadn't occurred to her that Joel had hung it incorrectly deliberately. Tears of frustration and anger clogged her throat. How *could* Joel have behaved so stupidly? He *must* have known what would happen, and all the extra shifts she had been working to pay the bills and to try to put a bit of money on one side would have to go towards paying for Daphne's wallpaper now.

'Too busy doing what?' she demanded. 'Wasting time with your friends? Joel, you know...'

'Mum, Dad's coaching the——'

'Be quiet, Paul,' Sally told him irritably. 'Go up to your rooms, both of you.'

Out of the corner of her eye Sally saw the looks Paul and Cathy exchanged as Paul shrugged and walked towards the door. She wasn't used to hearing either of them, but especially Paul, defend their father, and for some reason the fact that he had done so grated on her, adding to her anger.

'How could you be so irresponsible, Joel?' she demanded after they had gone. 'You must have known what would happen. Have you any idea how many extra hours I'll have to work to pay for that paper...?'

'We're not paying for it,' Joel told her.

'No,' Sally agreed fiercely. '*We're* not...*I* am. Something about the look on his face made her feel sore and unhappy inside, but somehow she couldn't stop the words from tumbling out. She had felt so guilty when Daphne had told her what he had done, torn between wanting to placate her sister and conversely wanting simply to put the phone down and walk away.

Couldn't Joel see that his petty revenge on Daphne for what he considered to be her snobbery was hurting her much more than it was her sister?

To tell the truth, Joel was beginning to feel guilty about what he had done: not on Daphne's account—nothing could change his opinion of her—but on Sally's.

But at the same time he was also angry at the way she automatically took her sister's side, refusing to see his point of view, dismissing his work at the centre as unimportant, a waste of time, making him feel useless, worthless.

'We'll have to pay for it now. I've told Daphne we would, and you'll have to go round and apologise to her.'

Joel swung round. 'Me, apologise to her?' His mouth hardened. 'No way,' he told Sally curtly.

'You can do it when you go round to repaper the room,' Sally continued doggedly. Panic was twisting her stomach. In order to get Daphne off the phone she had agreed with her that Joel must apologise, and if Joel continued to refuse to do so...

'I'm not going round,' Joel told her. 'Not to apologise and not to redo her bloody dining-room. As I just said, I've got better things to do.'

He watched her broodingly five minutes later as she left the room and went upstairs. She *did* look tired and drained, and a part of him had longed to go over to her and take her in his arms...to hold her as he used to...as she used to want him to do when they were first married and she had needed and wanted him.

He remembered how, when she was first pregnant with Cathy, her back aching with the weight of the baby, she had used to nestle gratefully in his arms while he held her and rubbed her aching muscles. He had felt so guilty and responsible for her discomfort, but she had laughed at him, saying that an aching back was a small price to pay for the baby they both wanted.

Now he felt equally guilty, but for different reasons. But how could he go to her and hold her, reassure her and comfort her, when both of them knew that he hadn't been able to keep the promises he had originally given her?

'I'm pregnant,' she had told him, awe and wonder in her voice, her expression quickly changing as she asked him, 'How will we manage, Joel, without my wages? I...'

'We'll manage,' he had said then. 'I've got a bit put by and I'm due to get a rise soon.'

How proud and confident she had made him feel as she'd looked up adoringly at him before snuggling back into his arms, her fears put to rest by his reassurance.

These days she'd treat that kind of comment from him with contempt and derision...and with good reason, he acknowledged grimly.

It was about a week later that the sound of the telephone ringing woke Sally up from a deep sleep. Joel had gone out, down to the leisure centre, no doubt, and the children were back at school.

Groggily she got out of bed and went downstairs to answer it.

'Sally...it's Kenneth.'

Her heart flipped over and then started to race. 'Kenneth...' She leaned weakly against the wall, her face flushed and hot.

'When can I see you?' she heard him asking.

She wasn't going to see him again; she had already made that decision. It was safer...wiser.

'I've got an appointment at the hospital on Monday,' Kenneth told her without waiting for her to reply. 'What time does your shift end?'

'Two o'clock,' she told him automatically, adding quickly, 'But Kenneth, I can't——'

'I'll be waiting for you,' he told her softly, cutting across her anxious objections.

He had hung up before she could make a firm denial. Shakily Sally leaned against the wall, cradling the receiver against her body as she closed her eyes guiltily.

She should not be doing this; she was a married woman and, no matter how physically platonic her relationship with Kenneth might be, she knew that her feelings for him, the happiness she experienced in his company, did threaten her relationship with Joel.

As she replaced the receiver, she swallowed uncomfortably. How many times recently had she inwardly made comparisons between Kenneth and Joel; how many times had she found herself looking at Joel, watching him, listening to him and wishing that...?

That what?

It was Joel's fault she was feeling like this, she reassured herself angrily. If he weren't so wrapped up in his own life, if just for once he asked her what she wanted, how she felt, if just for once he would give her the same consideration and support he expected to receive from her, things might be different.

Daphne and Kenneth were both right. He did take her for granted. He was selfish and inconsiderate.

But he was still her husband.

The phone rang again and she tensed immediately, her hand shaking slightly as she picked up the receiver. If it was Kenneth ringing again then she would tell him that she had changed her mind and that she couldn't meet him. Couldn't ever see him again...

She swallowed hard against the depression and sense of loss constricting her throat. But her caller wasn't Kenneth, it was her sister Daphne.

'Joel still hasn't been round to do that wallpapering,' Daphne informed her.

'I'll speak to him about it,' Sally promised her wearily ten minutes later, cutting through her sister's tirade.

Sally was still smarting from Daphne's criticisms and complaints half an hour later when Joel walked in. She saw him frown as he glanced across at her, and then placed the pile of books he was carrying down on the table. The table she had so recently cleared of all its accumulated clutter.

Her temper, so often recently on a short fuse, flared as she shouted, 'Don't you dare leave those there, Joel. Can't you see that I've only just finished cleaning up in here?'

She stopped abruptly. Her whole body was shaking inside; she felt sick and shocked, her sudden unprovoked outburst both frightening and yet exhilarating her somehow at the same time.

Joel said nothing, made no response to her anger—he just stood there, looking at her.

Couldn't he see that it was *his* fault that she was behaving like this? She could feel the anger surging through her again at his refusal to respond to or acknowledge her feelings.

'I'm going to be working a double shift on Monday,' she told him, turning her back to him as she spoke.

As soon as the words had left her mouth she wanted to recall them. That hadn't been what she had intended to say at all. Her face burned with heat; she felt light-headed and dizzy, like someone in shock, and she waited for Joel to say something, to object or protest, hoping almost that he would.

She had never lied to Joel before, never deliberately deceived him in any way, about anything—had never felt any need to—and yet here she was lying to him so that she could see another man... be with another man...

A man who treated her far better than Joel did, she reminded herself fiercely. A man who valued her... who put her first. A man who could see, as Joel apparently could not, how much she needed someone in her life to support her, to cherish her.

Still, though, she felt shaky and light-headed, frightened by the enormity of what she had done.

She waited for Joel to say something, accuse her, to sense her betrayal, but he was already turning away from her, uninterested in what she had said, unconcerned, unaware of what she was feeling.

The leisure centre seemed more important to him than she did these days, she reflected bitterly. He spent more time there than he did at home. He and Paul—listening to the two of them talking about events and people that meant nothing to her gave her a sense of alienation, made her feel excluded from their lives.

All she was to Joel these days was someone who paid the bills, she decided bitterly. He probably wouldn't have cared if she had told him about Kenneth. He never listened to her when she tried to talk to him.

Angry tears burned at the back of her eyes, but she refused to let them fall.

'Hello, there.'

Philippa tensed as she recognised Joel's voice, replacing the library book she had just been reading. Joel's eyebrows lifted as he read the title.

'*Home Maintenance Made Easy*? Having problems?' he asked her.

'It's the washing machine,' Philippa admitted. 'It isn't spinning properly and the service people charge twenty-five pounds just to come out...'

'I could come and take a look for you,' Joel offered.

Philippa flushed. 'No, it's all right,' she assured him uncomfortably, not wanting him to think that she had been deliberately trying to get him to offer to do so.

Or that she was using the washing machine as an excuse to see him again?

Her discomfort increased. He was a very attractive man and she had found herself thinking about him rather more than she liked. She had, of course, told herself that it was because he had been one of Andrew's employees and be-

cause they were, as he had so succinctly said, fellow victims
of Andrew's egomania, but somehow her arguments had
not been totally convincing.

'You don't trust me, eh ...?' Joel teased her.

'No... no, it isn't that,' Philippa hurried to assure him,
laughing herself when she saw the amusement in his eyes.

'You're learning to swim?' she asked him, eyeing his own
books.

'Not exactly,' Joel told her, briefly explaining why he
wanted the books.

'Coaching—of course, I should have realised,' Philippa
responded warmly. 'I thought it odd that you should just
be learning...'

'Too old?' he queried wryly.

Philippa shook her head, smiling.

'No, of course not... no, it's just that you don't
have... that you don't look... Well, you look as though
you would be good at sports,' she told him lamely.

What she had actually thought was that he had the kind
of body that looked as though he knew how to use it in
physical activities, but she had recognised as she'd started
to voice the words that her remark could be misinterpreted
as being sexually inviting, and the last thing she wanted
him to think was that she was trying to flirt with him.

'Coaching,' she continued quickly. 'How did you come
to get involved in that?'

Briefly Joel told her, warmed by her interest.

'Of course it doesn't pay anything,' he told her self-
deprecatingly, 'and, although Neil thinks I ought to try to
get some professional qualifications, there's no guarantee
that I can——'

'Oh, but that's wonderful!' Philippa interrupted him enthusiastically. 'And your wife must be thrilled as well?'

'Sally? She thinks I'm wasting my time and that I ought
to be out looking for a real job,' Joel told her bitterly.

Philippa looked at him. So things were no better between
him and his wife. She felt sorry for them both. Everyone
involved suffered when relationships went wrong.

'Look, it's really no problem to look at your washing machine,' Joel told her. 'In fact I could come back with you now if you like.' Sally had said something about working a double shift and he had no more classes at the leisure centre today.

'Well, if you're sure you don't mind.'

'I could even throw in a few swimming lessons as well if you want,' he added with a grin.

Philippa laughed.

It was a long time since he had heard Sally laugh, Joel recognised.

'There, that should do it.' Joel grunted as he gave the spanner a final twist. 'A nut had worked loose, that's all,' he told Philippa as he crawled out from behind the washing machine. 'You shouldn't have any problems with it now.'

'I'm really grateful to you,' Philippa told him ten minutes later as she poured him a cup of tea. 'Even with the benefit of the book I doubt that I'd have even been able to locate the problem, never mind fix it...'

'It didn't need much skill,' Joel responded wryly. 'Just a bit of brute force...'

'Don't do yourself down,' Philippa told him. 'Do you know how much I would have been charged if I'd called someone in to put it right?'

'Perhaps Daphne's right,' Joel commented. 'She's always telling Sally that I ought to be out trying to make a bit of money instead of wasting my time at the gym.'

'You're not wasting your time,' Philippa protested. 'Not from what you've told me. It must be very satisfying, helping people to achieve something...teaching them...' she said enviously.

'It is,' Joel agreed. 'Before I got involved at the leisure centre I suppose I'd have laughed at anyone who told me how good it would make me feel watching those kids... They really put everything they've got into it, you know. Neil's hoping that next year we'll be able to make up a junior team at competition level as well as the seniors. He's got this idea that if we can pick them out young enough——'

He broke off, shaking his head.

'Sorry, you don't want to hear all this...'

'Yes, I do,' Philippa contradicted him.

He paused to look at her and then smiled. 'Neil wants me to help out with the adult classes, but I'm not sure. It's one thing to teach kids...'

'You've got nothing to lose in trying,' Philippa told him.

He paused to take a bite of the cake she had cut him and frowned.

She had been to see the boys at the weekend and thanks to Susie's generosity she had been able to take them some of their favourite carrot and raisin cake. The slice she had just cut for Joel was a piece of it.

'What's wrong?' she asked him. 'If you don't like it...'

'No... I do. I was just wondering what was in it, that's all.'

'Oh, dear—are you allergic to...?'

'No, it's not that. It's just...well, since I've been reading up on all these training manuals, I've been doing a bit of experimenting ... with Sally working, she expects me to get some of the kids' meals and...they've been complaining that the only pudding I give them is fruit salad,' he explained bashfully, 'and I was wondering...'

'Oh, yes. I'm sure you'd be able to make this,' Philippa assured him, guessing what he wanted to ask. 'It's very easy and quite healthy as well ... my boys both love it. I'll write down the recipe for you if you like.'

How different she was from Sally, Joel reflected—Sally, who complained that she didn't like the way he had rearranged her kitchen cupboards, who said that he made too much mess when he cooked anything.

'It's quite cheap to make as well,' Philippa told him.

'Like my fruit salad,' Joel responded. 'How are things with you?' he asked her quietly as she got up to get some paper and a pen.

'Oh, not too bad,' Philippa fibbed lightly.

She was still waiting to hear from the bank and the wait was stretching her optimism to its limits. The small sum she received from the social services didn't go very far at all, and, if it weren't for Susie's insistence on constantly inviting her round for meals and then sending her home with the left-overs, Philippa suspected that she would be reduced to surviving on a very meagre diet indeed.

'I'm hoping to study for some qualifications myself,' she told Joel, 'although I'm not sure what it will be yet. I'd thought originally of taking a degree course, but with so many young people leaving university without a job to go to I've begun to wonder if I wouldn't be wiser going for something more practical, although I'm not sure what.'

'There.' She gave Joel the piece of paper with the recipe she had written down. 'It's quite easy to make. Do you...does your wife have a mixer?'

'Yes,' Joel confirmed, leaning closer then as he studied the piece of paper she had given him. 'What does this mean?' he asked her. 'Cream butter and...?'

'Oh, well, you have to...'

Joel listened intently to her while she explained. She was a nice woman, he decided. Warm and kind, and he would have liked her and felt drawn to her on the strength of that alone. But if it was her warmth and kindness that made him feel relaxed and reluctant to leave, that made it easy for him to talk to her and confide in her, it was her femininity, her softness, that small betraying tension he could sense within her, that made him respond to her physically and sexually—and dangerously!

'You see? It's really quite easy,' he heard her telling him earnestly.

He looked across at her. Her face was slightly flushed, her colour deepening slightly as she looked away from him. She was as aware of him as he was of her, Joel recognised. Aware of him and just a tiny little bit afraid. Not in the sense that she thought he might do anything to hurt or abuse her, he recognised, just femalely and intuitively afraid of his maleness and her own response to it.

Once, a long time ago...a long, long time ago...he had seen that look in Sally's eyes, felt her body tremble as he'd taken her in his arms, had known that when he touched her, kissed her, she would melt into eager response, wanting him...needing him.

She was behaving irrationally and ridiculously, as though she were a teenager, Philippa recognised as she tried to control her body's responses to Joel's proximity. She could feel herself starting to tremble, her legs threatening to buckle as she was filled by an overwhelming sensual yearning, a need to touch and be touched, to hold and be held.

Horrified that Joel might guess the effect he was having on her, she looked away, dipping her head so that her hair fell forward. Automatically she reached out to push the fair strands back behind her ear, only Joel beat her to it.

The pads of his fingers felt slightly rough but his touch was gentle and warm, stroking almost as though he was trying to soothe her. As though he recognised how she felt and was trying to comfort her, she acknowledged.

He was a very attractive, very sexy man, and no doubt he was well used to dealing with silly women who came on to him. And she was being silly...stupid, like an archetypal lonely housewife, so desperate for sex that...

'You're trembling...'

Philippa tensed, her mouth dry, her heart pounding; her face burned hot with embarrassment. She tried to turn away but Joel's hand was still lying against her jaw, cupping her face, turning it gently towards his.

'And you're not the only one,' he told her huskily as he took hold of her hand and lifted it towards his chest. 'Feel.'

The powerful fast thud of his heartbeat made her feel light-headed and dizzy—or was it the intensity of her own desire that was making the room spin round her, making her feel so weak that she had to cling to him for support?

'No...' she protested as he bent his head and she watched his mouth come closer to her own. 'No, we mustn't.'

His head stopped moving, his eyes searching her face.

'No,' he agreed sombrely. 'We mustn't.'

CHAPTER NINETEEN

SALLY glanced nervously at her watch. Almost half-past two. Surely Kenneth still wouldn't be waiting for her now?

He knew her shift finished at two and when she didn't appear he would know that she had changed her mind about seeing him.

If Joel hadn't made her so angry and upset she would never even have agreed to see him in the first place, no matter how much a part of her might have wanted to do so.

As she smoothed down the fabric of her skirt she noticed that her fingers were trembling slightly.

This was silly, she told herself firmly, sulking here like a little girl afraid of being caught out in some misdemeanour. She had done nothing wrong. Just because another man enjoyed her company and she enjoyed his, just because he made her feel protected and cosseted, just because he had told her... implied that he was falling in love with her, that did not mean...

Shakily she got up, tensing as the door to the staff restroom opened. The nurse who walked in raised her eyebrows when she saw Sally.

'Nice outfit,' she commented. 'Going somewhere special?'

'No... No, I...I just felt like a change,' Sally told her uncomfortably.

The outfit had originally belonged to her sister, a crunchy, soft-toned linen two-piece which Daphne had complained petulantly creased every time she wore it.

Guiltily Sally allowed her mind to escape from the admission that it was an outfit she normally only wore for very special occasions. So what if she had decided to get changed here at work before going home for once? What

did that mean? It was spring, the sun was shining; wasn't she as entitled as anyone else to wear something feminine and impractical?

She looked at her watch again. Almost a quarter to three—he would definitely have gone by now.

She *was* doing the right thing, she told herself fiercely as she left the building. For Kenneth's sake... For all their sakes.

She thought fleetingly of Joel who never seemed to have time for anything but the leisure centre these days. Once he would have known, sensed immediately that something was wrong. Look at the way he had objected at first when she'd insisted she was going to work full-time, and yet now, when she told him she was going to work a double shift...

She had been so nervous after she had told him, nervous and somehow elated at the same time, half afraid that he would accuse her of lying to him; that he would demand to know what she was really doing.

Perhaps because all he wanted from her was sex it never occurred to him that another man might fall in love with her.

Even the kids seemed to have changed towards her recently; it was Joel they talked to now...confided in...laughed with... She had seen the way they went quiet when she came home from work; the way they removed themselves from the room whenever she and Joel argued.

Perhaps Kenneth was right when he said that they were almost adults...that they no longer really needed her... except financially.

Tears blurred her eyes. Fiercely she blinked them away as she stepped out into the spring sunshine.

'At last... I was just beginning to worry that I'd missed you.'

Her body froze, her heart stopping and then starting to race.

Kenneth. He *had* waited for her after all. Dismay warred with pleasure. She truly hadn't expected him to wait, she assured herself. She had genuinely believed that he would have gone, but she knew that the smile curling her mouth was telling him how pleased she was to see him, and the feelings bubbling up inside her and making her feel almost as though she could walk on air betrayed the truth.

She had wanted to see him ... to be with him ... It was only her conscience, her awareness of what was right and what was wrong that had made her decide that she shouldn't.

'Now,' Kenneth was saying, 'where would you like to go...?'

To go? Sally gave him a startled look. She had been so convinced that he would have left that she hadn't thought any further ahead than that.

'After all, we've got plenty of time, haven't we...? Although eight hours is a mere tithe of the time I'd actually like to spend with you,' he added caressingly. 'A lifetime...no, several lifetimes would hardly be long enough. See how trite you're making me,' he added. 'It's a universal truth that a man in love becomes so besotted that he's reduced to the mere banal to express his emotions because he cannot find words magnificent enough to do his feelings justice...'

His hands touched her arm lightly, his fingers gently warm through the sleeve of her jacket. She liked the way he didn't make a grab for her, didn't make her feel sexually pressured or oppressed, Sally admitted.

It was reassuring to know that even if anyone had seen them together they would have found nothing to remark on in the way he was touching her; it was the polite gesture of any man to a woman he knew.

What he was saying to her, though, was a different matter altogether. It was exciting, enticing, flattering, giving without demanding any response from her, this verbal love play, reawakening echoes of the early days of Joel's courtship of her. Then Joel had treated her as carefully as though she were as fragile and precious as expensive glass.

He had dated other girls before her, girls who were far more sexually aware and experienced than she, but on their first date he had done nothing more than hold her hand ...

'I don't like you seeing him,' her mother had told her angrily. 'They're all the same, boys of that type... all after one thing...'

'He's not like that,' Sally had protested, blushing furiously at what her mother was implying. Sex was something that had not been openly discussed in their household apart from stern assertions from Sally's mother that she didn't want either of her daughters getting themselves into trouble.

Then Joel had loved her carefully and lovingly, but now...

When had he stopped courting her for sex, and started treating it instead as though it were a right...?

She could never imagine Kenneth behaving like that.

Eight hours... Eight hours alone with him... Her heart flipped over, her hands trembling. Where did she want to go?

'I...I don't know,' she told him. 'I...I hadn't really thought...'

'I had,' Kenneth told her softly. 'But if I told you where I'd really like to take you...'

He stopped speaking, his eyes darkening, and Sally felt her face flushing as she recognised the sexual innuendo and promise in his words.

'It's too soon for that yet, though, isn't it?' he asked her ruefully.

Kenneth was surprised how much it excited him, this prolonged drawn-out prologue to their relationship. The sheer headiness and euphoria of his anticipation had caught him off guard, like breathing in air that was short of oxygen, he recognised. Quick, urgent sex had never appealed to him; he enjoyed the power and self-control of a long period of foreplay.

His wife had once accused him of being narcissistic sexually, of enjoying the thought that he was arousing and controlling her, of bestowing on her the gift of orgasm more than he enjoyed his own release.

It had been shortly after that that she had stopped reaching orgasm, telling him that she refused to be used. to be studied as some kind of a laboratory specimen; th?.

she felt that his desire to get sexual satisfaction at second hand via her was a form of perversion.

He frowned angrily to himself. She had never really understood him; her reactions had been too coarse, too earthy. Sally was different: more sensitive and finely tuned. His desire for her was as much a form of mental arousal as a physical one.

The fact that today, when he could have chosen to take her home with him and have her all to himself, he had instead elected to be with her in public sharpened his desire for her, adding a fiercely keen edge to it.

'I know,' he told her now, as though the thought had just occurred to him. 'It's such a marvellous day—why don't we go to Farringdean?'

'Farringdean?' Sally frowned uncertainly. She had heard of the elegant Georgian House and its gardens, but it was somewhere she had never been.

'The house probably won't be open but the gardens will,' Kenneth told her. 'We can walk there and talk...get to know one another better.'

'That sounds lovely,' Sally told him gratefully. Had he guessed how mixed up and confused she felt, aware of his desire for her and her own response to it and yet at the same time reluctant to acknowledge it openly and to take their relationship a step further?

Just as long as she stayed on this side of the physical barrier that separated them, she could still tell herself that she was doing nothing wrong, but once she crossed it...

'So how are things at home?'

They had been walking through the gardens for almost half an hour, Sally unable to prevent herself from stopping every few minutes to admire them and exclaim over their beauty.

'Not too bad,' she told him.

They were walking slowly along the gravel paths of a formal garden, and Kenneth was holding her hand in his. She felt happy and relaxed, enjoying his physical closeness in the knowledge that it was not a prelude to a demand for sex, as it would have been with Joel.

'Joel's become very involved down at the leisure centre and he seems to spend nearly all his time down there.'

Kenneth was frowning. 'I thought he was supposed to be looking for a job,' he commented sharply.

'He was,' Sally agreed.

'But instead he goes out enjoying himself, leaving you to work to support him?' Kenneth's mouth hardened and Sally felt a small thrill of pleasure that he should be so angry on her behalf.

But her conscience prompted her to add, 'He is actually doing some voluntary work, coaching young swimmers...'

'But he doesn't get paid for it... Does he have any idea of how lucky he is to have a woman like you?' Kenneth asked her softly, stopping walking and turning to face her. His free hand touched her face lightly.

'He doesn't value you properly, Sally; you know that, don't you? I'd take any kind of work...do anything...' He stopped and shook his head. 'What is it?' Kenneth asked her. 'And don't say "nothing" because your eyes are already giving you away. I don't know what it is that's going through your mind, but I do know it's upsetting you...'

'It's nothing really...just something Joel did... My sister wanted him to do some wallpapering for her. She was having an important dinner party—her husband's headmaster and his wife—only Joel put the wallpaper on upside-down and now...'

She bit her lip. 'Daphne wants him to go back and re-paper the room, but he won't. That means I'll have to go and do it next Monday on my day off...'

She didn't add that she hadn't told Joel yet, nor that he would be furious with her for doing so, but what alternative did she have?

'You're too good for him,' Kenneth whispered, squeezing her hand. 'You shouldn't stay with him, you know...a man who doesn't appreciate or value you.'

Sally's mouth went dry. Her heart started to thump uncomfortably hard. Kenneth's words were only an echo of her sister's, and yet coming from him they held a much greater import.

'I...I can't leave him,' she protested in agitation. 'He...he needs me...'

'He's using you,' Kenneth told her forcefully. 'And besides, you shouldn't be asking yourself if he needs you, Sally, but whether you need him...if you want him...Do you still sleep together?' he asked her abruptly.

His question sent a shock of awareness thrilling through her. 'Yes...That is...we still share the same bed,' she told him huskily. 'But...'

'But you don't make love...you don't have sex,' Kenneth prompted softly.

'I...we...Joel wants to, but...' She closed her eyes, guiltily aware that every word she said increased her betrayal of Joel and their marriage, but it was such a relief to talk to someone who understood her, someone with whom she could be open and honest about her feelings. If Daphne had not been so antagonistic towards Joel she might have felt more able to confide in her, but with Daphne she was always uncomfortably aware that her sister was looking for faults in Joel, for something to criticise.

'I suppose it's just that men and women have a different attitude towards sex,' she told him ruefully. 'Joel just can't seem to understand that it isn't something I can...that I can't make myself...' She stopped, shaking her head.

'That you can't what?' Kenneth prompted. 'That you can't make yourself want him? And he still tries to force himself on you, knowing...' Kenneth began disgustedly, but Sally stopped him.

'It isn't like that,' she protested defensively. 'Joel doesn't...'

She stopped again. How could she explain to Kenneth...admit to him that the diminishment of her sex drive had meant that she almost preferred to have Joel get the whole thing over and done with rather than attempt to arouse her?

'You don't want him, and he has to know it,' Kenneth insisted. 'In my book that makes him...' He stopped,

shaking his head. 'There's an awful lot more to a relationship, to loving someone, than sex...'

'Yes,' Sally acknowledged sadly.

'You know how I feel about you,' Kenneth told her.
'Leave him, Sally, and come to me...'

'I can't,' she protested, panicky. It was too soon...too
much...she wasn't ready yet for that kind of decision, that
kind of commitment—and besides, how could she leave
Joel?

Kenneth watched her. He could afford to wait, to enjoy
the pleasure of anticipation, and sooner or later she would
come to him, he was sure of it.

If her husband was as sexually driven as she was implying, Kenneth doubted that he would be content to live
a semi-celibate life for very long. Sooner rather than later
there would be another woman, Kenneth reflected cynically, and once there was...

'I can't bear to think of you going back to him,' he told
Sally after they had gone round in circles for another ten
minutes. 'Being with him...sleeping with him...'

'Don't,' Sally protested, her eyes filling with tears. She
felt as though she was being pulled apart, her body and
her emotions wrenched into aching sickness by her conflicting needs.

Talking with Kenneth had underlined the emptiness of
her marriage and her relationship with Joel, and yet he was
her husband; she had committed herself to him. If she left
him...

'Don't look like that,' Kenneth told her. 'It's not your
fault. He's the one who's to blame for losing your love,
Sally, not you.' He turned her towards him, releasing her
hand to cup her face and look down at her. They were alone
in the garden, but Sally still looked anxiously over his
shoulder as Kenneth bent to kiss her. The sensation of his
mouth brushing delicately against hers with a gentle control
instead of the intense passion she had expected filled her
eyes with grateful tears.

'Right now there's nothing I want more than to take you
home with me and make love to you until you agree to

leave him and stay with me, but I can't do that...my conscience wouldn't let me. Just as I can't take hold of you now and force the issue between us by making us lovers.

'That isn't the way I want it to be between us, Sally,' he told her quietly. 'You are going to be mine, but I want our coming together, our sexual intimacy to be a celebration of our feelings for one another, not some frantic, urgent sexual coupling which leaves us both feeling as though we've been cheated... You mean too much to me for that.'

He had her now, Kenneth exulted. He could see from her face just how much his words were affecting her.

As a student he had won a commendation for his powers of oration. His ex-wife had derided him as a verbal poseur, a show-off, who enjoyed talking about sex more than he enjoyed doing it.

'I won't rush you,' he promised Sally. 'But I won't let you go, either. I need you, Sally...'

'Joel, we mustn't,' Philippa repeated shakily, but there was no real conviction in her voice, no real desire for his fingers to stop their gentle stroking of her scalp nor for his eyes to stop gazing down into hers, recognising her desire, responding to it, promising...

Her brain, her mind, her conscience told her one thing, but her body clamoured wildly for another, and if she really wanted him to stop then why was she turning her face up towards his, moving closer to him, staring at his mouth while her body shivered in sensual excitement and arousal?

He shouldn't being doing this, Joel recognised; he should have more restraint and more control... No matter how much he wanted her...ached for her, no matter how intense his desire...no matter how cold the bed he shared with Sally, he could not...should not. But then she moved against him, an unintentional, oddly innocent but wholly sensual small *frisson* of sensation that touched his own flesh and destroyed his will-power.

She was so caring...so warm and yielding, so responsive, and he ached so badly with his need for her.

felt bigger, harder than she could ever remember Andrew feeling, her awareness of the sensation of him within her intensely acute; the intensity of her orgasm, the urgency and swiftness with which it overwhelmed her were as unfamiliar as the extent of her desire.

She heard herself cry out and Joel make an answering guttural response, driving through her orgasm and carrying her with him, prolonging it until he reached his own peak.

Afterwards Joel held her tightly, stroking her damp hair back off her face, kissing her forehead, and then her mouth, gently, and then a second time, questioningly, before silently taking her hand and leading her upstairs.

This time their need was just as great, but their pace slower, so that she had time to marvel at the way the sunlight through the window played on his skin, highlighting the formation of the muscles that lay beneath it. She traced them, wandering with fingertips and then her mouth, kissing his throat and his chest, savouring the taste of him on her tongue, her senses excited by the maleness of him.

It had never occurred to her during her marriage to Andrew that a man's body could be something to admire, his arousal something to gloat secretly over in deep-seated female triumph. With Andrew the rare sight of his naked body had caused her to feel uncomfortable and faintly embarrassed for him as well as for herself. Now, without realising it, as she touched Joel she was making soft purring sounds of feminine approval and admiration, touching him, looking at him, Joel recognised as he watched her, as though his body was her greatest delight, giving him visually and verbally the approval and acceptance that every man's ego secretly yearned for.

There could be no greater delight than this . . . no deeper, richer pleasure than to lie next to a woman you had just made love to knowing you had pleased and satisfied her, hearing her making those soft cooing sounds of pleasure.

His throat tightening with emotion, Joel reached for her, drawing her back down against his body, holding her, Philippa recognised shakily, with the kind of tenderness that transformed what had happened between them from something purely physical to something far, far more dangerous.

Slowly Joel traced the bones of her face, his face shadowed and sombre. She felt so frail in his arms, so soft and vulnerable. He had felt her need in the way she'd clung to him and responded to him; the way her flesh had welcomed him. He felt his heart lurch against his breastbone. This was how it should be between a man and a woman...how...

'Philippa, I...'

Shakily Philippa reached out and placed her fingertips against his lips. 'No...please...don't say anything,' she begged him huskily. 'I don't want us to lie to one another, to make promises we can't keep.'

She watched as Joel closed his eyes against his emotions and then reached out and took hold of her wrist, kissing the fingertips she had placed against his mouth and then her wrist, the soft, vulnerable place inside her elbow.

Joel heard her moan as his mouth touched her throat and then her breasts. He teased her nipples gently, aware of his own desire to know and caress each and every part of her. Loving her was like a banquet, a feast of such unimaginable delicacy that he had to fight not to gorge himself but to savour and enjoy instead every individual sensation and flavour.

Philippa shivered as his mouth caressed her stomach, her skin tensing tightly against her muscles. Joel's tongue circled her navel and her quiver became an open shudder. His hands slid beneath her, holding her, lifting her.

'No,' she told him protestingly, shivering with the awareness of what he intended to do, torn between her physical longing for the intimacy of such a caress and her emotional fear of what the giving and taking of it could mean.

But either Joel hadn't heard her or didn't want to hear her, because his mouth was already moving delicately against her inner thigh and the sight of his dark head bent over her body made her heart turn over inside her chest in physical and emotional arousal.

Tears burned behind her closed eyelids as she recognised his tenderness and care, mingled with the hotter, more urgent thread of his desire, forming a skein of emotion and sensation that aroused her so intensely that it was impossible for her to control her body's response to him. It flooded through her, unstoppable, uncontrollable, charging through her body in fierce spurts of delight, as Joel's mouth caressed her until the final pulse of her pleasure had died away.

Later they made love again, and not just because she wanted to repay him the pleasure he had shown her, Philippa acknowledged drowsily as, to her own surprise and against her own expectations, she felt her body quicken against the slow, erotic thrust of his until she was urging him to move deeper and deeper within her, her hands reaching round him, holding him to her, her need for him a dam which, once breached, could not be restrained.

'Philippa, wake up.'

Sleepily she opened her eyes, her face flushing as she saw Joel leaning over her. He was fully dressed, holding a cup of tea, which he handed to her, saying, 'I . . . I brought you this . . .'

He watched her gravely while she struggled to sit up and take the tea from him and at the same time clutch the duvet protectively to her body.

Something in his eyes made her smile ruefully and let go of it.

'You must go,' she told him quietly. 'We shouldn't have . . .'

'*I* shouldn't . . .' Joel corrected her.

'It was an accident . . . a mistake . . .' Philippa pressed on doggedly, ignoring what she could hear in his voice. 'We must both forget that it ever happened. It should never have happened.'

'No,' Joel argued tensely, 'it shouldn't, but as for forgetting . . . do you know how long it's been since I felt like that...since I...?' He stopped abruptly and then told her, 'Have you any idea what it does to a man when a woman responds to him like that...needs him...makes him feel that she——?'

'Joel, you're married,' Philippa interrupted him desperately. 'You've got a wife...children. What happened between us...it must never happen again. We mustn't see each other again. I can't...' She stopped as she saw from the look in his eyes that a part of him was pleased by the knowledge that she feared his sexuality and her own responsiveness to it, and yet she couldn't blame or accuse him for it. She had felt an equally atavistic female thrill of pleasure as she'd dropped the duvet and watched as his eyes and his body responded to the sight of her.

'It was just sex,' she told him huskily. 'It doesn't mean anything. Just sex, that's all.' But she couldn't quite keep the forlorn note of loss out of her voice, and Joel, hearing it, leaned forward and touched her.

'No, it wasn't,' he corrected her gently, holding her.

'No,' Philippa agreed. 'But it still mustn't happen again—for all our sakes. If it does, I might not be able to stop myself becoming emotionally attached to you,' she told him with quiet honesty, 'and Sally—your wife—you love her...'

'Before today I thought I did,' Joel told her. 'But now...'

'It was a statement, not a question,' Philippa told him with a smile.

'It would be very easy for me to love you, Philippa,' Joel told her sombrely. 'In fact...'

'For a while,' Philippa conceded. 'And then it would be very, very hard...for both of us. We both know that if things were better for you at home you would never... Go home, Joel,' she told him softly. 'Go home and forget that this ever happened.'

'And if I can't...?'

'You must.'

She would cry later, when he had gone, because she already knew what she was turning her back on and rejecting, and how much she wished that things were different; that he were free.

What had happened between them was like a summer storm, intense and shocking when it happened, overshadowing everything else, but quickly forgotten once it had passed.

Easier to let him go now than to risk the heartache and pain that an affair with him was bound to bring.

Easier...? Easier than what? she asked herself grimly after he had gone.

CHAPTER TWENTY

FROWNING, Elizabeth surveyed the clothes she had laid out on the bed: trousers to travel in, the suit she planned to wear for the conference, underwear, tights, shoes, a sweater 'just in case', and a thin silky shirt she could wear in the evening with her black trousers just in case she needed to look a little bit more dressed up. Or ought she perhaps to take a dress?

'Richard, do you think I should put a dress in for the evening...?'

'It's a conference you're supposed to be going to, not a dinner party.'

The terseness of his reply startled her. He had been uncharacteristically irritable recently and she had put this down to the fact that she knew he was anxious about the siting of the new Fast Response Accident Unit. Now, however, her frown deepened slightly. A little wifely tolerance to oil life's wheels was one thing; an irritable, bad-tempered husband venting those feelings on her without explaining what was causing them was another.

Firmly she checked through the items she had placed on the bed before turning round and asking quietly, 'Something's bothering you, Richard. What is it...?'

'Nothing,' Richard lied shortly, and then added betrayingly, 'For God's sake, Liz, it's only a two-day conference you're going on. With all the fuss you're making, anyone would think you're going to a world summit... When I went to conferences...'

Elizabeth had heard enough.

'When you went to conferences, you had me to organise this kind of thing for you,' she told him with a sweep of her hand, indicating the things laid out neatly on the bed. 'Maybe I am over-reacting a little bit, but you see, this is

304

all still very new to me, Richard... New and—yes, I admit it—exciting as well... No doubt when I've attended as many conferences as you have I'll be as blasé about them as you are, but until then I'm afraid you'll just have to indulge me a little bit,' she told him tartly.

Ruefully Richard shook his head. 'Yes, you're right. I'm sorry, Liz,' he apologised.

'I know how worried you are about the Accident Unit,' Elizabeth told him gently, softening towards him. 'If you think it would help if we talked about it...'

'Save the counselling for your clients,' he suggested, his irritability returning.

When he saw the way Elizabeth folded her lips and quietly turned away from him he cursed himself under his breath. How could he explain to her how he felt? How could she possibly understand what it was like to feel as though you were constantly having to look over your shoulder to see how quickly younger men were catching up with you...what it felt like to wake up in the middle of the night in a panic because all you could see in front of you was a dead end, a blank wall, where once there had been a dozen different avenues of possibility and promise?

Of course Liz was excited about this conference, about the new life opening out in front of her, but her excitement, her opportunity was in such direct contrast to his own fears that he felt that it would be impossible for her really to understand... And besides, he didn't want to burden her with his fears; he didn't want to spoil things for her.

'Barbara has her own key,' Elizabeth told him, referring to the young single mother who came in to clean for them twice a week. 'And when I shop I'll get in a couple of ready-made meals you can microwave...'

'For God's sake, Liz, I'm not a child. I can put together a meal if necessary, you know. Besides, you're only going away for a couple of days, not a couple of months... I'll probably eat at the hospital anyway...'

'The hospital? I thought you'd want to get some golf in...'

'I've got some paperwork to catch up on,' Richard told her.

The budgets. He had seen the tiny frown in Brian's eyes the last time he had mentioned them and he had made himself a vow that despite his aversion to the whole principle of turning the National Health Service into a cost-effective exercise he would prove to David Howarth that he was perfectly capable of running his department just as efficiently financially as anyone else.

Just so long as that efficiency didn't prejudice the health of his patients.

'In fact I might do a couple of hours' work this evening,' he added.

'Oh, Richard, no,' Elizabeth protested. 'We're supposed to be going over to see Sara this afternoon. You can't have forgotten... It's weeks since you last saw your grandchild.'

He *had* forgotten, and watching the expression on his face made Elizabeth suddenly feel illogically anxious. It wasn't like Richard to be so irritable and withdrawn.

'Are you sure there's nothing wrong?' she persisted.

For a moment Richard wavered, tempted to tell her, but what could Elizabeth say to him that he had not already said to himself?

'Nothing's wrong,' he repeated, turning to leave the bedroom.

Elizabeth frowned as she watched him go. Something was bothering him, she knew that. Why was it that all men, even the most mature and well-adjusted of them, insisted on retreating behind this wall of protective male silence? What was, after all, really so threatening about simply saying what was on their minds?

She saw it time and time again with her clients, and sympathised with their female partners in their baffled frustration at their men's refusal to accept that being open about their feelings made them and their relationships stronger, not weaker.

But she understood how important the new Fast Response Accident Unit was to Richard and how hard he had worked to try to ensure that it was sited at the General.

Thoughtfully she went downstairs. Richard was in the kitchen making them both a cup of tea. Quietly she accepted his peace offering.

'I forgot to tell you—Brian and his wife are giving a dinner party to welcome our new psychiatrist and introduce him to everyone.'

'Is he anyone you know?' Elizabeth asked him.

'No. From the sound of it working at the General is going to be a bit of a step down for him. According to Brian he's been working in the States for the last few years, although he is British, but now, for family reasons, he wants to come back and doesn't mind taking a drop in status and income in order to do so... Brian was full of the innovative measures he's implemented at Johns Hopkins; apparently he believes in the psychiatric department working alongside the medical and surgical departments where necessary, treating the patient as a whole, not as a separate collection of needs. It seems that he's very keen on ensuring that medical and surgical patients get proper counselling to help them overcome any trauma they might be suffering...'

'Mmm... well, the two of you should get on well, then. That's something you've been campaigning for for years. You're always complaining that far too many patients come to you totally unprepared mentally for the effects of their surgery.'

'Brian and David seem to have a very high opinion of him. He's only thirty-eight...'

Elizabeth put down her tea, puzzled by the note of resentment she could hear in Richard's voice. He had always been a man who was very open to other people, but now, for some reason, he sounded almost truculent.

'He's done very well, then,' she commented. 'He must...'

'Why is it that everyone today is so obsessed by youth? What is it about being on the thirty side of forty that earns a man praise while being on the fifty side of it condemns him to the scrap heap...?'

Elizabeth gave him a startled look. 'You were the one who brought up the subject of his age,' she pointed out.

'But as far as Brian and David are concerned you'd think it mattered more than his professional qualifications. There was a time when a surgeon wasn't even considered experienced enough for a senior post until he had been operating for at least twenty years; these days if you haven't made it by the time you're thirty you might as well forget it.

'Do you know what David's trying to get Brian to do now? Bring in obligatory medicals for anyone over fifty...'

'You've often said yourself that more than half the operations you do might not be necessary if only people would give the same time and care to having their bodies checked out as they do their cars,' Elizabeth reminded him gently.

'Taking sensible health precautions is one thing,' Richard told her fiercely. 'Deliberately trying to make out that anyone over fifty isn't fit...' He stopped abruptly, shaking his head.

Brian's memo advising him that from the end of the quarter he intended to institute a system whereby everyone over fifty would have to undergo an obligatory medical test to prove that they were fit to do their job had been sitting on his desk for the last three days unanswered.

The arrogance of David Howarth! Did he really think that Richard would dream of operating on anyone if he thought that he wasn't competent to do so?

And no matter what David might think, being a good surgeon involved more than perfect eyesight and a steady hand. Those assets, no matter how good, were merely physical, and could not compensate for lack of experience, for the awareness, the knowledge that came with time, for the sixth sense one developed only with age.

Elizabeth sighed under her breath. No matter what David did, Richard would dislike it, because he disliked the man himself. Not that she could blame him for that—she didn't like him very much herself.

'It's time we left,' she told Richard. 'I promised Sara we'd be there for five...'

'And with the new funding we've been able to set up our own X-ray unit and take on a couple of extra nurses so that we can offer our female patients a specialised clinic, not just for routine smears, but for a variety of other aspects of their health as well, from a counselling service for teenagers wanting contraceptive advice right through to older women going through the menopause and wanting advice on HRT.

'Bernard's even talking about setting up a mini operating theatre. After all, we've got the space now that we've got this new purpose-built clinic up and running. You'll have to watch it,' Ian teased Richard. 'If you're not careful we're going to be putting you out of business altogether... You'll be able to take early retirement and spend all day on the golf course...

'*Have* you thought about taking early retirement?' Ian asked him. 'I know *my* father is considering it. My mother says she wants them to have some time together while they're still both young enough and fit enough to enjoy themselves.'

'Oh, Mum won't want Daddy retiring yet,' Sara informed her husband. 'Not now that her own career is just starting to take off... How are you going to manage while she's at this conference?' she asked Richard with a grin.

'Oh, for God's sake, Sara, I'm an adult, not a young child, and I'd appreciate it if you'd try to remember that...'

An uncomfortable silence fell over the table. Katie, Sara's four-year-old, looked at her mother unhappily, her bottom lip pouting as she lisped, 'Why is Grandpa croth...?'

'I'm not cross, Katie,' Richard assured her, giving his daughter an apologetic look. 'I'm sorry, Sara,' he apologised gruffly. 'I shouldn't have spoken to you like that...'

'It's OK, Dad. We all know how worried you are about the new unit. Have you any idea yet when you'll know who gets it...?'

'No...'

Across the table he saw the looks his daughter and son-in-law exchanged, and he wondered if Ian had heard the gossip on the medical grapevine that the Northern was favourite for getting the unit. He liked his son-in-law and got on well with him, but his loyalties lay in a different

direction from Richard's own, and Richard was reluctant
to discuss the General's budgeting problems with him in
case he inadvertently mentioned it to his partners, who
might in turn pass it on to their contacts at the Northern.

Not that he would be telling the Northern anything they
did not already know, he acknowledged sourly. He suspected that David had already made it clear where his
support really lay and why.

'Grandpa. You're really, really old, aren't you?' Katie
suddenly piped up.

'Katie!' Sara protested.

'But he is,' Katie insisted. 'Because all grandpas are old...
Will you soon be dead?' she asked Richard cheerfully.

'Not as soon as you,' Ian told his daughter threateningly.

Somehow Richard managed to laugh along with Elizabeth
as she insisted to Ian that no doubt to Katie at four years
old they did both seem 'really old'.

'Mum, what on earth's got into Dad? I've never known
him be so tetchy and irritable.'

Richard paused outside the kitchen door as he heard his
daughter's voice.

'He's worried about this new Accident Unit,' he heard
Elizabeth responding.

'No...it's more than that,' Sara protested. 'You don't
think...well, you don't think he's put out about your
success, do you...?'

'Put out...? *Jealous* of me, you mean?'

'Well, yes...' Richard could hear the discomfort in Sara's
voice. 'Well, it can't be easy for him, can it...? He's always
been used to having you at home and now here you are
going off on conferences, making an independent life for
yourself...'

'Oh, Sara, no. I'm sure you're wrong,' Elizabeth
answered. She said the words firmly enough, but Richard
caught the note of uncertainty that underlay them and it
hurt him.

He was proud of Elizabeth, proud of her and pleased
for her, and if he had started to contrast the upswing in

her career with the threatened downswing in his own it wasn't because he was jealous of her. Surely she knew that, even if Sara didn't?

He could hear Sara walking towards the half-open kitchen door, and quickly he stepped back from it. The last thing he wanted now was for his daughter to realise he had overheard what she had been saying.

He could tell that Elizabeth was surprised when he cut their visit short and said that he was tired.

'You were very grumpy this afternoon. I think Sara was hurt by the way you behaved.'

Sara was hurt ... Richard paused in the act of removing his shoes.

Elizabeth was already undressed and ready for bed. Unlike his, her hair was showing little signs of greying. Wrapped in a towel, with the light behind her as she padded round the bedroom, she looked almost as young as Sara.

She paused, bending to open the drawer and remove a clean nightdress.

'Richard...' He could hear the tension in her voice as she closed the drawer and then turned round. 'This ... this grumpiness ... it isn't anything to do with me, is it ... with the fact that I...?'

Angrily Richard threw down the sock he had just removed.

'With the fact that what? That you're an up-and-coming successful career woman while I'm just an old has-been, fit for nothing other than being pensioned off?

'What are you trying to ask me, Liz? If I'm jealous of you ... Is that what you think?'

'No, of course it isn't.' He could hear the shock in her voice. 'Why on earth should I think anything like that?' she asked him.

'I overheard you and Sara talking in the kitchen,' he told her flatly. 'It's almost a classic case history, isn't it? Ageing husband's jealousy of his dynamic independent wife, his fear that her independence will mean that he loses control of their relationship, his inevitable decline through anger to depression and then impotence as his wife's power and authority rises. Odd, isn't it, how sensitive a barometer a man's sexual organs are of his sense of self-worth and his status in a relationship, in society itself?'

He felt the bed depress as Elizabeth sat down beside him. 'Richard, what is it? I *know* you're not jealous of me...'

'Do you?' He turned to look at her. 'Liz, I heard the doubt in your voice this afternoon when you were talking to Sara...'

'Yes,' she admitted, 'but the doubt wasn't because I thought she was right. I know she isn't.'

'Then what was it for...?'

'Good old-fashioned female guilt,' Elizabeth told him ruefully. 'I know how worried you are about the new unit and part of me feels that I should be here beside you, worrying with you, just as part of me felt guilty because I couldn't be with Sara twenty-four hours a day worrying alongside her when Katie was ill.

'It's one of the things that being a woman is all about... Our *emotional* barometer, if you like—the thing that tells us we can't be truly a woman unless we're "there" for people we love...unless we can somehow wave a magic wand and make life perfect for them, take away all their pain and anxiety; that's how we judge whether or not we're successful,' she told him softly.

'The doubt you heard was because I was asking myself how I could be a good wife and still go away knowing how much you were worrying...and knowing too that you didn't want to share your worry with me...'

'Because I didn't want to spoil things for you. I know how much this conference means to you...'

'So there is something else, apart from the unit?' Elizabeth asked him quietly.

'Yes,' Richard admitted. He paused and then told her, 'I think David is trying to get rid of me...'

'Get rid of you? What do you mean? Sack you? But he can't do that...'

'No...not sack me. It's no secret that he's already got rid of most of the more senior men. I'm coming up to sixty...'

'You're fifty-five, that's all,' Elizabeth protested, 'and they opted to take early retirement...'

'Did they?' Richard asked her wryly.

Elizabeth stared at him.

'He's beginning to make me doubt my own judgement, Liz...to make me wonder if perhaps I am getting past it. I keep telling myself that fifty-five is no age, that, when I first started out, a surgeon wasn't considered to reach his peak until he was close to sixty; these days...

'He wants me out, I know that... All this rubbish about budgets is just a smokescreen. And I don't want to retire, Liz... I'm not ready for it. I don't want to be ready for it. Oh, I know it's always been there, an inevitable fact of life, but somehow it's always been safely in the distance...something that happened to other people.

'I don't want to retire...don't want to spend the rest of my life playing golf and reminiscing...waiting for death.'

'Richard!' Elizabeth protested.

'Well, what else is it? Limitless free time...empty time with nothing to fill it. It's a curse, not a gift. When I think of what it means, of what my life will be, I break out in a cold sweat. The thought of it fills me with panic and revulsion... I'm afraid of all that empty time...'

'Why haven't you said anything to me before...?'

He could hear the pain in her voice.

'It's never been an issue before... I didn't even realise how I felt about it myself until David began to drop unsubtle hints about my age. I suppose I ignored it because I didn't want to think about it.'

'But it needn't be the way you think,' Elizabeth told him. 'There are things you could do...consultancy work... part-time surgery...you heard what Ian was saying about them looking for a surgeon for the practice... Community work...'

'Doing what? Pushing wheelchairs and then in turn being pushed in one myself? Oh, hell, Liz, I'm sorry,' he apologised when he saw her face.

'It's all right,' Elizabeth told him.

His retirement was something they had never really discussed; the years had rushed by so quickly since Sara had left school, their lives had become so busy, and, like him, if she was honest, she had somehow assumed that his retirement was something that was still far away in the future.

She knew how much his work meant to him, but the feelings he was expressing to her now, the sense of fear and emptiness... She discovered that for all her training she was at a loss to know what to say to him.

'Do you know, I always used to feel sorry for men who dropped down dead in harness? The fatal heart attack, robbing them of their right to a well-earned retirement... Now I almost envy them...'

'*Richard!*'

'Oh, it's all right... David Howarth, for all that he thinks he's so damned powerful, can't make me retire, not even if he does bring in these damned compulsory medicals...'

He saw the troubled look she was giving him.

'But one day you will have to retire, Richard... You can't...' She stopped speaking.

'I can't what? Run away from the inevitable?' He smiled grimly. 'Do you think I don't know that? I should be making plans, thinking constructively, addressing the issue positively and confronting its challenge... that's what our new psychiatrist would undoubtedly tell me. My God... I've seen them up at the golf club, waiting to die, living on their memories.'

'Richard, it doesn't have to be like that...' Elizabeth protested.

'I can't face it, Liz,' he told her bleakly, ignoring her protest. 'I can't live like that, without my work... without any sense of purpose or order in my life. But if the Northern gets the new unit I'll have no option.'

'What? But why?'

'For two reasons. The first is that *I'll* be the one who has lost the General the unit. David Howarth has made no secret of the fact that he disapproves of the way I handle my budgets, that he feels that I'm not making enough economies . . . that I'm not carrying out enough operations. And the second is that, if the Northern does get the new unit, sooner or later all major surgery will be carried out there and the General will degenerate into a second-rate hospital staffed by junior surgeons doing minor operations, and it won't be able to justify the expense of carrying someone like me. I'll be too great a financial drain on its resources for it to keep me. So you see, either way I lose out. It's a matter of either jump or be pushed.'

'But it hasn't been decided yet that the Northern *will* get the unit. I thought the final decision rested with the Minister?' Elizabeth protested.

'It does,' Richard agreed sombrely. 'But she is bound to follow David's recommendation . . .'

'Oh, Richard . . .'

The sympathy in her voice made him smile crookedly. 'Perhaps Sara was right after all; perhaps a part of me is jealous of you, or envious rather.'

Immediately Elizabeth went over to him, reaching up to take him in her arms, holding him tenderly. 'That's rubbish,' she told him, 'and you know it.'

Gratefully he leaned his weight against her briefly, giving in to his need to brush his cheek against the softness of her hair as they stood silently together, holding one another. And then, as though the emotion of the moment was too much for him, he raised his head and asked her shakily, 'What do you say, Mrs Humphries? What do you counsel me to do? What's your solution to this problem?'

Elizabeth looked at him and shook her head. How could she tell him that the solution lay with him, and in his somehow finding for himself something that would give his life the purpose he obviously believed it would lose if he no longer had his work to harness himself to?

'It's all about changing one's attitude,' she told him gently. 'And that's the easiest thing in the world to say and the hardest thing to do.'

How often had she said those words to other people, preaching them like a litany and genuinely believing them? And yet now, when she said them to Richard, she discovered that they felt as empty and useless as he claimed his life would be without his career.

CHAPTER TWENTY-ONE

'RICHARD, are you sure you want to go tonight?' Elizabeth asked, casting a troubled look at his face. He had aged somehow over these last few weeks—not so much physically; it was more as though he had lost his normal appetite for life, the drive and vigour which had always made him respond so enthusiastically to life's challenges.

'We don't have any option,' Richard told her. 'Any refusal to turn up and socialise with the hospital's new luminary is bound to earn me another black mark with David.'

'Have you actually met him yet—the new psychiatrist?' Elizabeth asked him.

'Brian introduced us briefly the other day.'

Elizabeth frowned as she heard the reserve in his voice and knew the cause of it, just as she knew that there was nothing she could do to help him.

Oh, she could listen to him, talk to him, offer positive suggestions about how he might try to help himself come to terms with his fear of retirement, but she couldn't wave a magic wand and make life stand still for him. To comfort him by telling him that he might still have several years of work ahead of him before he did retire was not the answer, only a means of pushing the problem to one side and pretending it did not exist...

Brian and Grace Simmonds lived six or seven miles away in a neat modern house on a small luxury complex which personally Elizabeth would have found claustrophobically stifling but which suited Grace Simmonds' neat, orderly personality.

Despite the differences in their temperaments, Elizabeth got on well with Grace. She was six years younger than Elizabeth and yet behaved as though she were much older;

317

she was, Elizabeth recognised, one of those women who felt most comfortable assuming the protective mantle of a now old-fashioned type of female middle-age. Her life revolved around her three children, her garden and her bridge, while Brian was firmly kept to its periphery and his own male sphere of work, and golf.

It wasn't the kind of relationship which Elizabeth would have wanted, but it appeared to suit them and, knowing Grace as she did, she wasn't totally surprised following their arrival to discover that their hostess had seated her next to the 'guest of honour'.

Grace was the type of person who was instinctively defensive and suspicious of anything that involved curing the mind rather than the body. To her a psychiatrist would be someone to be avoided and kept at a distance, and since David was alone and Richard was the next most senior person present it would seem to Grace to be the 'right thing to do' to seat her next to the new man.

'He seems quite...normal,' Grace told Richard and Elizabeth in a nervous whisper as she glanced over her shoulder to where Brian and David Howarth were standing with a tall brown-haired man who Elizabeth assumed must be the new psychiatrist. 'It's a pity he isn't married, though...' she continued as Richard moved away. 'It makes things very awkward. I know the numbers are even because David is on his own as well, but...'

She had a habit of leaving her sentences trailing, which Elizabeth tended to find irritating. 'I had thought of inviting someone to even things out, but you never know, do you, and since this is more of a business dinner than a social occasion...? Brian is so unhelpful with anything like this,' she added fretfully, frowning in the direction of her husband.

'I'm sure you've made the right decision,' Elizabeth soothed tactfully, moving away to join Richard.

'Dreadful woman,' Richard muttered under his breath. 'How Brian has managed to live with her all these years without murdering her I don't know.'

Elizabeth said nothing. She knew that Richard's outburst sprang more from tension than from any real dislike of Grace Simmonds.

'Ah, good. I was hoping that you and I might get an opportunity to talk...'

Elizabeth raised an eyebrow but still smiled as Blake Hamilton politely pulled out her chair for her. He hadn't waited for Brian to introduce them, but had excused himself to Brian and David and come over to speak to Richard and to meet her as soon as he had seen them.

His good looks were something that Elizabeth discounted when assessing him—after all, she was married to an extremely good-looking man herself—but the warmth and openness of his manner was something that surprised her.

She had met other psychiatrists, both socially through Richard and through her own work, and, unlike Grace, she found them neither intimidating nor threatening; what many of them did have in common was a trait she had been told she must develop herself, and that was the ability to distance themselves from other people's emotions.

Blake Hamilton, though, was displaying an unexpected warmth and charm which her instincts as a woman told her was neither contrived nor shallow. Despite the years in the States there was no trace of any American accent in his voice, nor was there in his manner any hint of any kind of arrogant awareness of how fortunate the General was to have secured his services.

It had amused Elizabeth to see David's almost fawning attitude towards him, and it had hurt her at the same time when she compared it with the manner he adopted towards Richard.

In contrast, Blake had almost made a point of not just drawing Richard into the conversation, but of talking to him rather than to David.

'Your husband is a first-rate surgeon,' he commented now as they ate their first course.

'Yes,' Elizabeth agreed, knowing that it was the truth.

On her other side David, who had heard his comment, had started to frown, quite obviously disliking it.

'And a very innovative one as well,' Blake continued. 'I was speaking with one of his patients this morning, a woman on whom he had had to perform rather radical breast surgery. She was telling me that Richard had deliberately timed her operation in order to get the maximum benefit from her monthly cycle.'

To her left Elizabeth could hear David's derisory snort, but she didn't turn her head or betray in any way that she had heard him, simply concentrating instead on Blake.

'Richard had read a report which suggested that female patients had a better chance of recovery during certain phases of their menstrual cycle and he wanted to give her the optimum chance of recovery, especially in view of the serious nature of her operation. For a woman to lose her breast can't be anything but traumatic, no matter how well she is prepared for it...'

'No, I agree...'

'Organising operations by the phases of the menstrual cycle... Now I've heard everything,' David commented acidly. 'My God, no wonder the General's having so many problems... Perhaps it's the staff you ought to be counselling, Blake, not the patients,' he added with false jocularity.

Elizabeth knew that Richard must have heard his comment, but she stifled her own anger. In her view it simply confirmed what she had always thought of David, that he should use a semi-social occasion to try to humiliate Richard and score points off him was uncalled for.

'On the contrary,' she heard Blake contradicting coolly. 'In my view Richard is to be commended for his farsightedness. Far too many people on the surgical side overlook the fact that a human being is not merely a physical body. And I was very interested to see that Richard's patient is making a far better and mentally healthier recovery from her operation than a woman at the Northern who had much less radical surgery.

'After all, what are we about if we are not about helping people not merely to survive, but to live well and happily? Curing a patient isn't simply a matter of cutting away a piece of diseased flesh, and the more far-sighted surgeons, the ones who have the best overall success-rates, are the ones who recognise that fact.'

On her right David sat silently, but Elizabeth could feel his irritation and she wondered, a little dismayed, how much inadvertent harm Blake's unexpected championing of Richard might have done.

Anxious to steer the conversation into less controversial channels, she asked Blake quietly, 'Have you found anywhere to live yet or...?'

'Yes,' he told her. 'But finding a house is the least of my problems. The reason I've come back to this country is because I've suddenly and totally unexpectedly become the sole guardian of my late cousin's only child, a girl. I'm afraid to say that until I received the news of my cousin's and her husband's deaths I'd virtually forgotten that Anya existed.

'My cousin was always something of a rebel,' he explained. 'She dropped out of university when she became involved with a group of South American refugees who had been granted political asylum here. She went out to South America to work for the cause and it was there that she met her husband; in actual fact she helped to break him out of gaol. Luckily for them they managed to get out of the country before anyone caught up with them.

'At first when Lisa married Miguel I worried that he was using her, but in fact they were very much in love with one another. Both of them were inclined to be impetuous... take risks. Both of them thrived on danger and excitement.

'There's a small enclave of fellow refugees based in Leeds and they went to live there. They are a very tight-knit, wholly politically motivated community whose entire existence is devoted to freeing their homeland. An idealistic and impossible goal, I'm afraid, but one to which Lisa devoted herself whole-heartedly. Luckily Anya was born in this country and has British citizenship.

'Lisa was always a very dramatic character, and when she asked me if she could name me as Anya's legal guardian she dropped a lot of dark hints about political assassinations and so forth, and to be honest I agreed because it seemed the easiest thing to do; she was always very passionate about any cause she adopted, passionate *and* persistent... I must admit, though, that then I never expected their lives to end so suddenly...'

'Oh, no...how awful,' Elizabeth began. 'One reads about such things, but...'

'No, no,' Blake assured her. 'The cause of their deaths was not politically connected in any way; it was far more mundane. A car accident. None of the group had two pennies to rub together, and the police said after the accident that it was a wonder the car Lisa was driving had got them on to the motorway in the first place. They had no tax, of course, no insurance—such conventional bureaucratic necessities were anathema to Lisa, even if they had been able to afford them. Needless to say there was no provision for Anya...their flat was rented...'

Blake was frowning now.

'I suspect that, like me, Lisa had long ago forgotten asking me to be Anya's guardian and godfather, but in law that is exactly what I am, even if I am virtually a complete stranger to her.

'But if she's part of such a tight-knit community, surely they...'

'No,' Blake told her, guessing what she was about to say. 'As I said, the lives of the whole community revolve around overthrowing the government at home, and their children, while I am sure they are loved and wanted, are left very much to their own devices, and that includes in some cases not even speaking English properly, never mind attending school.

'There's no way the Social Services people would allow Anya to remain in that kind of environment. That's why I came home...'

'But you're not sure you've done the right thing,' Elizabeth guessed.

He gave her a wry smile. 'Does it show that much? I reacted impulsively, I have to admit—not always a good or wise thing to do. Legally I am responsible for Anya, nothing can change that, but the authorities, Social Services, have made it clear that they aren't too happy with the situation. For a child, any child to lose his or her parents has to be a very traumatic experience, and to add to that trauma by uprooting her from all that's familiar to her and take her to a completely unfamiliar, unknown environment, an unknown country, which is what I'd have been doing if I'd taken her back to America with me...' He shook his head.

'Fortunately my contract with Johns Hopkins had just come to an end. It would have been impossible for me to deal with the situation here from over there, so I came home...and set about looking for a new job in an environment suitable for Anya...'

Which explained the personal reasons for his taking a job which on the face of it was beneath him, Elizabeth recognised.

'Things aren't going to be easy for Anya...'

'Nor for you either,' Elizabeth commented.

He paused and looked at her. 'No,' he agreed. 'It's very easy to counsel other people not to make rash emotional decisions, but far harder to apply that advice to oneself...'

'Was there no one else who would take charge of her...someone closer to her?' Elizabeth asked him.

'No. It's either me or foster parents, and of the two the social services people have made it plain they consider foster parents to be a preferred option.

'As I said, finding a house was the least of my problems... I now need to find someone to give Anya what I am quite obviously not going to be able to give her...time,' he explained to Elizabeth. 'Time, care, reassurance and the security of a day-to-day, night-to-night dependable presence in her life. She needs that more than she needs anything else, which is just one of the reasons why I don't want her to go either into care or to foster parents. What Anya needs is someone who is prepared to be a mother substitute for her, someone who will love her and give her the security she so badly needs. So far all the agencies I've tried have only been able to come up with middle-aged housekeepers with terrifyingly formidable qualifications and references—the kind who I suspect will be more interested in keeping the house polished and immaculate than in Anya's welfare, or au pairs who will inevitably be more interested in boys than in Anya.

'What I need…what *Anya* needs is a woman who knows what it means to be a mother, someone old enough to be able to be firm and disciplined when necessary, and young enough for an eleven-year-old to relate to. She needs someone warm and loving to whom looking after her will be more than just a job…'

'I think I might know of someone,' Elizabeth told him quietly.

She saw the surprise in his eyes as he looked at her.

'A client of mine… She's all the things you've just specified; she has children of her own…two boys both at boarding-school.' Elizabeth frowned. 'Would that be a problem? When they're on holiday, I mean…?'

'No,' Blake told her. 'Not if she was the right person; in fact some contact with other children is just what I think Anya needs. But I'm not sure if a woman who sends her own sons to boarding-school…'

'It was her husband's decision, not hers, and she's keeping them there for the moment because…well…her husband committed suicide recently and left her with a lot of financial problems, including the threat of losing her home. It's all right,' Elizabeth told him with a smile. 'If you think I'm being interfering and that she isn't what you're looking for, please…'

'No. No, to be honest I'd far rather rely on your judgement than on agencies, and to be truthful she *can't* be any worse than the people I've already interviewed, so if you seriously think she might be interested…'

'I'll get in touch with her,' Elizabeth offered. 'Explain the situation and suggest that she ring you if she's interested.'

'Yes, please do. Here's my phone number... I haven't had time to get any cards done yet.'

He wrote down his phone number on a piece of paper he pulled from his pocket.

The job he was offering sounded ideal for Philippa Ryecart, Elizabeth reflected as she placed the piece of paper in her bag, and in her view Philippa would be the ideal person to take charge of his orphaned godchild. She was the kind of woman who instinctively and automatically opened her arms to life's waifs and strays, especially when they were children. She possessed that kind of warmth, that kind of genuine compassion for their need.

'What were you and Blake discussing so earnestly over dinner?' Richard asked her later as they drove home.

Elizabeth told him.

'Mmm... seems a sound enough sort of chap... Hope he doesn't find he's bitten off more than he can chew, though...'

'He's very enthusiastic about the new Accident Unit,' Elizabeth told him. 'I heard him telling David that it would be a good idea to include a facility for trauma counselling within its ambit.'

'Yes. He was saying something similar to me. Sounding me out about how I felt about it. Apparently the Northern isn't too keen on the idea of someone intruding on what it considers to be strictly its own territory, but personally I think he's right—it isn't just people's broken bodies we need to mend. Mind you, he'll have a hard time convincing David... he won't like the idea of any extra expense...'

'Well, Blake struck me as a man who's more than capable of dealing with the Davids of this world,' Elizabeth commented sagely. 'David's obviously slightly in awe of him, and he won't want to do anything that might make him think of terminating his contract. You never know, with Blake based at the General that might just be enough to swing David in its favour when it comes to the new unit...'

'Oh, yes... David's full of himself all right for having Blake at the General, but the only way he'll agree to our having the new unit is if I leave. You heard him tonight . . . saw . . .' His earlier good humour evaporated as he turned towards her. 'He wants me out, Liz; he's making that perfectly obvious.'

'He can't force you to leave . . .'

'No, but he knows damn well . . . The General needs that unit, Liz. It needs it a hell of a lot more than it needs me.'

'Oh, Richard . . .'

Dinner parties had never been events he had particularly cared for, Blake reflected; they smacked too much of people and places he would rather forget, of a lifestyle and a type of person he had always disliked.

Dinner parties had not been part of his experience as he grew up; his mother, widowed and working, had not moved in these kinds of circles. When he was a boy, dinner parties and the kind of people of who gave them had been surrounded by an aura of mystique and snobbish exclusivity, membership to a club for which he had had contempt rather than envy. When his mother had entertained, it had been informally, friends who dropped in and stayed on to eat, and in his memory the house of his childhood had always been filled with noise, laughter, conversation, good humour and good food, a home where he had sat silently listening to his mother dispensing advice, listening, talking, challenging.

Was it there that it had begun—his fascination with people's hopes and dreams—their minds?

But of course those happy childhood memories belonged to the time when his father was still alive, before his mother had become ill.

She was dead now. She had died while he was in the last year of his training, and six months after that . . . Automatically his thoughts changed path, obedient to his inner silent command.

These days dinner parties no longer held any mystique for him; they were no longer part of a world and a lifestyle which excluded him; rather now he was the one to exclude them. Their formality and self-consciousness irked and confined him; he considered them old-fashioned set pieces of stereotyped behaviour, show-pieces which brought out the worst aspects of certain types of human nature.

How, after all, could anyone expect to enjoy his or her food in such an atmosphere of contrived competitiveness? No wonder women like Grace always seemed to have such an anxious look about them.

It made him smile wryly to himself to recognise how once he would have felt not just slightly uncomfortable in such surroundings, but resentfully defensive as well.

During his years at university he had had a tendency to treat wealth and success with a certain degree of contempt and suspicion. He still didn't believe that focusing one's life on the attainment of money and status was a goal to be lauded and admired, but now his reservations were based on very different foundations.

In order to live one needed to have money; but in order to live well one needed to have something more, something that came from within the person themselves and which could not be bought.

It had taken him a long time to understand that, and even longer to be able to put it into practice. There had been years of his life which he had wasted living under a dark, bitter cloud of resentment and anger, refusing to accept that the goals he had set himself, the whole purpose of the life he was making for himself were not really his goals at all.

With hindsight it was so easy to see how self-destructive his behaviour had been, but then so many things were easy to see…with hindsight…with knowledge…with awareness.

Bleakly he closed his eyes.

He hadn't told Elizabeth the whole truth when he had responded to her interest about what had brought him here, what had made him choose to work at the General. With his connections it would have been easy enough for him to approach one of the major teaching hospitals, to take on a consultancy and go into semi-private practice; it would certainly have been far more lucrative, made far greater financial and career sense.

But something much more important to him than money and status had brought him here. When he had first seen the advertisement for the post at the General he had merely glanced at it, but when he had realised where it was . . .

He grimaced to himself, well aware of how the majority of his colleagues would have responded to an admission from him that he was allowing himself to be dictated to by fate. No, not *allowing* himself to be dictated to, simply taking advantage of the opportunity fate was offering him; there was a difference . . .

His guardianship of Anya meant that his whole life would have to be refocused, and, once he had got over the initial shock of recognising that fact, he acknowledged that it was perhaps also time for him to refocus himself inwardly as well as outwardly.

For far too long he had lived with too much of himself imprisoned in the past, his deepest emotions buried and denied because of the pain he was afraid they might cause him.

He had come back now determined to confront that past, to confront it and to lay an old ghost.

But certainly not in the biblical sense . . . His mouth curled self-derisively at the thought. No, there was scant chance that he would ever be allowed to do *that*. Or that he would want to?

He frowned away the question unanswered. What he had come back for was not to wallow in self-pity but simply to draw a line under a certain section of his life.

The past, after all, could always be analysed, understood, resolved and forgiven, but it could never truly be forgotten, deleted; and the effects of his past were woven so firmly within the fabric of his personality that to try to pull them free would be impossible.

His years in America had been good to him . . . good *for* him . . . He had gone there following his mother's death— a temporary escape at first, a place where by dint of hard work and determination he could totally transform himself and return like some mythological hero, victorious and clothed in gold; only the weight of that gold had oppressed him, its shine tarnished by the emptiness it hid and which only he could see ... and then after all there was no point in returning home—what point was there, when there was no one to recognise his success, his magnificence ... no one to marvel at and envy what he had achieved?

And so he had stayed in California, and when one of the new intake of college graduates had made it plain to him that she wanted him he had opened his arms to her and told himself that the sleekness of her suntanned body, the swing of her thick dark hair, the desire in her dark brown eyes, the lure of her sexuality and the skill with which she used it were more than adequate compensation for all that he had lost.

They had stayed together for three years and then she had left him for a man twenty years her senior, who, she had told him quite candidly, would make her a far better husband than he ever could.

He had watched from the sidelines the day she married him and had been surprised to discover how very distant he felt from what was happening ... how unmoved.

He had still been living in California the year Michael Waverly came to visit him, but he hadn't stayed on long after Mike had gone. Somehow by then the Californian lifestyle had begun to pall on him a little.

He had needed something more nourishing ... more sustaining, and so he had moved north and begun a new cycle, but he had still taken the baggage of his old self with him, only this time he had added the heavier weight of guilt.

And to some extent he still carried it. Which brought him back to Anya and the present and his determination to make sure, as far as it was within his power to do so, that he fulfilled the promise he had so carelessly given her mother.

Nothing could or would ever compensate her for the loss of her parents, but he was her only living relative and she deserved better, far, far better than that he abandon her to the impersonal care of an already overburdened Social Service.

Provided he was allowed to do so.

The situation would have been different had he been married, the social worker had told him, and he had known from her expression what she was thinking. After all, it wasn't the first time he had seen that look of critical suspicion in someone's eyes.

For a heterosexual man of his age to have remained unmarried was, he knew, unusual, giving rise to the suspicion in overly fertile minds that there might be something suspect and dangerous in his sexual inclinations, some refusal to acknowledge what he really was, and causing even the most generous and uncritical observer to question if there was perhaps some flaw in his nature that made it impossible for him to give a firm commitment to another human being, to form an emotional bond with them.

In today's modern society one of man's greatest sins was to remain emotionally detached. It was... interesting how many people confused emotional detachment with the trauma of emotions numbed by intense pain. Emotionally detached people did not live in fear of suffering a second bout of the pain they dreaded so much.

Men traditionally were not supposed to suffer that kind of pain. Their role was to inflict it and then to walk away from the destruction they had caused.

Walking away was something his sex were very good at, but, as he knew both from his work and personal experience, as a form of emotional management it wasn't very effective. You could walk away from people but you couldn't walk away from your own feelings; they went with you... and stayed with you.

He sat down on the edge of his bed and closed his eyes.

Maybe it hadn't been a good idea, coming back to Britain. It had brought back far too many memories, sharpening the focus that only years of careful self-control had managed to dull. It was pointless telling himself what he already knew: that once it was set in motion there was no turning back of life's clock, and even if there were... what could he morally have done differently...? Put his own needs first? What would that have gained him? A few brief hours of intense pleasure and the burden of years of guilt.

Then he would indeed have been playing God, and with potentially fatal consequences.

Odd that he hadn't realised until it was too late how very vulnerable he was. Even when it had happened he had assumed that the pain, although intense, would eventually go, that eventually he would love more appropriately and wisely.

He could have told Anya's social worker that his unmarried state was the result of his being distrustful of his ability to find someone to love.

'God, Blake, you really are ridiculously idealistic,' his last love had told him scornfully. 'People our age don't fall in love, not unless they're pathetically dependent ...'

She was a New Yorker, glamorous, brittle, witty, intelligent ... highly sexed, but intrinsically cold ... The kind of woman with whom he tended to form relationships because he knew that they would not look for what he could not give them.

In the end, though, it had not been their lack of mutual love which had driven them apart but his decreasing sexual desire for her.

Sex without love no longer held any appeal for him; it was an appetite he simply no longer needed to feed, and he had let it go without any regret.

She had claimed that it had been the time he had spent in Romania which had changed him, and perhaps she had been right. When he had answered the UN's call for qualified people to give their time free to help the orphaned victims of the regime he hadn't really known what to expect. The television footage shown on the news had been harrowing, particularly of the innocent children, but nothing could prepare any human being with any pretension to compassion for the gut-wrenching reality of those centuries-old eyes in the too small baby faces.

He was no stranger to people's emotional pain, but those children, babies most of them ...

It wasn't so much that it had changed his outlook on life, more that it had reinforced what he already knew and felt, compelled him to accept certain aspects of himself and his own emotional needs.

Which brought him back to Anya.

'Why do you want her?' the social worker had asked him scornfully.

Because she needs me, he could have answered, but that response was too simple and too complex. All he could have said was that he had seen in Anya's eyes that same look as in those children in Romania and that he had known that Anya needed someone of her own, someone who would invest time in loving her, not simply to repair the trauma and damage of losing her parents, but to give her something he suspected she had never known.

It was not that he thought that Lisa and Miguel had been bad parents; it was simply that other things had been more important to them. Physically, after all, they had been there for Anya, but emotionally...?

A foster home, going into care, no matter how good it was, was not the right environment for Anya. He had known that both emotionally and professionally, but Anya's social worker had also been right when she had pointed out that he could not give her the one-to-one attention he claimed she needed.

He could give her a home, a protected environment, financial security and his love, but he could not be there for her twenty-four hours a day. Finding someone who could was proving to be far more of a problem than he had envisaged—or rather finding the right *kind* of someone.

But now, thanks to Elizabeth Humphries, it looked as though his search might hopefully be over. She and Richard struck him as a well-matched couple, their relationship healthily balanced.

Richard. He frowned. He was a first-rate surgeon, admired by both his colleagues and his patients, but not evidently by David Howarth. It hadn't taken Blake long to discover David's hostility towards Richard, nor to guess at the cause of it.

His frown deepened. The last thing he needed right now was to complicate his life by becoming involved in hospital politics, but, like Richard, he was concerned that too much focus on finance and cost-cutting could ultimately lead to a dangerous and perhaps even life-threatening drop in medical standards.

David had mentioned this evening that the Minister was due to visit both hospitals.

'Officially she's the one who will make the final decision about which hospital gets the new unit, but in reality she will be relying on me to take that decision,' David had boasted to Blake.

Thoughtfully he removed his shirt and padded barefoot into his bathroom.

'You've got a very, very sexy body,' Holly had told him purringly the first time they had made love. She had used almost exactly the same words, but in a far different tone and with the added rider, 'Pity all it does is look sexy,' the last time.

Wryly he reflected how in the end none of her experienced, knowledgeable caresses had been able to arouse him to any real desire, and yet at night in his dreams, and sometimes even in his conscious hours, all it took to make him ache and throb with intense sexual need was the blurred memory of a certain face... a certain voice, her smile, her scent... her memory... the way he was beginning to ache now...

CHAPTER TWENTY-TWO

FOR four days Philippa managed to convince herself that nothing had really happened and that she had safely dismissed Joel and all that she had experienced in his arms to a small sealed container which could easily be buried beneath all the other detritus in her life, and then, five nights after they had made love, she woke up alone and aching in the dark, her face wet with tears.

What was she really crying for? she asked herself as she fought to suppress the sharp clarity of the pain that had woken her, the sense of loss, not just of her present and her future as a sexually functioning desirable woman, but her past as well.

The woman who had responded so passionately to Joel's touch was not the same woman who had lived so passively for all those years as Andrew's wife. And now, when it was too late, she could recognise just why she had crouched timidly beneath the protective cover of that passivity and acceptance for all those years; the reality of accepting her needs as a woman was acutely painful.

Now that the euphoria of expressing her sexuality so freely and so uninhibitedly was over, she was left with the cold, raw emptiness of the loneliness which had taken its place.

But Joel was another woman's husband, a woman who he believed no longer wanted him.

She wanted him, Philippa recognised. She wanted him very badly indeed.

She got up and went downstairs to make herself a cup of tea. Through the kitchen window she could see the first feeble, pale rays of light trying to break through the darkness. It seemed impossible that they would do so, and yet of course they would.

She put down her cup of tea. Was it really Joel she wanted, or just someone to cling to, someone to transfer her troubles to, someone to make her feel that her life had a viable purpose to it? Was she really so weak, so *afraid*?

Even if Joel were free to form a relationship with her, she was not free to have one with him, she acknowledged honestly; there was too much other unfinished business in her life.

And besides, she mocked herself wryly as she stood by the window and watched the first pale lemon warming of the spring sun lightening the grey sky, didn't she need to learn to love herself before she could start trying to convince herself that she loved someone else?

Five hours later, when Susie called round to invite her to go out to lunch with her, she found her halfway up a ladder cleaning windows.

'Spring-cleaning,' she commented ruefully. 'You're making me feel very guilty; I haven't touched mine yet.'

'Mmm. Well, this is more a form of therapy than good housewifeliness,' Philippa admitted as climbed down the rungs and pushed her hair off her face. She looked tired and thin, Susie noticed, but at the same time there was a new determination about her, a new energy.

'Therapy?' Susie quizzed her and then added teasingly, 'What you need is a new man in your life, not——'

She broke off, appalled by her own lack of tact when she saw the look of pain that crossed Philippa's eyes.

'Oh, Pip, I'm sorry,' she apologised. 'I didn't mean to be so tactless—I know Andrew was...'

'It isn't Andrew,' Philippa stopped her. She made a faint grimace. 'Even I can't be that much of a hypocrite. You know how Andrew and I lived, Susie, what our relationship was.' She got up and walked over to the sink, keeping her back to her friend as she told her, 'It never really bothered me that Andrew and I didn't have much of a sex life; to be blunt about it, I was almost glad.

'It's odd, isn't it, how things change? Ten years ago the worst thing you could possibly admit to was having a low sex drive. Any woman who couldn't manage to have an orgasm to order, never mind admitting that she didn't even want to, would have been classed by her peers as an oddity— a complete failure.

'I was almost grateful to Andrew for not wanting to discuss the lack of sexual desire between us; it made it easier for me to pretend that I was just like everyone else.

'Fashions change, though, don't they, and now it's almost acceptable for a woman to lay claim to a certain amount of loss of libido, provided she can back it up with the combined demands of a high-profile career, motherhood and if possible half a dozen other balls to juggle in the air as well?'

She turned round and gave Susie a smile that was half rueful and half sad. 'The trouble with me is that I never seem to quite make it in step with fashion...'

Susie digested and unravelled her small speech and then said carefully, 'If you're trying to tell me that you've met someone else and that you want to have sex with him——'

'Wanted to and have done,' Philippa interrupted her, and then added gravely, 'But that's as far as it goes. He's married and if I'm honest with myself I know that at least half the reason the sex between us was so...so explosive was because of our joint need...

'That's the trouble with our sex, isn't it, Susie? We have sex with a man and suddenly we have to invest what is really only a physical act with a full battery of emotional baggage.'

'You mean he took you to bed and then dropped you?' Susie demanded angrily. 'What a rat! He...'

'No... It wasn't like that. I...he...I was the one who said that it couldn't go any further. It shouldn't have gone as far as it did.'

Her eyes filled with tears as she said softly, 'He was so tender, Susie, so loving, so giving; he made me feel so...so sexually strong and powerful. He made me realise something that all those years of marriage to Andrew never did.

I woke up last night aching for him...wanting him... envying, hating his wife almost, wondering how on earth she could be so indifferent, so unmoved by a man who is such a wonderful lover...'

'He could be lying to you, Pip,' Susie warned her gently. 'Men do, you know, especially when...'

'When they want to get you into bed. Yes, I *know*...' Susie's expression lightened as Philippa laughed.

'No...it wasn't like that. It wasn't planned or contrived and I already knew, despite his gallant attempts to deny it, that he loves his wife.

'And even if he didn't, the last thing I want is to be responsible for the break-up of someone else's marriage. It's just...it's just that it hurts so much knowing how good what we had together was and knowing that it can never happen again. Logically I know that it's only my body that aches and yearns for him, Susie, but because I'm a woman...'

'And because right now you're far too damned vulnerable,' Susie supplied for her. 'Oh, Pip, I'm so sorry...'

Philippa shook her head and gave her a brief smile. 'Don't be. I'm not. Not really. Even while I was lying in bed crying for him this morning, a part of me was...' She stopped and shook her head. 'When I was in my teens I had a mammoth crush on a friend of my brother's. When he rejected me and I married Andrew I thought my sexuality was something that only my first love could arouse. Discovering that I was wrong is like being set free from an imprisoning cage.

'It's hard to explain properly, but I feel as though the control of my sexuality, which subconsciously I believed I had handed over to him, has been returned to me. That I am now the one who can choose and decide to whom I do and don't respond.'

'It's all right,' she assured her friend when she saw the way she was looking at her. 'Right now I feel bad, but I know that it's something that will pass, like a bad bout of flu.

'Even if Joel were free to have a relationship with me, it's too soon for me. There are things I need to do, problems I need to resolve first, emotionally as well as practically.

'Don't feel sad for me, Susie—I can do that all too well for myself—it isn't pity I need, it's love. Yes,' Philippa laughed now, 'love.'

'There, that should be OK now.'

Joel smiled reassuringly at the small tow-headed boy whose bike he had just been fixing, dusting off the knees of his jeans before getting up to watch him ride off.

He was going to be late home—again, he acknowledged as he walked across the leisure centre car park and unlocked the door of his car.

It had felt good knowing that he could afford to pay for things like petrol for his car himself.

'Where did you get the money for these?' Sally had demanded when he had taken her home some flowers. Her voice had been full of suspicion, destroying his pleasure in being able to afford to give her the small gift.

'I earned it,' he had told her. 'Remember I told you last week that one of the parents had asked me to give her little girl some private swimming lessons?'

'Estelle just doesn't seem to be getting anywhere with her swimming,' the woman had confided to him as she'd stood watching him coach her son. 'We've just become members at the new private health club that's opened at Deighton Hall, and I hear they've got a pool there and I was wondering if you gave private swimming lessons.'

He had bought the flowers on impulse on his way home, remembering how Sally's face used to glow with pleasure when she arranged the flowers she had occasionally bought herself, confessing that they were a treat she hadn't been able to resist; but instead of being pleased she had almost thrown the flowers down on to the kitchen worktop, threatening their delicate stems, her face flushed with temper and her mouth tight as she'd criticised him for wasting money.

In the town centre the traffic lights were on red and, as he waited for them to change he glanced to his right and the road which led to Philippa's house.

'We mustn't see each other again,' she had said, and although the firm tone of her voice had told him that she meant it he had seen the way her mouth trembled slightly and her eyes grew shadowed. 'And Sally—your wife—you love her,' she had told him.

The lights changed and quickly, before he could give in to the temptation, he drove straight on.

It wasn't just sex that made his thoughts turn to Philippa at odd times during the day and, even more betrayingly, when he lay awake beside Sally at night. He had liked her honesty and her humour, the way she sat watching him so attentively while she listened to him.

No, it wasn't just the small throaty cries of pleasure she had given when he had touched her, nor the way she had touched him.

'It doesn't mean anything', she had told him. 'It was just sex', and he had known that she was lying, that what was there between them could, if they allowed it to do so, become far, far more than physical lust.

He could feel his throat tightening with pain and an aching sense of loss. It didn't matter how hard he tried to reach out to Sally these days; all she did was reject him.

In the peace of Philippa's kitchen and in the warmth of her bed he had found a pleasure and sense of relaxation he had long ago forgotten existed, simply holding her and talking to her, knowing that he would be listened to, that his opinions and views were valued, that he was valued; he had felt a sense of companionship with her, of closeness to her, that had brought into painfully sharp focus the emptiness of his relationship with Sally.

'You've got a wife...children', Philippa had told him softly.

He had known what she was saying.

Six months ago he would have shrugged aside her comment, telling her that his children barely knew he existed, that it was their mother they related to, but now things were different and yet Sally was still just as critical of his relationship with them now as she had been in the days when she used to accuse him of not taking enough interest in them and not spending enough time with them, of being jealous of them; only now she complained that he spoiled them and undermined her authority over them.

In fact, she had changed so much recently that she no longer seemed like his Sally, the girl he had fallen in love with and married.

Sally tensed as she heard Joel opening the kitchen door.

She was constantly on edge in his presence these days, terrified that she would somehow betray herself and that he would guess what she was doing, and yet, at the same time as she feared his discovery of her relationship with Kenneth, another part of her felt very let down and angry because he was so oblivious to what was happening to her, to the fear and panic that swept over her like lightning, piercing the dull, thick cloud of an oppressive, overcast sky, sharply illuminating changes she would really rather not have seen.

Some days she felt as though the Sally who was so drawn to Kenneth was someone who wasn't really a part of her, but rather a dangerous stranger who took over the real Sally, and then at other times it was her life with Joel that didn't seem real.

Sometimes when she looked at Joel she was overwhelmed by a feeling of panic, of her life being out of control, and the small, tight pain inside her became a huge, enveloping feeling of anger and resentment against Joel for being so oblivious to what was happening to her, for being deaf and blind to the fact that another man wanted to take her away from him.

But then Joel wasn't really interested in her feelings, was he? The leisure centre and the new friends he had made there—that was all he wanted to talk about.

A small knife-sharp pain twisted inside her as she remembered a comment one of the other nurses had made the previous day.

Everyone knew that Donna fancied herself and that she was a bit of a man-eater, always hinting at having men running after her, and normally Sally didn't pay much attention to anything she said, but yesterday she had made a point of seeking Sally out and saying purringly to her, 'I saw your Joel down at the leisure centre yesterday... he certainly looks good in a pair of swimming-trunks, doesn't he? I wouldn't mind getting a few private lessons from him myself,' she had added.

Joel had always been an attractive man and Sally had never been blind to the looks he attracted from other women, but this was the first time she had actually felt threatened—and upset by another woman's interest in him.

And yet why should she be? Surely the very best thing that could happen now was for Joel to find someone else. That way she would be free to go to Kenneth without feeling any guilt.

'You are going to be mine,' Kenneth had promised her. 'I won't let you go. I need you, Sally,' he had told her.

Once Joel and the children had needed her, but not any more. These days they scarcely seemed aware of her existence, she recognised bitterly.

Watching their children with Joel, she felt sometimes as though she was an outsider, invisible and unwanted, and her feelings gave her a frightening feeling of disorientation, of not, somehow, actually existing.

It was Kenneth who made her feel real... who made her feel she was important to him.

'But how will they manage without me?' she had whispered to Kenneth when he'd told her that he wanted her to leave Joel.

'How will *I*?' he had asked her in return.

'You're late,' she told Joel, interrupting the conversation he had been having with Cathy.

The look in his eyes as he glanced at her over their daughter's head hurt her somehow.

'I'm sorry,' Joel apologised quietly. 'Neil wanted to discuss a new training programme he wants to try with me and——'

'And that was far more important than getting back here so that I could leave for work on time,' Sally interrupted him bitterly. 'It's all right for you, Joel—you can do as you please; your time's your own. I don't have that choice— I have to go out to work...'

Sally actually loved nursing and she enjoyed the companionship of the other medical staff, but with the family financially dependent on her, and the increasing talk of cuts having to be made and of jobs being lost, didn't Joel realise how frightened and alone she felt?

She had always loved her home, too, but these days it didn't somehow feel as though it was hers any more.

It was Joel who had suggested that it might be an idea to put up a dado rail in the living-room and to redecorate it, Joel who had noticed that the bathroom tiles needed regrouting and suggested that it might be an idea to consider replacing their shower with a modern and efficient one.

'And how are we supposed to pay for that?' she had demanded.

The phone rang just as she was putting on her coat and she froze as Joel went to answer it. She saw him frown and then replace the receiver with a brief shrug.

'Who was it?' she asked him nervously.

Did her voice sound as rough and anxious to him as it did to her?

Apparently not, because there was not a trace of any suspicion or concern in Joel's voice when he told her carelessly, 'I don't know; they hung up. Must have been a wrong number.'

Kenneth; it had to be Kenneth. He had rung several times at home already even though she had begged him not to do so.

As Joel looked across at Sally he was suddenly made aware again of just how tired and pale she looked.

As he watched her she lifted her hand and pushed her hair back off her face. A painful knot of emotion tightened inside him.

'Sal...'

Warily she looked at him.

'It's your day off tomorrow. Why don't we go out some-where together...just the two of us?'

'Go somewhere? How can we?' She sighed. 'Have you really forgotten what I've got to do tomorrow, Joel?'

He was frowning now, the warmth gone from his voice, leaving it sharp with irritation.

'You're not still going on about your sister's damn wall-paper, are you? I told you. I am *not* redoing it...'

'Then *I'll* have to, won't I?'

'Sally,' Joel protested wearily, 'you...'

But it was too late; she was already halfway out of the door and plainly not interested in listening to whatever he had to say.

Didn't she realise how it would make him look if she went ahead and did it—how it would make that sister of hers crow? Couldn't she just for once have supported him...taken his side...seen his point of view instead of immediately siding with her sister, without even bothering to listen to him?

Sally felt as though Joel was a stranger to her these days, a different man from the one she had married—a different man even from the one who had been made redundant from Kilcoyne's.

He had been so unhappy, unable to talk or think about anything else. Now, though, Joel didn't seem to care any longer that he was out of work; he sang and whistled in the house, joked with the children, laughed and played with them in a way she had never known him do before.

He actually seemed to be enjoying life, as though...as though... As she struggled with her thoughts, fresh tears filled her eyes.

Once he would never have let her leave the house like that with an argument between them unresolved. Once he would have been the one to go to Daphne's and redo the wallpapering; once he would have been the first to notice that something was wrong and to demand to know what it was. Once he would have been immediately aware and suspicious of Kenneth's presence in her life; once he had thrown the warmth of his protection and his love around her as possessively as he had thrown his leg over her body in bed at night, drawing her close to him, securing her to him.

She shivered suddenly. He slept with his back to her now, leaving a cold, empty space in the bed between them.

Once he had told her that he would love and look after her forever.

Silently Joel watched as Sally carefully assembled everything she would need.

She hadn't spoken to him once this morning, studiously ignoring him, just as she had ignored the cup of tea he had made her, making herself a fresh one instead.

His irritation clashed with the guilt he was feeling.

He wished now he had never given in to that crazy impulse to ignore his suspicion that he was hanging the wallpaper the wrong way, but he was dammed if he was going to back down and give Daphne the triumph of belittling him a second time. Couldn't Sally see that her sister was just using him ... them; couldn't she see just how she was playing into her hands by giving in to her?

He looked across at her. She had her back to him, and she looked tired and vulnerable, her shoulders slightly hunched. A feeling of pain and guilt swept over him. He put down his mug and walked over to her.

'All right, Sal,' he told her quietly. 'I'll do it. You...'

Angrily Sally whirled round. 'Oh, no, you won't,' she told him. 'Do you think I'd risk letting you touch that wallpaper after what you did the first time?'

She was over-reacting, Sally knew, but she couldn't help it. She was so tired and so confused that all she wanted to do was to spend the day in bed, safe from the rest of the world and all her problems. She knew that a part of her had been deliberately trying to goad and force Joel to do the wallpapering for her, and yet now that he had said that he would she felt irrationally angry with him, as though somehow by giving in to her he was in some way letting her down. As though he cared so little for her that it was easier to give in to her than to ask her what was wrong.

Joel did not care . . . it was like receiving an electric shock direct to her heart; it jerked violently against her breastbone and then started to thud frantically at high speed.

'I don't want you going anywhere near my sister's wall-papering,' she heard herself saying shakily to him. 'And I don't want you coming anywhere near me either,' she added, checking him as he took a step towards her.

She waited for Joel to say something, to explode and demand an explanation, but instead he simply looked at her. At her and then through her, she recognised numbly, as though she were a stranger—no, she corrected herself, as though she simply did not exist.

And then he turned away from her and walked over to the table, picking up his jacket and his car keys.

'Joel, where are you going?' Panic sharpened her voice but Joel didn't even turn round to look at her as he responded flatly,

'What the hell do you care?'

CHAPTER TWENTY-THREE

JOEL drove around for two hours before finally giving in and doing what he had wanted to do, ached to do from the moment he had closed the back door behind him and driven away.

He saw the shock on her face as Philippa opened the door to him—and he saw something else as well.

She made no attempt to resist him as he took her in his arms, gathering her up against himself with gentle care. She felt slender and fragile, warm and softly woman-scented.

His body trembled with the fight to control his emotions as he kissed her with tender restraint and then kissed her again with no restraint at all when he felt her response to him.

'I had to see you,' he told her as he held her, kissing the top of her head, wrapping her tightly in his arms as though he never intended to let her go. But ultimately he would have to let her go, Philippa recognised; ultimately they would have to let one another go.

'You shouldn't be here,' she told him. 'We agreed——'

'That we couldn't be lovers,' Joel interrupted her. His hands cupped her face, tilting it upwards so that he could look down at her. 'But we can still talk, can't we? Still be ... friends ...?'

'Oh, Joel. This ... this thing between us isn't really real, you know,' she told him sadly. 'It's ... it's just a ... a fantasy...a...a mirage we've both conjured up because...'

'Oh, it's real to me,' Joel said fiercely. 'As real as the way I feel when I hold you in my arms ... as real as the ache in my body when I lie awake wanting you at night ...'

'You mustn't say that to me... You're married... No matter how strong my feelings for you were, I couldn't live with the knowledge that I'd broken up your marriage...'

'What marriage?' Joel asked her bitterly. 'Sally and I don't have a marriage any more. You can't break up something that no longer exists.'

Philippa could feel herself weakening. The feel of his body next to hers, the now dangerously familiar male scent of him, the warmth of him, his need and emotion were like a drug to her senses, senses which she was only just beginning to recognise that she had deliberately denied and starved into virtual non-existence for years in an attempt to conform to others' demands of her; a betrayal of herself as a woman.

She knew how much she wanted Joel, but she knew as well how vulnerable she was; habit had made her cautious, wary of expecting too much for herself.

Instinct told her that, no matter how much Joel might believe now that he wanted her, no matter how strongly he might believe that his marriage was dead, he still loved his wife. He had released her face and was holding one of her hands, lifting it to his mouth, gently caressing her palm and then her wrist with his lips.

'Don't send me away,' he begged her.

'Come into the kitchen,' Philippa told him, weakening, hoping that the more mundane workaday atmosphere there might ease the intensity of the sexual tension she could feel building between them. Here in the hallway with the stairs behind her and her mind and body already flooded with awareness of him, as well as the potency of her memories of their previous lovemaking, it would be all too tempting to turn round and take him by the hand, to give in to the need she knew they were both feeling.

'I know what you're thinking,' Joel told her drily as she offered him a cup of tea. 'But I didn't come here looking for sex. No matter what Sally seems to think, that's not... Every time I try to touch her or hold her she accuses me of wanting sex, as though it's some kind of punishment

I'm inflicting on her...some kind of payment she has to make...

'She lies there next to me, her body tense and unmoving, willing me to get it over with. That's sex; that's what our relationship has been reduced to. What you and I shared...

'I'd forgotten how good it feels to hold a woman who's warm and responsive, who wants you as much as you want her, who doesn't turn her head away when you kiss her, or tense her body when you touch her.'

Philippa could feel her throat starting to ache as she listened to him. Did he realise how much he was betraying with every word he said? She could hear the anger in his voice when he spoke of his wife's lack of response to him, and she could hear the yearning and the pain as well.

Stupid, stupid and totally irrational of her to feel jealous of this unknown woman, and yet totally predictable that she should, as well.

Joel eventually shook his head. 'I'm sorry; you can't want to hear all this.'

She ought not to want to hear it, Philippa acknowledged, if only from a sense of self-preservation, but there was a morbid, self-destructive fascination in hearing about Joel's marriage, his relationship with his wife.

'All relationships suffer...change when there's a switch in their power base.' Philippa smiled as she saw the way Joel was watching her. 'I'm trying to be detached now,' she admitted wryly. 'To...to listen to you as a friend and not as...'

'A lover,' Joel supplied for her. 'I didn't plan what happened between us, Philippa, but it wasn't just a knee-jerk reaction to the fact that you were there and I wanted sex. If it were just sex I wanted, there are plenty...' He caught himself up. The last thing he wanted was for Philippa to think he was the kind of man who needed to brag about his sexuality, but there had been enough subtle and sometimes not so subtle come-ons from other women over the years for him to know that he could have quite easily found elsewhere the sexual satisfaction his marriage no longer gave him, if he had really wanted to.

That was what hurt, he acknowledged: the fact that Sally relentlessly accused him of being sexually obsessed when the reality was that for him sexual desire had to be accompanied by something deeper; and he had thought that Sally knew that.

'I suppose you think the same as Sally—that I'm a selfish, thoughtless bastard who——'

'No,' Philippa interrupted him, shaking her head. 'It's just that as a woman...' She paused. Her marriage was not his, and to tell him that she too knew what it was like to lie intimately sexually entwined with a man with her body while her mind and emotions remained totally unengaged would be to open doors she preferred to keep closed. 'As a woman,' she continued, 'I know that it isn't always easy trying to combine so many different roles, especially when one of those roles involves being a mother...'

'I sometimes used to feel that our kids—especially Paul— meant far more to Sally than I did,' Joel admitted.

'Fathers often do feel a little bit jealous of their sons,' Philippa commented.

'Did *your* husband?'

She paused and then answered honestly, 'I don't know... Andrew and I never discussed our feelings. *I* was the one who wanted children; he...he never seemed to have any strong feelings for them one way or the other...' Or for me, she could have added, but she stopped herself, not wanting to sound self-pitying, and besides, wasn't at least half the truth that she and Andrew had never talked about their feelings because there hadn't been any real feelings between them to discuss—something she had always known and yet been afraid of confronting, preferring inertia to action, passive acceptance to passionate aggression?

'Sally and I used to talk a lot once... In bed at night after we'd...she used to lie there in my arms and tell me about her day... That all stopped once Paul was born. He was a difficult baby, restless at night, never wanting to go down, and she used to complain that if we made any noise we'd wake him up.

'Even when we made love all she seemed to want to do was to get it over with as quickly and quietly as possible.

'But at least then she still needed me...I could still support her...all of them... Now...'

'Can't you see, Joel?' Philippa told him gently. 'Her anger is because she's afraid...because she feels insecure...because she's worried about the way you're taking over her role...'

The baffled look he gave her made Philippa smile slightly.

'I'm just doing what she wants me to do...'

'Yes, but you're also usurping her role within the family, just as with her going out to work to support you all you feel she's usurping yours. It's like...it's like when someone does something for us that we're supposed to be grateful for... Logically we know we *should* be grateful, but inside a tiny part of us resents them for it, and knowing we feel that resentment makes us feel mean and uncomfortable with ourselves... None of us likes admitting to the darker side of our nature, even though we've all got one.

'I used to feel that my husband never gave our children enough time and attention, and yet I know that deep down inside me a part of me was secretly pleased that it was me they turned to and me they wanted, even though I knew that they needed love and attention from both of us.

'It's the same for all of us, whether we want to admit it or not; I suppose we're all programmed to feel protective and possessive about certain aspects of our most personal lives, about the things we do that give us status, if you like, in our own eyes. While we're quite happy to compete in a broader circle, when it comes to our most intimate relationships we each want and need to feel confident of supremacy in our own particular sphere.

'That's why it's so difficult for any of us to adapt to the kind of role reversal you and Sally are having to go through. Think about it, Joel. Deep down inside, aren't you perhaps just a little bit resentful of the fact that Sally is able to work and support you all, even though logically you know you should feel grateful for the fact that she can...?'

He was quiet for so long that Philippa thought she had gone too far, pressed on him too hard, but when he lifted his head and looked at her she expressed her pent-up breath in a small, leaky sigh of relief.

'Yes,' he admitted. 'Yes, I suppose I am...'

'And it's the same for Sally. She *knows* she needs your support at home and that she can't do everything but at the same time she feels hurt because she feels that you and the children no longer seem to need her.'

'She might be hurt because of the kids, but not because of me,' Joel denied.

'When a woman withdraws sexually from a man it doesn't necessarily mean that she's stopped loving him,' Philippa told him, but she saw from his expression that she hadn't sounded as positive as she would have liked and that he had picked up on her real feelings.

'Talk to her, Joel,' she urged him. 'Talk to her the way you've just talked to me...ask her why...what's wrong... Surely your marriage is worth that much of an effort...'

'And trying to work things out with Sally will stop me coming round here and pestering you...is that it?'

'No...no...' She could see the pain in his eyes. He deserved her honesty, Philippa recognised, both of them deserved it.

'It would be the easiest thing in the world to let what's started between us develop into... Until I met you I'd never thought of myself as a sexually hungry woman; far from it.

'I don't know whether to be ashamed of how much I want you or proud of it, but on balance feeling proud wins out. And I know myself well enough to guess that if a sexual relationship developed between us I'd become emotionally committed to you as well, emotionally dependent on you, and that wouldn't be healthy for either of us. Can't you see, Joel, that both of us, for different reasons, would be using what we have between us to cover up other problems, to avoid dealing with them...? We'd be using each other as a means of escape, and to me that would be the worst kind of betrayal—of ourselves and each other.

'It isn't that I don't care, but that I'm afraid of caring too much and for all the wrong reasons. What was it that first attracted you to your Sally, Joel...?'

He paused and then told her quietly, 'Her gentleness; the fact that she needed me...looked up to me, I suppose...it made me feel good...it made me feel...'

'Valued and wanted,' Philippa supplied for him. 'And now it's my need that your senses and emotions are responding to, but it's still Sally you love.'

'No,' Joel denied, but his voice lacked the conviction it had held earlier when he had told her that his marriage was over.

'It's time for you to go,' Philippa told him gently.

She walked with him to the front door and paused while he turned to her and took her in his arms.

'We would have been good together, you and I,' he told her huskily.

'Yes,' she agreed. Her throat ached and her mouth trembled as he lowered his own to touch it, but she didn't try to turn away.

Tears burned behind her closed eyelids, her ears buzzing with the agonised cry of her silenced emotions. She neither moved nor touched him, making no attempt to hold on to him or keep him, but her lips clung betrayingly to his for a handful of seconds after their kiss ended, and she knew that if he pushed her now, if he begged her or pleaded, she wouldn't have the strength to resist him. She suspected he knew it too.

But he *didn't* say or do anything other than simply touch her mouth with his fingertips in a silent gesture of farewell before opening the door and walking away from her.

The phone started to ring as she walked back to the kitchen. She picked up the receiver, automatically forcing herself to sound bright and optimistic, using the lessons learned over the weeks of her widowhood. 'Never mind love thy neighbour,' Susie had once told her grimly. 'It's love thyself that really matters.' Love herself, value herself, depend on herself, know herself—because her own self was all that stood between her and the rest of the world now, Philippa admitted.

She recognised Elizabeth Humphries' voice before the other woman gave her name, her stomach tensing with familiar apprehension. Like her mind, her body had learned to dread the arrival of unheralded visitors and telephone calls, of letters and bills.

'The reason I'm ringing,' Elizabeth told her, 'is that the other evening at a dinner party I was talking with a colleague of my husband's who has just moved into the area and he was telling me about the problems he's having finding someone suitable to employ to take charge of both his orphaned god-daughter and his home.

'He stressed that he didn't want either a nanny or a traditional housekeeper but someone who could be to his god-daughter a sort of surrogate-mother figure, without usurping the role of the child's dead mother... He wants someone who can act on her own initiative and who is used to dealing with children; someone the child can relate to and whom he can trust not just to look after her physically, but to help her emotionally as well.

'It immediately occurred to me that you would be perfect for such a role.'

'Me? But I don't have any qualifications for that kind of thing,' Philippa protested. 'I'm not...'

'You're a mother,' Elizabeth reminded her, and added drily, 'And reading between the lines, as well as going on my own judgement, I'd say you are more than adequately qualified for the role he's got in mind. He stressed to me that he considers it far more important that whoever he employs is more concerned about his god-daughter's emotional welfare than running a spotlessly clean house; that he wants someone young enough to be a mother figure to the girl and old enough to be left completely in charge of her.'

'You said she was orphaned...'

'Yes,' Elizabeth agreed.

Philippa hesitated. She could all too easily imagine the trauma such a child must be experiencing and the anxiety of the man apparently responsible for her.

'I...I don't know... A child like that would need someone who could make a long-term commitment to her. Has he— her godfather—has he no wife, no female relatives?'

'Apparently not. I'm not trying to push you into something you don't wish to do, and of course it will be the child's needs that come first; her godfather was quite adamant about that. He did say, however, that if you proved suitable he would be quite willing for you to have both your boys with you during the school holidays; in fact he seemed to think that would be a plus point—company for his goddaughter. He's got a large house with plenty of room to spare. The salary he mentioned is a good one; the girl is eleven and of course in full-time schooling so you would have some free time on your hands to study for that Open University course you discussed with me.'

'I... I don't know what to say,' Philippa admitted. 'It...it would solve a lot of my problems. I still haven't heard from the bank about the house, though...'

'Well, think about it,' Elizabeth counselled her. 'I've got his telephone number here if you want it; I left it with him that you'd telephone and make an appointment for an interview if you were interested. He knows something of your circumstances, by the way—not the full details, just the fact that you've recently been widowed and your financial situation; as a potential employer...'

'Yes, yes, of course...a housekeeper. I'd never thought...'

'Rather more than just a housekeeper,' Elizabeth corrected her firmly. 'I think you'll find he will place far more emphasis on how you will relate to his god-daughter than how well you can run a home, although I suspect that, like most men, he won't be averse to finding that his house is both well-run and comfortable; and, of course, his position at the hospital will mean that he could be involved in a certain amount of domestic entertaining, but that is something you would have to discuss with him if and when you meet him. It would be quite a challenge,' Elizabeth remarked.

'Oh...does he have a very large house? I...'

'Not the house, the little girl. Apparently he had quite a battle with the Social Services to convince them that he was the best person to take charge of her. There was a great deal of talk of placing her with foster parents. Of course, they're bound to be jittery these days about the wisdom of placing any child, male or female, into sole male care, and I suspect he's very conscious of the need to provide her with the right kind of female companionship and care.

'I wouldn't have recommended you for the job if I hadn't genuinely thought you could do it,' Elizabeth told her quietly.

Eleven years old and orphaned, both her parents lost to her, poor child; Philippa could all too easily imagine the pain and fear she must be suffering.

She had always wanted another child, a girl...a daughter... She grimaced at her own sentimentality.

This child would *not* be her child, her daughter...they might not even get on... The godfather might not even like or want her.

'Do you want his number?' Elizabeth asked.

Philippa's mouth had gone dry.

'Yes. Yes, please,' she told her.

'What are you looking so pleased about?' Richard asked as he walked into the sitting-room and found his wife sitting in a chair with a very self-satisfied smile on her mouth.

'Nothing...well, if you must know, I was just congratulating myself on being a wonderful judge of character,' she told him, grinning at him.

'Such modesty... Why? What have you done?'

'You remember your new psychiatrist saying the other evening that he was looking for someone to take charge of his orphaned god-daughter...?'

'Vaguely,' Richard admitted.

'Well, I'd thought of the perfect person, but, as I knew she would, she protested that she didn't think she was up to the job, until I pointed out to her how much the little girl needed her.

'She's one of these women with too soft a heart for her own good. Securing her own financial future couldn't sway her judgement, but believing that another human being needed her could and did.'

'Didn't that used to be called emotional blackmail?' Richard asked her drily.

'Not by me,' Elizabeth assured him. 'I look upon it more as finding the right piece for the right place in a particularly complicated jigsaw...'

She laughed as she heard Richard murmuring under his breath, 'Egomaniac,' as he left the room.

She didn't normally indulge herself by playing *Deus ex machina* with other people's lives—her training had taught her the dangers of doing that—but in this instance...

'I've got an interview for a job...well, potentially at least,' Philippa announced after Susie had picked up the phone.

She had dialled her friend's number almost immediately she had finished speaking with Elizabeth, and now quickly she explained to her friend what had happened.

'It sounds perfect for you,' Susie told her enthusiastically. 'Ring him up now, and if you don't I'll come round and stand over you until you do.'

Happily Philippa started to dial the number Elizabeth had given her, a rush of nervous anticipation singing through her body.

CHAPTER TWENTY-FOUR

DEBORAH stared bleakly round the silent flat. It had been three weeks and even now sometimes she still forgot, still opened the door and expected to see Mark there, still thought she heard his footsteps...still thought she could smell him next to her in bed at night.

At work, of course, she had to pretend that she didn't care, to smile dismissively when people asked her if she still heard from him or if she knew how he was getting on.

She was under no illusions about the reasons for their curiosity. The news of their split, so quickly followed by Mark's departure from the partnership, had obviously been a subject of intense speculation and gossip.

She still felt numbed by it all; not just by his ending of their relationship but by the speed with which he had completely disappeared from her life.

The partnership had let him go without insisting on his serving out any period of notice; he had removed his things from the flat that same day, having told her that he had found work with an agency.

He had been in touch with her only once, leaving a message on their—now her—answering machine with a forwarding address for his mail.

His address and a telephone number. In case she changed her mind and gave in...left the partnership; accepted the limitations he had put on their future...on *her* future.

Tears blurred her eyes. Only she knew how much she had been tempted to do just that, but how could she? She knew herself too well. It would never work if she did that. Sooner rather than later she would start to lose not just her respect for him but her respect for herself as well.

'You don't need me,' Mark had said bitterly, but he had been wrong. She did need him, and that was what hurt her most of all: the fact he had not recognised and understood the need; the fact that he had allowed himself to be blinded to that need by the opinions and false judgements of others.

The fact that she had been promoted while he had not had made no difference to the way she valued him. Even though he had accused her of treating him differently, of reinforcing his own growing sense of 'coming second' in their relationship, it was simply not true. She had never felt like that about him. He was the one who...

Tiredly she shook her head. What was the point in going over and over what had been said? Mark had gone and the only way they could be together again would be for her to capitulate to his terms. It wasn't pride that stopped her and it certainly wasn't ambition...her career... No, it was more than that. It was the knowledge that in giving up her job and allowing him to dictate the terms of their relationship she would be helping him to destroy something very precious and rare—and she would be destroying herself as well. To give up her job would demean her as a human being...as a woman, just as Mark had claimed that having to take second place to her at work had demeaned him.

Angry tears filled her eyes; desolately she brushed them away.

Ryan had been openly contemptuous of Mark's departure from the office. Whenever he asked about what he was doing, she parried his questions—or ignored them.

Despite her insistence to Mark that Ryan had offered her promotion on merit alone, she was beginning to feel increasingly wary of doing or saying anything that might lead Ryan to believe that she wanted anything other than a strictly professional relationship with him.

Bitterly she told herself that there was one point at least on which both Ryan and Mark thought alike, and that was that sexually she was vulnerable to Ryan.

Both of them were wrong. No matter how sexually frustrated she might feel—and she did—going to bed with Ryan was the last thing she was likely to do.

He kept on subtly pressuring her, though, full of praise for her one moment, fiercely critical of her the next, slowly isolating her from her peers, she recognised, publicly making it plain that she was *his* personal protégée...his personal property, ostensibly elevating and supporting her, but at the same time subtly undermining her position with the others.

And yet there was nothing he had said or done that she could actually complain about. He was far too subtle for that.

Only yesterday, when he had rebuked her in public, treating her as though she were a mere junior, she had challenged him about her promotion.

'You're still on trial—remember,' he had warned her silkily. 'Nothing's official...yet.'

Silently Deborah had digested that warning along with the unpalatable suspicions that went with it. She knew she was good at her job; she knew she had earned and deserved her promotion. But now Ryan seemed to be teasing her with it like an adult offering and then withholding a bag of sweets.

The comparison was too uncomfortable for her to dwell on too deeply.

It was Friday evening and the weekend loomed emptily ahead of her. She missed Mark so much. Ached for him, emotionally, mentally and physically, but how could she pay the price he had set on their love? *His* love. Hers was given freely, unconditionally—too freely and too unconditionally?

She walked into the bedroom and took off her office suit, changing into leggings and a loose sweater.

In the hallway were the cans of paint she had bought on the way home. Grimly she surveyed the bedroom walls. 'Right,' she told the room grittily. 'This time tomorrow you'll look so different I won't be able to come in here and see Mark everywhere.'

She looked at the bed. She had even bought new bedding. Hers still smelled of Mark, she swore, even though she had washed it a number of times since he had gone.

She went into the kitchen and opened the fridge door, grimacing as she remembered that she had forgotten to buy food. A forlorn bottle of wine caught her eye. She reached for it.

She ought to be in the bedroom painting, not lying here on the settee drinking wine, Deborah told herself severely.

She was, she admitted to herself, distinctly tipsy. Tipsy? She was damn near drunk, she corrected herself.

The doorbell rang, the sound cutting sharply through the silence of the flat, reinforcing her awareness of her loneliness.

The doorbell... Mark... She swung her feet to the floor and got up hurriedly, grimacing as she almost lost her balance and fell over.

Mark... Mark had come back. She hurried to open the door.

'Dee... Hi... how are you? Where's Mark?'

'Garth...'

Stupidly Deborah stepped back to let her visitor come in.

Garth Preston and Mark had been in the same year at university and the three of them had been close friends, spending a great deal of time in one another's company until Garth had gone to work abroad. Now they kept in touch via sporadic letters and even more sporadic visits from Garth whenever he came home.

'Mark's gone,' Deborah told him and then suddenly she was crying, crying like a baby, while Garth scooped her up in his arms and carried her over to the settee.

He was shorter than Mark but still taller than she was and chunkily built, square-bodied and square-faced with thick, curly dark hair and innocently round blue eyes.

Women loved him, and he loved them. Unlike Ryan, he did not deliberately set out to seduce, and unlike Ryan he did genuinely love his victims, for victims they were, as Mark and Deborah had often agreed, because as quickly as Garth fell in love so too did he fall out of it, and in love with the next adoring woman to catch his eye.

Not that that stopped Deborah from liking him. You couldn't not like Garth. He was that kind of man.

'Mark's gone...gone where?' he asked her.

'Gone...' Deborah repeated tearfully. 'Gone...left... He doesn't want me any more...'

Fresh tears fell...It must be the wine she had drunk that was making her react like this, she told herself muzzily. This just wasn't her...she just *wasn't* the 'tears and helpless vulnerability' type. Her feelings were normally something she kept strictly to herself.

'Mark's left you? Impossible,' Garth was saying. He was wearing a soft woollen jumper that felt good against her skin, the warmth of his arms holding her making her feel cosseted and protected, reminding her of Mark, reminding her of all that her body had missed since Mark had gone.

'Hey, come on; stop crying and tell me exactly what's happened,' Garth cajoled while he stroked her hair gently, pushing her hair back off her face and settling her more comfortably in his arms. 'Come on; tell Uncle Garth...' he coaxed teasingly.

Reluctantly Deborah smiled.

'That's better,' Garth encouraged as he touched her mouth, pretending to hold her lips in their smile.

The pads of his fingers felt slightly rough, their touch against her skin unexpectedly sensual, reminding her of that last quarrel with Mark, of what had happened beforehand, of the way her body, her breasts had ached with such delicious anticipation for the touch of his skin against them...they were aching now, she recognised. In fact her whole body was aching. There hadn't been a night since Mark had gone when she had not lain awake wanting him. It had hurt her that he had accused her of being too sexually aggressive, especially when in the past he had always told her how much her sexual openness and honesty had turned him on.

Why did men feel that they had to control a woman's sexuality, that they should be the ones to give her permission to exercise it? Who ever heard of a man being ashamed of having a strong sex drive, and how many women did she know who were equally proud to acknowledge theirs?

'You're too thin,' she heard Garth accusing her. 'What have you been doing to yourself...?'

Deborah blinked up at him. It felt so good being physically close to another human being. In her mouth she could still taste the wine she had drunk, its taste sweetly sour on her tongue.

'I'm not too thin here,' she told him huskily, and she reached for his hand and placed it against her breast, and then, before he could say anything, she reached up and covered his mouth with her own, letting herself drown in the sensation of his hand reacting instinctively to the provocation of her warm, hard-tipped breast bare beneath the soft covering of her sweater, the response of his mouth to the demand of hers.

His thumb touched her nipple. Achingly she pressed herself closer to him. She felt so empty inside, so needy...

'Dee...no...we can't do this. What are you doing to me, you witch? You know how much I've always wanted you,' Garth protested.

If he wanted her then why was it he had stopped kissing her...touching her?

She saw Garth frown as he accidentally kicked over the wine bottle, swiftly reaching for it, his frown deepening as he looked at her.

'It's empty,' he told her.

'I was thirsty,' Deborah defended. 'Garth...take me to bed...make love to me... I need...'

She closed her eyes, willing back the tears she could feel forming behind them.

Garth was picking her up, carrying her...asking her the way to the bedroom.

Deborah groaned as she opened her eyes. The light felt like ice-picks, the pain in her head agonisingly sharp, the taste in her mouth...

Groggily she tried to sit up and then stopped as she felt her stomach heave and then it heaved again as the events of the previous evening came back to her.

Garth...oh, God... What had she done...?

Queasily she swung her feet to the floor and then froze as the bedroom door opened.

'Ah, so you *are* awake; I thought I could hear you...'

'Garth...'

'Feeling hung over?' he asked sympathetically. 'Never mind; I know just the cure...'

'Garth...' she repeated anxiously.

He stopped beside her bed, sat down on it and looked at her. 'It's OK,' he told her quietly. 'Nothing happened.'

'*Nothing* happened...?' Deborah stared at him.

'More fool me,' Garth added, grinning. 'All these years I've been waiting for you to look past Mark and see me and what happens when you finally do...? I go and get a fit of conscience and do the gentlemanly thing——'

'You mean my coming on to you turned you off as much as it does Mark?' Deborah interrupted him bitterly.

'No way.' He reached out and took hold of her hand between his own, ignoring her attempts to pull away from him. 'Listen to me and listen good. If I'd thought for one moment that it was me you wanted last night, then nothing, and I mean nothing, would have kept me out of your bed... Even though I'd have probably had to wait until this morning to get you to fulfil those promises you were making me,' he added ruefully.

Deborah looked at him.

'You'd passed out by the time I carried you in here,' he told her.

'Passed out!' Deborah stared at him.

'The wine...remember?' Garth prompted her.

Remember? How could she forget?

'Want to talk about it?'

'The wine?'

'No, not the wine,' he told her softly. 'Mark...Mark, and the reason he... Mark...and what's happened to the pair of you.'

'What's happened.' Deborah gave him a twisted smile. 'Are you sure you really want to know?'

'I'm sure,' Garth told her.

* * *

'Well, there's one thing I can tell quite categorically,' Garth announced half an hour later when Deborah had finished speaking. They were seated at the kitchen table, Deborah still grasping the now cold mug of coffee he had made for her.

She was still wearing the clothes he had put her to bed in the previous night. Her face was pale and drawn as she relived the unhappiness of losing Mark.

'It isn't you Mark's stopped loving, Dee, it's himself.'

'Himself...?' She shook her head. 'No.'

'Yes,' Garth insisted. 'Look, take it from me—I'm a man, I know, and even now there's still a tiny, ineradicable, deeply programmed part of us that says, Me man...me hunter...me winner...'

Deborah stared at him and then shook her head.

'No,' she insisted. 'Mark isn't like that——'

'Balls,' Garth interrupted her forcefully. '*All* men are like that. Look, I'm not saying that Mark is deliberately trying to offload his own sense of failure on you, to blame you for it, to punish *you* for being more successful than he is, but you can be damned sure that somewhere deep inside him, even if he doesn't consciously recognise it, that's exactly what's going on.

'It's all down to the loss of face, you see, Dee. Boys... men...are geared, genetically programmed if you like, to view other men as their rivals and to compete with them; there's nothing a man—any man, every man—fears more than the contempt of his male peers, of being seen to fall below the standard they set themselves. It starts from the moment we're born and we learn that we can take our mother's attention away from the other man in her life— our father. It takes a hold of us right there where it really hurts and it keeps the pressure up on us every day of our entire life.'

'But that's ridiculous,' Deborah protested. 'Mark has always encouraged me.'

'He loves you,' Garth told her. 'And anyway, knowing you're ambitious is one thing; having to deal with the results of it is another. You've beaten him in his own field,

Dee, and what's more you've done it in front of other men... That's a hard thing for any man to take, even one like Mark——'

'You mean his own ego is more important to him than I am?' Deborah asked quietly.

'He can't live without it, Dee,' he told her gently. 'No man can. All human beings need to have pride in themselves and self-respect, and we men, because we're that much weaker and more mortal than you women—well, we need that little bit extra help as well.'

He grinned at the look Deborah gave him. 'OK, well, maybe some of us need it more than others...

'Mark's no egotist, Dee,' he added. 'If you'd worked in different areas, or even different firms...'

'Or if I'd played the traditional female role and put his ego before my career?' Deborah suggested grimly.

Garth caught the note of anger in her voice.

'It's not as cut and dried as that, Dee, and you know it. Of course Mark wants you to succeed, of course he's proud of you, but it's a tough old world out there and when we're among our own kind we men are still supposed to show that we've got what it takes to come out on top. Don't give up on Mark, Dee...'

'What else can I do?' Deborah asked him, her eyes bright with tears. 'Give up my job...' She shook her head. 'Oh, it might work in the short term, but that's all.

'I *never* thought Mark would do something like this, Garth... Not Mark.'

CHAPTER TWENTY-FIVE

TIREDLY Sally surveyed her sister's stripped dining-room walls. Her back ached, not just with the effort of removing the wallpaper, but with the tension of suppressed resentment and anger as well.

Joel should have been the one doing this, as her sister had already self-righteously told her—more than once—and since she did agree with her why was it that she was finding she had to grit her teeth and bite back a wave of irritation against her almost as strong as her anger against Joel?

Half an hour ago her sister had come in to see how she was getting on. She had just returned from the hairdressers, her hair a smooth, shiny, elegant bob, reminding Sally of how much she needed to get her own hair cut, her face, immaculately made-up, grimacing as she carefully avoided the damp shreds of wallpaper matting on the floor at Sally's feet.

'Will you be much longer?' she had asked. 'Only Clifford has just rung to say that he's bringing a colleague home for drinks...'

'No, I've almost finished,' Sally had assured her tiredly, correctly interpreting the message hidden in her sister's speech.

Daphne obviously didn't want her around when Clifford and his colleague arrived... Sally knew her sister well enough to know how little she would relish having to introduce her as her sister, but she was still prepared to make use of her to get her dining-room wallpapered cheaply, Sally acknowledged.

Once she and Joel would have laughed together over her sister's meanness and snobbery. Once nothing would have made her want to trade places with Daphne, to exchange her own world with Joel for Daphne's far more affluent lifestyle. Once it had never occurred to her to envy Daphne a husband who had a secure, well-paid job.

Fiercely she squeezed back the tears of tiredness and self-pity burning in the back of her eyes.

'Joel's doing the best he can, working hard at the leisure centre,' she had automatically defended her husband when Daphne had raised the subject earlier of Joel's finding a job. 'In fact the leisure centre manager has suggested that it might be worthwhile considering making coaching and training a full-time career...retraining to...'

Her sister's exclamation of contempt had silenced her. '*Joel*, retrain? Oh, come on, Sally—you must know as well as I do that to make any kind of success in that field Joel will need proper academic qualifications. The country's full of graduates who can't get jobs, so how on earth someone like Joel, who left school without so much as a single quali- fication to his name, can even begin to think that he——' She had broken off, shrugging disdainfully.

'Of course he always could wind you round his little finger. Mark my words: if you're not careful, ten years from now he'll still be telling the same old tale, and you'll still be working full-time to support him while he enjoys himself playing at earning a living.

'I hear he's been giving private coaching lessons to Carol Lucas's little girl. I'd keep an eye on him if I were you, Sally... I'm not suggesting anything, of course,' she had added hastily as she'd seen the look Sally was giving her, 'but one hears *such* things and after all he has always been a very physical sort of man, hasn't he...?'

'If you mean he's always had a strong sex drive then yes, he has,' Sally had agreed steadily, 'but Joel is the last man who would ever let a woman pay him for sex, if that's what you're implying...'

'No, of course not...no such thing. You misunderstand me completely,' Daphne had back-pedalled furiously, her colour high, but Sally knew that she had not misunder- stood her at all.

The thought of Joel of all men allowing some rich, bored woman to pay him for sex was indeed totally ridiculous; that pride of his would get in the way for starters...

But supposing he did meet someone else—a woman whom he was attracted to, a woman who was attracted to him...

Her heart skipped a beat and then started to thump painfully. She was uncomfortably aware of how often she had turned away from him recently, rejecting his sexual advances, but marriage, loving someone wasn't just about sex, and surely she had just as much right to have *her* needs respected as he did when he had been the one going out to work, supporting them all, worrying about how they would pay the bills. She had often put his needs before her own then, but now that their positions were reversed he was making no attempt to do the same for her.

After she had returned to work on the dining-room she had continued to brood over Joel's selfishness—the fact that he still seemed to expect her to do whatever he wanted, even though *she* was now the one who controlled the purse strings.

Abruptly she put down her scraper.

Was that really how she thought of sex...of marriage...?

She shivered abruptly, feeling oddly sick, and dizzy tears suddenly filling her eyes. Tears not for herself, she recognised, but for the dreams and ideals which somewhere along the road of her life she had lost, and for the disillusionment which had taken their place.

When she had married Joel she had thought that life could hold no greater pleasure than being his wife. In bed at night, held safe in his arms, she would sometimes feel as though her heart might almost burst with happiness, and she had marvelled daily that she should be singled out for such joy.

Then the thought of making love with Joel had filled her not with dread but with incoherent excitement and delight, and if the things he had whispered to her, the way he had touched her had sometimes half shocked her, it had been a pleasurable, expectant kind of shock.

Had she ever disappointed Joel in those early days with her shyness and inhibition? If she had, he had never said so, she acknowledged. Then he had been patient with her, tender, wooing her slowly into a state of ecstatic ardour.

But that kind of sexual intensity didn't last. One only had to ask any long-married couple.

Now when Joel turned to her in the night she knew it wasn't the intensity of his love for her that motivated him, but simply his own physical need.

It was Kenneth, with his restraint and his appreciation of her as a human being, and not just a body in his bed, who loved her, not Joel.

So why was she standing here with her heart thumping and her stomach churning with nausea at the thought of Joel touching another woman? If she didn't want him any more... if she didn't love him...

She frowned as she saw her brother-in-law's car turning into the drive. The room was stripped but she still had to clear up and Daphne wouldn't be at all pleased that she was still here.

Still, with a bit of luck she could finish off and sneak out the back door without Clifford's 'colleague' knowing that she was here—or who she was.

She could hear voices in the hallway outside, her brother-in-law's, thin and slightly petulant and another man's—deeper and very familiar.

Her heart thumped into her ribs in shock.

'My wife must be in the kitchen; I'll just get her,' she could hear Clifford saying and then the dining-room opened and Kenneth was standing there apologising,

'Oh, I'm sorry—wrong door,' and then as he saw her he exclaimed in surprise, 'Sally! Good heavens...what on earth are you doing here...?'

'You know my sister-in-law...?'

Clifford couldn't quite keep the disbelief out of his voice or the disapproval out of his expression as he looked at her, Sally noticed.

'Sally is your sister-in-law? You're a very lucky man.'

Kenneth was talking to Clifford but looking at her, and Sally thought faintly that if Clifford had been anything like as intelligent and observant as he liked to pretend he must surely have noticed the intensity, the possessiveness in Kenneth's eyes as he watched her. *She* could certainly see it.

'Sally was my nurse when I was in hospital. And a very good nurse she was as well. I've missed her...'

Sally could feel her face starting to burn. Kenneth, please be careful, she begged silently. If Daphne came in and saw the way he was looking at her...

She ought to have trusted him, she acknowledged mentally ten minutes later as her sister, plainly flattered and overwhelmed by the attention he was paying her, allowed Kenneth to manipulate the situation so that as though by magic the four of them were sitting in her sister's over-fussy sitting-room, drinking glasses of sherry, while Kenneth pandered to her sister's ever-hungry ego by relating how impressed he had been by Clifford's reputation and how he thought that Clifford was wasted as a teacher at a mere comprehensive.

'Of course that's what I've always told him,' Daphne gushed.

'But Clifford believes that he owes it to his pupils to stay where he is, even though from my and Edward's point of view it would be far better if he applied for his own headmastership.'

Watching from the sidelines, Sally could imagine all too well what Joel would have had to say about her sister's behaviour.

She had known immediately from the look he gave her that the only reason Kenneth was here in Daphne's house was because of her, and yet even while a part of her thrilled with pride that he should want her so much, another part retreated from the knowledge that he was deliberately using her family... deliberately and quite callously encouraging Daphne to make a complete fool of herself as he played on her susceptibilities. His charm, his friendliness, his quiet and yet somehow too knowing questions which led to her sister's arrogantly, blithely revealing the poverty and ugliness of her personality, the arrogance, the vanity, the lack of awareness or concern for the feelings of others...this reduction of her sister to all her most base parts was, Sally discovered, somehow hurtful to her.

It was almost, she recognised uncomfortably, as though Kenneth was enjoying not just manipulating her sister and husband, but humiliating them as well. Hastily she dismissed her thoughts; she was letting her imagination run away with her. Kenneth wasn't like that, he was kind, thoughtful, caring; it was just an unfortunate coincidence that his questions should bring out the worst in Daphne.

Not, of course, that her sister was at all aware of what she was revealing. On the contrary, Daphne was revelling in Kenneth's attention, patently semi-awestruck by the fact that he as an academic and a university lecturer should seek out her husband to express to him his admiration of him.

That he should actually know her sister as well was something she dismissed as a mere coincidence.

'Oh, Sally has just come round to help us out getting our dining-room ready for redecoration,' she had said hastily when Kenneth had commented not just on Sally's presence but on her appearance as well.

As she glanced down at her feet Sally saw that a couple of stray pieces of once damp wallpaper had now dried on to her shoes. No wonder Kenneth had grimaced a little in distaste when he had first seen her; she probably did look a sight wearing her old jeans and an even older shirt of Joel's, her hair caught back in a ponytail and her face free of make-up.

'We wanted a change of style in our dining-room,' Daphne confided, 'and our regular decorator could only manage to fit us in if he only had the repapering to do.'

'Ah . . . of course,' was Kenneth's response. 'Of course, I should have guessed; naturally you wouldn't expect your sister to do your redecorating—not when she already has so much to do.'

'No, of course not,' Daphne agreed, shooting Sally a fiercely warning look that dared her to contradict what she was saying.

Kenneth and Clifford were discussing a paper Kenneth had apparently recently submitted on economics and Sally's thoughts wandered, the wallpaper on her shoe catching her eye a second time. Her fingers itched to bend down and remove it but Daphne would be furious with her if she did and it marked the pristine newness of her sitting-room carpet.

There was an itch beneath her left shoulder-blade—another errant piece of paper, she suspected.

Somehow she was always the one who managed to get herself covered with either wallpaper or paint when they were decorating, she acknowledged ruefully, while Joel never did.

She could remember the first decorating job they had ever tackled together after they were first married, stripping the hideous brown-painted wallpaper off the room which was to be their bedroom.

It had been summer, the small room hot and airless, shreds of damp paper sticking themselves persistently to her clothes and face, her body hot and uncomfortable beneath the protective layers of clothes she was wearing.

'Take them off,' Joel had suggested when she had complained for the umpteenth time about her discomfort.

'I can't!' she had protested, half laughing, half shocked, but in the end she had and Joel had too, and somehow she hadn't noticed any discomfort at all later when they had made love on the floor among the tangle of discarded paper and clothes.

She dipped her head towards the floor, not to examine the paper clinging to her shoe this time but to conceal the hot colour burning her face.

What on earth had made her think of something like that...and so vividly as well that for a moment she had almost been able to smell the hot, aroused scent of Joel's body, his skin tanned, gleaming like oiled silk, his hands sliding over her body as he marvelled at its softness? Oh,

Joel... A feeling of such intense yearning and loss filled her that it actually brought tears to her eyes, burning the dry sockets, making her blink rapidly to disperse them.

'Oh, but that's a wonderful idea, we'd love to, wouldn't we, Sally...?'

Abruptly she lifted her head and stared at her sister. She had been so absorbed in her own thoughts that she had completely lost track of the conversation going on around her.

'Er—I——'

'Your sister has just been telling me about her garden and I've just invited you all to come round and see mine...'

'Oh, I don't think...' Sally protested, but Daphne was already overruling her, telling her firmly,

'Of course you can go...'

'Good; so that's settled, then.' Kenneth smiled as he stood up. 'Shall we say some time next week... Thursday afternoon...?'

Next week, when she was on earlies and would be at home during the afternoon. Sally gave him a brief look and then looked quickly away again, afraid that she might betray what she was thinking.

'I want you to see my home,' Kenneth had told her the last time they had met. 'It will be a perfect setting for you.'

'I can't,' she had protested. 'I...'

'You can and you will,' he had contradicted her softly. 'Wait and see.'

She had thought that he meant she would change her mind, not that he would manipulate events so that she would have a perfectly acceptable excuse for visiting him.

His behaviour reminded her slightly of the way Joel had taken charge of her when she was at school. The feeling of knowing there was someone else there, someone that she could rely on was comfortingly familiar.

Now, as Kenneth reached the door, he paused and turned to smile at her.

* * *

His car had barely turned into the road before Daphne was questioning her, demanding to know all she knew about him.

'He was a patient, that's all,' Sally fibbed, grateful that her sister's ego prevented her from suspecting the truth. Daphne quite plainly had no conception of the real reason for Kenneth's visit, thank goodness.

'You'll have to come with us, of course,' Sally heard Daphne telling her. 'It would look odd if you didn't, but for heaven's sake, Sally, try and make a bit of an effort to smarten yourself up a bit. That dreadful shirt and those jeans...'

'I was working,' Sally reminded her. 'I've finished the stripping,' she added, 'but I'm not sure when I'll be able to start the papering...'

'Oh, yes. I meant to have a word with you about that. Teresa Craven has a decorator who is marvellous, apparently, and quite cheap. We've decided to ask him to do the work; after all, we can't afford to have a second set of paper ruined. You should have made Joel come back and put it right, you know, Sally. You're far too soft with him. You could never imagine someone like Kenneth allowing his wife to shoulder his responsibilities, could you?'

'No,' Sally agreed quietly. 'I couldn't.'

As she collected her things she acknowledged that Joel had probably been quite right when he'd insisted that it wasn't so much her dining-room wallpapering that Daphne wanted, but to humiliate him. But if she hadn't come round she wouldn't have seen Kenneth... Kenneth, who had obviously remembered that comment she had made about having to do her sister's wallpapering on her day off and acted upon it.

Kenneth who had very cleverly and subtly worked with her sister's vanity and not against it as Joel did.

Philippa tensed, her fingers curling nervously round the receiver as the number she had dialled rang out.

When it did there was a brief initial silence. Her excitement faded as she recognised the tell-tale signs of an answering machine. She would just have to leave a message and her number and wait for her prospective employer to ring her back, she recognised in disappointment. She started to rehearse her message mentally and then froze as the cool, firm tones of a male voice filled her ear—a voice and name she recognised immediately even though she had not heard it for years, and when she had, the last time she had, it had not been as it was now—cool and pleasant—but hotly, furiously, bitingly angry, hard with a contempt which had lashed her sensitivities and her pride red raw with whip-thin acid strokes of dismissal and dislike.

Her reactions were instinctive and immediate, her face draining of colour as she frantically replaced the receiver, cutting off the voice in mid-sentence, her hand trembling so much that it took her several attempts to replace the receiver properly, her heart thumping as hard as though she had just woken up from a nightmare of terror.

She stared at the telephone as though she half expected it to ring and then she would hear Blake's voice angrily demanding to know what it was she wanted, why she had hung up; why she had rung him in the first place when she knew just exactly what he thought of her.

Caught as she was in a web of shock, paralysed by it and by her own emotions, it was minutes rather than seconds before she had even enough control over herself to accept the irrationality of her own fears.

Of course Blake wasn't going to ring her back. How could he? He had no idea who she was. When he reran his machine he would simply assume that she was yet another person who balked at the thought of using an answering machine.

Her thoughts formed slowly like tired swimmers fighting desperately against a too swift current.

Blake was a colleague of Elizabeth's husband, a man in need of a woman to take charge of his orphaned godchild; could coincidence really stretch a long arm so far?

To the best of her knowledge Blake was still working abroad. America somewhere, her brother Michael had said the last time he had mentioned him. Before that he had spent some time working with disturbed children, some of the victims in Romania, his time and skill given free, so her brother had told her.

How could he now be working at a relatively small local hospital in a part of the country with which he had no connections?

It was impossible; she must have imagined it… She stared at the telephone, willing herself to find the courage to dial the number again. When she did so, the voice declaring the name 'Blake Hamilton' and the phone number was as cool and precise as before. Her mouth dry, her heart pounding, she replaced the receiver, a cold sweat had engulfed her body, making her shiver.

Thank God Elizabeth had arranged things so that she was the one to get in touch with him.

'He knows something of your circumstances, by the way—not the full details,' Elizabeth had told her. Had that 'something' included her name and, if it had, had he recognised it?

Obviously not, otherwise he would never have agreed to interview her.

A bubble of hysterical laughter choked her throat.

'You would be perfect for such a role,' Elizabeth had told her.

The bubble exploded in a sharp high sound that shocked her into silence. It was the cackle, the shriek of a mad woman, someone on the verge of completely losing control.

There was no way she could ever apply for the job now, and no way that Blake would want her.

Her mouth twisted in grim recognition of her betraying choice of verb. She would have to come up with some sort of explanation for Elizabeth, some sort of excuse, some sort of lie.

Clinically her brain observed and assessed the physical weakness of her body and her emotions.

Funny how the sound of a voice which had once had the power to transport her into a teenage seventh heaven of sexual and emotional delight should now almost have the reverse effect upon her, sending instead a cold, shocked *frisson* of fear and panic racing down her spine, triggering off acute nausea in her stomach, making her recognise that she was still as ill-equipped to deal with the effects of severe emotional trauma at thirty-odd as she had been at eighteen.

Which was it she was most afraid of having to face— Blake, or her own awareness of just how much of a fool she had made of herself in front of him?

It was a shame about the job, of course, much more than a shame, even though she tried to be philosophical about it and remind herself that after all she was really no worse off than she had been when she woke up this morning... before Elizabeth had spoken to her.

She had, after all, already survived potentially worse blows: the death of her husband and the subsequent scandal, the loss of her financial security, her place in local society, the loss of people who had purported to be her friends, the loss of a man who could have become far more to her than just her physical lover. What could one more small loss matter? She hadn't, in any case, been totally sure that she was right for the job... or that she would get it, despite Elizabeth's reassurances.

Blake Hamilton... Was it tragedy or comedy that had so nearly brought him back into her life? Or was it perhaps neither, but fate offering her a chance to prove that she had meant what she had said about taking charge of her own life, being her own person... taunting her with the knowledge that there were still some aspects of her personality she could neither change nor escape?

Blake frowned as he listened to his answering machine and found that two calls had come in, but both times the person at the other end had hung up.

Why did people do that? he wondered irritably. What was it about a simple recorded message that they found so daunting?

He had been in meetings virtually all day sorting out a myriad small details of his new appointment. That was something that never changed no matter what part of the world he worked in: bureaucracy... red tape... officialdom;

and a part of him, for all his self-examination and teaching, still found it tedious and time-consuming, absorbing energy and assets which would have been far better employed on his patients.

He ran the tape through to the end, grimacing as he realised that the woman Elizabeth Humphries had recommended to him had not rung.

According to Elizabeth she was perfect for the job, and with her professional training he had no reason to doubt her judgement. He had never realised before how difficult it was to find someone to take charge of one young child. He had had far fewer problems employing and staffing an entire department. Far... far fewer.

His frown deepened. Perhaps those friends and colleagues who had advised him to let the authorities take charge of Anya had been right after all. After all, what did he really know about bringing up an eleven-year-old girl? Nothing.

But he had seen the look on her face when the social worker had suggested taking her into care.

Care, despair... The two words had formed a relentless rhythm, pounding against his brain and his conscience, reminding him of the moral responsibility he had taken on when he'd first agreed to be the child's guardian. Him, a guardian.

He hadn't needed the Social Services to point out that he had no legal responsibility for the child; there was no estate to speak of. Lisa and Miguel, both of them idealists, had worked tirelessly for their cause from their English base with other patriots, but their small council flat had been damp and ill-furnished and their daughter, who had inherited her father's South American colouring, had looked sallow and undernourished, her huge dark eyes following Blake's every movement.

Some of Miguel's co-refugees had offered to take charge of Anya, informally adopting her into their semi-commune-like existence, but the authorities had balked at this even more than they had at Blake's decision to take charge of her.

He closed his eyes briefly, all too aware of the problems that lay ahead of him, of them both.

There was no psychiatrist yet who could ever totally manage to dissociate himself completely and apply his knowledge unemotionally to his own family or those closest to him; even to apply it in many ways to himself; that was why it was so important that he find exactly the right person to take charge of Anya.

The house felt stuffy after being closed up all day. He strode into the sitting-room and threw open the French windows.

He had bought the house after a single viewing on a flying visit to confirm that he would take up the post the hospital was offering him. The chief executive, an accountant, with, Blake suspected, meanness and suspicion locked into his soul, had not seemed able to believe that he actually intended to take the job.

'But it's a considerable drop in salary,' he had commented several times. Blake had said nothing, volunteered no explanation to satisfy his curiosity.

He paused in front of the open windows, studying the untidy green lawn. The house was Victorian and large with an equally large garden, a family home far too big for one man and a child—but he had seen the green lawn, the shabby summer house, the trees and had immediately thought of his own childhood... and Anya's.

He had told himself that the house was a bargain, hard to sell due to the recession, and that ultimately when things picked up he could always convert it and sell it off as separate apartments at a profit.

Sometimes he thought he had almost forgotten what real man-to-woman emotion was, questioning even if he had ever experienced it at all, and then something would remind him, some trick of his memory, a woman's scent, a voice... a laugh... the unexpected glimpse of a half-familiar face, bringing it all back to him again.

In the early days he had often wondered what might have happened if things had been different, if he had been different, but even then his priorities had been set; they had

had to be—his mother—and he had been younger too, his principles and beliefs far less flexible, his judgement of others arrogantly harsh. He had learned better since.

Why hadn't that blasted woman rung? Time was running short. The Social Services were already nipping at his heels, issuing warnings and ultimatums.

Why the hell was he bothering anyway, disrupting his life for the sake of one small unknown eleven-year-old? Out of a sense of moral duty? Out of guilt because for the last ten years he had almost forgotten her existence apart from the obligatory Christmas cheque?

If the woman really wasn't interested in the job then he would have to start going through agencies again.

He reached into his jacket and removed his wallet, flicking out the business card Elizabeth had given him on which she had written her home number. He would give her a ring...find out what was happening.

'She hasn't been in touch with you. Oh, that's odd. I spoke to her today and she said she was going to ring you straight away,' Elizabeth told him.

'Look, why don't you give *me* her number,' Blake suggested, 'or better still her address...? I'll go round and see her...'

Elizabeth hesitated about disclosing Philippa's details, but she knew enough about Blake to be able to trust him. 'Yes, of course,' she agreed. 'Her name is Philippa Ryecart and her address is Green Lawn, Larchmount Avenue.'

Philippa Ryecart... Philippa.

As he thanked Elizabeth, Blake's glance flicked back to the name he had just written down, noting the betrayingly heavy strokes he had used, as heavy as the hammer-strikes of his heartbeat.

A widow, Elizabeth had said. His mouth tightened as he remembered the careful way she had sketched in the story: the husband a failed businessman who had committed suicide, leaving his wife virtually destitute and alone.

Philippa, alone—and common sense warned him to be

cautious, to wait, to think. This was something he had not been prepared for—had not anticipated.

'No matter what happens, Pip will stay with him, she's fiercely loyal to him. Too loyal in my view,' Michael had told him during that long-ago Californian summer. He had told him other things as well—made him see himself in a completely new light . . . a very unflattering light—the same light that Philippa would see him in?

He reached for the phone and then put it down.

Perhaps it would save time, circumvent unnecessary delays if he went round to see her instead, he decided, ignoring the inner voice that mocked and taunted him.

He went upstairs to shower and change. He had bought the house already furnished; the previous owners had gone to live in Spain where they had no need or room for the heavy old furniture that clothed the house.

Its empty silence was faintly depressing. He wondered how easy it would be for Anya to adjust to it after the cramped smallness of the council flat. Easier, no doubt, than adjusting to her parents' death.

He had dealt with many traumatised children, children who had suffered far, far more in their short, tragic lives than Anya would ever know, and yet something about her had reached out to him, not as a psychiatrist, but as a man.

Perhaps it had been something in her expression, some likeness to her mother, or perhaps it had been the look of resignation and hopelessness in her eyes, her unchildlike awareness of the decision he had almost made that her best interests would be served by allowing the state to take charge of her. *Her* best interests, or his?

In the future, would she bless him or curse him for making the choice he had? That, he already knew, depended very much on the woman he chose to look after her.

Elizabeth Humphries had assured him that Philippa *was* the right woman.

For Anya's sake he could not afford to ignore that advice.

And that fierce unexpected upsurge in his heartbeat had of course nothing to do with the thoughts going through his mind and the memories they had stirred, but were simply the natural physical after-effects of a man of thirty-odd going up a flight of stairs too fast.

CHAPTER TWENTY-SIX

'MUM, what will happen during the summer holidays?'

Philippa tensed as she heard the anxiety in her elder son's voice. As her fingers tightened around the telephone receiver she could picture him so clearly, that small frown he had when anything worried him crinkling his forehead, his eyes watching, waiting for her to say the magic words that would put his world to rights again.

Only he wasn't a little boy any more, he was almost an adolescent, too old to deceive with ambiguities and well intentioned lies, no matter how much she might want to protect him.

'Stuart Drayton says that when his uncle was made bankrupt his aunt and cousins didn't have anywhere to live any more...'

Philippa's heart sank. She should have been expecting something like this, she recognised; the headmaster had after all told her himself that her sons weren't the only boys in the school in families which were suffering financial setbacks.

'His cousins had to go and live with their grandmother...' Rory added.

Philippa closed her eyes. 'Darling, you mustn't worry,' she told him gently. 'I promise you that you and Daniel won't have to go and live anywhere you don't want to or with anyone you don't like,' she added.

Was it her fault that there was this distance between her sons and their grandparents? She had tried not to let her own feelings colour the relationship between them, but young children were very good at picking up on unexpressed adult emotions.

'And we'll be able to come home for the summer holidays—we won't have to stay at school?' Rory pressed her.

'Yes,' Philippa promised, superstitiously crossing her fingers.

Why hadn't the bank been in touch with her yet about her proposal that she be allowed to stay on in the house? She suspected that they were playing a game of cat and mouse with her, testing her strength and determination, and for that reason she could not be the one to get in touch with them. Whatever happened with the house she would somehow find a way of keeping her promise to Rory, she decided fiercely; she could not, *would* not allow her sons to suffer.

As she replaced the receiver, she saw the piece of paper on which she had written Blake's number. That job would have been ideal for her. She liked children, of all ages, and found it easy to get on with them, perhaps because her memories of her own childhood made her sensitive to their emotional needs.

Had things been different she would have liked a larger family—two girls, perhaps...four was a good well-rounded number.

Visiting the hospital with Susie, she had always found herself drawn towards the children's wards. The little ones were especially heart-aching, but it had been the teenagers who had moved her the most with their strength and their vulnerability.

If her prospective employer had been anyone other than Blake Hamilton she would have welcomed both him and his job with open arms.

'He's got a large house with plenty of room to spare,' Elizabeth had told her.

Rory's anxiety still at the forefront of her mind, she started to hurry back to the kitchen to write him a letter, but the doorbell ringing stopped her. She had very few visitors these days apart from Susie, who she knew was over at her mother's and wouldn't be returning until the morning, and so her heart thudded against her chest wall and then started to race.

Had Joel ignored what she had said and come back? And, if so, would she have the strength to send him away again?

Unsteadily she went to open the door.

For a moment, when she saw who her visitor actually was, she almost started to panic and close the door in his face, until she registered his expression. Her recognition of his grim determination and her relief that he was not, after all, Joel gave her the strength to say quietly and somewhat to her own surprise, 'Hello, Blake. You'd better come in.'

Blake was caught off guard by her reaction as well; she could see it in his eyes.

What had he been expecting? she wondered—that she would blush like a schoolgirl and fall at his feet in a fit of swooning adoration? She wasn't that idealistic, infatuated teenager any more.

'You sound as though you've been expecting me.'

His voice sounded deeper, harsher than it had done on the answering machine. She could hear his emotions in it: tension, impatience, irritation... Tension? Why should he be tense?

'Not really,' she told him, responding automatically to his question.

'No? But you did recognise my voice on the answering machine.'

'Yes, I did,' Philippa agreed. What was the point in lying?

'And, having recognised it, you decided not to bother going ahead and making an appointment to see me.'

'It seemed the best thing to do,' Philippa told him.

It came to her suddenly that this was not the man she remembered, the all-powerful, godlike hero-figure she had worshipped and adored; this was a human being who right now seemed more thrown off guard by the situation than she was.

It was a disconcerting sensation recognising that fact; it gave her a dizzying, unfamiliar sense of freedom, changing things so that the balance of power between them had swung slightly in her direction, bringing home to her the fact that she was after all no longer that shy, adoring girl whose image had remained trapped in her memories, but an adult woman with far more important things to concern her than the urgings of her immature adolescent emotions and body.

Physically Blake might hardly have changed at all; his body, she recognised, was still as lean and powerfully male as she remembered, even if now he was dressed in the imposing formality of a dark suit and an immaculately ironed white shirt rather than the T-shirt and jeans she remembered. His eyes were just as clear and assessing as they had been, the dark, almost black iris banded by a rim of much clearer pale green; the high cheekbones still gave his face a faintly austere aura of sexual masculinity; and his mouth still possessed that full bottom curve of sexuality and passion. But *she* had changed, without knowing it, without even recognising it until now, because, although she was aware of all those things about him which had once made her heart and pulse race and her fevered sensual imaginings a physical torture to live with, now they no longer had any power to affect her.

Yes, she was aware of him as a very sexually powerful man, but it was her memories of Joel's lovemaking that made her body ache with sweet heaviness, not Blake's presence here in her house.

It was an odd, disconcerting feeling, a combination of relief and foolishness, like waking up from a terrifying nightmare to discover that the shadow which had haunted her sleep had been nothing more than a dress hanging on the wardrobe door.

'How is the little girl?' she asked him compassionately, dismissing her own feelings. 'Poor child, she must be suffering dreadfully...'

As he heard the genuine warmth and concern in her voice, Blake acknowledged that Elizabeth Humphries knew what she was doing. Philippa had been the only person he had interviewed for the job who had mentioned Anya first.

Only of course he was not interviewing her, and nor, he suspected, was he going to get the opportunity to do so.

This calm, slightly distant, wholly mature woman was nothing like the Philippa he would have expected to find given the circumstances Elizabeth had briefly outlined to him. The metamorphosis in her from the girl he had known both intrigued and slightly chagrined him.

The fact that her startling prettiness had not diminished over the years did not surprise him, but the fact that she herself was so unaware of it, so careless almost of it, did, he acknowledged.

Despite what Michael had told him about her he had still half expected her to fit into a very different image, given her upbringing: designer clothes, immaculately coiffured hair, polished nails; in fact, the kind of artificiality he had always found a turn-off in any woman.

That was how he had visualised the woman she would become, not this jeans- and T-shirt-clad woman with her softly tousled fair hair and short blunt nails, her face free from make-up and her manner equally free of any artifice or constraint.

As a teenager, looking as she did today would have been something her parents would never have allowed.

Then she had looked like an immaculate, untouchable little doll. Now she looked like a wholly and enticingly touchable woman; the kind of woman who laughed and cried, who was warm and giving, the kind of woman who would take a lonely, frightened child to her heart and wrap her in the safe security of her love.

How had she become that woman...? Via a man...her husband?

Immediately he suppressed his thoughts, answering Philippa's questions.

'Anya is naturally very unhappy and confused. She's a quiet child, mature for her age in some ways and very immature in others. She hasn't had much contact with other children and her parents' death has made her retreat into herself...' Blake frowned. 'Why did you change your mind about applying for the job, Philippa? I know that you...'

'That I what...? That I need the money?' Philippa supplied for him steadily. 'Yes, I do,' she admitted honestly. 'But you can have as little desire to have me working for you as——'

'I am not concerned with *my* desires,' Blake interrupted her curtly. 'Only Anya's needs.'

He saw from Philippa's expression that his words had hit home. She always had been emotionally vulnerable, and it had been because of that— He stopped his thoughts, refusing to let them go any further. It was Anya he was here for, not...

'I won't be manipulated, Blake,' Philippa warned him steadily. 'And to be honest I'm surprised that you want me.'

Philippa stopped, abruptly silenced by her own choice of words and cursing herself inwardly, but if Blake was aware of what she was thinking he was not showing it.

'I haven't got much time left,' he told her abruptly. 'The Social Services have never been happy with the idea of me taking charge of Anya; they're already pressuring me to prove that she's going to be better off with me than under their care...'

'And you're getting desperate,' Philippa half mocked him.

'Yes, I'm desperate,' he admitted. 'But not so desperate that I'm prepared to employ someone who isn't one hundred and ten per cent the right person to have charge of Anya...'

'And you think that *I'm* that person?'

It was impossible for her to keep the cynicism out of her voice, and she could tell that Blake had recognised it.

'So...not quite everything about you has changed,' he told her softly. 'The Philippa I knew always did lack self-esteem.'

Not only did she not desire him any more, she didn't much like him either, Philippa decided.

'The Philippa you knew doesn't exist any more,' she told him icily. 'She was a girl...a child... I am a woman...'

'Yes...'

Why, after the control she had felt and exhibited, did that one slow, soft word make her feel as though her entire body was suddenly engulfed in a wave of self-conscious heat?

'I'm sorry, Blake,' she told him tersely. 'But I can't work for you.' She turned away from him. 'It just wouldn't work and I have the boys to consider now, as well . . .'

'That would be no handicap as far as I am concerned—far from it.'

Philippa looked back at him.

'Anya has been too isolated, she needs contact with other children, but I suspect that, thrown into a new school and with the trauma of her parents' death to cope with, instead of reaching out to her peers, she's far more likely to retreat from them completely.

'To have the opportunity to mix with other children in her own home, a home she shared with them, would be of enormous benefit to her.'

'Is that Anya's guardian speaking or her psychiatrist?' Philippa asked him sharply.

'Anya is my charge, not my patient,' Blake responded equally curtly, adding angrily, 'And if you're suggesting that I want to use her emotional vulnerability in some kind of absurd professional experiment . . .!'

She hadn't been; all she had wanted to do was to irritate him a little, scratch him to see if he really bled, a small compensation for the bruises she had received from flinging herself against the implacable rock of his uninterest. But someone obviously had suggested that. Who? Philippa wondered. The Social Services?

His temperament was far more mercurial than she had realised, she recognised, his emotions far closer to the surface.

'Why should I?' she told him, adding drily, 'I'm not the guardian of your conscience, Blake. I've got far more important things to worry about . . . like my sons . . .'

'Their father . . . your husband . . . did you love him?'

Philippa stared at him, unable to conceal her shock.

Blake was shocked as well, she recognised, as though his question had been as unanticipated by him as it had been by her. For a second she was tempted to lie, to abide by convention and regress to the person her parents had brought her up to be, but her pride wouldn't let her. Why should she, after all?

'No,' she told him, her head held high, her eyes defying him to criticise her. 'But I was grateful to him.'

'Grateful?' He was frowning.

'Because he wanted me...needed me, approved of me...because he reinforced my self-esteem, because he gave my life a purpose and a focus. Because,' she told him quietly, 'he provided an escape route from my parents.

'And you, Blake. Have you ever married?'

'No.'

Their eyes met and it was Blake who looked away first, Philippa noticed in surprise.

'I'd still like you to reconsider taking the job...'

He meant it, Philippa realised.

'Don't give me your final answer yet. Think it over for a couple of days,' he urged her. 'Anya needs you, Philippa.'

'That's emotional blackmail,' Philippa told him bluntly. 'And you don't even know yet how Anya will react to me.'

'Oh, but you're wrong,' Blake contradicted her softly. 'That is the one thing I do know...'

'Is that your professional judgement?' Philippa's mouth twisted slightly as she spoke.

'Yes...and it's my judgement as a human being as well...as a man...'

He was already turning towards the door, leaving while he felt he had the upper hand, Philippa realised, knowing that she was on ground that was far too unstable for her to challenge him. It didn't make any difference, though; she might as well allow him his small victory, because she wasn't going to change her mind...she wasn't going to take the job.

Why not? She had already proved to herself that she was immune to him now both emotionally and sexually.

In the empty kitchen she shook her head in silent rejection of her own unspoken question.

She just wasn't, that was all; she didn't need to give logical reasons, explanations, excuses... She just wasn't.

* * *

The letter arrived with the morning's post. She saw the bank's stamp on it and reached for it first, her fingers trembling as she opened it, knowing by some instinct that it contained a response to her request.

She read it once and then a second time as the sickening sense of shock and disappointment spread outwards through her body.

The bank was sorry, but it could not agree to her request.

There was a lot more to it than that, of course, but essentially that was what they were saying...a firm and unequivocal 'no'.

It was several minutes before she realised that there was a second page to their letter. Its contents only reinforced the message of the first page. It named the estate agents who would be acting for them and warned her that the agents had been instructed to go for a quick sale.

So much for her promise to Rory that they would all be together for the summer holidays... Together where? At her parents'?

The temptation to give in to her own fear and misery was almost overwhelming, but what was the point? What good would it do?

When the phone rang she raced to answer it, illogically hoping that it might be the bank ringing to say they had changed their mind, but instead it was Susie.

'Hey, where are you?' Susie asked her cheerfully. 'You were supposed to be coming round here for coffee and a natter this morning—remember?'

'Yes...yes... I'm sorry...I was just about to leave...'

'Philippa, what is it? What's wrong?'

'I heard from the bank this morning,' Philippa told her. 'They aren't prepared to let me stay on in the house and apparently they've instructed the agents and asked them to look for a quick sale.'

'Oh...oh... I'm so sorry...'

Susie's quick sympathy made her eyes sting with tears.

'Well, it isn't all bad news,' Philippa told her. 'Believe it or not I have actually been offered a job...'

She stopped speaking abruptly. What on earth had made her say that? She hadn't intended to discuss Blake's visit, nor his job offer, with anyone. What was the point, when she had already decided not to take it?

It was that stupid pride of hers again, she recognised grimly, over-reacting against the sympathetic pity she had heard in Susie's voice.

'A job... The little girl?' Susie guessed excitedly. 'Tell me all about it.' Philippa sketched the details. 'It sounds marvellous,' Susie enthused. 'When do you start?'

'I don't. There's a problem,' Philippa told her.

'A problem. What kind of problem, minor, major or mega?'

'That,' Philippa told her, 'depends on how you look at it.'

Quietly she went on to explain.

'Mmm—curiouser and curiouser,' was Susie's only comment, but when Philippa pressed her to explain what she meant she refused to do so.

'But if you don't feel attracted to him any more——'

'I don't,' Philippa interrupted her sharply.

'Then there isn't really a problem, is there?' Susie pointed out gently. 'He obviously isn't concerned about what happened in the past; if he were he wouldn't be so keen to employ you, would he? And from your own point of view there's obviously nothing to fear, since you don't lust after him any more. Which brings us to another point.

'I don't want to sound preachy, but there are other reasons why it might be a good idea for you to take this job, apart from the more obvious commercial ones, that is—or don't you agree?'

Philippa sighed. She knew what Susie meant.

'You mean Joel,' she acknowledged wryly.

'If that's his name, then yes. You said yourself that it couldn't go anywhere; that he was married and that the last thing you wanted was to be responsible for another woman's potential unhappiness,' Susie reminded her.

'Yes. I know...'

'So, here's your chance to end it—after all, if you're living with another man...'

'As his employee...' Philippa reminded her quickly.

'Well, yes, of course, but you've got to admit it wouldn't be as easy to entertain a lover under someone else's roof as it would under your own.'

'Yes, you're right,' Philippa acknowledged. 'Everything you say makes sense, I know, but...'

'Have you thought that it might not be your fear that Blake might think you still have a crush on him that's holding you back, but your change of status...?' Susie suggested gently.

'No...no, of course it isn't,' Philippa denied indignantly.

'Then take the job,' Susie counselled her. 'After all,' she added cheerfully, 'you can always leave if it doesn't work out.'

'No...that's the one thing I *can't* do,' Philippa contradicted her. 'Not once I've made a commitment to Anya. She's been through so much already, lost so much... I don't know why Blake is so keen to employ *me*,' she burst out. 'I mean, there must be dozens of other women far better qualified for the job than I am.'

'It depends what you mean by better qualified,' Susie told her. 'I imagine he wants you for the same reason that Elizabeth Humphries recommended you for the job in the first place. And that's quite simply because he knows that to you it won't just be a job. Take it, Pip,' Susie advised her firmly. 'After all, what other real option do you actually have?'

'None,' Philippa admitted tiredly.

The letter from the bank was still on the kitchen table, her promise to Rory very much to the forefront of her mind.

Susie was right. What real option did she have?

'Ring him now and tell him that you've thought it over and that you've decided to take the job,' Susie urged her.

Numbly, Philippa stared at the telephone.

It was pointless trying to put off what she knew had to be done.

She picked up the receiver and slowly punched out Blake's number.

The answering machine was on again. She waited for the tone before leaving her message.

There, it was done. There was no going back now, unless Anya took a dislike to her.

The phone rang as she stood there, her stomach still churning with reaction to what she had done.

'Philippa?'

'Blake.' She hadn't expected him to ring back so quickly.

'I was working at home,' he told her. 'But you rang off before I could reach the phone. I'm glad you changed your mind.' He paused. 'I'm due to collect Anya from the foster mother who has been looking after her tomorrow. If you're free it might be a good idea if you come with me.'

'Wouldn't you prefer to get Anya settled first, let her find her feet a little...?' Philippa protested.

'Philippa, I might be a psychiatrist, but I'm also a man; what I know about pre-teenagers and their problems might fill half a dozen textbooks in theory, but theory is exactly what it is. The thought of applying that theory to good old-fashioned hands-on reality terrifies me and so do the thoughts I can almost see running through the mind of the Social Services people.

'What Anya needs more than anything right now is a bit of human warmth and comfort. I can't give her that. She might be my god-daughter, but she's also a stranger to me. I've seen her once since Lisa and Miguel were killed...until all this happened, I hadn't seen her since she was christened...'

Philippa could hear the exasperation in his voice. It made him seem more human.

'I'm not asking you to come with me as some kind of Macchiavellian psychological test,' he told her drily. 'I'm asking you to come because Anya needs you and so do I.'

It was the last admission she had expected him to make, and hearing it shocked her into complete silence.

'Philippa... Pippa... Are you still there?'

'Yes. Yes... I'm still here.'

Why was it that she only had to hear anxiety in someone's voice, sense their need, and she was hooked? Blake might claim that he was not manipulating her, but she wasn't so sure.

'Well...what do you say? Will you come with me?'

Philippa took a deep breath.

'Yes...' she told him quietly. 'Yes, I'll come...'

After she had put the phone down she reminded herself very firmly that there was nothing for her to fear. Not any more; after all, she was hardly likely to be stupid enough to fall in love with him a second time, was she?

CHAPTER TWENTY-SEVEN

'MARK... Please come in.'

Mark smiled and then turned to follow the immaculately dressed dark-haired woman as she led the way through the house to her office.

She had good legs, he thought—like Deborah. His body tensed against the thought... against his memories.

It was almost two months now, during which he had slowly started to rebuild his crumbling self-respect.

He had hesitated at first when the agency had offered him this long-term temporary work in a small market town practice, but he liked the work, and the people. It was a single-partner practice with William Harcourt, the partner, close to retirement and anxious to get on top of the backlog of work caused by a recent illness before he put the practice up for sale.

He and Mark had jelled straight away and it had been William who'd suggested that Mark take over full responsibility for the accountancy affairs of the firm's biggest client.

'I never thought when she first started that it would turn out to be so successful. None of us did... There's even been talk of making the company public, but I doubt that Stephanie would ever agree. She enjoys being in charge too much for that.'

Stephanie Pargeter had intrigued Mark before he had even met her. She was a millionairess several times over; she owned and ran her own highly successful business which she had built up from nothing, and she was also an attractive woman... extremely attractive, Mark noted as he followed the elegant sway of her body down the hallway to her office.

'I'm sorry to drag you out here on a Saturday morning,' she apologised to Mark as she showed him into the elegant, book-lined room, 'but there were one or two points I needed to go over with you on the takeover.'

'No problem,' Mark assured her. 'I was only going to play golf with William...'

'Don't,' Stephanie advised him, laughing. 'He's a terrible cheat...'

Her smile robbed the words of any criticism. For a woman in her early forties she had an oddly youthful face, the look in her eyes often mischievous and teasing.

She didn't look like the stereotyped image of a successful woman; the clothes she normally wore were soft and fluid, her hair fell just short of her shoulders in an unfussy silky bob, the only jewellery she wore was her wedding-ring and a watch...but successful she most certainly was.

'Tea or coffee?' she asked Mark now as she invited him to sit down.

'Coffee, please...'

While she went to get it, Mark studied the room. It was decorated in a soft, pretty shade of lemon that made the room feel sunny and warm. Clever touches of dark blue broke up its softness and the desk in the corner was a large, solid, no-nonsense piece of furniture.

He was looking towards the desk when Stephanie came back with their coffee.

'Hideous things, aren't they?' she commented, wrinkling her nose with disgust as she looked at the computer. 'Hideous but necessary...like far too many things in life,' she added wryly.

'Including men?' Mark asked slyly as he took his coffee from her.

They had developed a very good working relationship in the month he had been here and he knew his comment would not cause her any offence. It was no secret locally that, after her husband had left her, taking with him her twenty-two-year-old PA and a large portion of her fortune, she had announced that that was the first and last time that any man would make such a fool of her.

'Some of them,' she agreed, mischief darkening her eyes as she looked directly at him and added softly, 'Although I do *sometimes* make an exception . . . in certain cases . . .'

Mark held her gaze. He wasn't quite sure if she was actually coming on to him, or if she was just playing a game with him, testing him . . . but either way she was a very, very attractive woman; older than he was, but still extremely desirable.

She was, he recognised on a sudden sharp spear of pain, exactly what Deborah would be in fifteen years' time.

'Odd, isn't it?' Stephanie commented drily. 'You think that by running away from something you're escaping but still somehow it manages to come after you.

'What is it exactly *you're* running from, Mark . . . or is it a *someone* rather than a something?'

'Both,' Mark admitted.

'Ah . . . And you don't want to talk about either it or her? Well, why should you?' she asked drily. 'After all none of us likes admitting to a failure . . .'

A failure . . . Mark frowned. What was she implying? How could she know . . . ?

'If you're running from a woman, a relationship, there has to have been a failure,' she told him, apparently reading his mind. 'A failure of communication . . . understanding . . . sharing . . . loving . . .' She gave a small shrug. 'That's something we women tend to forget far too easily—that when we embrace a lover we're also embracing the risk of failure and of loss.'

'You make it sound as though women are always the victims in relationships.'

'Most of the time they are,' she told him succinctly. 'We bring it upon ourselves, of course . . . take on far too willingly the responsibility for making it work, for being the one to nourish and sustain . . .' She stopped and shook her head.

'I'm sorry. I'm getting too maudlin . . . Now, where are those balance sheets?'

She went over to her desk, picked up a file and came and sat down opposite him.

'On the face of it the purchase of this company will be a good asset for us. They have a good distribution network for the flowers they grow, selling into the areas where we don't as yet have much penetration, but I have a feeling, an instinct, if you like, that they're hiding something from us. If the figures are as good as they seem, why are they so anxious to sell?'

'It's a family business, with no one to take it over,' Mark reminded her.

'Not true.' Stephanie shook her head. 'There's a grandson, born illegitimately to the daughter... and besides... bear with me, Mark; I have a gut feeling about this one... it's too perfect... too tempting.'

'Without a few more acquisitions you could be very vulnerable to takeover yourself,' Mark warned her.

'Don't remind me...'

The company had fought off a takeover only the previous year and Mark knew how determined Stephanie was that it remain under her control. It seemed incredible that she could have built up such a successful business in so short a space of time, almost by accident.

She had initially started doing dried-flower arrangements merely as a hobby, and it had been curiosity initially which had led her to seek out suppliers direct as she searched for flowers that were not readily available.

She had bought her first wholesale business, ailing and run-down, from a small legacy left to her by her parents. Now she owned not only several wholesale businesses, but their suppliers as well—the growers. Her company owned growing fields in England and abroad, particularly Holland.

She was, he reflected, a very clever woman; a very shrewd woman; a very sexy woman... Like Deborah.

He fought to pull his attention back to what Stephanie was saying to him.

'You must be very proud of all that you've achieved,' Mark commented later.

'Why? Because I'm a woman?' She put down the file and gave him a level look. 'That's a very sexist remark,' she told him. 'And one you wouldn't have made were I a man.'

Mark flushed uncomfortably. 'I'm sorry. I...'

'Don't apologise,' she told him. 'Yes, I am proud...proud and lonely.'

She saw the look on his face and gave him a small half-smile.

'What is it, Mark? Did you expect me to behave like a man and claim that I'm better off without my husband? It isn't because I hate him that there hasn't been anyone else in my life, you know...'

She got up and walked over to the window.

'The year I made my first million I bought myself a Mercedes sports car. Not so much as a reward for doing so well, but as compensation for losing so much...' She turned round. 'My husband...he grew tired of being the husband of a successful woman, of having publicly to take second place, of feeling that my success demeaned him in the eyes of other men. In the end it was easier for him to bow to that peer pressure, to prove that he was still a "man" by leaving me for another woman, a younger, prettier woman—trophy wives, they call them in America, I understand—than to stay with me...

'Easier on him, easier on his pride...easier on the collective male psyche of his "friends", but it certainly wasn't easier on me.

'I wonder if any man can really understand what a woman goes through when she loses someone to whom she has given her trust, her love...her life? It destroys something inside us that I don't believe can ever be replaced.'

She pulled a wry face, and Mark saw that there was no trace of any mischief at all in her eyes now, only intense sadness.

'His affair wasn't the *cause* of our break-up, but the culmination of it. At first, in fact, he was proud of me, encouraged me...but then slowly he started distancing himself from me. Initially he blamed me for not having enough time for him, for making him feel that he wasn't important to me any more... Then he stopped making love to me.'

She gave him a brief look. 'Have you any idea what it does to a woman when a man, *her* man rejects her sexually... how demeaning it is to discover what you thought was a temporary incapacity on his part turns out to be a far more serious failure on yours? If a woman tells a man he's failed to arouse her, he can always save his ego by telling himself that she's lying. But when a woman fails to arouse a man...' She shook her head.

'That's how it starts; and the way it ends... It wasn't his sexual infidelity with another woman I couldn't forgive, but his infidelity towards the bond which I believed existed between us. He was the rock on which I had built my whole life; it was the security of believing I had *his* love that gave me the self-confidence to become the woman that on my own I had hardly dared believe I could be.

'He claimed that fulfilment and growth came at his expense, but that was *his* view of the situation, not mine. And the most ridiculous thing of all about it was that I never particularly wanted to be successful... initially it was just something for me to do while he forged ahead with his career... Just something to bring me in a little bit of pin-money so that he wouldn't feel I was totally dependent on him.

'Sometimes on a bad day I wake up in the morning feeling that I know how Midas must have felt... but do you know the worst thing of all?'

Mark shook his head. His muscles were tense, his heart thudding uncomfortably, his mind trying to close itself off from what his emotions were telling him.

'Success is like a drug—once you've tasted it there's no going back—for anyone. You become addicted to it... dependent on it, and very soon there isn't room for anything else in your life. All your energy, all of you is given over to feeding its voracious appetite; you daren't leave it or ignore it because it's all you've got left.

'Mark...' she said suddenly. 'What is it...what's wrong?'

'Nothing,' he denied. 'Nothing.'

* * *

'Of course, it's no wonder he left her. Everyone knows that the only reason she got that promotion in the first place is because ...'

'Shush ...'

Deborah tensed as the two girls chatting by the coffee machine fell silent as she walked past. She pretended that she hadn't heard them. What else could she do?

She knew, of course, that it had been her they had been gossiping about, putting two and two together and doing a bit of 'creative accounting' with it.

'You look a bit down ... Not still missing the boyfriend, I hope. You're better off without him.'

Deborah froze as she felt Ryan moving close to her. Too close, she decided wearily as she moved back from him.

'You're doing a nice job with the Kilcoyne liquidation,' he told her approvingly. 'I had the bank on this morning full of praise for the way you're handling things ...'

Deborah said nothing. Three days ago he had been complaining that she wasn't showing enough aggression towards the company's debtors, and besides, Ryan never gave a compliment without demanding repayment for it—one way or another.

'We got a new case in this morning ... I'd like you to have a look at it,' he added.

A new case ... Had he forgotten that only last week he'd given her five case-files to work on, all of them involving an enormous amount of careful checking and cross-checking, dull, boring routine work ... the kind of work she had thought she had left behind in her first junior job?

'I'm not sure if I've got time,' she began, but he overruled her, raising his eyebrows and telling her vigorously,

'Then you must make time ... Delegate ...'

'Delegate. To whom?'

When they had initially discussed her promotion, the package he had described had included extra staff to work under her, but so far they had not been forthcoming. She pointed this out to him now, watching as he shrugged and gave her a charming, lazy smile.

'I know...but there's nothing I can do, I'm afraid. Not until the partners ratify your promotion officially...'

'And when will that be?' Deborah asked him, trying not to sound too anxious. She was tired of the looks and innuendoes she was constantly intercepting, implying that her promotion was still not 'official' and that there was therefore something suspect about it.

Ryan shrugged carelessly. 'Not for a while yet. There isn't another full partners' meeting until the end of the month. But don't worry,' he told her, smiling at her. 'There won't be any problem.'

His capriciousness was wearing her down, she admitted after he had gone. It made her feel uncomfortable and on edge; wary and defensive. She had begun to feel so isolated and alone here since Mark had gone...isolated, alone... and...and vulnerable.

She shouldn't have changed the décor of the bedroom in such a rush, Deborah acknowledged as she stripped off her suit and pulled on her leggings and a thick sweater. The blue which had looked so pretty on the paint chart seemed cold and hard on the walls, the bedlinen she had chosen too stark and plain. The room still smelled of paint and she woke up in the morning with her head aching.

Increasingly she felt reluctant to go home at night, dreading the moment when she would open the door and walk into the empty flat.

She went into the kitchen and made herself a meal which she then pushed around her plate for twenty minutes before admitting that she didn't want it.

She was just scraping her food into the waste-bin when the doorbell rang. Automatically her stomach muscles locked even though logically she knew it wouldn't be Mark.

It wasn't...it was Ryan.

She stared at him blankly for several seconds until he stepped past her and into the flat.

'Ah, good, you are in... I was just leaving the office when I remembered that I hadn't gone through those files with you. So I nipped back and got them. You're not doing anything, are you...?'

'No... No, I'm not doing anything,' Deborah agreed, too surprised at seeing him to say anything else.

'Good, that gives us the whole evening...without any interruptions.'

Warning bells rang suddenly in her brain. But it was too late; he was already inside...

'Good... You've got a nice quick mind, Deborah. I like that,' Ryan told her approvingly as he closed the last file.

He leaned back against the settee, stretching luxuriously, his chest wall lifting against his shirt as he breathed deeply. He had discarded his jacket earlier, pulling off his tie as he did so. Beneath the fine cotton of his shirt Deborah could see the dark shadow of his body hair. He was a man who exulted in his own sexuality, she recognised; a man who was vain of his masculinity...proud of it...arrogant about it.

Watching him now, as he stretched, she realised that it wasn't only the muscles of his chest that were being revealed for her admiration, and it was hard work for her not to fall into the trap of hurriedly averting her eyes; of being flustered into pretending she had not seen the way the fine wool of his trousers had momentarily pulled against his thighs and crotch.

Somehow that brief outlining of his body had been more erotic than if he had had a full erection, and she suspected that he knew it...and had deliberately manufactured it? His action irritated her.

'How about some coffee?' he suggested. For a moment Deborah was tempted to refuse, but decided she was probably over-reacting.

Tonight, apart from that one provocative stretch, he had behaved towards her as the perfect male mentor, praising, explaining, encouraging without any hint of sexuality in his manner towards her, until now...

He had even managed to make her laugh as well, to forget, even if only for a handful of seconds, her own unhappiness as he'd related a couple of incidents from his own early career. But now she felt uneasy and edgy and would really have preferred him to leave.

She had just finished making the coffee when she heard him coming into the kitchen. She tensed automatically, turning round to face him, and then saw that he was laughing at her.

'Why so nervous?' he asked her. 'Not because you're alone with me, surely? Is it me you're really afraid of, Deborah... or is it yourself? It must be hard... being on your own...'

He was moving close to her, coming between her and the kitchen door, and in the constricted space of the small room there was nowhere for her to go.

As she tried to edge past him he caught hold of her, swinging her towards him as he told her, 'Don't play coy with me... You know how much I want you... and what you do to me... don't you...?'

He was holding her waist with one hand and her wrist with the other and now, as he spoke, he took hold of her hand and carried it down his body, watching her as he held it against his erection, moving his body against her palm, blatantly enjoying what he was doing, and equally blatantly impervious to her shock.

'Mmm... doesn't that feel good?' he asked her as he leaned forward. 'Very, very good,' he murmured against her ear as he wedged her between the worktop and his body, the hand which had been on her waist travelling up towards her breast. 'Bigger that what you're used to, is it?' he laughed. 'Well, you just wait until you've got it inside you... I promise you, you'll...' His hand was on her breast, his thumb pushing aside the fabric of her sweater.

Anger galvanised Deborah into life. She pushed hard against his chest and pulled fiercely away from him. 'Ryan, stop it!' she demanded. 'You've got it all wrong; I'm *not* interested.'

'No...?' He was still smiling at her.

'No,' she told him evenly, adding quietly, 'I've always made it clear to you that I'm not in the market for an affair...for sex. You know that...'

Determinedly she held his gaze while he looked at her.

'I hope you know what you're doing...just what you're throwing away,' Ryan told her silkily. 'We could have been very good together, you and I...in bed and out of it...'

Deborah suppressed her anger. 'Professionally, I value your advice and friendship, Ryan, but I won't sleep with you,' she told him steadily.

'No? Isn't it a bit too late to tell me that now...?'

'Too late?'

'Come on, Deborah, you're an intelligent woman. You know the score...'

'I thought I did,' she agreed. 'But now I'm not so sure.' Her heart was beating heavily and painfully. Mark, it seemed, had been right after all, and yet she had been so sure that he was wrong, that she could handle Ryan, that she had made it clear to him that she was not prepared to trade sex for promotion. She had believed also that Ryan knew and accepted this.

'Perhaps you'd better enlighten me, Ryan.' She lifted her head and stared directly at him. 'When you promoted me I believed that promotion was given on merit...*professional* merit...'

'What promotion?' he taunted her softly. 'You haven't got it yet.'

Deborah felt as though her whole body had been immersed in icy water, disbelief following shock.

'You offered me that promotion on *merit*,' she protested, but even as she said the words she was remembering the other women who had walked this road ahead of her.

'Grow up, Deborah,' Ryan advised her. 'Nothing in this world comes for free. You should have learned that by now. After all, it's a fine old tradition in business...the giving and taking of favours...in one way or another...

'Networking, I believe they call it today,' he told her. 'The name is maybe different but the principle is the same.

We all bargain for what we want with what we've got. That, my dear Deborah, is the way of the world.'

'Are you saying that the only reason you offered me promotion was because you wanted to go to bed with me?'

She couldn't quite keep the anger or the disillusionment out of her voice.

'Not the *only* reason,' Ryan told her with a smile. 'I have my position within the partnership to consider, and if I hadn't thought you were up to the job...' He gave a small shrug. 'The job was there; someone had to have it...why not give it to you and kill two birds with one stone...?'

'By using promotion as a means of blackmailing me into sex?'

'Blackmailing you?' He almost looked hurt. He was over the loss of control, of superiority her rejection had caused, Deborah recognised now, and if anything he was almost enjoying taunting her, forcing her to acknowledge his power over her, professionally if not sexually. 'Hardly. What I had in mind was something that would have been a mutual pleasure...a mutual benefit. Promoting you would simply have made it easier for us to be together...for me to show you how much I enjoyed and valued you...'

Deborah digested the words and their past tense in silence.

'You're a good accountant, in fact you're a *very* good accountant, but it takes more than professional skill to succeed, and if I could give you a small piece of advice...

'People-management, Deborah...you need to polish up the way you relate to your colleagues... I hate to say it, but there have been one or two comments about the way you seem to have let your new role distance you a little too much. Kim Wright mentioned to me the other day that you were rather off with her.'

Deborah bit down hard on the words about to spring to her lips.

Don't drop down to his level, she warned herself, he was playing games with her now and he was enjoying it.

'There is far more involved in running your own department than merely getting through the workload. Have you ever considered taking a staff-management course of any kind?'

'Yes, as a matter of fact I did one when I was with Crook's,' she told him quietly. 'It was on my c.v.'

She wasn't going to remind him that she had received a very high commendation from the tutor on the course for the work she had done; after all, no course could teach her or anyone else to become as expertly manipulative of other people as Ryan was. That was something you were born with... or without...

'Pity...' Ryan told her just before he turned away from her. 'I was looking forward to having you as my... protégée...'

After he had gone, Deborah sat down in a chair and closed her eyes. Oh, Mark, she thought tiredly.

She had his phone number. He had left it and his address on the answerphone, the answerphone he had insisted she keep, just as he tried to insist that he would continue paying half the rent on the flat. She had taken the phone but refused the rent. After all, why should he pay for something he no longer wanted?

She looked at the telephone, and then, before she could give in to her own weakness, she got up and walked quickly away from it.

Mark frowned as he looked down at the papers in front of him. He was supposed to be studying the accounts of the French company Stephanie was planning to buy, not wasting his time doodling.

As he looked at the letter 'D' he had meticulously made out of a series of figures he grimaced and pushed the papers away.

The French firm was quite a large one, almost as large as Stephanie's, although nothing like as profitable. A disastrous venture, trying to grow flowers for the perfume industry, had resulted in years of heavy losses, although, as Stephanie had said, potentially the scope for the company was very good. 'It will extend the range of flowers I can supply and the growing season.'

'And it could also leave you very vulnerable to a take-over bid,' Mark had warned her. 'In fact... it isn't unheard of, you know, for a company to be lured into over-committing itself to make it more vulnerable for a takeover...'

'My biggest rivals at the moment are Dutch and not French,' Stephanie had told him.

He was due to fly out to France with her later in the month to see the French business at first hand.

'I could do with you working for me full-time,' she had commented half jokingly to him. 'Not to handle the day-to-day wages and general finances—I have someone to do that—but to act more as a financial-adviser-cum-PA...'

She hadn't mentioned it a second time and Mark hadn't taken her up on it; it was the kind of work that would appeal to Deborah far more than it did to him—a real high-flying job. Deborah... He looked down at his doodling again. The remarks Stephanie had made about her own ex-husband and her marriage had caught him on a raw nerve. Listening to her, he had immediately been filled with in-dignation on her behalf and contempt for the man, any man who could treat a woman who loved him so gener-ously and genuinely that badly, who could hurt her so much simply to salve his ego.

And then it had come home to him that she might just as easily have been talking about him.

But the two situations were completely different. Stephanie had made no secret of the fact that she had loved and needed her husband, that the business success was something set apart from their relationship.

Deborah did not need him, and their personal and pro-fessional lives were so closely entwined that they could not be kept separate.

Stephanie had been compassionately aware of her hus-band's feelings; Deborah had totally ignored his.

And yet the picture Stephanie had unwittingly drawn for him of her husband as a spoiled, selfish man behaving like a child, punishing his wife for his own failings, and the uncomfortable feelings it raised in his own conscience, would not go away.

He had had no option other than to do what he did... If he had stayed...

Was he more like Stephanie's husband than he wanted to admit? *Had* he only been able to handle Deborah's success just as long as it did not overtake his, as she had accused? He had denied that accusation vehemently and angrily then.

Too vehemently? Too angrily?

He closed the file he was studying and walked over to stand in front of the window of the small cottage he was renting.

It was one in a series of three just outside the town; originally farmworkers' cottages, they had been modernised by the farmer who owned and rented them out.

Their peace and relative isolation suited Mark. He had never liked city life as much as Deborah had. A country practice like this one would suit him down to the ground, he admitted... and drive Deborah crazy with boredom.

His eyes burned drily in their sockets, his throat felt raw with emotion.

He might have stopped wanting her, but he sure as hell hadn't stopped caring about her... loving her.

He glanced across at the telephone and then turned back to the window.

She probably wouldn't be in anyway... There was no way Ryan would have lost any time in offering her comfort and solace.

A car went down the lane, its windows open, its radio blasting out pop music. Cher sang raunchily about wishing she could turn back time, and Mark closed his eyes against the pain he could feel welling up inside him.

CHAPTER TWENTY-EIGHT

'RICHARD, do you remember that woman you operated on for breast cancer, the one whose operation you timed to coincide with her menstrual cycle? Well, there's an article here about it in the *Gazette*.'

Richard put down his toast.

'They've given it a full-page spread as well,' Elizabeth told him. She passed the paper over to him. 'They're running a women's health awareness campaign. It's a very complimentary article, good publicity for the hospital...'

'I doubt David will see it that way,' Richard told her grimly. 'He already thinks I'm past it; when he sees this he'll probably try to get me certified. He hasn't got any time for any kind of holistic approach. Samuel Tozer was complaining the other day because he's refused to authorise funds for massage therapy for his geriatric patients. It's a proven fact that massage provides emotional as well as physical benefits for elderly patients, but David virtually accused him of trying to run some kind of seedy massage parlour aimed at corrupting his patients. Samuel was livid.'

'But the article is full of praise for your concern for your patients... It even contrasts the treatment your cancer patient received and her recovery with the experiences of other women locally. And it calls for lists to be made available to patients comparing operational success-rates — something you've always said they have the right to see. Has David said anything more to you about wanting you to retire...?'

'Not directly, but there have been hints. It's virtually common knowledge now that the Northern is the favourite to get the Accident Unit.'

Elizabeth watched him sympathetically.

'When David sees this it will probably just confirm what he's already decided—that I'm no longer fit to be in charge of a surgical unit!'

'Brian, have you seen this article in the *Gazette*? What...?'

'Yes, I have,' Brian confirmed, adding enthusiastically, 'It's excellent publicity for us, David, and not just for us but for the Health Service as a whole. It shows just how innovative and forward-thinking we can be, and how open to exploring new ideas and acting on them...'

'New ideas...deciding when to operate by the time of the month...?'

'The story's been picked up by a couple of the nationals already,' Brian continued. 'The *Telegraph* were particularly keen to run an article on it...'

'What? That means the Minister's bound to see it. Have you any idea what fools it's going to make us look?'

'*Fools?*' Brian protested. 'Some of the teaching hospitals are already considering running serious trials based on the premises that Richard used... That's how seriously they're taking it...'

'We'll be the laughing stock of the country,' David continued, overriding Brian's protest. 'I warned you months ago, Brian, that Humphries was a liability, and I'm afraid I shall have to tell the Minister so. She's bound to raise the matter next week when she comes down.

'If you want my advice, your wisest course would be to dissociate yourself as much as you possibly can from what's happened. You'll have to accept *some* responsibility, of course... It's a pity you spoke to the Press without consulting me first. Still, it does mean that at least we've got a perfect excuse for getting rid of Humphries now. We could hardly do anything else. It's bound to affect his credibility, people's faith in him as a surgeon, and indirectly, through him, their faith in the General as a hospital.

'The Northern have cut their staff down quite dramatically along with shortening their waiting lists by weeding out what turned out to be a good many unnecessary operations,' David told him smoothly. 'Christopher Jeffries agrees with me that patients who refuse to take proper care of their health and who in fact prejudice their own chances of recovery and therefore waste both the Authority's time and money must be made to realise that they really cannot expect the Health Service to put right what amounts to self-inflicted damage.'

'You can't legislate against people like that,' Brian protested. 'It goes against the whole ethos of the Health Service...'

'It's for their own good,' David contradicted him smoothly. 'Smokers, drinkers—they need to realise that they are responsible for their own health problems. Now that is what I call forward-thinking...not some idiotic belief that the position of the moon affects a patient's chances of recovery from an operation.'

Smokers...drinkers...what next? Brian wondered tiredly as he replaced the receiver. Drug addicts, suicide attempts...the elderly...would they be considered to be responsible for their own ill health and treatment refused them accordingly?

He sat back in his chair, appalled by the knowledge of what might potentially happen when human beings took it upon themselves to play God.

One rule for the rich, another for the poor. He had thought the Health Service had come into being to put an end to that.

Suddenly he felt very tired and very old.

'I hope you didn't mind...about my giving that interview to the *Gazette*,' Hannah Jacobs told Richard hesitantly as he finished examining her. 'Only it was Mr Hamilton who suggested it. He said that since I obviously felt so strongly about what you had done, the trouble you had taken, I should share it with other women...give them the opportunity to benefit as I had done; and then when the *Gazette* approached me I remembered what he'd said and gave them the interview...'

Richard frowned. Blake Hamilton had said nothing to him about giving her any such advice, although they had discussed the case.

'I don't mind at all,' Richard assured her only semi-truthfully. Both the *Mail* and the *Telegraph* had run stories on the article. Ian had rung him up to tease him about his publicity and so, of course, had a variety of other medical colleagues.

What exactly was Blake Hamilton trying to do? He had not struck Richard as a particularly manipulative type of man; they had got on well together and had seemed to share corresponding views, and yet there was no doubt in Richard's mind after listening to his patient that Hamilton had manipulated her... For what purpose: to discredit him further with David? But how could that possibly benefit Blake Hamilton, who had seemed to share his own contempt for David?

'I don't understand why he should have involved himself,' Richard told Elizabeth later. 'What is he trying to do...?'

'Why don't you ask him?' Elizabeth suggested reasonably.

'It isn't as simple or as straightforward as that,' Richard told her. 'We've got the Minister visiting us tomorrow. Brian's in a real flap about it. It looks as if the Northern is going to get the new Accident Unit,' he added quietly. 'Nothing official has been said yet, but...'

Elizabeth watched him unhappily. No matter what she said to him or how much she tried to comfort him, to help him adopt a positive attitude towards the prospect of his retirement, it would achieve nothing unless Richard himself changed.

She had thought quite often recently about what would happen if he stopped work; there was no use trying to pretend or to avoid acknowledging that if Richard did retire it would change her life as well as his own.

In the early days of their marriage she had always put Richard and his needs, the needs of his career first—girls and young women had done that in those days—and then her daughter had been born and her needs too had seemed more important than her own.

But things...life had changed. She wasn't that same young woman any more. She was enjoying the excitement of discovering how far she could push herself, how much she could achieve, how her mind, her brain was enjoying the feeling of being stretched and used in much the same way as her muscles did after a good exercise class... She was thriving on the challenges she was being offered far too much to give it all up and to stay at home now and help nurse Richard's bruised ego...to comfort him in his self-inflicted self-pity... No, she couldn't...

Quickly she turned her head away, not wanting Richard to see her expression. How often had she counselled other women that it was healthy and good for them to be selfish sometimes, to put themselves and their own needs first; that their respect for themselves engendered respect in others?

Giving such advice was one thing...acting on it was another... 'Richard, have you thought of having a word with...with someone about how you feel about re-tiring...?' she suggested quietly.

She saw immediately that she had said the wrong thing. 'For God's sake Liz, you might have been brainwashed into believing that counselling is an instant cure for every-thing... Try telling that to someone who's suffering from a perforated ulcer or a malignant cancer,' he told her sourly.

Elizabeth paused, tempted to point out the ineffec-tiveness of the evasive and defensive tactics he was adopting, but putting him in the wrong and trying to make him ac-knowledge what he was doing was hardly likely to help.

'I'm beginning to wish I'd never brought the subject up in the first place,' he continued testily. 'Just because I don't feel that I'm ready to retire, and that I'm being forced into it, it doesn't automatically make me a candidate for the shrink's couch.'

Guiltily Richard avoided meeting Elizabeth's eyes. He knew that he was over-reacting, but even the very mention of the word 'retirement' had become like touching a raw nerve, his body so sensitive to the anticipated pain that it reacted almost before that nerve was touched.

And besides, what could counselling tell him that he didn't already know himself? That his fear of retirement represented a very male fear of no longer commanding respect, being needed, having a defined role to play, being in control of life? And what the hell good would that do him?

'And this, Minister, is Mr Humphries, our senior surgeon.'

'Mr Humphries.' The Minister extended her hand towards Richard with a warm smile. 'I've been hearing and reading some very good things about you. It's a very welcome change to see us getting some good publicity for once, and to know that our senior people are so open to exploring new avenues of healing, especially when they're connected with such an important issue as women's health,' she told Richard approvingly.

At the Minister's side, Richard could see David frowning as he tried to edge her away from him.

'I understand that you were the initial instigator of the plan to open an Accident Unit locally, and that you've been one of the prime campaigners to raise funds towards it, and arouse local interest.'

'The new motorway links opened locally have meant that we're seeing far more road accident cases than we used to,' Richard replied. 'It's a proven fact that the victims of these accidents stand a far better chance of surviving if their injuries are dealt with immediately by experienced staff...staff who are trained to recognise the nature of their injuries and how to deal with them. And of course we're not just talking about when they actually reach hospital,' Richard told her, warming to his theme. 'Medical teams in the ambulances——'

'Thank you, Richard,' David cut in testily, glaring at him. 'But I'm sure the Minister doesn't need a lecture from you on...'

'On the contrary,' the Minister stopped David smoothly. 'I consider it part of my remit, and certainly my responsibility, to be as well-informed as I can.'

Richard could see that David was growing increasingly impatient.

'Er—I don't wish to rush you, Minister,' he started saying, 'but if I could just introduce you to our newly appointed psychiatrist, Mr...'

'Blake!' the Minister exclaimed warmly as she turned round. Ignoring his outstretched hand, she clasped Blake Hamilton warmly by the forearms.

'Minister,' Richard heard Blake responding formally.

'What on earth are you doing here?' she demanded, ignoring his attempt at formality. 'I thought you'd gone back to Johns Hopkins...'

'I did,' Blake confirmed. 'But...I had to come back for personal reasons.'

'And you're working *here*?' she asked him, her eyebrows lifting a little.

'Like Richard, I believe that the future lies in treating the patients as a whole, not as a variety of different needs.'

'So...you and...Mr Humphries would be working together in the new unit,' she commented thoughtfully. She frowned as she looked at David. 'I didn't read any mention of this in your last report, Mr Howarth?'

'Er...we hadn't quite finalised our plans then,' David told her.

His colour was unusually high, Richard noticed, both with temper and mortification, but he made no attempt to challenge what Blake had said.

'Of course initially it will mean some extra expense,' Blake was adding quietly. 'And we all appreciate the difficult situation the Health Service is in, with so many calls upon its finances, but from my work at Johns Hopkins I know that early counselling not only aids the patients' speed of recovery but also ultimately is cost-effective, in that the counselling itself is far more effective in the early days after the trauma.'

'It's certainly a very innovative idea,' the Minister commented.

'And one with considerable media appeal,' Blake told her.

Richard saw the slightly sharp look she gave him, her mouth pursing slightly as she told him, 'It's the health of our patients that is our prime concern, not the approval of the media.' But then her expression softened slightly as she added, 'But you're right, of course, Blake. It would be good publicity—show that we are forward-thinking and not wholly bound up with cost-cutting and bureaucracy, as so many of our detractors appear to think.

'The PM is very anxious to improve the Health Ministry's public image——'. She broke off, frowning. One of the aides behind her leaned forward to murmur something in her ear, and looked significantly at his watch.

'It's been interesting talking with you,' she told Richard as she shook his hand a second time, her mouth curled into a small smile as she added, 'I shall look forward to seeing the results your new unit achieves, although not, I dare say, its budgets. However, health care can never be wholly about finance. Good money-management is important, of course—we must never forget that we are housekeepers of the nation's funds, not our own—but good health is even more so.' Her eyes darkened a little and became slightly shadowed as she turned to Blake and told him, 'We must arrange to have dinner and talk properly, Blake. It's been a long time since Romania...'

'You should have seen David's face when she made that comment about looking forward to seeing the results of the new unit,' Richard told Elizabeth later as he related the day's events to her. 'He looked as though he was about to have a thrombosis...'

'But I thought you said he was going to recommend the Northern for the unit...'

'He was, but the Minister never gave him the chance...'

'Can she *do* that? Go against his recommendations...?'

'She *is* the Minister,' Richard told her drily, 'and before she left she apparently saw Brian and confirmed to him that we were to get the unit. He's cock-a-hoop with it ... and——'

'He's not the only one,' Elizabeth interrupted him with smile.

'You should have seen David's reaction when the Minister saw Blake Hamilton. It seems the two of them met when he was out working in Romania for one of the relief agencies and she was there as a government adviser.'

'That kind of experience must have a bonding effect on the people who share it,' Elizabeth responded. 'Those poor children, I don't think any of us will ever forget the news footage we saw. To have witnessed the reality of what their poor little lives were at first hand must have left its mark on the people who were there.'

'Mmm. Well, Blake had obviously impressed the Minister.'

'And not only Blake. To judge from what you've told me, you did your fair share of impressing her yourself...' Elizabeth commented.

'Oh, she made some remark about the good publicity we'd got,' Richard agreed, 'but without Blake I doubt that it would have been enough to swing her decision our way... He's a very clever man, is our Blake. Very clever...

'After she'd gone I asked him why he encouraged her to come down on our side, when he could quite easily have put pressure on David to use him at the Northern where he could have had equally easy access to the new unit.'

'What did he say?' Elizabeth asked him curiously.

'He said that, like me, he believed saving people's lives should come before saving money, and that he felt that Christopher Jeffries was too easily influenced by David. "He's a good surgeon," he told me, "but rather too easily put upon..." The Minister wants the new unit to come into operation as soon as possible and she's told Brian that she wants estimates in straight away—and she's given him the go-ahead to make enquiries about that specially equipped ambulance-cum-mobile-operating unit we wanted.

'God, half of me still can't believe it. The relief...after what I'd been dreading... You've no idea...' He stopped and smiled at her, buoyant with enthusiasm and excitement. 'Call Sara; see if she and Ian are free this weekend; we'll take them out somewhere to celebrate.'

'Richard...' Elizabeth began, and then stopped. Now was perhaps not the time to raise the subject that was troubling her. It seemed unkind to broach it while he was so ebulliently happy, but the issues raised by his reaction to his threatened retirement were still there, even if events had pushed them into abeyance.

One day, ultimately, they would have to be faced, even if right now she felt a cowardly relief that they were not going to have to face them yet.

Whether Richard chose to see his brief foretaste of what ultimately lay ahead as something constructive or destructive could only rest with him.

And if he chose to ignore what he had learned?

'Liz...'

She looked up to find he was watching her.

'Let's enjoy today for what it is...'

'And forget about tomorrow?' she suggested wryly.

'And forget about it—no...' He came over to her and folded her in his arms, resting his chin on top of her head, his hand slowly stroking her hair. 'I know what you're thinking,' he told her huskily, 'and I know you're right. I promise I'll do my best to try to cultivate a more positive attitude...

'This afternoon, when I'd started to come down a little, I told myself how lucky I've been...not just because of the unit, but because I've been given a chance to...to see what lies ahead and to prepare for it.

'I'm not going to lie to you and pretend I feel any differently about it—I don't...but perhaps I can *learn* to feel differently. In fact,' he added softly, drawing her closer, 'I've already thought of one way I can make very good use of all this free time I'm ultimately going to have—a leisure activity eminently suitable for a man of my age with a proven beneficial effect on the cardiovascular system. You haven't got anything planned for this evening, have you...?'

'This evening...?' Elizabeth laughed, and teased him, '*All* evening...?' as his hand stroked up over her body and lingered caressingly against her breast.

'All evening,' Richard confirmed, laughing with her.

'Mmm...' Her mouth curled into a smile as he kissed the side of her throat. 'Fifty pence says you can't...'

'You're on,' Richard told her.

Elizabeth felt him move slightly, and as she peered over his shoulder she saw that he had the fingers of his free hand crossed behind his back.

She was still laughing as she turned to walk upstairs with him.

CHAPTER TWENTY-NINE

THE Volvo estate car Blake arrived to pick her up in wasn't somehow the kind of car she had expected a man of his professional stature to drive; a top-of-the-range Jaguar, BMW or Mercedes would have been more the type of car Philippa would have expected him to own—shiny and expensive, rather than merely comfortable and clean.

Andrew would have been highly disdainful, but then Andrew had always placed too much emphasis on outward show and material possessions.

It had been hard to know exactly what to wear this morning—or perhaps easier to worry about her clothes than all the other issues her decision to accept Blake's job offer had raised. Had she been working in an office it would have been much easier—a suit, a skirt and blouse—but what did a housekeeper-cum-surrogate mother wear?

Bearing in mind the fact that she was going to be meeting Anya's social worker as well as Anya herself, Philippa had opted for a simple plain white T-shirt and her jeans, but had brought with her a navy jacket she could wear to add a touch of formality if it proved necessary.

A little to her surprise, Blake was wearing almost exactly the same sort of outfit, except that he did not have the jacket, and the T-shirt he was wearing moulded the contours of his body far more snugly than her own did hers.

Inadvertently she found herself looking at him for just that little bit too long.

His forearms were taut and sinewy, with far more muscle than she would have expected in a man whose occupation was mainly sedentary; his skin was tanned a warm golden-brown, a legacy from the time he had spent in America, she guessed.

Even the soft furring of hair on his arms had a faint golden sheen to it... Would the rest of his body hair be the same colour or slightly darker still, the way she remembered it?

Her stomach did a somersault.

'Are you OK?' he asked.

'Yes... Yes, I'm fine...' Instinctively she took a step back from him, widening the gap between them before risking meeting his eyes.

When she saw that they were registering only good-mannered concern, she relaxed slightly.

'I'm glad you've dressed casually,' he approved as he opened the car door for her. 'Anya's parents were more concerned with their cause than their appearance and she tends to be slightly afraid of anyone dressed too formally or in uniform.

'She's never actually been to South America, of course, but her parents still lived there spiritually in many ways. An overriding point in my favour as far as the Social Services were concerned is the fact that with me she would have the opportunity to become more integrated into the mainstream of everyday life; she's completely fluent in Spanish, but she's never had a doll and appears more knowledgeable about the difficulties of arming revolutionaries than she does about playing games with other children.'

'That isn't necessarily a disadvantage,' Philippa commented drily. 'In fact I should think it would make her extremely popular with her peers. Children are all potential revolutionaries...'

'With adults their oppressors?' Blake suggested, laughing.

As Philippa shared his laughter she was sharply aware of how much shared adult male-to-female laughter had been missing from her life.

Andrew had not had a good sense of humour, frowning disapprovingly whenever he'd heard the boys telling her jokes. Philippa had the suspicion that he'd considered that spontaneous genuine laughter in a woman was somehow something not quite acceptable...like spontaneous genuine enjoyment of sex?

Quickly she dismissed the thought, clipping on her seatbelt as Blake started the car. As she glanced over her shoulder she noticed a dog guard lying in the back of the car.

'Have you got a dog?' she asked him curiously.

Blake, following her glance, shook his head, and then told her slightly self-consciously, 'No... At least not yet... I had thought...pets can be very therapeutic for people going through trauma; they can often express their emotions through animals far more easily than they can through their contact with other human beings. That's one of the reasons I bought this car. Plenty of room for a family and for a dog as well. Don't you like animals...?'

'Yes, as a matter of fact I do, but Andrew never cared for pets, and with the boys at boarding-school...'

Philippa saw the look he was giving her and, correctly interpreting it, told him quietly, 'It wasn't my decision. Andrew insisted and...' She hesitated, searching for the right words, reluctant to betray to him what she perceived as her own weakness. 'There was family pressure as well...'

'From your father,' Blake guessed. His voice was suddenly much harder and colder, Philippa noticed. 'What did he do?' he asked her harshly. 'Tell you that you were being selfish and emotional in wanting to keep them at home, putting your own needs before theirs?'

Startled by his perception, Philippa stared at him.

'How did you know that...?' she began, and then fell silent. Blake and her father had never liked one another and habit prevented her from criticising someone to whom she was supposed to be close to someone who wasn't.

'Oh...I suppose it's your training,' she hazarded. 'You must...'

'No...it isn't my training,' Blake contradicted her. He sounded angry, she recognised. Male anger had always alarmed her and unnerved her, and she had to fight to suppress the instinctive urge to placate him in the way that she had been taught... in the way that her father and elder brother had demanded and expected.

Those days were gone now; she was not responsible for Blake's emotions, they were his responsibility, she told herself firmly.

'It isn't my training,' he repeated. 'Just the fact that I know your father.'

And I know you, he might have added, Philippa acknowledged silently. I know how weak you are.

'It seemed better to let them go to school rather than keep them at home in a bad atmosphere,' she said in defence of herself. 'I didn't want them growing up like my father, like Robert, like Andrew, to think that being a man means that you have to withdraw from any kind of emotional contact with anyone.

'As it happens, the fact that they are away at school has meant that it's been easier for them to come to terms with Andrew's death. They never really knew him, you see. He never really had time for them...' Or for me, she could have added, but she didn't. She was in danger of becoming over-emotional as it was. 'And thankfully they're still both young enough not to feel any guilt...'

She stopped speaking. She had already said enough...too much really, but there was something about the quality of Blake's silence that made it easy to talk to him.

All part of his training, no doubt.

'You love them very much.'

His statement was as unexpected as the soft roughness in his voice.

'Yes,' Philippa agreed chokily.

'When do they come home for the summer holidays?'

'Not until the end of the month,' Philippa told him, grateful for the switch from emotional to practical matters.

'Three weeks. Good... That should give Anya some time to get settled in first.'

'Three weeks isn't very long,' Philippa said. 'It's bound to be difficult for her, and not just because of the trauma of losing her parents. The change from living in a city, in a small flat to living somewhere rural... She's bound to find it confusing.'

'Yes, I know. The one good point is that she starts secondary school in September, which means that at least she will be on a par with her peers there.'

'To some extent,' Philippa agreed.

'Having second thoughts?' Blake asked her lightly.

Why was he asking her that? Was *he* having second thoughts himself, perhaps judging her too emotional for the role he wanted her to play after hearing her speak about her sons?

'No,' Philippa denied. 'Are you?'

'No, I'm not.' He took advantage of a slowing down of the traffic to turn his head and look at her. 'What makes you think I might?'

His questions made her feel slightly uncomfortable, vulnerable almost.

She gave a small shrug, unwilling to express the self-doubt or the self-knowledge that had given rise to her question, and said instead, obliquely, 'I'm still my parents' child.'

There was a moment's pause, and then Blake asked her softly, 'Are you? Somehow I don't think so. I would have said that now you're very much your own woman.'

His compliment, so unexpected and so unlooked for, caught Philippa off guard; she could feel her skin starting to heat and she was probably gaping at him like a raw adolescent, she told herself fiercely as she willed her body heat to subside and turned her head away from him.

Very much her own woman; they were words to be treasured and savoured, bright stars lighting the darkness of her own voyage of self-discovery, and would have been no matter who had given them to her; but to have received them from Blake of all people.

Be careful, she warned herself... Be very, very careful.

The outskirts of Leeds were similar to those of any other large industrial city, the block of flats where Anya was staying depressingly familiar.

How could any child thrive, living in such surroundings? Philippa wondered sadly. It was like planting flowers where they would be deprived of sunlight.

The flat where Anya was staying was halfway up one of the larger blocks; the lifts were out of order so Philippa and Blake had to walk.

She would have felt very uneasy about using these stairs on her own, Philippa acknowledged as she carefully avoided any eye-contact with the silent group of youths gathered together on one of the landings, and she was a healthy, relatively young woman. How must it feel to be old and alone, living in one of these places?

It was Anya herself who opened the door to them. Her skin, which Philippa suspected would have gleamed warm honey-gold in a warmer climate, looked sallow, clinging to the thin bones of her face and body, and her huge brown eyes watched them in silence as they entered the small flat.

The clothes she was wearing were too small and shabby.

It wasn't so much that she looked undernourished, Philippa recognised, rather than that she looked underloved.

A huge rush of emotion seized her, a need to take hold of Anya's thin body and hold her protectively in her arms, but Philippa sensibly resisted it. To overwhelm Anya with unfamiliar and probably unwanted physical affection would be the worst possible thing she could do. *Her* needs were not the ones that were paramount—Anya's were.

There were two other people in the small cramped sitting-room—an older grey-haired woman, who Philippa guessed was the foster mother the council had had looking after Anya since her parents' death, and a younger woman who quickly introduced herself as Anya's social worker.

It was obvious from the slight stiffness in her manner towards Blake that she did not totally approve of the situation. Her manner towards *her* was slightly warmer, Philippa recognised, and she mentally applauded the girl's professionalism in putting her responsibility towards Anya before her own personal reactions.

While she listened to her and responded to her questions, Philippa watched Anya, aware that despite her physical withdrawal from the adults discussing her future she was fully aware of what was going on.

Philippa's heart went out to her. She knew all too well how it felt to have other people in control of your life, to feel powerless to have any say in the decisions they were making.

'Has anyone asked Anya what she would prefer to do?' she asked quietly when the social worker had finished speaking.

Immediately the younger woman bridled resentfully, 'Of course,' she told Philippa crisply. 'Naturally. It is always the child's needs that are of paramount importance...'

When it was time to leave, Anya did so in an apathetic silence which caught at Philippa's heart. The social worker walked with them to the car. She was so plainly determined not to be impressed by Blake that Philippa had to hide her amusement.

'It's all right for you,' Blake muttered to her as the other woman left them. 'You're not a potential child molester.'

'It's their job to be concerned...' Philippa pointed out quietly,

'Yes, I know,' Blake agreed as he placed Anya's suitcase in the back of the estate car. 'But it still isn't...' He shook his head and added feelingly, 'God, I'd hate to be a parent, a father caught up in an alleged abuse case...'

'Yes,' Philippa agreed with a small shiver. There were worse things than being an emotionally absent father as Andrew had been; far, far worse.

Anya looked surprised when Philippa got in the back of the car with her, but she didn't, as Philippa had half expected her to do, retreat into the far corner, putting as much physical distance between them as she could.

'We'll have to stop somewhere for lunch,' Philippa warned Blake as he started the car.

'What kind of things do you like to eat, Anya?' he asked as he drove off.

Silence. A small, anxious frown pleated the sallow forehead.

'For a special treat my sons love going to McDonald's,' Philippa offered, and was rewarded with a relieved look from Anya's brown eyes and a brief hint of a smile.

'McDonald's, eh?' Philippa had to fight hard not to laugh as she saw Blake's expression.

'Are you OK back there, Philippa?' Blake asked quietly.

Philippa nodded. Anya had fallen asleep with her head on Philippa's shoulder half an hour after they had resumed their journey after their stop for lunch. Now, as she gently eased her into a more comfortable position, Philippa didn't risk waking her up by speaking.

Her appetite was healthy enough at any rate, she reflected, judging from the way she had demolished her lunch, although Philippa would have preferred to see her eating a healthier diet.

'What am I to call you?' she had asked Philippa politely when Blake had gone to get their food.

'What would you like to call me? My name is Philippa, but you can call me Pip, or Pippa if you prefer,' Philippa had offered.

'Pippa—it's a bit like Nanna, isn't it?' Anya had told her, adding quietly, 'I don't have a grandmother, or a grandfather. They're dead. The secret police killed them...' She'd said it matter-of-factly. 'I don't have anyone else at all now,' she'd added.

'You have us,' Philippa had told her, swallowing down the emotion threatening her.

'Yes, but you don't really belong to me, do you?' Anya had replied levelly.

There was nothing that Philippa could say, no words that could give Anya back what she had lost, she'd acknowledged, and it would be an insult to the child to pretend any different.

She had failed her already, Philippa had thought hollowly as Blake had come back with their food, including

a huge sweet milkshake for her, which she knew she had
not ordered.

'I thought you would like it,' Blake had told her innocently when she'd pushed it away after one taste, but there
had been laughter in his eyes as he'd watched her expression and rueful acknowledgement in her own.

'She's really taken to you,' Blake whispered softly now.

'What's that?' Philippa responded drily after checking
that Anya was still sound asleep. 'Your professional opinion
or wishful thinking?'

'Neither,' he responded promptly. 'If you like, it's just
a plain basic male interpretation of the fact that she prefers
to be close to you, that she relaxes and lets down her guard
with you…responds to you in a way that she certainly hasn't
shown any signs of doing with me. I'd like you to move in
with us as soon as you can. Anya obviously prefers your
company to mine.'

'She doesn't seem to have had a lot of contact with her
own father,' Philippa told him. 'She's probably just not
used to men.'

'You spend so much time protecting others' sensitivities,
but who, I wonder, protects yours?'

'Mine don't need protecting,' Philippa responded lightly,
but inwardly his perception had jolted her, touching a vulnerable nerve. Once she would have been overjoyed at the
thought that he had actually noticed something, anything
about her, but now the knowledge that he had been studying
her made her feel wary.

What else had she given away about herself to him
without knowing it?

She had felt almost relaxed travelling back from Leeds
with him, her attention concentrated not on the past, but
on Anya, her awareness of how easy it would have been
for her actually to enjoy being with him firmly pushed safely
out of harm's way.

Anya was a warm, slight weight against her arm, familiar from holding her sons and yet at the same time
very different.

'I'll drop you off first,' Blake announced as they reached the outskirts of their town.

They had already told Anya that tonight Philippa would be staying in her own home but that soon she would be moving into Blake's house to take care of her.

Philippa nodded and then froze as she glanced out of the window and saw Joel standing on the opposite side of the road.

He hadn't seen her. He was waiting for the lights to change so that he could cross the road, his attention fixed on the traffic.

Her heart turned over inside her chest, her throat closing on a surge of mixed emotions: her body's instant physical response to the sight of him, her emotional urge to reach out to him, her mind's reminder of all the reasons why she could not do so.

She had not loved him, nor he her, she knew that, but the possibility of love developing between them had been there and a part of her still ached with loss for the tenderness of his lovemaking, the sense of being needed, wanted, protected.

Through his driving mirror Blake watched her face. He had seen the man standing on the pavement and her reaction to him, and for a moment the intensity of his emotions had caught him unprepared.

'Want me to stop?' he offered harshly.

Philippa stared at the back of his head, her face flushing as she realised how much she had betrayed.

'No, thank you,' she told him quietly.

'An old friend?' Blake persisted.

Philippa could sense his anger and was confused by it. So he had seen her looking at Joel and guessed...something. That was no reason for him to cross-question her...or judge her. She was not ashamed of what she had shared with Joel.

'Not a friend, no...' she said steadily. 'If you must know, we were briefly lovers...very briefly...'

As she watched Blake's hands tighten on the steering-wheel she knew that she had surprised him.

'It's over now,' she added quietly. 'What's wrong, Blake?' she challenged him when he remained silent. 'You asked, I told you—or am I not allowed to be truthful? Do you, like my father, prefer me to conform to your values and judgements? Well, I'm sorry, but the only values that matter to me now are my own. I'm not ashamed of what I had with Joel. What *would* make me ashamed would be hiding or denying it. He gave me something that no one else has ever given me, showed me a part of myself I didn't think existed, gave me back a part of myself I thought I'd lost forever.'

'Was that why you took this job with me?' Blake asked her harshly. 'Because your affair with him was over?'

'No,' Philippa told him. 'I took it so that our affair could never get the opportunity to start ... among other reasons.'

Somewhere in among the turmoil of jealousy he could feel seething through him there was also awareness and respect, Blake acknowledged.

Awareness, respect, and an overwhelming sense of loss.

Many times over the years he had allowed himself the indulgence of imagining what manner of woman she had become. He had not done her justice, though, he acknowledged tiredly—nowhere near.

'Here, let me take her.'

Philippa tensed as Blake reached into the back of the car to lift Anya's still sleeping body from her arms so that she could get out, but there was no need for that wary tensing of her muscles, she recognised; Blake was scrupulously careful about not touching her, not even by the merest brush of his fingertips, as he lifted Anya away from her.

A sense of forlornness, of aloneness filled her as she relinquished Anya to him. What was it about the sight of a big man with a small child in his arms that tugged so emotionally at the heart-strings?

'Would you like me to come inside with you...make sure...?'

'No... You mustn't wake Anya,' Philippa told him, shaking her head. 'What time tomorrow...?'

'Whatever time best suits you,' Blake told her.

As she turned to walk away, he said quietly to her, 'Philippa, I'm sorry. What I said earlier...your private life is your own affair.'

'I have no private life—at least not in the context you mean,' Philippa told him steadily. 'But you're right, it is my own affair. I intend that the only arbiter of what I may or may not do or be shall be me. It's *your* choice, *your* right to judge me as you wish, Blake, just as it's mine to decide whether or not to allow that judgement to have any power over me or any jurisdiction over my life.'

As she walked away from him, Philippa told herself that she had broken free of the shackles which had once bound both her life and her, and that no one, not even Blake, could be allowed to reimprison her in them.

Not *even* Blake.

Why the 'even'? He was no more important, no more special to her than anyone else. Less so, in fact; much, much less so.

Blake felt Anya stir slightly in his arms. It was too late for regrets now, he reminded himself, too late to dwell on what he had lost and denied himself.

But it didn't stop him thinking...remembering, he admitted to himself later when Anya was in bed.

Even without closing his eyes he could still visualise the expression on Robert's face, the afternoon he had told him that his parents—his father—wanted him to leave and why.

'Thing is that Philippa is going through a bit of a difficult stage at the moment. Personally I'm surprised at the old man's patience with her,' Robert had told him, 'and to be blunt with you, old boy, having you here isn't making things any easier. Girls of that age...' He had given a brief shrug. 'Well, you know how it is—it's obvious she's got a bit of a thing about you and for both your sakes really we feel it would be best if you left.

'After all, it's not as though anything could come of it,' Robert had gone on, apparently oblivious to Blake's reactions to what he was saying. 'Philippa is the kind of girl who's going to need to marry someone who'll be able to take care of her properly—I'm sure I don't need to say any more...'

'Oh, but I think you do,' Blake had told him, his voice dangerously low and calm.

Philippa's feelings for him were of course no secret to him but he had been so careful about not using them, about not abusing the position he felt he was in...about not taking advantage of her youth and innocence.

As long ago as that first summer he had known what his own feelings were, but she had only been sixteen then, far too young for him to...

Now she was eighteen, and in between worrying about his mother and working and studying he had allowed himself to dream...to imagine.

He would be so careful with her, so slow and tender, so that he didn't frighten or repulse her with the intensity of his desire for her... his love for her.

He had been pleased when she had first shyly confided to him her wish to go to university. He had never liked the way her parents and especially her father treated her; the way they controlled her life.

Michael had been embarrassed when he had raised the subject with him. But Blake had sensed that he agreed with him.

He had felt that it would do Philippa good to get away from her parents, that it would give her a much needed opportunity to mature and become independent. In lots of ways she was very young for her age.

If Blake was honest with himself he would have admitted that he didn't particularly like Philippa's parents, especially her father. Victor Waverly had very fixed ideas and attitudes about life, but most especially about status and wealth.

It was obvious not only that he liked the fact that he was the wealthiest man in the small neighbourhood in which they lived, but that he also seemed to need to be held slightly in awe by others.

The fact that the small business he had inherited from his father had been taken over by a much larger and very successful company and that Victor had been astute enough to negotiate for himself a place on that company's main board—a position that was more of a sinecure than anything else from what Blake had seen—seemed to Blake to have given him an exaggerated idea of his own importance.

That his family should reflect that importance very obviously mattered far more to him than their own personal happiness. Blake had witnessed Michael's unhappiness over his father's lack of interest in his own chosen career in design, and the constant unfavourable comparisons between him and his elder brother, Robert, who was not just his father's favourite but also very much cast in the same mould.

Over the years Blake had seen how Philippa's father treated those whom he considered lower down the social and financial scale than he was himself, *and* those who were above him.

There might not be anything vulgar or ostentatious about the way Philippa's parents displayed their wealth—that would not have fitted in with Victor's image of himself at all—but his desire to overpower and overawe others with what he had and what he owned was still there.

Like the public pride he took in Philippa's prettiness . . . Blake had marvelled at the quiet calm with which Philippa endured her father's attitude towards her and he was determined that he was never going to allow himself to be trapped by his love for her into trying to manipulate or dominate her in the way her father did.

No, before he even mentioned marriage to her he wanted her to have the freedom that going to university would give, the opportunity to make her own choices, her own decisions. In doing so he might be risking losing her but it was a risk he had to take, for both their sakes.

Now, as he'd listened to Robert, his anger had overwhelmed him.

'I think you need to say a lot more,' he had told him. 'One *hell* of a lot more...'

It had pleased him to see Robert looking flustered and uncomfortable as he blustered, 'Oh, come on, old man. I don't want to offend you, but it must be obvious to you that my father would never allow Philippa to become seriously involved with you...'

'What about what Philippa might want?' Blake had asked him. 'Or doesn't that come into it?'

'She's far too young to know what she wants...she can't even make up her mind which dress to buy and has to come home with them both.'

'Is she?' Blake had challenged him softly. 'She's not too young to think she's in love with me.' It was an underhand move, but it was one that Robert had forced him to make.

Blake could see how uncomfortable he had made him, his skin flushing as he'd avoided looking directly at Blake.

'She's far too young to know what love is... Oh, she might imagine she knows, but do you honestly believe those feelings would last five minutes once she realised what she'd be giving up?

'The pearls my father gave her for Christmas probably cost more than you could earn in a whole year. She treats them like glass beads. She isn't a girl who knows the meaning of the word "economy". She has never had to go without anything...*anything*,' Robert had emphasised.

'On the contrary,' Blake had told him. 'I believe she's had to go without a great deal.'

It had been Blake who had heard the door open, who had seen Philippa coming towards them. She had been playing tennis and her face was flushed, her skin as soft and clear as the pearls she had asked him to fasten for her two evenings ago—the pearls her father had bought her. She was wearing a tennis dress with a brief fluted skirt and a neat fitted bodice, a discreet logo proclaiming its expensive manufacturer, and Blake knew that the club where she had been playing was exclusive and private, with very very high fees.

As he'd looked at her, Blake had suddenly seen her with new eyes.

How would she really fare in his world? How would she adapt to wearing cheap chainstore clothes, to having to economise, having to go without?

He had left that evening while Philippa was out with her parents, but he hadn't given up hope . . . not then . . . Then he was still convinced that she loved him, that somehow he would find a way of breaking the hold her parents had on her.

But then his mother's debilitating condition had worsened and he had had no option other than to finance round-the-clock care for her. Struggling to make ends meet and to keep on with his studies as well as worrying about his mother, he had recognised grimly that Robert was quite right. There was no way he could afford to have Philippa in his life.

And then she had come to see him, just when he had reached rock-bottom, when he was wondering whether he would have to abandon his training completely and find work—any work just so long as it earned him enough to pay to make his mother's life just a little more comfortable.

He had had no alternative other than to send her away, to deny them what he knew they both wanted. To have even tried explaining to her would have strained his fragile self-control well beyond his limits; he had known quite well that one soft helpless look . . . one single tear . . . one small plea from her and he would have been lost, unable to deny any longer what he felt for her . . .

And then she had told him that she wasn't going to go to university because 'Daddy' wouldn't let her and to his own shock he had found himself wondering if after all Robert hadn't been right...if she was after all far more her father's daughter than he had ever imagined.

He had watched her driving away in the car 'Daddy' had given her and he hadn't been sure which of them he had hated the most—her father or himself.

He had seen how much he had hurt her, but he was hurting as well. A part of him still hurt.

His mother's condition had worsened over the following six months and it had been a release for her, and for him, he acknowledged sadly, when she'd died. Michael had attended the funeral. Philippa had been away on honeymoon with her new husband, Andrew Ryecart.

Angry and embittered, he had left for the States just as soon as he had completed his studies. Once there, he had continued training and working with furious energy to prove to the Ryecart family in general and Philippa in particular that when it came to earning power and status he was streets...leagues ahead of the man she had married.

It had taken Michael to bring him to his senses and show him what he was doing to himself.

It had taken Romania to show him how man's cruelty and greed for power and wealth brutally destroyed the innocent and unprotected.

It had taken meeting Philippa again to show him just how much he had lost...denied himself...out of false pride and lack of faith.

He had come back expecting to find a dull, ageing woman passively accepting her role in life, devoting herself to it, tied securely by loyalty and habit to her husband—by them and their children. But instead he had found...instead he had found Philippa...

And this time...this time... Anya cried out in her sleep, disturbing the silence of the house. When he went up to see what was wrong she was sitting up in bed awake.

'Where's Philippa?' she asked him. 'I want her...'

'She'll be here tomorrow,' he assured her. How easy to be a child and to have no inhibitions about stating one's desires... one's needs.

Tiredly he got up and went back downstairs.

CHAPTER THIRTY

SALLY stiffened guiltily as she heard Joel coming upstairs. Her hand was trembling so much that she had deposited more mascara on her skin than on her lashes. She reached for a tissue to clean it off, glancing anxiously over her shoulder as Joel walked into the bedroom.

'I thought you were going out.'

Joel's mouth tightened as he heard the accusatory note in her voice. Cynically he noted the way Sally reached for her dressing-gown, quickly pulling it on over her underclothes.

She still had a good figure, slightly softer now than it had been when they had first married, rather more curved, but then she was a woman now, not a girl.

'I am,' he told her curtly in response to her comment. 'I just came up to get my jacket.'

In the early days of their marriage he had watched, entranced and fascinated, as she went through the routine of putting on her make-up, sometimes sneaking up behind her to wrap his arms around her and start nuzzling the side of her neck, teasing her with light kisses until she had abandoned her task and turned round in his arms.

Then, the last thing she would have wanted to do would have been to conceal her body from him; and now, although she didn't know it, it was the last thing she *needed* to do.

The comparison between her coldness towards him and her rejection of him and Philippa's warmth twisted into an aching pain of resentment inside him.

Sally watched him as he opened the wardrobe door and removed his jacket, holding her breath. He had made no comment when she had told him she was spending the afternoon with her sister and brother-in-law. As she watched him shrug on his jacket she tried not to glance betrayingly at the clothes she had laid out on the bed...her best ones.

She felt uncomfortable and uneasy with Joel in the bedroom with her while she was getting ready to see another man.

Even though outwardly her visit to Kenneth's home seemed perfectly respectable and even mundane, she knew how carefully and skilfully it had been contrived, and that it was her company Kenneth wanted and not her sister's and brother-in-law's.

The bathroom door was open, and as he walked past it Joel caught the faint scent of Sally's perfume.

He frowned, pausing. Anyone would think it was royalty Sally was going out with, from all the fuss she was making, not just her sister and her husband.

His mouth grew bitter, causing Sally to stop abruptly as she walked out on to the landing. She had thought that Joel had already gone downstairs and she touched her skirt nervously as she waited for him to make some comment on her appearance, to question and query, and her heart started to hammer frantically against her ribs as he looked at her and said sourly, 'It's easy to see who matters most to *you* these days. That sister of yours...'

He stopped speaking as the doorbell rang, turning to go downstairs. As she followed him, Sally could feel her stomach churning sickly. She had barely been able to eat anything all week, she felt so nervous and on edge, and now she felt uncomfortably light-headed and queasy.

She knew that it couldn't possibly be Kenneth at the door—the arrangement was that she would travel to his house with Daphne and Clifford—but she still stood halfway down the stairs, her body as stiff and wary as a hunted animal's, as she waited for Joel to open the door.

When he did, she realised that the man standing outside was a complete stranger to her, and to Joel too apparently, she recognised distantly as her panic-induced surge of adrenalin receded, leaving her feeling weaker than ever.

She watched as the man introduced himself to Joel. His car was parked outside the house; it looked new and expensive, like the clothes the man was wearing.

'I've just come round to thank you for fixing my boy's bike the other day,' she heard him telling Joel. 'I'd have come round before but I've been away on business... I'm always telling him about looking after his things properly... Modern kids—they don't appreciate the things you give them... You're working down at the leisure centre parttime, I understand, as a swimming instructor.'

'On a voluntary basis,' Joel acknowledged.

'I hear you're very good...'

Sally saw the surprise in Joel's eyes.

'Carol Lucas is a friend of my wife's,' the man added. 'She says that her daughter, Estelle, has come on by leaps and bounds since you've been giving her private tuition. My son tells me that you've been giving the older ones a few informal lessons on simple home-maintenance jobs...'

Sally could see from the way that Joel shrugged that he was slightly embarrassed. 'One of them was complaining that the computer he'd bought second-hand didn't have a plug on it. I happened to have a spare one in my car, so it wasn't any big problem to show him how to fit it.'

As the other man thanked Joel again and turned to leave, Sally frowned. Their visitor, with his expensive car and clothes, had quite plainly been impressed with Joel; Sally had heard the admiration and respect in his voice.

He was a man who from his outward appearance would fit into the same social circle as her sister and her husband, but there had been none of their disdain and contempt for Joel in his manner—far from it.

Sally remembered how after Paul had first been born Daphne had come to the hospital to visit her and had commented tactlessly, 'Of course, he'll never have the opportunities Edward will have—not with Joel as his father.'

'Don't take any notice,' the woman in the bed next to Sally had told her firmly when Daphne had gone. 'It's as plain as the nose on your face that she's jealous of you and envies you having a real man for a husband, instead of that poor pathetic weed she's married to.'

Sally had dismissed her comment with a polite smile. Daphne, jealous of *her* . . .? How could she be?

As he closed the front door, Joel turned round and saw Sally standing on the stairs behind him. She looked pretty in her pastel-coloured suit and with her hair all newly washed and soft.

You love her, Philippa had told him.

'Sal . . . There's a sixties dance down at the leisure centre the Saturday after next, if you fancy going . . .'

'I can't . . .' Her panicky reaction was so swift that it even took Sally by surprise. As she saw the look in Joel's eyes she felt an unexpected sense of loss and disappointment, but how could she have said yes?

She was afraid of being alone with Joel now, she recognised, afraid of what she might accidentally betray, afraid that he might somehow guess. 'I'm working that night,' she told him lamely.

Joel was already turning away. 'Forget it; it doesn't really matter,' he told her distantly.

After Joel had gone Sally moved restlessly around the kitchen. It was still almost an hour before her sister was due.

She went into the kitchen and saw that Cathy had left some of her school-books on the table. She frowned as she saw them. Cathy had been complaining this morning that she wasn't feeling very well, and Sally had panicked, instantly worrying that if her daughter stayed at home she might have to cancel her visit to Kenneth's and knowing that she wouldn't be able to get in touch with him to let him know.

'She looks fine to me,' she had commented hardily when Joel had started to comment that perhaps Cathy ought to stay at home.

'Yeah, Mum's right—I'm fine,' Cathy had agreed. 'Stop fussing, Dad . . .'

She had been nervous and on edge with Joel in the house, blaming his presence for her feelings, but now that he had gone she didn't feel any better. She paced the living-room restlessly, tensing every time she heard a car going past outside, wondering why, when she wanted to be with Kenneth, when she had been looking forward to seeing him all week, she should now almost be dreading doing so.

It wasn't as though Joel had even noticed anything different about her, had even realised the significance of what she was wearing, where she was going.

She heard a car pulling up outside and knew instinctively that it was Daphne. The palms of her hands were damp and when she looked into the mirror her face looked far too pale and set and her eyes correspondingly huge and over-brilliant.

She looked like some of her patients after she had given them their drugs, she recognised, but the only drug in her system was too much adrenalin.

'It's such a shame that some parts of the city have been spoiled by new buildings,' Daphne was commenting snobbishly as Clifford drove towards the university. 'Kenneth is very wise to have moved out of the immediate environs of the university. The houses there must have been so gracious once, but most of them have been turned over to student flats now...'

Sally gritted her teeth. Her sister's inane, self-satisfied chatter felt like a drill being applied to a raw nerve.

'I'm glad to see you've taken a bit more trouble with your appearance today, Sally,' Daphne approved, adding bossily, 'Although you really ought to have your hair properly cut and styled. It's far too long and untidy for a woman of your age... Kenneth could be very important to Clifford's career. With his connections at the university...'

Kenneth doesn't give a damn about Clifford or his career, Sally wanted to tell her, but somehow she managed to hold back the words.

Kenneth's house was at the far end of a cul-de-sac of similar tall, narrow Edwardian houses. Its red-brick façade, rather than being warming, had a repressive starkness about it, Sally felt as she studied it through the car window. The bricks were red and shiny, cold and hard, the house free of the softening effects of the ivies and climbing roses which adorned the other houses. The front garden, like the exterior of the house, was starkly immaculate, and mentally she contrasted it with their own garden and the clutter of bikes which adorned their pathway.

Something about the house made her feel uncomfortable, but before she could question what it was Kenneth was opening the front door and waiting to greet them.

Sally stood back while her sister gushed effusively.

Kenneth might be pretending to listen to Daphne but he was looking at her, Sally recognised.

'Please come in...'

Somehow or another Kenneth managed to manipulate things so that he could take her arm as they walked into the hallway. It was wider than her own, the stripped, matt floorboards so free of any marks or dust that Sally almost felt afraid to walk on them.

The hallway was painted white and so was the sitting-room Kenneth showed them into. There were no expensive fitted carpets here like the ones Daphne had, just those bare, immaculate floorboards covered with neutral-coloured rugs. There was no colour anywhere in the room; everything was pale and neutral, immaculate and stark; even Daphne seemed to have lost some of her normal self-confidence and arrogance as the room imposed its austerity on them. Sally could see her looking round uncertainly.

Kenneth was watching Daphne and there was a look on his face that Sally couldn't quite define. It was almost as though he was somehow enjoying Daphne's discomfort. Sally frowned. It was the lack of any personal belongings that made the room seem so austere, she decided; there were no *things*...no books, no magazines, no photographs.

Where were Kenneth's photographs of his family, his sons? Perhaps he kept them upstairs in his bedroom, she decided, her skin flushing slightly at what she was thinking.

'Let's go out into the garden, shall we?' Kenneth was saying. Once again he managed things so that he fell into step beside her.

'You're looking very pretty,' he told her softly as he leaned towards her.

'It's a suit Daphne gave me,' Sally confessed.

Kenneth's, 'Yes, I thought it might be,' made her tense a little bit. There had been something in the tone of his voice that once again disturbed her without her being able to put her finger on why it should.

Once she was his, the first thing he intended to do was to buy her a new wardrobe, Kenneth decided. Subtle, elegant clothes in subdued neutral colours...natural fabrics, not that appalling man-made mixture she was wearing now. His colleagues would have a field day if they saw her dressed like that. The sister would have to be held at a distance as well—very much at a distance.

He shepherded them towards the French windows and the garden beyond it. Sally caught her breath as they stepped outside, and Kenneth, hearing the tiny betraying sound she made, turned to smile down at her.

'Like it?' he asked her, plainly pleased by her reaction.

'It's beautiful,' Sally told him truthfully, and indeed it was; perfect green lawns gave way to deep borders filled with flowers and foliage in every possible shade of white and green, the colour scheme mirroring the neutrality of the room they had just left behind. A dark green yew hedge bisected the garden and as Kenneth guided them along the path that led to the opening in it Sally could hear Daphne enthusing in front of her, chagrin mingling in her voice with her praise.

Beyond the yew hedge lay a small formal garden, secret and shadowy with its green lawn and dark yew boundaries. Even the seats in it were painted dark green and set perfectly opposite one another.

There was no doubt that the garden was spectacular, Sally acknowledged, even her untrained eye could see that, but it was impossible to imagine Paul running around in it playing with his football; impossible to imagine any child at all, no matter how well-behaved, being allowed to play in such surroundings...or wanting to?

For once even Daphne was silent. Was she contrasting this silent green perfection with her own flamboyant, brilliantly hued flowerbeds? Sally wondered. To judge from the look on her sister's face, Sally suspected that Clifford would soon be being bullied and chivvied into replacing them.

'I like to walk here at night, just as it grows dusk,' Kenneth murmured to her. 'Sometimes it is almost possible to imagine oneself a true inhabitant of the Renaissance; to capture a small echo of its perfection.

'I want to walk here with you, Sally. You don't know how often I imagine that you are already here with me.'

Sally could feel herself starting to tremble, caught up in the magnetism of his personality, aware suddenly and sharply of just how strong-willed he must be. A man who could impose this degree of perfection on nature had to be ruthless... She shivered again, not liking the sensation the word conjured up. It suggested someone with an implacable ego, a determination to enforce his own will on everyone and everything around him, a selfishness...and Kenneth was none of those things.

They had tea in the immaculate, austere sitting-room, where Sally felt too nervous to do more than sip at the clear pale liquid Kenneth had served her. Even the cups were plain and white, eggshell-thin and so fragile that she was terrified of even holding them.

'Oh, by the way,' she heard Kenneth telling Clifford, 'I didn't realise that Slater Hobbs was an old friend of yours. I happened to mention that I had met you and he told me that the two of you had met over the debating table in your younger days. He suggested that if you had time you might like to call in on him in his rooms before you leave...?'

Sally had no idea who Slater Hobbs was, but he must be someone important, to judge from Clifford's expression.

'I'd like to call and see him,' Clifford began cautiously, 'but——'

'Oh, don't worry about Sally,' Kenneth interrupted him. 'I've got an appointment at the hospital for a check-up, as it happens, and I'd be delighted to give her a lift back to town...'

'Oh, no, we couldn't let you do that——' Daphne was saying, but for once Clifford overruled her, interrupting her to say enthusiastically,

'Well, if you're sure it wouldn't be any trouble... You remember Slater, Daphne,' he added, turning to his wife. 'I introduced you to him at one of the Head's social evenings. He's head of the university's maths department now, I understand.'

'Yes... a very influential post, of course, but then you'll already know that...'

Both Kenneth's voice and manner were casually calm, but Sally wasn't deceived. This Slater Hobbs, whoever he was, was obviously very important to Clifford, and she suspected this invitation to call and see him had not come about by any idle chance but had been deliberately contrived by Kenneth—so that they could be alone?

Half an hour later, when her sister and brother-in-law had gone, she voiced her suspicions to him. Kenneth laughed.

'You credit me with rather more influence than I possess, I'm afraid... Who am I, a mere lecturer, to the likes of a senior chair...?'

Sally looked at him uncertainly. There was an acid edge to his voice which made her suddenly realise that there was a lot about him that she didn't know.

'So, now that we're alone, what do you think of my home...? Do you think you could be happy here?'

He said it indulgently, like an adult teasing a child, sure already of her answer, but Sally was uncomfortably aware that, beautiful though the house was, it didn't feel like a home.

She could not imagine either of her children living here, for instance.

Rather than lie to him, she changed the subject, saying quickly, 'Your sons—I thought you'd have had photographs of them somewhere...'

'Photographs? What on earth for? The last thing I need is to be reminded——' He broke off, seeing her face, adding more gently, 'You're far too sentimental, do you know that? I shall have to teach you better,' he added lightly. 'And, speaking of sentiment, you know, don't you, that things can't go on much longer as they are? I want you here with me, Sally, where I can look after you instead of knowing that you're slaving away looking after that unappreciative husband of yours. Have you any idea how it makes me feel, knowing that you're with him when I want you so much? Leave him, my darling; he isn't worthy of you. He doesn't appreciate you...'

'I can't leave him just like that,' Sally protested huskily. 'And the children...'

Try as she might she could not imagine their living here... or Kenneth wanting them to live here?

Quickly she dismissed the thought and the panic that came with it.

'Please don't rush me, Kenneth. I need time... Joel and the children need me and...'

'Do they?' Kenneth questioned her softly. 'Or are they just using you? Look at me, Sally,' he commanded.

Uncertainly she did so. What he had just said to her had touched a too painful nerve.

'*I* need you,' he told her fiercely. 'I need you...not them.'

For a moment Sally thought he was going to take hold of her and kiss her, but although his hands did cup her face he almost immediately released her.

'No,' he told her thickly. 'Not now...not yet...'

Sally felt his hands tremble slightly as he held her and a sharp *frisson* of corresponding excitement flared through her own body. It was a wonderful feeling, knowing how much he wanted her and knowing at the same time that he was prepared to control that wanting for her sake... to put her first.

It wouldn't be long now, Kenneth promised himself as he looked down into Sally's upturned face and saw her expression. And the first thing he intended to do was to teach her how to dress properly. The first time he took her to bed, she would be wearing a soft flowing nightdress in pure natural silk, or perhaps fine unbleached cotton. He hoped she wasn't the kind of woman who had a lot of body hair. He remembered with a sharp sense of revulsion how his ex-wife had almost taken delight in flaunting the dark thatch of thick, coarse curls that grew between her legs, angrily refusing his hints that she ought to remove it.

Such a profusion of hair was not aesthetically pleasing in a woman; it was too coarse, too... too aggressively sexual.

No, Sally would not be like that, he assured himself, and unlike Rebecca she would be grateful to him for everything he did for her. How could she not be, when she compared the life she had now with everything that he could give her?

The sister might become a problem, but Kenneth knew that he would be more than a match for her.

'Stop worrying,' he told Sally gently when he saw her expression. 'Everything's going to be all right. I promise...'

'I don't want to hurt Joel,' Sally whispered.

'He deserves to lose you,' Kenneth told her.

'Me, yes... but not the children...'

She felt Kenneth tense slightly. 'Sally,' he began. 'I don't...'

As he moved his arm to release her, Sally glanced at his watch, shocked to see how late it was.

'Oh, Kenneth, I must go; Paul and Cathy will be home from school soon and I don't want Joel getting suspicious...'

She was already hurrying towards the front door, her body tense and anxious. She had stayed longer than she had anticipated...

'No, you'd better drop me off here,' she told Kenneth some time later as he turned into her road.

'I'll ring you soon,' he promised her as he stopped his car and she got out.

'Not at home...' Sally begged him. 'Joel...'

'At work,' he agreed.

As she started to straighten up he caught hold of her hand and lifted it to his mouth, gently kissing each individual finger.

Nervously Sally glanced over her shoulder to make sure that no one was watching.

'One day soon I'm going to do that to every single inch of your skin,' Kenneth promised her softly. 'One day, very, very soon now, Sally.'

Her face still felt hot and flushed when she unlocked the back door. The untidiness of her own kitchen, instead of irritating her as it normally did, felt oddly relaxing.

The pale, clean austerity of Kenneth's house had made her feel uncomfortable, she acknowledged; it was too perfect, too immaculate... not really a home at all. She'd felt constantly on edge the whole time she was there, afraid that she might drop something, damage something, ruin that perfect paleness.

She shivered suddenly, the euphoria induced by Kenneth's company and his flattery abruptly deserting her. No matter how hard she tried she just could not imagine her children living in Kenneth's immaculate home.

Or wanting to leave Joel?

The tiny nagging feeling that somehow over these last months Joel had supplanted her in their children's affections suddenly crystallised into a full-blown fear that, asked to make a choice between them, they might actually choose their father.

The children had always been closer to her than to Joel, not by her choice or design, but surely mothers generally always *were* closer to their offspring?

Now Joel was the one they turned to, not her; Joel was the one...

She froze as she caught sight of the note propped up on the kitchen table, panic exploding inside her as she frantically ran across the kitchen and picked it up.

'Cathy in hospital,' Joel had written baldly, his handwriting hurried and unsteady.

Sickly Sally put down the note. Cathy—in hospital. Why... when... how...?

Picking up her car keys, she ran towards the door. It didn't matter that it would be easier and quicker to ring up and find out what had happened... she had to be with her daughter.

As she drove towards the hospital she realised for the first time what it felt like to be on the other side of things, what it felt like to be a mother whose child lay ill or injured in alien surroundings.

It wasn't Sally the professional, the nurse who parked her car haphazardly and then ran all the way to the hospital entrance, but Sally the mother.

She saw Joel first.

He was standing with his back towards her outside the doors that led to the children's ward.

'Joel, where's Cathy?' she demanded as he turned round and saw her. 'What happened... what's wrong...?'

'They don't know,' Joel told her tersely. 'They think it could be appendicitis.'

Appendicitis... Sally felt the floor start to give way beneath her as her legs threatened to buckle.

They had had a teenager in only last month but his condition had been caught too late, after the appendix had burst, and he had died soon after admission.

Appendicitis—the word trickled into her consciousness like ice-cold water filtering through her brain, ice-cold water tinged with an acid which left an afterburn that made her want to scream in pain and denial.

Why on earth hadn't she *listened* this morning when Cathy had complained that she didn't feel well? But she had been more concerned with seeing Kenneth than her daughter's health, she told herself bitterly...

'Where is she...? I must see her.'

'You can't...the specialist is with her. Where the *hell* have you been?' Joel added, demanding, 'I've been ringing your bloody sister's for the last two hours.'

'I—we got delayed,' Sally told him.

Oh, why wasn't I here; why didn't I know? Anguish and guilt filled her.

'Where's Paul?' she demanded anxiously. 'He...'

'He's just gone to get us both a cup of coffee. I thought it would give him something to do. I rang the school and asked them to send him straight here. I didn't want him going home and being on his own, worrying...'

Sally flinched as she caught the accusatory note in his voice. 'It wasn't *my* fault I wasn't there,' she protested defensively.

'No, but you were the one who insisted on Cathy going to school this morning, weren't you, just so that you could go out with your bloody sister?'

Joel knew he was over-reacting, punishing Sally for something that was not her fault, but he had never felt so afraid or so alone in all his life as he had done when Cathy had turned up at the leisure centre looking so very ill.

'The teacher at school said I should come home, but no one was there so I came here,' she had told him. 'You don't mind, do you, Dad?'

'No, of course not!' Joel had been able to see that she was in great pain. They had gone home, but as the pain had got worse Joel had decided he needed to get her straight to hospital. Frantic with worry, but trying not to show it, he had attempted to reach Sally on the phone, having to leave her a hasty note when his calls went unanswered. Cathy had been terrified when he had insisted on bringing her to hospital, but too weak to do anything about it when he had handed her gently into the car.

He had never needed or wanted Sally more in all his life, but the minutes and then the hours had ticked away and still Sally hadn't come, nor had anyone answered at Daphne's even then.

Now his fear had turned to anger, and, although he wanted to call back his words when he saw Sally's white face, somehow he just couldn't do so.

Not man enough, an inner voice taunted him, but before he could answer it the ward doors swung open and a nurse came hurrying towards them.

'Ah, Sally, you finally made it,' she greeted Sally, and then, turning her back on her, she addressed herself to Joel, telling him, 'It's all right, Mr Bruton. The specialist is sure that it isn't appendicitis. He thinks it's more likely to be a particularly virulent strain of stomach bug that's been doing the rounds recently, but we'll keep her in overnight just to be on the safe side.'

Sister Fuller had never liked her, Sally acknowledged. She was one of the old school, devoted to her young patients, but thoroughly disapproving of mothers who worked, even if it was in the field of nursing.

'You can see your daughter now if you like,' she continued, still keeping her back to Sally and addressing herself to Joel.

A movement at the far end of the corridor caught Sally's eye and as she turned her head she saw Paul coming towards them. When he saw the nurse talking to Joel he tensed and started to run.

'It's all right,' Joel reassured him, reaching out to him before Sally could say or do anything, putting his arm around his shoulders and drawing him protectively towards him as he told him, 'Cathy's going to be OK.'

Watching the two of them together, the way Joel's arm curved protectively around his son's body, the warmth and reassurance in his voice, the closeness and intimacy between them, Sally suddenly felt like an outsider, unwanted and unnecessary, an intruder into their private circle—a world she no longer had the right to enter. Hot tears stung her eyes and burned her throat.

Over Paul's shoulder Joel suddenly noticed Sally's downbent head and the betraying shine of tears in her eyes. Remorsefully he gently started to push Paul to one side and reach for Sally.

He had been unfairly hard on her. It wasn't her fault she had been too preoccupied this morning to see how ill Cathy had been. It was only fear and panic that had made him speak so savagely to her, the knowledge of how completely helpless and alone he had felt . . . how much he had needed her.

He called her name softly, but she was already turning away from him and heading towards the ward, walking so quickly that she was almost at the ward doors before he could catch up with her, stiffly holding herself aloof from him as he fell into step beside her.

'I'm sure there's really nothing to worry about,' the specialist was telling them gently a few minutes later as he met them outside the ward. 'Although your husband was quite right to bring her in.'

'I panicked,' Joel admitted gruffly. 'I didn't know what to do when she was in such pain.' He shook his head, unable to find the words to express what he had felt.

Sally watched him. Reaction had started to set in, her body cold with the realisation not of the fact that Cathy was safe and only suffering from some bug, but what she would now be feeling had her appendix really burst.

As a nurse she knew better than most how important time was in diagnosing an inflamed appendix, so important that minutes and sometimes even seconds could make the difference between life and death. But she had been away, unavailable, oblivious, uncaring, unknowing, unreachable for hours. Hours when the fight for Cathy's life could have been waged and lost.

A cold, numbing sensation spread through her, her head threatening to burst under the pressure of her thoughts as she tried to imagine how she would have felt walking into the hospital which was so familiar to her to learn that her child had died while she...

What kind of mother was she...? What kind of person...?

'Sister said that you wanted to keep Cathy in overnight,' Joel was saying.

'Yes, but that's only as a precaution,' the specialist was reassuring him.

'I want to stay here with her...tonight...' Sally announced croakily. 'I——'

'I'll stay,' Joel interrupted her, reminding her, 'You've got an early shift in the morning...'

'I really wouldn't advise either of you to stay. I promise you it isn't necessary and, besides, I'm afraid we just don't have the room,' the specialist informed them. 'You can see her now, of course.'

Although the nurses had done their best to cheer up the children's ward, it had a spartan, almost bleak appearance, far too reminiscent of Kenneth's unnaturally perfect rooms for Sally's comfort. The knowledge of where she had been and with whom while her child lay ill spread across her conscience like a heavy weight she couldn't remove.

She needed someone else to help her lift it, she acknowledged, but who was there who could do that...who *wanted* to do that for her...?

Not Cathy, who lay still and unnaturally quiet in the pristine white bed, averting her face when Sally approached her; and certainly not Joel, who had done everything bar wave a banner to proclaim her an unfit mother.

'It's OK, you're going to be fine,' she heard Joel saying. 'But they're going to keep you in overnight...'

'Oh, Dad. I was so frightened...'

Sally could hear the emotion in her voice, but when she instinctively reached to take hold of her hand Cathy pulled away from her, ignoring her, her attention fixed on Joel.

'I know. You and me both,' Joel responded feelingly. 'But it's OK now, and your mum's here...'

Sally flinched beneath the look Cathy gave her.

'When they let me leave tomorrow you'll come for me, won't you, Dad...?'

Across the bed Joel looked at Sally's downbent head. He could see how upset she was but now was not the time to tell Cathy off for the way she was behaving.

He might be flavour of the month now, Joel recognised wryly, but it had been her mother Cathy had cried for this afternoon when she'd come to the leisure centre. Perhaps it was only to be expected that she should want to punish Sally a little now for not being there...even if it was unfair.

'Of course I will,' he assured her.

'Time to leave now,' the nurse told them briskly, coming up to bundle them out.

'Dad, I'm hungry—can we go to McDonald's?' Paul demanded plaintively at Joel's side.

Once *she* would have been the one he had asked. Not Joel...

Kenneth was right; they didn't need her any more...not any of them. There was no place in their lives for her now...

No place, no need...no desire...no love...no anything.

CHAPTER THIRTY-ONE

'AH, DEBORAH, there you are...let me introduce you to Kay...' Ryan announced with smooth malice. 'She'll be joining our accountancy team from next week. The partners have decided that the workload on this side of the business has increased so much that we need to take on new staff...'

So, Ryan had already picked the girl who would take her place, Deborah reflected cynically as she smiled at the younger woman and shook her hand and then watched as Ryan steered her protectively towards the general office. She was small and blonde and, Deborah suspected, spectacularly curvy beneath her Armani suit. And, to judge from the look Deborah had seen in her eyes, she was by no means as kittenish and naïve as she looked.

She and Ryan would suit one another very well. Kay would have no qualms about 'networking' to promote her career.

Bitch, Deborah cautioned herself mentally, but what was the point in denying the truth? Her days here now were numbered; they had to be. She could stay and accept that she would never get her promotion, live with the humiliation of being 'sidelined', relegated back to the general office and all the speculation and amusement that would go with such a demotion, or she could press sexual harassment charges against Ryan—or she could do what she suspected Ryan now wanted her to do and find a job elsewhere.

Had he ever really expected her to sleep with him, or had that unexpected move on her on his part simply been his way of removing her to make way for this other girl? she wondered wryly. Despite what he had said to her, a part of her still refused to accept that he had not known right from the start that she would *not* sleep with him, and he was, as she had good cause to know—as Mark had often warned her—a master tactician.

Officially she was still working on the liquidation, still waiting for official recognition of her promotion, but she was under no illusions. Like Kilcoyne's employees, she too was now effectively redundant.

She had spent the last few evenings ringing round her old friends and contacts trying to find another job. So far, things didn't look very hopeful. There was a possibility that there might be a job going at her old firm in London, although of course it would mean a drop in salary, and status.

Perhaps in the end, like Mark, she might have to do temporary filling-in work until she found something suitable. The thought depressed her. She was in her late twenties now; what if she hadn't made the next rung up the ladder by the time she was thirty...? She decided to go home for the day.

When she got to the flat, tiredly Deborah turned her key in the lock and walked inside, shrugging off her jacket and then opening the sitting-room door.

'Mark!'

She stared at him in disbelief, frowning. 'What are you doing here...how did you get in...?'

'I still have my key. I'm sorry if I gave you a shock...'

A shock! Quickly Deborah turned her back on him, not wanting him to see the emotions she suspected were all too clearly revealed in her eyes.

He had been standing by the fireplace but now, as she turned around, she saw that he was walking towards her.

Immediately she made a tense, defensive movement with her body, and Mark stopped.

'Can we talk?' he asked her quietly.

Deborah pushed her hand into her dark chestnut hair. Mark looked tanned and well, making her feel depressingly aware of her own weary tension. She started to shake her head. What, after all, was there for them to talk about? But Mark stopped her.

'Please, Deb. I promise it won't take too long.'

Wearily Deborah nodded her head. It would be easier to listen to him than to argue with him.

As she sat down on the settee she saw him frowning. 'You look tired,' he said abruptly.

'Thanks,' Deborah told him drily, and then reminded him, 'You said you wanted to talk.'

'Yes.' He sat down opposite her, the soft fabric of his jeans stretching against his thighs. Her body gave a small, dangerous jerk of sexual recognition which she instantly suppressed.

Ryan would probably not believe it, but as far as she was concerned, when it came to male visual and physical sex appeal, in any contest between them Mark would have won hands down. She remembered how once in their early days together he had laughed at the way she had buried her face in his chest, nuzzling at his flesh and breathing his scent.

'I love the way you feel,' she had told him then. 'Like a lovely firm, cuddly, soft teddy bear... You're so gorgeous to snuggle up to, Mark—so warm and safe...'

'Oh, thanks,' he had laughed, but she had meant what she said; to her his body—firmly muscled, broad-shouldered and softly furred with light golden hair—was overwhelmingly sensually appealing.

It was the combination of sexuality and security which he represented to her that had made it possible for her to express her own sexuality with far greater freedom than she had ever known before.

Now, watching him sitting there in front of her, legs apart as he leaned forward, watching her earnestly, she could feel the aching need flooding her body.

Funny how easy she had found it to resist Ryan, she reflected absently, and how very, very hard it was to stop herself from going over to Mark and...

'I've been doing a lot of thinking recently, Deb, a lot of heart-searching and trying to be honest with myself. When I left it was because I'd convinced myself that you were the one who was responsible for my problems.'

He shook his head.

'I suppose the truth is that I couldn't bear to admit, even to myself, what was so obvious to you: that I felt threatened by your success, jealous of it and afraid that it would take you away from me.

'I resented the fact that your success demeaned me in the eyes of the other men, and because of that...' He paused.

'I thought that by walking away from you I was being a man, proving myself... and in reality all I was proving was that I was a fool, throwing away something of irreplaceable value... *someone* of irreplaceable value.

He looked up at her.

'I still love you,' he told her emotionally.

Deborah closed her eyes. The longing to go over to him, to touch him, to hold him, to be touched and held by him was so strong that it rocked her body like a giant hand trying physically to propel her towards him.

'You said you didn't want me,' she reminded him quietly. 'You didn't want to make love to me...'

'Yes,' he agreed.

'You were punishing me, Mark, withholding sex from me... using sex and my need for you to try and control me... We can't go back,' she told him, trying to keep her voice steady. 'It wouldn't work... Sooner or later we'd be facing the same problems all over again. I can't live with that fear hanging over me; you know how important my career is to me... That won't change. I *can't* change, and I can't live with the fear of wanting professional success and yet dreading how you'll react to it.

'Can't you see what would happen... how I'd be compelled to start pretending... playing down my career... creating an unreal persona, a disguise for myself in case the real me threatened or upset you...?

'You've always known what I am, Mark, what I want from life... I've never tried to deceive you about that...'

'No,' he replied quietly. 'I'm the only one who's been guilty of deception... not just of you, but of myself as well... But not deliberately, Deb—never that... It's different now, though—I've——'

'How can it be different?' Deborah demanded painfully. 'It's only been a few weeks. People don't change just like that...'

'No, they don't,' he agreed. 'I'm not trying to claim that I've changed, only that I think I've come to terms with myself, with what I am and what I'm not, with what's important to me and what isn't... with whose definition of what it takes to be a real man is most important to me— mine, or that of people like the Ryan Bridgeses of this world. I'm not competitive, Deb. I never have been, but these last few months I've felt as though that lack of competitiveness made me a failure as a man...'

'Oh, Mark,' Deborah protested sadly. 'I thought you knew that in my eyes it made you more of a man, not less of one, that you never needed me to put you up on some kind of pedestal, to make a false pretence of deferring to you, to boost your ego at the expense of my own, to have to hide from you how I felt about my career. To me those kinds of needs are a male weakness, not a male strength, and most other women feel the same.

'I admired and respected you more because you *didn't* need those false trappings of manhood, because you *didn't* follow the herd, bow down to the rules men have imposed on society... I loved you *because* of what you are, not in spite of it,' she told him.

'Loved me?' he repeated quietly.

Deborah turned away from him. What point was there in allowing him to know that she still loved him? What point could there be in their love if it was always going to be in conflict with her other needs? There was no point in deceiving either herself or Mark; she could not make him the whole focus of her life, become dependent on him and live only for him, and she had thought that he understood; that his love for her was like hers for him; that he loved the person she was and had no desire to change her.

'I can't give up my ambitions, my career...'

'No... How are things going, by the way...?'

'Fine,' she told him.

'Liar.'

Deborah stared at him.

'I had a phone call this morning from Gil Bennett and he wanted to know why I hadn't been in touch to let him know we were coming back to London. He'd heard on the grapevine that you were looking for a new job...'

'You know I've always preferred living in the city,' Deborah hedged. 'The only reason I moved out here was because of you...'

'Because of me and because the promotion prospects were better,' Mark corrected her.

'All right, all right... I admit it, Mark, you were right and I was wrong. The only reason Ryan offered me promotion was because he wanted to get me into bed. Satisfied...?'

'What...? You—he's trying to force you out because you wouldn't sleep with him...?'

At any other time the outrage on Mark's face would have been welcome, but it had hurt to have to admit the truth to him.

'Not force me out exactly, but he's made it plain that I won't be getting any promotion,' Deborah admitted wearily. 'Go on, gloat, Mark... I'm sure you must want to...'

'Gloat? That's the last thing I feel like doing... You can't let him do this to you, Deborah. It's sexual harassment and——'

'And what? I could take him to court? Would you, in my shoes...? Oh, yes... that would look good on my c.v., wouldn't it? No, I shan't do a damn thing about it and he knows it... He even had the gall to introduce me to the other girl whom he's hired to train in my place. Apparently my managerial skills aren't all that they might be... I don't handle people very well...' She gave a small bitter smile as her feelings broke through her control.

'Balls,' Mark told her forcefully. 'That's not true and you know it. You deserved that promotion, and if he's trying to renege on it now... Why didn't you let me know...?'

Deborah shrugged. 'There didn't seem any point. It wasn't your problem...and to be honest,' she added tiredly, 'being told "I told you so" was the last thing I was in the mood for.'

His quiet, 'Thanks,' made her look at him. 'Is that really what you think...? That all I'd have wanted to do was gloat?'

The pain in his voice caught at her own vulnerable emotions. She shook her head.

'I don't know. I just...' She stopped, recognising the truth: that she hadn't wanted him to know, not because she'd thought he would gloat, but because of the blow it would have given her own pride.

Her *pride*? Since when had that mattered? Since when had it been important for her to prove herself to Mark, to protect herself from the risk of his seeing her defeated?

Something in his expression made her add shakily, 'I would have got in touch with you... told you...'

'Would you?' he asked her quietly. 'What's happened to us, Deb? I used to think our love was so strong; that we...that we trusted one another...that *nothing* could ever come between us...'

'Perhaps we made the gods jealous,' Deborah replied wryly, a ghost of a smile touching her mouth.

She looked older, thinner, drained of her normal vivacity and self-confidence. His heart ached for her and for the ability to restore them to her and his body ached even more with desire for her.

He took a step towards her and then another.

'No,' Deborah told him huskily as she put out a hand to hold him off. 'This isn't the answer, Mark... This isn't...' But her lips were already clinging hungrily to his and the hand she had put out to reject him was now resting against his body, feeling the heavy pounding of his heart.

* * *

It was like the early days when they had first met all over again, his touch on her body so lovingly tender that it seemed to make her very bones melt with longing for him.

'This wasn't supposed to happen,' he told her ruefully as he leaned over her, gently circling her nipple with his tongue.

Stretching herself luxuriously beneath his caress, Deborah responded wryly, 'It wasn't exactly on my agenda for the evening either.'

She waited for him to ask her if she wanted him to stop, to put the onus of making any decision on her, but to her surprise he didn't.

Instead he opened his mouth over her nipple and caressed it with such slow sweetness that it made her cry out in pleasure as she slid her hands into his hair and held him against her body.

She felt the slightly rough grate of his teeth against her flesh, the sensation so fiercely erotic that a shiver of pleasure gripped her. The weeks without him had made her body extraordinarily sensitive and responsive to his touch.

She heard him groan as his hand covered her sex and he buried his hot face between her breasts.

There was laughter as well as chagrin in his voice as he told her thickly, 'Oh, God, Deb, I'm so sorry, but I don't think...'

Against all the evidence that her senses were giving her to the contrary, she immediately thought that he was trying to tell her that he didn't want her, that he couldn't... It wasn't just sexual frustration that was clogging her throat with tears and making her heart ache with pain, she recognised as she pulled away from him, shivering as she reached for the duvet.

It was a shock to feel his arms coming round her, pulling her back against him, his mouth warm against her ear as he told her, 'I'm sorry...I feel like a raw kid again, desperate to prove how much of a man I am and instead proving only that I haven't got an ounce of self-control.

'It's all these weeks of celibacy without you. Can we try again?' he asked her softly. 'And this time I promise I'll do my best to hold on at least until I'm inside you...'

When she realised what he had said, Deborah turned round in his arms.

'Blame it on the pleasure of being back here with you,' Mark murmured against her mouth. 'On the need I have for you. Oh, Deborah... I could make love to you all night long and still want you...'

Despite the fact that her body was trembling as it recognised the passion and desire in his voice, she still laughed, albeit a little shakily.

'Not on recent evidence, you couldn't,' she teased him.

'Oh, no?'

Her breath caught in her throat as Mark took her hand and placed it on his body. Beneath her fingers his flesh felt silky hot and familiar. She had missed him so much... The feel of his body next to her own, the scent and taste of him, the strength of him inside her... her mouth curled in a small secret smile.

'What is it?' Mark asked her.

'Nothing,' she told him.

When it came to showing off in the showers she suspected that Ryan would definitely lose out to Mark. Quite definitely.

She held him firmly, caressing him with the slow, sure strokes she knew pleased him best, feeling her own body's excitement grow to match his, sensuously anticipating the pleasure of having him inside her, her body quickening as she urged him not to wait any longer.

Her climax was quick and intense, over almost before she had had time to appreciate it, but Mark knew her well enough to know her needs without her having to voice them.

It had been so long since they had made love like this, she thought drowsily as she felt the warm drift of his mouth moving teasingly over her stomach—spending so much time indulging in all the small erotic pleasures of love-play. Lying together, sometimes simply kissing and gently touching just for the pleasure of breathing in one another's scent, of tasting one another's skin.

She couldn't imagine ever having a more perfect lover than Mark. He was so attuned to her needs...to her moods, so aware of every small nuance of her body's silent communication with his.

They made love again and this time Deborah was unusually silent, clinging to him, fiercely protective of the pleasure he was giving her and her own vulnerability to it, aching already with the pain of knowing that it couldn't last.

Mark woke up abruptly. The bedroom was in darkness but he could still see Deborah's silent figure standing by the window.

He got out of bed, swinging his feet to the floor and padding over to join her.

Deborah tensed as she felt him touch her. She had woken up over an hour ago, curled up against him, warm, relaxed, content, happy, and her mouth had curled into a soft smile of pleasure as she'd reached out to stroke her fingertips down his arm in a soft caress of loving possession...and then she'd remembered...

'What is it?' Mark asked her. She stiffened as he drew her back against him but he ignored her resistance, wrapping his arms round her, holding her in the warmth of his body.

'You're cold,' he told her. 'Come back to bed...'

Deborah shook her head. She could feel the tears burning behind her eyes, and she didn't want to Mark to see her crying.

'This doesn't make any difference, Mark,' she told him painfully. 'What happened between us tonight...it doesn't change anything... I wish to God it could,' she admitted. 'I love you and I want you...'

'And I love and want you,' Mark assured her roughly.

'But don't you see that isn't enough...? Not any more...'

She felt him stiffen against her.

'You want me *now*, Mark... *Now*, when I'm vulnerable and in need——'

'What is it... what are you trying to say?' he interrupted her.

'That I'm afraid,' Deborah admitted. 'Afraid that you only really want me when I'm vulnerable... when I'm dependent and needy. But that isn't what *I* want. I don't want to be that person. I don't *want* to be your inferior. I've seen what that does to women, how it makes them sacrifice themselves... Can't you see, Mark? I need you to want *me*... the real me... I need you to want me when things are going well for me... when I'm strong and powerful. I want to share that feeling with you, for you to rejoice in it with me, not turn away from me... to celebrate it with me... I'm sorry that I can't be the woman you want, but...'

'You *are* the woman I want,' Mark contradicted her fiercely. 'I made a mistake... I admit it. Punish me for it if you want to, Deb, but don't punish yourself as well... There was something else I came here to tell you...'

He paused and then continued, 'This partnership I've been working in is up for sale. I want to buy it. All right, I know what you're thinking and you're right; it's a small country practice that will just about earn me a living, and there won't be any glory or power; but those aren't the things I want. Life in the fast lane isn't for me... not because I'm not good enough but because it simply isn't my choice. I know myself now, Deb, and I know what's right for me.

'I've been working at this practice long enough now to know that I'd forgotten what it felt like actually to enjoy my work... to get a real feeling of satisfaction out of it, to enjoy the contact I have with other people, to wake up in the morning and look forward to the day ahead. And if in Ryan's eyes and those of men like him that makes me a failure, then so be it. I certainly don't feel any less of a man for having different goals from them...'

'Nor should you,' Deborah agreed. Mark was right; her heart had started to beat too heavily. What was he going to suggest—that she join him in his country idyll? But to her such an existence would be a trap, a dead end. She could feel her eyes filling with tears and for the first time in her adult life she came close to wishing she were different, that Mark and his love were all she wanted.

'It sounds perfect for you, Mark.'

'But not for you.'

It was, she realised, a statement and not a question.

'No,' she agreed sadly, 'not for me... I need more than that... I'm not like you. I like to be challenged... stretched; I need a job that takes me out into the world, not shuts me away from it...'

'Yes. And that's one of the reasons I came to see you. I have a client, a woman... a very, very successful woman who's looking for someone to work alongside her as her second in command——'

'A company accountant?' Deborah interrupted him. 'Oh, Mark, I don't think I——'

'No...she already has a company accountant... Stephanie is an empire-builder and what she wants is a colonel-in-chief to check out the land ahead of her, so to speak, and to guide her through its dangers.'

'And she wants me for this job...'

Mark paused.

'No—well, no... as a matter of fact she wanted me,' he told her ruefully. 'She isn't very keen on the idea of working with another woman, especially one young enough to suddenly decide that she wants to trade in her career for motherhood...'

'What?' Deborah turned round angrily. 'Is it any wonder that women find it too hard to climb the career ladder when our own sex——?'

'Of course, I told her that you might not even want the job,' Mark went on. 'After all, it's a pretty big step to move out of the comparative security of the profession for industry; no one would blame you if you felt wary about wanting to take on that kind of challenge.'

Deborah was thinking furiously. It was impossible, of course. Work for another woman... another woman who already seemed ambivalent about employing her... who would have preferred Mark... Give up her career plan of working in the profession...

She couldn't do it; she would be a fool even to *think* of doing it.

She turned round to tell Mark as much, but he was standing so close to her that she walked right into his arms.

'Mark, no. Stop it...' she mumbled under his kiss.

'Why not come and find out for yourself?' he suggested softly.

Deborah looked at him with narrowed eyes. 'It won't work,' she warned him. 'I know what you're trying to do, Mark, but life isn't like that; it doesn't come with fairy-tale endings.'

'It's OK,' he told her straight-faced. 'I know what you're thinking. It is a big step to take; you'd only have yourself to rely on, no professional back-up team to fall back on and blame if things go wrong, and Stephanie does set almost impossibly high standards, expecting everyone to be as enthusiastic about her company as she is herself, expecting them to give the total commitment *she* gives it. She'd drive you as hard as she drives herself and expect you to make the kind of decisions I admit I wouldn't want to make. You'd be out there on your own, and it would be one hell of a risk to take——'

'What are you trying to say?' Deborah interrupted him indignantly. 'That I'm not good enough for this woman?'

She stopped abruptly, eyeing him suspiciously when she saw the amusement in his eyes. Laughter struggled with irritation, a wry smile curling her mouth. 'All right. You always did know how to wind me up,' she complained ruefully.

'At least come and meet Stephanie,' Mark urged her.

'It won't work,' Deborah repeated, forced to mumble the words through his kiss.

'It will if we want it to,' Mark insisted. He lifted his mouth from hers and studied her face. 'Isn't what we have together worth at least giving it a try?' he asked her emotionally.

Deborah drew a shaky breath. 'I'm not promising anything,' she warned him. 'Your Stephanie and I will probably loathe one another at first sight.' But she was smiling as she said it, her body warm and fluid as he drew her back into his arms.

CHAPTER THIRTY-TWO

SALLY winced inwardly as her daughter turned her head towards her with obvious reluctance.

She had been at work since six and almost halfway through her shift Sister had allowed her an extra ten minutes' break, despite the fact that they were short-staffed, so that she could come down here to see her daughter.

She had looked in on her when she'd first arrived but Cathy had been fast asleep then, unaware of Sally's presence as she'd straightened the bedclothes and tenderly touched her, holding her breath until her fingertips came into contact with the warm, living flesh.

The loss of a child must surely be every parent's worst nightmare, and its echoes haunted Sally still as her heart ached with pain at her daughter's rejection of her.

'When's Dad coming?' Cathy demanded now. 'He promised he'd be here.'

The hunched shoulder and sulky pout which accompanied her demand left Sally in no doubt how little she wanted *her* company.

'He's coming to collect you later,' Sally told her quietly. 'Once Mr Davies, the specialist, has been to see you.'

The specialist's round was later in the afternoon, after she had gone off duty. She had wanted to wait and take Cathy home herself but what was the point when Cathy had made it so obvious that the parent she wanted was her father?

'All you do these days is nag,' Cathy had accused her only the previous week when Sally had asked her to tidy up her room. 'And all you care about now is money, not us,' she had added hurtfully as she'd slammed the door closed on Sally's reminder of how expensive and wasteful

472

it was when Cathy spent far too long on the telephone talking to her friends.

As Cathy continued to keep her back turned towards her, Sally stood up, blinking back her tears.

As she left the ward, she paused for a moment, looking back at the small, still form of her daughter, remembering how the previous evening she had felt so shut out and unwanted as she'd watched Joel bending over Cathy's bed, comforting her, his arm around Paul's shoulders, the three of them a complete self-sufficient unit in which there was no place for her.

Even the specialist had directed his comments to Joel and not to her.

Depression filled her, saturating her thoughts, surrounding her like a thick grey cloud of dull misery.

There was no place for her in Joel's or her children's lives any more, she decided as she went back to the ward. Financially they might need her, but that was all... If she weren't there... She took a deep breath and closed her eyes.

Leave him and come to me, Kenneth had urged her.

She couldn't, she had protested. They needed her...

But that wasn't true any longer, was it?

By the time she had finished her shift she knew what she had to do.

Joel would soon find someone else to take her place; he was, after all, a very sexually attractive man, as she was constantly being told.

Her hands trembled on the steering-wheel of her car as she stopped in a queue of traffic, catching her breath on the sharp, hurtful pain that bit so deeply into her as she visualised Joel with someone else, holding her, touching her.

It confused her that she should feel so intensely emotionally and sexually jealous, hating already the woman who would lie in her bed, in Joel's arms, responding eagerly to his touch, drawing from him soft sounds of pleasure and excitement... Sounds he no longer made for her.

Behind her another driver punched his horn impatiently and she realised that the road ahead of her was now clear.

The children wouldn't miss her either. Not now that they had Joel, and she couldn't have taken them to Kenneth's with her anyway; she knew that and had known it from the moment she'd entered Kenneth's house.

How would Cathy, with her love of loud pop music, her untidiness, her giggling friends who liked to practise the latest dance steps on the bedroom carpet and make up one another's faces, leaving brightly coloured pieces of cotton wool and sticky bits of make-up all over the bathroom and Cathy's dressing-table, ever be able to fit in or feel comfortable in Kenneth's immaculate rooms?

And Paul, who took his bike to bits outside the back door and then scattered oil and dirt all over the kitchen floor, who left his muddy football boots on the kitchen table and argued volubly with Cathy about whose turn it was to choose the tapes on the video. Would Kenneth welcome and want him?

She already knew the answer.

Kenneth liked order and discipline in his life; she had absorbed that knowledge instinctively; those ruthlessly weeded flowerbeds, those empty, immaculate rooms—her children would stifle and choke in them...

As perhaps Kenneth's had done.

She dismissed the traitorous thought. Kenneth loved her. He wanted her. He would make her feel safe and protected...as Joel had once done.

She gave a small shiver. Some women were designed to be independent...needed to feel that independence; but she wasn't like that. It hurt acknowledging this weakness within herself; she had always tried to keep it hidden from other people, ashamed of being so needy in a world where women were expected to be so much more than she had always felt she was.

Back at home, she went slowly upstairs to hers and Joel's bedroom, walking like someone in a semi-trance.

The house was empty, as she had known it would be; Paul was at school and Joel was down at the leisure centre— where else? He had said last night that he would go straight from there to the hospital to collect Cathy.

The bedroom looked unfamiliarly tidy. Joel had made the bed before he left.

There was nothing particularly special about the room— there were thousands upon thousands like it all over the country, decorated in much the same way: a pretty floral wallpaper, enlivened by a matching border, a soft pastel carpet... matching bedlinen, the peach and grey colour-scheme designed to be warm and comforting.

She had been so thrilled when she and Joel had rede-corated this room, she remembered as her hand smoothed absently over the pillowcase on Joel's side of the bed, just as she had been thrilled when years before Joel had made the row of built-in wardrobes which housed their clothes.

Kenneth would hate this kind of bedroom, she recog-nised... His would probably look like those she had seen and felt repelled by in glossy magazines on her rare visits to the hairdressers.

Kenneth. She closed her eyes, squeezing back the tears she could feel threatening her.

Why was she crying when this was what she *wanted*? When she *wanted* to be with him... to go to him?

Like a sleepwalker she opened the wardrobe doors and then pulled open a drawer, carefully removing the underwear stored in it.

For her birthday the previous year the girls at work had bought her this delicate lacy set of bra, briefs and sus-pender-belt. She had never worn them. Wearing stockings was something that always made her feel slightly un-comfortable... not tarty exactly, but somehow sexually available.

She hadn't shown the set to Joel, knowing how he would react. He used to love her wearing pretty, feminine underwear...

She showered slowly and carefully, not using the perfume which Joel had bought her for Christmas, but a different one which Daphne had given her.

When she slid on her stockings her fingers trembled violently. She avoided looking at her own reflection in the mirror.

She was doing what she wanted to do, she reminded herself. Making this commitment to Kenneth, taking this step that, once taken, meant that she could never, ever turn back, was her decision.

Giving herself sexually to Kenneth was crossing a chasm which could never be re-crossed; an act of symbolism and sacrifice...

Sacrifice? What was she sacrificing? A marriage that was just a hollow, empty sham, a family, children who had already outgrown her.

There could be no betrayal like this one... no greater way of destroying her marriage... not so much because of the sex itself but because she was giving to Kenneth something she had withheld from Joel; and something, moreover, that Joel had greatly valued.

But she wasn't doing it to punish Joel, she was doing it because... Tears blurred her eyes as she stood up and reached for her dress. She was doing it because even now half of her was still afraid... still, like a coward, wanting things to change... to go back to the way they had been.

With Joel on the outside and *her* the one the children wanted, had Joel ever felt as she did, unwanted, alone... afraid...?

It was too late now to feel regret, to wish that... that what? That she had talked to Joel... asked him...?

What had happened to the sense of power, of control she had felt when she had gone back to work? When had it become resentment and anger and an awareness that it had not brought her the things she had expected; that feeling that as the only breadwinner she had the right to expect Joel to acknowledge that she was the one to impose her control of their relationship on him, to refuse him sex in much the same way as she had felt he had demanded it from her?

Kenneth would never impose that kind of subtle sexual pressure on her; he just wasn't that kind of man. He would know, too, that in coming to him now, in giving herself to him, she was making an unchangeable choice between him and Joel.

She opened the wardrobe to remove her jacket, pausing as her hand brushed against one of Joel's sweaters. It felt soft and warm, her touch releasing a faint scent of his aftershave... of Joel himself.

Fresh tears blurred her eyes.

What had happened to them... to their marriage? It frightened her, made her feel threatened and resentful that Joel had changed, adapted to their new way of life, deserting her almost, leaving her alone to face worries, carry burdens she just wasn't able to manage.

The house felt silent... too silent... but it was a silence she would have to grow used to.

She went downstairs and walked to the back door, opening it slowly.

There was no point in looking over her shoulder, hesitating... there was no one there to see her go... no one to care that she was going.

She felt cold and calm, her body almost weightless, her thoughts and emotions all suspended in the relief, the release of knowing that there would be no more indecision, no more worry or anxiety...

It hadn't occurred to her to ring Kenneth to warn him of her arrival, and she could see the startled surprise in his eyes as he opened the door to her.

'Sally...'

She saw him glance uncertainly, uneasily almost, past her as though concerned that someone might have seen her, before he ushered her inside.

The stairs lay ahead of her, bleached and bare; they seemed to rise up steeply in silent, jeering challenge, mockingly aware of her weakness and apprehension.

As Kenneth closed the door she started to climb them.

She heard Kenneth saying her name, his voice sharp and anxious, but she didn't stop to respond to him. If she did... if she tried to explain... She dared not let anything break the fierce wall of concentration she had built so protectively round herself.

Joel had been her only lover and it was her nature to let him be the one to take control sexually, to approach her... To know that she was the one inviting, initiating sex was something that she could not consciously allow herself to acknowledge, and if she stopped now to talk to Kenneth...

She heard him climbing the stairs behind her but she still didn't look back.

Several doors led off the landing; she automatically headed for the closest and pushed it open. The bedroom beyond it was furnished just as starkly as she had imagined, its décor reminiscent of pictures she had seen of interiors of monasteries, she decided absently.

Kenneth had followed her inside the room.

She stopped at the foot of the bed and turned round to face him.

He looked different somehow, his features sharper, clearer, unfamiliar in some odd way.

Slowly she started to unbutton her dress, keeping her eyes fixed on his face. She could hear the sound of her own breath, shallow and nervous. Her mouth was dry, her body icy cold, apart from her face which felt burningly hot.

The room was airless, a vacuum that seemed to suck up and drain all the emotion from her, so that she felt she was just a collection of bones and muscles and flesh, that this woman carefully removing her dress was not really her but someone else.

Once the dress was unfastened she took it off, carefully folding it neatly and putting it on the bed.

It was time now... Time to do what she had come here to do... time to...

She froze as she heard the sharp, ragged indrawn sound of Kenneth's breathing, her body tensing in anticipation of his touch, of his sexual arousal and need, even though she had come here expressly so that they could be lovers. Nervously she waited for him to come to her, to hold her, to cover her nakedness and vulnerability with the warm protection of his body...to drown out her doubts and fears with the heat of his desire.

'Oh, my God...no...'

She heard the words, but her brain, her awareness, was several seconds late in translating their real meaning, several seconds during which she simply stood there waiting, not recognising that the look in his eyes, the tone of his voice signified not passion but revulsion.

At first she couldn't believe it...couldn't accept the evidence of her own senses, couldn't understand why he simply stood there and stared at her in a white-faced mixture of anger and disgust, looking at her as though her body, her nakedness, her availability was something shameful and embarrassing.

'Kenneth...' Her voice was a cracked, shocked, pleading protest expressing her need and fear, but he ignored her, shaking his head and turning towards the door.

'Please get dressed,' he told her. 'I've got a colleague coming round in fifteen minutes. He mustn't find you here...like this...

'My God...' he demanded as he reached the door and turned round to look at her. 'How could you? How could you come here dressed like some cheap joke of a tart, soliciting sex? I thought you were different...I thought you...

'Why couldn't you wait?' he asked her almost sorrowfully. 'I had it all planned... It would have been so perfect between us, so aesthetic and pure, not coarse and vulgar like a cheap harlot selling her wares, gross and demanding... My God, look at you...' Sally saw him shudder with distaste. Her throat was thick with tears, her body cold with shock.

Trembling violently, she pulled on her dress. The knowledge that she had been sexually rejected burned her skin like acid; the look she had seen in Kenneth's eyes was something she would never, ever forget.

She felt cheap and dirty, choked almost on the sterile, thin air the house seemed to possess.

How could she ever have thought that Kenneth loved her? That she loved him? Why on earth had he ever said that he *wanted* her when it was obvious that he didn't, or at least not in the way she had always thought of a man wanting a woman? It was like waking up abruptly from a dream or a nightmare.

Now the lack of sexual contact between them, the lack of sexual pressure on her from him which had pleased her so much, seemed cast in a different light, and all the doubts she had previously suppressed came rushing to the surface: the knowledge, for example, that a man who could so easily dismiss his own children from his life must surely have an intrinsic coldness about him, a coldness confirmed by his attitudes...his surroundings...and his rejection of her?

Her tears stung her eyes. She had never felt so degraded or humiliated, and it didn't help knowing that she had brought it on herself by coming here.

As she hurried downstairs Kenneth was saying something to her, but she ignored him, her stomach churning with revulsion—against him and against herself.

He was right, she *had* behaved like a tart, dressing herself up like that...asking for sex.

In the hallway Kenneth reached out to touch her, but she stepped back from him.

'No...' she told him fiercely. 'It's over, Kenneth. It's over...' She was crying as she ran out to her car, in her mind the image of herself as he must have seen her forever etched in painful clarity, her body, her clothes a gross parody of her sexuality.

She had gone to him expecting to be received with open arms and joyful passion, expecting him to honour the gift she had given him with tenderness, with an acknowledgement of just what the step she had taken meant, and instead he had looked at her with disgust and horror...

Angrily Kenneth watched her drive away. How could she do this to him...Sally, whom he had been ready to lift up on to the pedestal he had kept waiting for her? It had taken him a long time to meet a woman fit to occupy that place, and in Sally he had believed he had found someone he could mould and teach, someone malleable and grateful enough to appreciate all that he would do for her. He had thought she knew, understood that sex was something that he felt could only be justified if it was stripped clean of all lust and passion... A physical need which could only be satisfied if its darkness was lightened by purity...a purity which only he could control and approve.

To see Sally standing there in that cheap tarty outfit, like some back-street prostitute...stockings, suspenders, a form of bondage designed to titillate the male appetite—and, worse still, to wear such garments in white, the symbol of purity and innocence...

Sally had disillusioned him completely. He had thought she understood, that she shared his feelings...

The last thing he had ever expected was that she would come here dressed like that, looking for sex.

It was just as well he had discovered the truth before it was too late.

The hallway smelled of her of the perfume she had worn. Distastefully he opened the windows. Yes, it was just as well he had discovered what she was really like... And if he was honest with himself hadn't he always had that small doubt about her, the way she had talked almost incessantly about her children and demanded to know about his? He had always deplored that kind of foolish sentimentality. Personally he had been glad, relieved when his ex-wife had severed all contact with him, between himself and his sons.

He had never wanted children in the first place; Rebecca had tricked him into marriage by becoming pregnant. All women were adept at deceit; it was a natural instinct for them—even Sally, who he had thought had not had the intelligence for it.

Well, at least he would no longer have to worry about cultivating that appalling sister of hers and her husband, and socially Sally would probably have never quite fitted into his circle, no matter how patiently or well he had groomed her.

No, on balance he was glad it was over and that she had revealed herself to him in her true colours.

Unsteadily Sally walked up the garden path. The car was parked behind her at an angle in the road although she had no knowledge of actually driving it home. She must have done so, though. She shuddered, trembling violently as she searched in her bag for her key and unlocked the back door.

The house was still empty and silent. Joel had obviously not returned from the hospital.

She went upstairs slowly and painfully. She felt so old...drained...exhausted...terrified of letting her concentration slip in case she started visualising all over again the way Kenneth had looked at her.

Nothing in her life had prepared her for what had happened. The thought of being sexually repugnant to a man who had claimed that he loved her, of being rejected by him, was completely outside her personal experience, alien to the way she believed men and women related to one another.

It had never crossed her mind that Kenneth would react to what she was doing with anything other than eagerness and desire. Whenever she had voluntarily dressed prettily for Joel, shown him that she wanted sex, he had always responded positively to her. She had heard other women complaining about their husbands' lack of physical interest in them, of course, especially some of the older and more outspoken nurses on the wards, but it had never occurred to her that it might be something that could happen to *her*.

She had been stupidly naïve, she admitted...naïve and worse...but she had thought that Kenneth wanted her...that he wanted...

She froze as she heard a car pull up outside. Joel was back.

Joel frowned as he saw how Sally had parked her car. He still felt guilty about the way he had over-reacted and criticised her in the hospital but he had been so terrified of doing the wrong thing, his fear shocking him into the realisation of how many times when the children were growing up Sally must have felt as he had done—alone...afraid; but she had never let him see it...never taken it out on him the way he...

She had looked so hurt when it had been him Cathy had turned to and not her. He understood just how that felt.

He opened the kitchen door, expecting to find Sally in the kitchen. Cathy had insisted on being dropped off at her best friend's so that she could relate every detail of her 'ordeal' to her, and Joel suspected that Sally would be annoyed with him for giving in and letting her.

Paul was down at the leisure centre, now that the danger to his sister was over returning their relationship to the state of semi-siege which existed between them.

He had shown last night where his true feelings lay, though, Joel reflected, remembering his son's frightened face.

The house felt disturbingly silent, a small, worrying thread of instinct tightening warningly inside him.

Without knowing why, he took the stairs two at a time. Sally heard him and cowered back against the bed. She couldn't face Joel now... Not now. Tears filled her eyes and ran helplessly down her face while her body trembled uncontrollably. Distantly her trained mind registered what was happening, had made its clinical diagnosis... Shock...she was in shock... Talk to the patient calmly,

reassure her...keep her warm...but she was the patient,
wasn't she, and so how could she do any of those things...?

'Sally...'

Joel pushed open the door and then stopped abruptly.
'Sally, what is it...what's wrong?'

Instinctively he lowered his voice, speaking slowly and
gently as he moved towards her.

She was shaking violently, her body racked by intense
bouts of shivering, tears flooding silently and slowly from
her eyes.

It was like watching someone crying blood. He had never
seen her looking so shaken or afraid. Automatically he responded to her need, reaching out for her, taking her gently
in his arms, holding her, rocking her, soothing her as he
stroked her hair, crooning soft words of comfort in her ear.

This was the Joel she had loved, Sally recognised through
her pain, the Joel she had needed and missed so desperately.

This was what she had gone to Kenneth expecting to find.
The appalling irony that she should find it now, here in
Joel's arms after what she had done, sliced her with a pain
so intense that she cried out against it.

'Sally, what is it...what's happened?'

She could hear the concern, the alarm in Joel's voice but
instead of answering him she simply burrowed closer against
him. The feel of him, his smell, his warmth, his familiarity
were suddenly the only security she had.

Beneath the thinness of her dress Joel's hand registered
the presence of her suspender belt and stockings.

A cold shock of male knowledge numbed him. There
could only be one reason for Sally to dress like that.

He had told Philippa that their marriage was over, their
love dead, but now the thought of Sally, his wife, in the
arms of another man made him realise the truth. It wasn't
just jealousy that seared and burned him, he recognised,
it was fear for Sally as well; fear for her and a wild, fierce
anger against the man responsible for her grief.

As he started to pull away from her, Sally clung to him.
She didn't want Joel to let her go...not now...not ever...

She didn't ever again want to be that woman whom Kenneth had stared at with such disgust and distaste. She wanted to be what she had always wanted to be; she wanted to be protected by Joel's love, to be held safe by it and by him.

As he saw how distressed she was, Joel felt his jealousy turn to compassion and pity, his need to reassure her overwhelming his desire to know what had happened.

'It's all right...' he told her soothingly. 'It's all right... Whatever happened...'

'Nothing happened... nothing...'

Sally was shivering violently, her teeth chattering, but as Joel heard the agony in her voice he knew, without knowing how he knew it, that, whatever impulse had led to her dressing so obviously for sex, it had not been desire that had motivated her, and it was not from the arms of her lover or from his bed that she had come back home in such a state of distress.

Unfair and illogical of him to feel relieved that she had not been physically unfaithful to him, he knew...

'Hold me, Joel... Make love to me... take me to bed... Make love to me...'

Sally was as shocked to hear her words as Joel looked, but when Joel hesitated, watching her, her shock gave way to panic. Kenneth had rejected her; what if Joel did too?

'Joel... please...'

It hurt him hearing her beg him like this, looking at her and seeing the fear and panic in her eyes... he wanted to take hold of her and wipe it away, to tell her there was no need for her to punish herself like this, to pretend to want him when he could see from her eyes and her body that sex was the last thing she really wanted; but he wasn't sure he was capable of finding the right words, words that would comfort and not hurt, and so instead he cupped her face in his hands, smoothing back her hair, damp and sticky from her tears, her skin hot and flushed beneath his hands, her eyes more terrified than they had been that very first time she had let him touch her intimately.

But then she had trusted him . . . and wanted him as well, even though shyness had made her loath to admit it . . .

'It's all right, Sally, everything's going to be all right.' He kissed her gently and without passion, stilling the trembling of her mouth with the slow, sure warmth of his own.

A kiss of peace and knowledge rather than one of desire.

'How can everything be all right?' Sally asked him wretchedly when he stopped kissing her. 'How can anything ever be all right again . . . ?'

Slowly trying to feel his way through her pain without adding to the distress she had already suffered, Joel told her, 'It can if we want it to be. If that's what we both want. What do you want, Sal . . . ?'

'I want everything to be the way it used to be,' Sally told him brokenly. 'Joel, I'm so frightened,' she whispered to him. 'Everything's changed so much . . . No one wants me or needs me any more . . .'

'*I* need you,' Joel told her quietly, and as he said the words he knew, illuminatingly, that they were true. 'You love her,' Philippa had told him, and he had denied it . . . His heart ached with shame and guilt.

It hurt him seeing her like this, afraid and vulnerable, and it hurt him even more knowing that he was partly to blame; that he had punished her for his own sense of inadequacy in losing his job, letting her shoulder burdens he had had no right to expect her to carry, simply because his own ego could not accept the reversal of their traditional roles.

He had blamed her for turning away from him and making him seek sexual consolation with someone else. Did she similarly blame him?

Beneath his hands he could feel her body trembling still.

'Make love to me . . . take me to bed . . .' she had begged him, and perhaps after all it would be a good thing to do; the making of a new commitment to one another; the acknowledgement that there were things they were leaving behind, things too painful to discuss now but which would have to be dealt with ultimately.

Sally tensed as she felt Joel sliding free the buttons fastening her dress. It had been a long time since he had undressed her like this, she acknowledged, his mouth caressing her skin as he exposed it to his gaze and touch.

Her awareness of his arousal and desire were reassuringly familiar even though her relieved gratitude for them was not.

She tensed momentarily as he slid off her dress, holding her breath while she waited for him to make some comment about her choice of underwear, but all he did was gently remove it and then tell her softly, 'That's better—this is how I like you best . . . with nothing to come between us.'

Sally gazed uncertainly at him. Had he chosen those words deliberately? Had he after all guessed and was now trying to tell her . . . ?

She trembled on the brink of guilt and anxiety, her eyes searching his as she began uncertainly, 'Joel, there's something I should tell you . . .'

'There's only one thing I need to hear you say,' Joel told her softly. 'Do you still love me?' he prompted her when she stared at him in confusion. 'Because that's all that really matters, isn't it, Sal . . . all that should matter? That we love one another . . . The rest . . . well, we can find a way of sorting that out later . . .'

She did love him, Sally recognised as her body trembled with relief and joy . . . Because this was the Joel she had originally fallen in love with, the Joel who had always loved and protected her.

'Yes . . . yes. I love you,' she told him.

It might not have been the most passionate and intensely sexual lovemaking he had ever known, Joel reflected an hour later as he lay on his side, Sally's sleeping body curled up back against his as though even in sleep she needed to know he was close to her, but there had been a special quality about it nevertheless, a sense of shared intimacy and awareness of the significance of what they were doing, an acknowledgement of what still lay ahead of them.

Perhaps neither of them would ever discuss fully with the other exactly what had happened, not out of deceit but out of love and the need to protect one another. Some things were far more hurtful to hear than to say. It was enough for him now that he knew Sally was here with him through her own choice, that for whatever reason she had held back from making a sexual or emotional commitment to the man she had dressed so sensually for, and if it hurt him to know that she would never have chosen willingly to dress like that for him, then perhaps he ought to look at his own responsibility for that, instead of assuming that all the responsibility was hers.

Perhaps he had been guilty of focusing too much on the sexual aspects of their relationship in the past, expecting her to know that for him sex and love were two different faces of the same coin.

'I need to know that you want, need me... that you love me,' she had whispered to him as he held her. 'I need it to be more than just a physical thing, just a body for you to use to satisfy yourself, Joel.'

'You've never been that,' he had assured her. 'Never... It's just that sex has sometimes been the only way I could get your attention... I need to feel needed as well,' he had told her gruffly. 'I need to feel that I'm loved and not just a useless waste of space who can't even look after you financially any more... Have you any idea how much that hurts me... how bad it makes me feel?' he had asked her softly, and he had seen from her expression that she hadn't.

'It hurts like hell, Sally... It makes me feel that I'm a failure—that I've failed *you*.'

'No, you haven't,' she'd assured him. 'It's not your fault the factory closed, and you never know—this work you're doing at the leisure centre could lead to something,' she had added gently.

'Maybe... but don't count on it,' Joel had warned her. 'We could manage on less, you know,' he added. 'I hate seeing you looking so tired all the time... knowing... We don't need two cars. We could get rid of mine... I could buy a bike and become a real environmentalist,' he had teased her when she had started to protest. 'I could advertise and maybe get some more private pupils. A couple of the guys who go down to the leisure centre who are out of work are talking about setting up a sort of self-help group...a sort of trade and barter system with everyone pitching in with what they can do. It won't bring in much money, but if we're careful we could manage on less and——'

'I could go back to working part-time,' Sally had interrupted him.

'Not unless it's what you want,' Joel had told her quietly after a small pause. 'I'm not trying to dictate to you what you should and shouldn't do, Sal. I've already made that mistake once. You have as much right to what you want from life as the rest of us. I've realised while I've been at home with the kids how much of yourself you've sacrificed for them...for us. All I want now is for you to have a choice... If you want to work full-time, fine; if you don't...'

'Oh, Joel...'

'Now what have I said?' he had demanded as she'd collapsed in tears against him, soaking his chest with them as she'd hugged him with fierce joy and genuine emotion.

Some time she would have to tell him about Kenneth, to try to explain, and perhaps, if she was brave enough, to ask him where he had learned that new sexual gentleness and patience that was so unfamiliar to her.

She had shivered a little before curling up in his arms.

She had come far too close to losing what she now recognised was so important to her to want to risk spoiling this new harmony between them before it had had time to grow into something a little bit stronger.

In her sleep, Sally gave a small, sharp, frightened cry. Instantly Joel's arms tightened around her.

'It's all right, Sal...everything's all right,' he whispered to her.

'Joel.' She turned her head to look at him, her voice trembling slightly as she told him, 'I dreamed that you weren't here...'

'Of course I'm here,' he reassured her. 'Where else would I be...where else would either of us be? We belong together, you and I, Sal...here with each other...with the kids...'

'Joel!' Sally sat bolt upright in the bed. 'Cathy...Paul—where are they...?'

'Come back here and kiss me,' Joel demanded, grinning at her. 'Otherwise I'm not going to tell you...'

'Joel,' Sally threatened.

'No kiss...no kids...' Joel threatened back, straight-faced, laughing as Sally picked up her pillow and hit him with it.

'Things are going to be all right, aren't they, Joel?' Sally asked him, her face suddenly grave and anxious.

'Of course they are,' he told her, pushing aside the pillow. 'Of course they are.'

And he prayed that his words would prove true.

CHAPTER THIRTY-THREE

'NOT too close to the house,' Philippa called out warningly through the kitchen window as she watched Rory and Anya setting up their tennis net.

It was just over two months now since she had moved into Blake's large, comfortable house to take charge of Anya. Two months... in some ways it felt as though she and the boys had lived here forever; in others...

Outside, Rory was patiently demonstrating to Anya how to hold her racket. It had been an unexpected bonus, this rapport which had developed between her elder son and Anya.

It amused her to watch the protective fraternal manner he had adopted towards her and to observe Anya's very determined insistence that he should treat her as an equal.

After an initial three weeks on her own with Anya, gently and compassionately trying to help her to adjust to her new life, she had been very anxious about how her sons, who had after all never had to share her time or attention with another child, especially a female one, would react to Anya's presence.

'Stop worrying,' Blake had instructed her quietly when they'd gone to collect the boys from school. 'You can't protect them from all of life's hazards, you know, and it wouldn't be good for them if you could. They'll find a way of co-existing...'

'I was thinking of Anya just as much as the boys,' Philippa had defended herself.

'I know you were,' Blake had told her.

When she'd shot him a surprised look he had turned his head and smiled at her.

'You ruffle up like a protective mother hen the moment you feel that anything threatens her...'

491

'It's my job,' Philippa had protested, unconvincingly, she knew.

Looking after Anya, helping her to make the adjustment from her old life to her new one, could never be just a job to her, and hadn't been from the first moment she had set eyes on her.

Temperamentally and in almost every other way as well they were poles apart, and yet she had sensed in Anya a loss of personal identity similar to her own as a girl; she was determined that Anya, unlike her, would never be forced into a mould of someone else's making.

The look in Blake's eyes had shown her that he knew the truth just as well as she did herself.

'Your *job*?' he had repeated, his eyebrows lifting. 'Who are you trying to convince, Philippa, me or yourself? If it's me you're wasting your time. Do you know what I see when I watch you with Anya?'

She had shaken her head.

'I see love...love in its purest, most selfless and giving form, and I see Anya growing in the warmth of that love like a starved plant.'

'She has grown, hasn't she?' Philippa had agreed quickly, anxious to change the subject. His compliments warmed her heart in much the same way that his presence warmed her life, and that knowledge, that admission was something far too dangerous for her to dwell on...

'I think she's put on weight as well,' she had continued, speaking, she knew, far too quickly. 'I was going to ask you if it would be all right to buy some new clothes. I expect I'll have to buy the boys some things anyway...'

But the boys' clothes would be second-hand, while the allowance Blake had set aside for her to use for Anya's needs was so generous that she could buy an entire new wardrobe without making much of a dent in it.

Blake had already told her that he was perfectly happy to leave it to her discretion how much she spent and on what, but she was scrupulously careful about checking with him first before she bought anything, something which she felt sometimes irritated him for some reason.

'Fine,' he said now. 'Why don't you leave it a few days, though, until they've all settled down, and then I'll take a day off and we'll have a proper shopping trip?'

Philippa glanced across at him, digesting his suggestion in silence. Blake had revealed several unexpected traits over these last few weeks, not the least his desire to be involved not just with Anya's day-to-day life, but, it seemed, with her sons' lives as well.

He had already mentioned taking time off to take them all out on various day trips to enliven the long summer holiday, and when Philippa had demurred that there was no need for him to feel he had to include her sons in his plans he had reminded her of his original conversation with her. 'It will be good for Anya to mix with her peers in a family situation.'

'We don't know how well they get on with one another yet,' she had reminded him.

'Probably not very well at first,' he had surprised her by saying. 'Learning to interact with others in a close family unit isn't easy even when you've been doing it from birth.'

When she had moved into Blake's large rambling house he had made over one of the downstairs rooms to her as her own private sitting-room, an act which Philippa had assumed was more to protect his privacy than hers.

But in the evening after supper, when she and the boys had retreated to this sitting-room, Anya had wanted to come too, and of course Philippa hadn't felt it was fair to exclude her, so that the room, instead of being somewhere where she spent the evening alone as befitted Blake's employee, had become instead the focal point of their joint lives.

And not just for Anya but for Blake too.

Of course it was only natural that he would want to spend time with Anya and develop his relationship with her, but some evenings it was her sons who gravitated towards Blake, bombarding him with questions about some apparently wholly masculine pursuit, while Anya curled up on the sofa with her.

It had amazed her to hear Rory talking quite openly and easily to Blake about his relationship with his father, amazed her and humbled her a little as well as she'd recognised the man already growing in her elder son in that he had quite obviously felt he had to protect her from the concerns she'd overheard him expressing to Blake.

Perhaps it was only natural that her sons should relate more easily to another male—they were, after all, used to being at an all-male school and used to relating to their male teachers—but she didn't want them to grow up isolated from contact and familiarity with her own sex. Perhaps now that she was going to send them to a local mixed school for their next school year, that would help redress the balance.

Although she had tried to insist on Blake's reducing her salary to cover the cost of the boys' food and board, he had been so grimly sarcastic about it that she had had no option but to give in.

'Oh, yes, feeding a couple of half-grown boys is going to make me bankrupt, is that what you think?' he had asked her, and then she had heard him curse as he saw her wince, and immediately apologise for his unfortunate choice of words.

'I'm sorry,' he had said. 'I didn't think...'

He had been standing close enough to her to catch hold of her hand, holding it between both of his own in a gesture of comfort and remorse.

For a moment she had been terrified that she might make a complete fool of herself and actually cry.

There had been no physical displays of affection for her from her father when she was growing up, and not really from her mother either, and, while she had made sure that both her sons knew what it was to give and receive spontaneous physical affection, Andrew had been cast in much the same mould as her father.

To be touched like this by a man in a gesture of physical apology and reassurance was so rare that she couldn't even remember the last time it had happened.

And, not for the first time since she had come to live with Blake, she had been starkly aware of the bleakness and paucity of her emotional life.

Watching him with Anya, and with Rory and Daniel, seeing the way all three of them responded to him and he to them, the natural gestures of affection and comradeship they exchanged, made her achingly aware of the difference between her and Andrew's relationship and the relationship a man like Blake would have with a woman with whom he was intimately involved.

'When's Blake coming home?' Rory asked her now, walking into the kitchen. 'He said we could play that new computer game he got us tonight.'

'I don't know,' Philippa responded, adding firmly, 'And when he does, you mustn't pester him...'

'Oh, he won't mind,' Rory assured her. 'He's not like Dad,' he added innocently. 'He likes being with us. What's for tea, Mum? I'm starving...'

Philippa closed her eyes on the wave of emotion.

Yes, it was all working out far better than she had imagined. Even her decision not to see Joel again had now become something she genuinely believed had been the right decision for both of them, her brief relationship with him something she could view with tender pleasure and not pain, instead of a forced acceptance of what she knew morally she ought to feel while privately wishing that things could have been different.

Blake had been generous in his praise for the way she was dealing with Anya, and Susie had commented only the previous day that she seriously ought to consider training for some sort of work with children.

Even her parents and Robert had not raised as many objections about her working for Blake as she had expected— probably far too relieved to be freed from any responsibility towards her, Philippa recognised drily.

So, given that everything was so perfectly wonderful and marvellous, why was it that she woke up in the morning with a feeling like a lead weight in her heart?

Why? What was it she had said to herself about only a fool falling in love with Blake a second time when she'd taken the job? she asked herself grimly.

But the emotions she felt now had nothing to do with those fevered teenage yearnings; now it was his tenderness, his warmth, his sense of humour that made her ache helplessly with longing; now it was the reality of him that she loved, not the fantasy she had conjured up for herself.

She didn't just love him, she admitted as she checked the oven, she liked him as well—liked the way he treated her as an equal, seeking her opinions and her views, discussing things with her, sharing... Showing her sons by his example that being a man was not about taking charge and being in control, that it did not involve the denial of one's emotions, the distancing of oneself from others, that it allowed for mistakes, errors and vulnerabilities in others as well as in himself; like the way he was setting down for Anya the pattern of the kind of man she would one day look for, a man who would value her and respect her, a man who would love her.

It was hard concealing her emotional responsiveness to him, and even harder sometimes concealing her physical desire.

All right, so she was no longer the teenager who had lain in her bed night after night imagining what he would be like as a lover, but that didn't stop her from having to fight against that betraying feminine ache deep within her body far, far too often.

No, it wasn't easy concealing her love for him. Not easy but essential.

It wasn't just the financial security of working for him she didn't want to lose. There was Anya to consider, and her needs had to come before her own.

So far, she congratulated herself wryly, she was rather proud of the very neat job of containment she had done on her emotions. Not even Susie suspected how she really felt.

'Mmm...he's definitely worth leaving home for,' had been her approving comment the first time she had met Blake. 'He's so sexy you could almost bottle it and sell it. God knows how he's managed to stay single...why is it that with some men you can just look at them and know that in bed and out of it they just can't help but turn you on?

'I mean, he isn't just sexy, he's old-fashioned nice as well. I'm glad I'm not in your shoes—I don't know how I'd be able to keep my hands off him...' she had added frankly, and then apologised quickly, 'Oh, hell, Pip, I'd forgotten for a moment what you told me...'

'It's all right,' Pippa had assured her. 'That was years ago, a teenage crush, that's all.'

Then, she had believed it.

She smiled valiantly to herself. Well, at least now she was sensible enough not to waste her time indulging in impossible daydreams, to cherish every smile Blake gave her, to place far too much significance on the conversations they shared, the compliments he gave her; these were, she reminded herself, no more than any appreciative employer would give to an employee he or she wished to keep; and Blake did wish to keep her, he had made that very plain, though not for any personal reasons.

It was Anya's welfare that was at the forefront of his mind when he told her approvingly how much more of a real home she had made the house; Anya's happiness he was considering when he told her there was no need to shush the children when they were outside playing while he was working in his study, and that he enjoyed hearing the sound of their laughter; Anya's emotional welfare that brought that warm, almost tender look to his eyes when he commented on the bond of physical affection developing between Anya and herself.

No, the woman she had become would never make the same mistakes as the girl she had once been, never attempt to deceive herself about Blake's feelings for her, never take the risk of inviting his rejection a second time.

She frowned as she glanced up at the kitchen clock and then opened the back door to call the children in, reminding them that they had the supermarket shopping to do.

'All right, everyone, upstairs, hands and faces washed and hair combed,' she announced firmly, ignoring Daniel's, 'Must we . . . ?'

Twenty minutes later, just as she was about to lock the back door, Blake's Volvo came sweeping up the drive.

'Ah, good, I've caught you,' Blake announced as he climbed out of the car and came over to her. 'I hoped I might.'

'Why, is something wrong?' Philippa asked him uncertainly.

'No . . . nothing. But I managed to finish early and so I decided to come home and give you a hand with the supermarket shopping. You mentioned this morning that you intended to do it today and I thought it might be easier if we went in the Volvo.'

'Yes . . . yes, it would,' Philippa agreed.

He wasn't wearing his suit jacket and the sleeves of his shirt were rolled up to reveal his forearms. His skin was tanned, the muscles beneath strong and firm, a legacy no doubt from the summer he had spent crewing for a fellow colleague at Johns Hopkins who was a keen yachtsman. Blake had told her how much he had enjoyed the sport one evening when they had been chatting. He had offered to teach the boys if she thought they might be interested, and she hadn't been able to help contrasting his attitude towards them with Andrew's.

That had also been the evening he had first mentioned his American girl-friend and the relationship they had shared.

She had kept to herself the fact that, no matter how much the girl might have stressed that their affair was founded on mutual sexual interest and had no deep emotional basis, she found it very hard to accept that any woman could have that kind of long term relationship with a man, especially a man like Blake, without loving him.

She had also kept to herself her belief that the American had perhaps kept her feelings private because she had sensed that Blake did not return her love.

Now, as she saw the way the sunlight glinted on the hair on his arms, turning it from brown to gold, highlighting the underlying muscles in a way that made her stomach lurch disconcertingly and a *frisson* of sharply dangerous sexual awareness and longing shoot through her, she wasn't sure if she envied the girl or pitied her.

One thing she did know, and that was that for her a merely sexual relationship with Blake would never be enough, no matter how physically fulfilled her body might feel. Her heart and her mind would still ache and yearn for more.

That was what loving someone did to you. The simple purity of luxuriating in the satisfaction of plain physical need that she had experienced with Joel would never be enough to satisfy her with Blake; she would always long for more, so much, much more... for his love.

'Philippa...'

Suddenly realising how long she must have been staring at him, she blushed as furiously as an embarrassed schoolgirl when Blake said her name, dipping her head so that her hair swung forward to conceal her flushed face.

'You really didn't need to do this, you know,' she told Blake over an hour later as she negotiated the heavy trolley out of the supermarket's automatic doors while Blake took charge of the children.

The supermarket's car park was busy; it was the school holiday season after all, and Philippa was wryly aware of the envious looks they were attracting from other mothers struggling on their own with both trolley and offspring.

No doubt in their eyes she and Blake represented the perfect family picture. If only they knew the truth.

'I wanted to do it,' she heard Blake telling her quietly as they waited to cross the road.

Her heart had started to thump far too fast. Will you stop it? she ordered the recalcitrant organ with silent firmness, warning it that it was getting far too excited over nothing, and that if it didn't stop she was going to have to take very severe action.

Determined not to betray to Blake what she was feeling and prejudice the friendly relationship they had built up, she forced herself to smile and challenge him teasingly, 'Why? Don't you think I can be trusted with a shopping trolley?'

'On the contrary,' he told her softly, 'I think...'

He broke off to step aside, to make way for another shopper to pass them, while Philippa headed determinedly towards the car, feeling thoroughly flustered.

What was the matter with her? Anyone would think that a man had never paid her a compliment before... never tried to flirt with her.

Blake... flirting with *her*... impossible... Now she *was* letting her imagination get out of control.

She had almost reached the Volvo when Blake caught up with her, unlocking the doors for her and then opening the boot.

'Here, let me do that,' he insisted as she leaned forward to lift the first of the paper cartons out of the trolley. As they both leaned forward at the same time their bodies collided briefly.

'Whoops...' As Blake apologised, Philippa laughed. She was facing the sun, its warmth pleasant against her skin, the air current across the car park, which on a cold day could feel as icily bitter as though it had come from Siberia, today a lulling, fresh caress, tousling her hair so that she automatically lifted her hand to push the soft curls off her face.

And then she saw her shadow on the tarmac, saw the way the breeze had flattened her top against her body, the way her lifted arm was throwing the curve of her breast into prominence, the way her whole body seemed to be leaning yearningly towards Blake... Blake, who was standing there, his body completely immobile, his expression hidden from her by the shadow cast by the sun. He moved, leaning towards her, his hand lifted as though to touch her, and shame poured through her as she saw herself as he must be seeing her, practically inviting his touch...his kiss, showing him that she was after all still the same old Philippa...still stupid enough to want...

Quickly she pulled back from him, her body trembling as she turned away and quickly reached into the trolley, her movements jerky and unco-ordinated.

Bleakly Blake watched her, silently cursing himself for his crassness. The way she had pulled away from him just now had been quite unmistakable...told him everything he wanted to know, or rather everything he *didn't* want to know! He had seen the look of shock, of horror almost in her eyes when she'd thought he was going to touch her. He had been a fool to think he could resurrect what she had once felt for him; to imagine the woman she had become would even want to be reminded of it, never mind...

Well, he wouldn't add to her obvious embarrassment and disgust by repeating his mistake. In future he would make sure that he kept his distance from her, physically and emotionally. That was quite obviously what *she* wanted to do.

His interpretation of the conversations they had shared, of the laughter...of the way she had seemed to listen with such interest when he had told her about his life, her head held slightly to one side, her eyes sometimes alight with laughter, other times soft with emotion, but always, like her, alive and warm, quick to respond to the need in others, had quite obviously been the wrong one. He had quite obviously mistaken mere politeness for something far more personal, and that was his fault and not hers. He turned away from her, his eyes narrowing as he looked into the sun.

He had come back to draw a line under the past, fully
expecting that the reality of the woman she had become
would finally banish the image of the girl she had been
from his heart and his memories.

But instead. He closed his eyes. Watching her just now,
seeing the laughter in her eyes, the curve of her mouth, her
body, knowing how he felt about her, he had ached so much
with love and need ... had wanted so much to reach out
and just touch her, if only to reassure himself that she was
real. Behind the darkness of his closed eyelids he waited
for the familiar pain to roll over him in its dull, relentless,
unmerciful dragging surge.

He would have to do something, he knew that. Otherwise...

'You get in the car with the children,' he told Philippa
harshly. 'I'll see to this...'

Philippa didn't bother to argue... It was obvious that
he wanted to distance himself from her, and of course she
knew exactly why.

Blake was late. He was normally home by this time.
Philippa tensed as the phone rang. She went to answer it,
her heart flipping over unsteadily when she heard Blake's
voice.

'I'm afraid I'm going to be held up at work,' he told
her. 'Don't wait supper for me. I'm not sure what time I'll
be back.'

'But that's the second time this week he's been late,' Rory
protested later over supper, adding with a scowl as he kicked
the leg of his chair, 'It isn't the same having supper without
him.'

No, it wasn't, Philippa agreed silently. Was Blake genuinely very busy at work, or was he simply avoiding spending
time with them ... with her?

Since that incident in the car park, an uncomfortable
and tense atmosphere had built up between them. Philippa
tried her best to behave as naturally as she could, for the
children's and especially Anya's sake, but it was difficult

when every time she looked at Blake she remembered the way she had leaned towards him, looking at him…inviting him…

'Philippa, may I have a word, please?'

Philippa tensed as she caught the formal note in Blake's voice and saw the way he was frowning.

'Of course,' she agreed, trying to keep her voice as steady as she could.

Anya and the boys were in bed and Philippa had been just about to go upstairs herself when the door of the small room that Blake used as his study had opened and Blake himself had come out.

Now, as she followed him back inside, Philippa felt rather like a schoolgirl called in to see her head teacher.

They hadn't seen much of Blake this last week, he had worked late most evenings and left early in the morning. While the children complained vociferously about his absence she remained silent, even though she missed him every bit as much as they did.

Blake was standing with his back to her, facing the window.

He removed his jacket and his shirt was stretched tightly across his back and shoulders, revealing the tension in his muscles.

'There isn't any easy way to say this,' he told her brusquely. 'Things aren't working out the way I'd hoped…'

Philippa stared at him, her heart thudding painfully, shock churning her stomach. What did he mean, things weren't working out? She could feel the panic starting to flare inside her.

'Oh, it's nothing to do with the way you're dealing with Anya; no one could have done a better job.'

A better job? Helplessly Philippa fought down her feelings. Caring for Anya wasn't just a job to her. Hadn't Blake himself been the one to tell her that?

Suddenly he was the cold, impervious man she remembered from all those years ago from her visit to his flat, hard and unyielding in the face of her emotional need. Well, this time she was not going to humiliate herself, to...

'No, it isn't Anya,' she heard him saying roughly. 'It's... It's...there are other issues...I don't want to be specific—some things are better left unsaid—but I suspect you already know what I mean.'

Philippa's mouth had gone dry. She had to clear her throat twice before she could manage a thin, whispered, 'Yes.'

And she thought she had been so clever...so contained...so good at hiding what she felt. How long had he known? Was that why he had been 'working late' so often recently—to avoid her...? Oh, God. She closed her eyes as the twin pains of despair and loss savaged her.

'For Anya's sake I don't want you to leave. She needs the stability you've given her more than what I can offer her on my own. I've decided that the best thing to do would be for me to move into rooms at the hospital, temporarily at least...'

'You can't do that,' Philippa protested. 'This is your home—if anyone leaves it should be me...'

'It's Anya's home as well,' Blake pointed out quietly, 'and she needs you here with her.'

'She needs you as well,' Philippa told him.

He turned round. She could see the stress in his eyes and on his face, and guilt was added to all her other burdens.

She had done this... She, with her stupid unwanted betrayal of a love she already knew he didn't want.

'She loves you, Philippa, and to be honest I'm not too sure that the Social Services would allow me to bring her up alone. No. The best solution is for me to move out.'

No, she wanted to protest, the best solution is for you to be here where you're loved and needed. I should be the one to go, to pay the price of loving you, not the other way round.

'I think it best that for the time being at least we tell the children that it's only a temporary arrangement...'

'Lie to them, you mean?' Philippa asked harshly.

'I don't like doing it any more than you do, but this isn't something we can explain to them, you know that...'

'You don't have to go...'

Oh, God, why had she said that? In her own voice she had heard the forlorn cry of a frightened child.

'We could...I could...'

'No,' Blake stopped her. 'No, Philippa... You see, I couldn't.'

Tears filled her eyes; fiercely she blinked them away.

Well, she had asked for it, she told herself grittily. It wasn't Blake's fault that she had pushed him to the point where he had to be so blunt.

'When...when will you go...?' Her voice was a croaky whisper forced past the huge, painful lump in her throat.

'Tomorrow.' He ignored her small, shocked protest. 'There's no point in delaying things. I'll tell the children in the morning at breakfast.'

Tiredly Philippa picked up the cup of tea she had just made for herself and wandered into the sitting-room, switching on the television and then curling up on the sofa.

It was now almost two weeks since Blake had left and if anything she was missing him more rather than less.

Tomorrow was Saturday. He had telephoned her during the week to say that he would be coming home for the weekend and she had determinedly made plans to spend as much time as she could away from the house while he was there. It seemed the only decent thing to do.

The agents had apparently had two separate people showing interest in her own house, or rather the bank's house, and the bank had informed her that it was optimistic about an early sale.

It seemed there was also a small...a very small possibility that a buyer might be found for the company, but she was not to get her hopes up too high, the bank had told her—any sale would only be for a very modest figure and it was by no means definite that the business would be sold. If it was started up again it would certainly only be with a very much reduced workforce, Neville Wilson had told her in response to her query.

She had gone up to bed over an hour ago, but lying there unable to sleep had brought her down again to make herself a cup of tea. Now, too restless mentally to focus on the television she had switched on, she closed her eyes.

Her body was tired even if her mind wasn't.

The house was almost completely in darkness, only a small light showing through the window of Philippa's sitting-room, Blake saw as he stopped his car and got out.

Originally he had not planned to come home until the morning and he was still not sure why he had been foolish enough to give in to the savage clamouring of the needs which had driven him away in the first place and come back now.

He had never really thought of himself as a masochist, enjoying self-inflicted pain for its own sake.

He unlocked the front door and then stood for a moment in the hallway. From Philippa's sitting-room he could hear the subdued murmur of the television.

It was hardly surprising that she had not come out to greet him, he reflected with self-contempt, but who could blame her for avoiding him? How arrogant he had been, assuming just because he was over fifteen years older that he was also fifteen years wiser.

But then fifteen years ago his reasons for refusing to give in to temptation had been reinforced by his knowledge of her own youth, his awareness of how limited her real experience of life actually was, his fear that she would be damaged in the inevitable battle between him and her father.

And of course then he had been afflicted with all the arrogance of his own youth, the magnanimity of his own noble rejection of his own needs in favour of hers.

He pushed open the sitting-room door and then stopped.

Philippa was not watching the television, as he had imagined, but was instead fast asleep on the sofa, curled up on it like a small child—only the slim bare legs and the softly curved body revealed by the thin nightshirt she was wearing were not those of a child.

The speed of his physical response to her caught him off guard. What had happened to the self-control his lovers had congratulated him on—and complained about when their relationships had drifted to their inevitable close?

He started to back out of the room, but something had obviously alerted Philippa to his presence, for her eyes opened. She focused on him and then blinked slowly.

'Blake.'

Still groggy with sleep and the shock of seeing him standing there, Philippa sat up, her face flushing as she realised how she must look, fair hair tousled, face free of make-up, and wearing nothing but a thin piece of cotton which had ridden up while she slept so that it was now wrapped tightly round her thighs, making it impossible for her to move properly without revealing far more of her body than Blake could possibly want to see.

'I...I thought you weren't coming back until tomorrow...'

'I wasn't.'

'The children have missed you,' she told him awkwardly, relinquishing her battle with her nightshirt to give in to her need to look properly at him.

He looked tired, haggard almost, and her heart ached with love for him.

'I've missed them too.' She could tell from his voice that it was true.

'Blake, please come back,' she begged him. 'We can work something out; I'll...'

'Can we? How?' he demanded harshly. 'My God, I've been back in the house five minutes and already——' He broke off abruptly, rubbing his hand along the side of his jaw in a betrayal of what he was feeling.

'I can't come back, Philippa,' he told her roughly. 'I thought being away from you would make it easier, not...' When he saw the shock in her eyes his mouth twisted bitterly.

'You see what I mean? Look at the way you're reacting to just the words. How do you think you're going to feel if I try to put them into action?'

Please, please don't let me cry, Philippa begged herself. The smile she forced her mouth to frame felt as brittle as old glass, mirroring every aching crack in her heart.

'You're quite safe, you know,' she told him, trying to keep her voice light. 'I promise you that I'm not going to invade your bedroom the way I once invaded your flat...'

'*I'm* quite safe? What the hell are you talking about?'

Strangely, his anger didn't even make her flinch. She had come too far now for that.

'I'm talking about us, Blake, you and me, and the fact that I've stupidly gone and fallen in love with you—again. But my feelings are *my* problem, *my* responsibility, and I promise you that... Blake, what are you doing?' she protested huskily as he crossed the distance between them and physically lifted her off the sofa and into his arms.

'I am doing,' he told her thickly, 'what I should have done years ago and what I've certainly wanted to do from the moment you opened your front door to me...'

There wasn't any time for her to question or protest. Blake's arms were wrapping her tightly against his body, his mouth touching hers, caressing it with delicate tenderness.

Caught between disbelief and desire, Philippa moaned his name against his mouth. She was trembling so violently she could hardly stand up. Blake was shaking as well. His mouth left hers, his lips whispering a husky reassurance before he reclaimed hers, his earlier delicacy abandoned as passion overwhelmed him.

His hands stroked her hair, her face, her body as he kissed her and told her how much he needed her, loved her and wanted her... how much he always had done, the words running helplessly into kisses that turned her responses into incoherent soft murmurs of pleasure and response.

'I love you so much.'

His hand touched her breast and she shivered in anticipatory pleasure. 'No, not yet,' he told her thickly as he bent his head to brush his mouth against her cotton-covered nipple. Leaning against him, shivering in helpless delight, feeling the hard arousal of him against her, she closed her eyes on a shudder of sensual pleasure.

Blake's mouth returned to her breast, his hand sliding the fabric aside.

As the sharp, high sound she made arced across the silence she could feel the deep shudders of response racking his body.

'Eighteen years ago, I wanted you like this,' he told her thickly. 'You were sixteen, a child still, a child who looked at me with the eyes of a woman. I couldn't believe what was happening to me. The last thing I had expected, the last thing I had wanted was to fall in love, but it was too late. And so I waited and watched you, knowing that I had to give you time to grow up, that I couldn't, *must* not take advantage of what I could see in your eyes.'

'But you rejected me,' Philippa reminded him huskily. 'When I came to you, you sent me away...'

Blake's heart ached as he caught the echo of her pain in her voice.

'I know, I know... I didn't want to hurt you, but...'

He released her slightly, holding her gently away from him, smoothing her hair back off her face as he looked down at her.

'Believe me, my darling... hurting you was the very last thing I wanted to do.'

'Then why did you?' Philippa asked him simply.

For a moment she thought he wasn't going to reply, but then he started to speak, choosing his words carefully, hesitantly almost.

'That last summer... the year you were eighteen... Robert told me that your father was... concerned about you and about the fact that you... about your feelings for me... He pointed out to me how young you were, how you had been brought up to expect a far different lifestyle from the one I could give you... He told me that your father wanted me to leave——'

Philippa had started to frown, and abruptly she interrupted him, demanding, 'It was that afternoon, wasn't it, the afternoon I came back from tennis? I thought then that you and Robert were quarrelling...but you denied it...you said you had to leave...

'I had been so convinced that somehow things were going to change between us...that at last you were going to see me as a woman and not a child...that you were going to...' She stopped speaking, swallowing painfully. 'I loved you so much, Blake, and I thought that you...'

'I know, I know,' Blake groaned, taking her back in his arms, rocking her gently against his body, his voice muffled against her hair. 'But I couldn't stay, not after Robert had made it so plain that I wasn't welcome...'

'You could have written to me...telephoned...'

'I wanted to, but everything that Robert had said kept coming back to me. I knew he was right, you see—I knew that I *couldn't* provide you with the kind of lifestyle you were used to. I could barely manage to feed myself, never mind... I had to put my mother first, Pip... She was so ill...'

'Yes, of course you did,' Philippa agreed fiercely. 'But surely you knew...must have known that you were far more important to me than material possessions?'

She saw his face and cried out in distress. 'Oh, Blake. No...no...you must have known...'

'Yes. Deep down inside I think I did, but at the same time... You were so very young, Pip,' he reminded her gently. 'So very vulnerable...so very dependent on your parents. I couldn't——'

'*I* made you think that, didn't I?' Philippa cut in painfully. 'I only reinforced everything that Robert had said to you by not defying my father and going to university.' She closed her eyes, trying not to think about how different things might have been if only she... 'That's why you were so angry with me, so harsh, when you claimed that if I'd really wanted to I could have worked to finance myself, wasn't it...?' Tears filled her eyes. 'Oh, Blake...Robert had no right to interfere,' she began bitterly, 'to tell you...'

'He thought what he was doing was best for you,' Blake told her gently.

'No, he didn't,' Philippa denied sadly. 'He knew he was doing the best thing for *him*, for him and for my father... Neither of them ever...' She bit her lip and looked up at him.

'Do you know, after Andrew's death, Robert actually tried to pretend that he had never wanted me to marry him in the first place? Andrew was Robert's friend, you know... They were at school together. Robert was very impressed by Andrew's *expectations*.' Her mouth curled derisively.

'Poor Andrew; nothing in his life quite ever lived up to those expectations—not his marriage to me, not his work...and certainly not the reality of his great-aunt's will.'

Briefly she explained to Blake what had happened and then added quietly, 'I didn't marry Andrew for his money, though...'

'I know that,' Blake told her quietly. She stopped speaking and waited. 'When I first heard about you marrying Ryecart, I almost hated you,' Blake admitted gruffly. 'I went to America determined to show you, to show your family just what a mistake you'd all made, that if it was money and status you'd really wanted, then I could have given you so much more; that I could be more successful than your father; richer than your husband.' He looked at her sombrely.

'I was a fool and worse in those days, Pip, and it took Michael to bring me to my senses.

'He came out to visit me one summer and he made it obvious that he was shocked at how much I'd changed, at what I was doing to myself. His honesty forced me to be equally honest, and I found myself admitting how I felt...and most especially how I felt about you...how bitter your marriage had made me.

'He told me the truth about your marriage. That he didn't think you loved your husband. That you'd married him because it was what your father wanted, not because it was what you wanted. He said that you'd married him so quickly that it was almost as though you'd been running away from something, or from someone.'

He paused, and Philippa admitted shakily, 'Yes... I was running away from you and from myself... from the pain of loving you and being rejected by you... I was so immature, Blake,' she admitted honestly. 'I should never...'

'No... your father is the one to blame, not you,' Blake corrected her. 'He should never have allowed you to marry him, never mind pushed you into it.

'Michael told me that he didn't believe you were happy, but that he felt you would stay with Andrew out of loyalty and because of the boys... I was so tempted to come back then, to see you and... but I'd already hurt you once, and very badly; I knew I couldn't do so a second time, so I stayed away...told myself it was time to make a fresh start. I threw myself into my work, not this time out of my desire to make money or achieve status, but simply as a means of drowning out all the things I couldn't bear to think about.

'And then I went to Romania... That changed everything, including me. It finally enabled me to leave behind my bitterness, my resentment against your father... to put down the chip I was carrying on my shoulder. But it didn't stop me wishing that things could have been different...'

He touched her face, his eyes so bleak with remembered pain that Philippa had to blink away fresh tears.

'When I heard the news about Anya's parents I knew that I had to come back. When I was looking for a suitable post and I saw the job at the General advertised it seemed as though fate was urging me to make a final attempt to get my life in order, finally to draw a line under the past.

'I told myself that it would be churlish, and worse still, cowardly to refuse that chance; that I had to come back and lay a few old ghosts...'

Philippa's eyebrows rose and he laughed.

'Mmm... that thought has crossed my mind too,' he admitted, making her laugh with him. 'Fascinating, isn't it, how our choice of language often betrays us even when we think we've got everything under control, all our secrets safely hidden?'

'Yes, well, never mind about your hidden motives,' Philippa mock scolded him. 'What concerns me most is your use of the word "ghosts" in the plural.'

'There is no plural,' Blake assured her, 'only one single, very singular, very special, very, very real and alive ghost who...'

Philippa laughed again, teasing him until he reached out for her and wrapped his arms round her, silencing her as he had once done a long, long time ago, only this time there was no anger in the fierce passion of his kiss, no pain or threat, no bitterness, only the long, slow sweetness of a love that had come to full maturity.

When he had finally released her Philippa asked him huskily, 'What were you really expecting to find when you came back, Blake...?'

'Not this,' he admitted quietly. 'I imagined that if we did happen to meet it would not be the girl I loved I would see, but a comfortably married woman whose main concerns in life were her family. The sort of woman who diligently involved herself in local charities, who would not have much time at all for a man who had once behaved so badly towards her; the sort of woman who was far too sensible and content to even want to think about resurrecting such a painful past.

'I pictured you comfortably ensconced in your home, surrounded by your family and friends...'

'You're talking about me as though I'm closer to fifty-odd than thirty-four,' Philippa protested indignantly, her expression changing and becoming very sad as she added quietly, 'You're drawing a picture of a woman like my mother, Blake... not me...'

'Yes. I know,' he agreed. 'But don't you see...if I hadn't done that I couldn't have come back? It was safer to imagine you like that, Pip, than to risk visualising the truth...safer for me and safer for you as well. After all, what right did I have to come back and disrupt your whole life? I guessed from what Michael told me how much I must have hurt you but it was too late then to do anything about it. You were married, you had the boys, and Michael had stressed to me how loyal you were to Andrew...'

'I never *loved* Andrew,' she told him quietly. 'I married him because he was my escape route and he married me because I was my father's daughter; both of us were too cowardly, too afraid to reach out for what we really wanted from life; too insecure in one way or another to believe that we could stand alone and be valued for what we were. I've learned that since Andrew's death, and I've learned as well that it's much easier to forgive another's weakness than it is your own.

'It doesn't feel very good looking back and seeing myself as others do...' She heard the small sound of denial Blake made and a faint smile touched her mouth. 'I've begun to learn to accept Andrew's weaknesses, so hopefully it shouldn't be too long before I can accept and forgive my own, and in truth, compared with some marriages, ours wasn't so bad. Andrew was never abusive or unkind. His work, worldly success—they were what mattered most to him; sexually...' She gave a small, revealing shrug. 'When he first died I felt so angry with him because of what he had done, the way he had locked me out of his life and left me so unprepared for living on my own, for coping with the mess he had left behind; but then I started to see that I had *helped* him to lock me out, even encouraged him in some ways.

'I didn't *want* our marriage to be any different because I didn't want that kind of intimacy with Andrew. Quite what that makes me...'

'It makes you human, and honest,' Blake told her huskily, 'and it makes *me* glad.'

When he saw the questioning look she was giving him he told her, 'It makes it easier for me to deal with my jealousy of him and of the years he had with you knowing that you didn't really love him, knowing that when you and I marry we'll be making a completely fresh start; that he won't be a ghost in our lives or our bed.

'With a bit of luck we should be able to arrange things so that we can get married before Christmas. I don't know how you feel about it, but a holiday away somewhere with the kids over the Christmas break rather than a honeymoon might...'

'I can't marry you, Blake.'

'What?'

The look in his eyes made her reach out towards him, gripping his hands tightly in her own. Had she ever really thought this man unemotional, cold, hard? How blind... how juvenile...how self-obsessed she had been!

'I don't mean not ever...I just mean not yet.'

'Not yet? But you said you loved me. If you're not sure about how you feel...'

'I am sure. It isn't anything to do with how I feel about you.' She touched his face lightly. 'There's nothing I want more than to marry you, Blake, to commit my life to you and to know that you've committed yours to me, but if I marry you now, with the company's bankruptcy and my own financial problems still hanging over me, unresolved...'

'You're afraid of what people might say...that they'd think you married me for my money?' he asked her roughly.

'No, of course not. It isn't anything to do with what other people might think, it's us, Blake. You and me... I want us to be equals in our relationship, not me some pathetic Cinderella needing to be rescued from the mess she's made of her life by you, her prince. I want to participate actively in our future together, not sit back passively and let you take all my problems off my shoulders. I...please try to understand.' Her voice shook slightly, betraying the depth and intensity of her emotions. 'I need to prove to myself that I have learned something from this whole mess, that I have grown...that I have coped. I want to be for you the woman that you deserve,' she told him softly, 'for you *and* for myself.'

Blake groaned. 'You already are that woman... More woman than I ever thought I would be lucky enough to find.'

'To marry you now would be a betrayal not just of my love for you but of myself as well. I don't want to come to you burdened by the detritus from my and Andrew's marriage, either emotionally or financially,' Philippa told him firmly, but she couldn't quite keep the small tremor out of her voice. It told him not just how important what she was saying was, but how important *he* was as well.

'I need to be able to respect myself, and I still have to earn that respect,' she told him.

'The way we feel about one another is bound to show,' Blake pointed out. 'Others will see it and you know what they're going to say, don't you?'

'That you're sleeping with the hired help?' Philippa hazarded. She gave a small shrug. 'Other people's words and opinions can't hurt me any more, Blake, but if you're concerned that that kind of gossip might affect your career...'

He shook his head. 'No. But your family won't like it. Your parents, your brother Robert...'

'Tough. Their likes and dislikes are their own problem, not mine,' Philippa told him squarely. 'When you and I marry, become partners, I want us to become *equal* partners; I want to show my sons and Anya, by our example, all the good ways in which a man and a woman can relate to one another. I want Anya to grow up with the self-respect and the self-confidence that I never had. I want her not just to believe it but to accept without question that a woman has the right sometimes to be selfish about her own needs, to put herself first, and that those who genuinely love her will accept her as she is; that in a good relationship both partners make sacrifices for one another sometimes and, equally, both partners put themselves first sometimes. I want my sons to grow up with a respect and admiration for my sex . . . I want our children, if we should have any . . .'

She stopped when she saw his face . . .

'What is it—don't you want children?' she asked him hesitantly.

'Not *want* them . . . your children . . . *our* children . . . ? Oh, my God, Philippa . . .'

As he reached for her and then withdrew she leaned forward and told him huskily, 'As a teenager I wasted so many hours fantasising about what it would be like if you and I were lovers. I don't want to waste any more hours fantasising, Blake. I want to know *now* . . .'

After he had finished kissing her, he warned her ruefully, 'I'm only a man, you know . . . Those teenage fantasies . . . I'm not sure I'm going to be able to live up to them . . .'

The uncertainty, the vulnerability, the love in his voice made her heart and her body ache with answering emotion. How well she knew what it was like to feel that vulnerability.

She cupped his face in her hands and looked up into his eyes.

'I am,' she told him softly, and suddenly, gloriously, unequivocally and irrevocably, she knew she was.

'Mmm—what time is it?' Sleepily Blake lifted his arm from around Philippa's waist to look at his watch. 'I suppose I'd better make a move and get back to my own bed before the children wake up and find me here with you.'

'Mmm,' Philippa acknowledged, but instead of moving away from him she curled herself more securely round him, her mouth lifting in a smile he couldn't see as he gave a soft groan and his hand cupped and stroked her breast.

It felt so right being here with him like this, so natural. Last night, after they had made love, she had told him about Joel, banishing the look she had seen in his eyes with a tiny shake of her head.

'I thought I might fall in love with him, but in reality both of us were looking for someone to displace our individual pain.' Her face had clouded a little. 'I hope he and his wife resolve their problems.'

She had enjoyed making love with Joel, discovering her sexuality, feeling desired and wanted, but from the first moment that Blake touched her she had known she need have no fear that Joel's ghost would ever come between them in any sexual sense.

It wasn't a matter of degree of experience or expertise, it was much simpler than that—and much, much more complex as well.

It was the difference between knowing that Joel was not her man and that Blake was. A 'coming home' that both heightened her sexuality and her responsiveness to him and deepened it, so that the emotional rapport between them was as intense as the sexual one.

'Don't go yet,' she whispered to Blake as she removed his hand from her breast and slowly started to lick and then suck his fingers.

It was surprising how sexually inventive and instinctively knowing you could be once you had the confidence of being certain you were wanted, desired . . . loved . . . your feelings and needs reciprocated.

'You do understand why I can't marry you yet, don't you?' she asked Blake gravely just before he pulled on his clothes to go to his own room.

'I understand, yes,' he agreed. 'But that still doesn't stop me from wishing you'd change your mind.'

'No,' Philippa told him firmly.

'No,' he agreed ruefully, 'but you can't blame me for trying, especially not now.'

From her bed Philippa smiled at him.

'I love you,' she told him.

In the bedroom next to her, Anya coughed sleepily. 'We aren't going to be able to keep this a secret for long, you know,' Blake warned her.

'I don't want to,' Philippa told him, and it was only when she saw the way he looked at her that she realised how afraid he had actually been, despite her reassurance, that a part of her was holding back from committing herself to him.

As she held out her arms to him and he came into them he told her thickly, 'I love you too much to bear the thought of losing you now, but...'

'You won't lose me,' she promised him.

When he held her face in his hands and pushed her hair back off her face, cradling her jaw as he bent to kiss her, she was filled with a sense of strength and purpose, an awareness of being in control of her own destiny; of knowing that Blake loved and accepted her as she was, unconditionally and without any reservation.

As she loved him.

The future they would all share was there waiting for them, but to reach out greedily for it, to act in panic rather than in the sure knowledge that their love would endure, would be a step backwards in time for her, back to the old insecurity and lack of self-esteem she was only just beginning to recognise and push aside.

Their love would be all the better, all the stronger, all the more mature if she listened to what her intelligence was telling her as well as her heart—and so would she.

Knowing that Blake understood and accepted how she felt made her feel, not insecure that because he wasn't trying to push her into an immediate marriage he didn't love her enough, as the old Philippa would have felt, but aware instead of just how deep his love actually was.

EPILOGUE

Three years later

'RIGHT—have we got everyone ...?'

Philippa smiled as she heard the chorus of response to Blake's question.

'I'll take Rachel, shall I?' Anya offered, softly removing one of the sleeping babies from the rear of the car before calling over her shoulder, 'Come on, Rory—you take Simon.'

Over their heads she and Blake exchanged glances. Life wasn't always as harmonious as this, especially when the twins were awake.

They would be one in two months' time, walking and creating even more havoc. A rueful smile curled her mouth.

She had been in the second year of her Open University course when she had discovered she was pregnant. At first she hadn't been sure how Blake would react. After a year of marriage had resulted in her failure to conceive they had agreed that enough was enough; they had three children, after all. Blake was heavily involved in helping to raise finance for the new children's ward they were hoping to open, Anya and the boys were already teenagers, and they shared a happy and fulfilling life together.

She had started doing part-time voluntary work at the hospital in the children's ward and concentrating on her studies.

On her birthday they had celebrated with a small family party; and, as she had told Blake lovingly in bed later that night, she felt she had a lot to celebrate.

Four days later, when she woke up in the morning, she had felt oddly queasy.

Idiotically, she had put it down to delayed stress after the effects of the difficult months before she and Blake had married, when she had struggled to sort out the financial mess Andrew had left behind him.

When the factory had ultimately been sold at a knock-down price nowhere near its real value, she hadn't known whether to laugh or cry. After the house had been sold the bank had decided to write off what remained of its losses. Andrew's personal debts she had managed to pay off herself... after a fashion. Without the salary Blake had insisted on paying her before they married she wouldn't have stood a chance of doing so.

She *had* earned the money, he'd insisted, adding that if she didn't take it he would begin to believe that she did not want to marry him after all.

'Stress?' Susie had laughed when she'd told her how ill she'd felt. 'Sounds more like you're pregnant to me...'

Blake had come home to find her sitting in the kitchen staring into space.

'What's wrong?' he'd asked her.

'I'm not sure,' she had told him. 'Blake... do you still want children...?'

He had sighed, taking hold of her and telling her softly, 'I thought we'd agreed that what we've got is more than enough. I may not have fathered the boys or Anya but to me they *are* my children, Pip.'

'So you don't *want* any more children?' she had asked him intensely, plucking at his jacket with her fingertips.

'I have what I want,' he had told her gently. '*All* that I want... Pip, what is it?' he'd asked when he'd seen that she was crying.

'Oh, Blake, Susie thinks I could be pregnant, but you don't want me to be,' she had wailed against his chest.

Later they had agreed that her reaction had probably been caused by her burgeoning hormones. There was certainly no other reason for her to have acted so ridiculously, she had acknowledged.

Blake had been thrilled by her news, doubly so when they learned she could be carrying twins.

'It will mean you putting your career plans on hold,' he had warned her, watching her.

'Mmm,' she had agreed, laughing. 'Looks as if I never was destined to get that degree.'

'I'll push them,' Anya told Rory firmly.

'Are you sure we're not going to spoil your image, turning up *en masse* like this?' Philippa teased Blake. The hospital car park was already almost full.

It had been a unanimous decision by the senior staff that this opening of the combined children's surgical and pyschiatric ward they had all campaigned so hard for should be attended, not by a mass of local dignitaries, but by those who had done the most to make the ward's opening possible: the staff and their families and those who had done the most to raise the money for it.

The ward was in many ways Blake's baby, the idea born originally out of the success of the Fast Response Accident Unit where they had combined surgical and counselling procedures in an innovative, ground-breaking venture.

Semi-reluctantly the authorities had given in to Blake's badgering for a similar unit for children, with the proviso that they must raise half the money themselves.

On Monday the ward would open officially to its first patients, but today it was empty of beds, and was being used to celebrate the fact that against all the odds they had managed to bring it into existence.

It was worth all those cold, wet Saturdays spent in town with her collecting tin, all those car boot sales, all those fund-raising lunches and other events to see what their efforts had achieved.

The walls of the ward had been painted with bright murals, their design a gift from a talented local artist. The work itself had been done by groups of local children of varying ages, all of whom would be here this afternoon proudly showing their families their handiwork.

The walls of Blake's consulting-room were painted a warm, soft yellow. Philippa's smile faded temporarily as she reflected on the pain that would fill this room as his young patients relived their various traumas.

There was a gymnasium filled with equipment donated by local firms, and—Richard Humphries' pride and joy— a swimming-pool to help children suffering from paralysis and other forms of limb weakness, the entire cost of which had been donated by one single person.

Philippa glanced over her shoulder. Anya was talking to one of her friends, at the same time fiddling importantly with the twins' clothes and safety harnesses while the friend watched slightly enviously. Encouragingly, the twins' birth had seemed to give Anya the confidence she had previously lacked, bringing her out of the shell she sometimes retreated into.

Philippa looked round for Blake to check that the boys were with him. It was perhaps natural that now that they were growing up that they should attach themselves more to Blake than they did to her.

She had wondered at one time if Blake ever felt constricted or that his skills were not being put to their best use here in a small country hospital, but when she had tentatively suggested it to him he had shaken his head.

'Moving to a larger hospital would ultimately mean teaching instead of practising, and that isn't what I want. My career is important to me, but you and the children and the life we have built together here are far more important...'

'You could take us with you...' she had told him.

'To a city environment where I would spend almost as many hours travelling as I do working? No, that isn't what I want...'

Their time together had deepened her love for Blake and his love for her had given her a fertile soil to flourish and grow in; to mature and become far more at ease with herself.

Love, she had discovered, the right kind of love, did not constrain and impoverish, but instead conferred freedom and independence, enriching every aspect of her life.

Smiling to herself, she walked over to where Blake was standing talking to someone, slipping her hand through his arm as he turned towards her and drew her slightly closer while he introduced her to his companion. She listened to their conversation with half an ear while she studied the other guests, her attention suddenly caught by a familiar face.

Quietly she watched as she saw Joel turn towards his wife. His arm rested easily on his son's shoulders, and his wife's mouth was curled into a smile as she spoke to him. Their daughter, taller than her mother, laughed at whatever it was her mother had said.

As though he was suddenly aware of her scrutiny, Joel turned his head and looked at her.

Briefly their eyes met and then disengaged. She had no regrets about what they had shared, at least not for herself. From the desolation and despair which had been, in its different ways, Andrew's cruel legacy to them both, she knew she had come through a stronger, more emotionally balanced woman.

It had after all been a major turning point in her life, a recognition of her right to express herself sexually as a woman. What she had shared with Joel had unlocked the door which had allowed her to step confidently into her new life with Blake.

Without the knowledge of her sexual response to Joel, she might have hesitated, unsure if what she was experiencing wasn't merely a throwback to her teenage crush.

No. She had no regrets. Had Joel?

As Joel turned away from watching Philippa he saw that Sally was watching him, a faint shadow smudging her eyes.

He reached out to touch her, but before he could say anything Neil Saunders came up to him.

'Have you got a minute, Joel?' he asked him.

Excusing himself to Sally, Joel turned to listen to what he wanted to say.

'I wouldn't mind specialising in paediatric nursing...once I've qualified,' Cathy commented to Sally enthusiastically. Her decision to train as a nurse had surprised and pleased Sally, and she had encouraged and helped her as much as she could.

She was working part-time again now, a decision she and Joel had made together when he had discovered how uncomfortable she felt with the transposition of their traditional roles.

It hadn't been easy, talking about how she felt...for either of them.

There had been times when she had wondered if they or their marriage could survive such painful honesty, but Joel had refused to give up or to let her do so and in his determination she had recognised the same strength which had originally drawn her to him.

It had been Joel too who had suggested that they go for counselling and that it might be easier for them to be open and honest about the sexual problems within their marriage in front of someone else. 'It isn't a matter of blaming or accusing,' he had told her when she had cried and said that she knew he thought it was all her fault. 'I still love you, Sal, and you still love me...but we both know that that isn't enough.'

And he had been right; it had been easier to say how she felt through an intermediary. It had made the whole issue somehow less emotive.

'When we've had a row or a disagreement about something...when you've ignored me all evening, I can't suddenly switch off from that when we go to bed and become sexually turned on,' she had told Joel.

'I need to feel that you want me...not just for sex...that you're prepared to take the trouble to...to arouse me before we go to bed,' she had told him uncomfortably when the counsellor had invited her to explain her feelings...

'How can I do that when whenever I come near you you push me away?' Joel had countered. 'You complain if I touch you in front of the kids, and the bedroom's the only place where we have any privacy...where we're on our own...'

Both of them had almost been equally surprised when she had told the counsellor how ambivalent she had felt about Joel's vasectomy, how although on one level she had known he had made the right decision, on another she had felt almost cheated.

Joel had been openly distressed by her admission. He too would have liked another child, other children, he had admitted, and he had felt guilty at not being in a position to support a larger family. The spectre of his own childhood poverty had haunted him, though, along with his embarrassment over their hand-to-mouth existence and his father's lack of status.

It was only now that he was actually coming to terms with those feelings and becoming able to value his father's good points, rather than to focus on the others which as a child had caused him so much embarrassment.

Listening to him falteringly and uncomfortably revealing how he had felt about his childhood had moved Sally unbearably, rekindling all the tenderness and emotion she had felt for him when they first met.

It had been his offer to undergo a reversal of his vasectomy operation if that was what she wanted that had touched her the most, though.

'No. You were right,' she had told him softly. 'We couldn't have afforded another baby, and now I'm content with the children we have.'

It had taken some months of counselling before she felt able to respond properly to Joel in bed, and it had been a little while after that before, totally unexpectedly and out of the blue one morning, when he was making love to her, she had realised that she was going to climax.

That had been a memorable milestone, but nowhere near as memorable as the afternoon she had paused in her housework, frowning over the unfamiliar feeling flickering through her body, not even recognising it properly for what it was until she heard Joel's voice in the kitchen and felt her stomach twist in reactive anticipation.

She hadn't said anything, almost more alarmed than pleased by what she was experiencing.

She had told Joel she wanted an early night and had then spent over an hour in the bathroom, showering, smoothing scented body lotion on to her skin, looking at herself uncertainly in the mirror, wondering if he still found the sight of her naked body arousing. She never normally initiated any lovemaking between them, and her humiliation by Kenneth had left a small, painful scar which had never quite healed.

She went to bed and lay there tensely waiting for Joel, listening to the quiet hum of the television downstairs.

An hour later, still lying there waiting, she gave in to the anger and, pulling on her dressing-gown, went downstairs.

'Sally, what is it—what's wrong?' Joel had asked her anxiously when he saw her.

What was wrong? Did he honestly not know?

Furiously she had opened her mouth to tell him and then the humour of the situation had struck her and instead she had started to laugh.

'Sal...'

Joel had got up and come towards her. Still laughing, she had held out her arms to him, the dressing-gown falling open to reveal her naked body.

They had ended up making love downstairs on the floor in front of the fire as quickly and as urgently as a couple of teenagers. And for once Joel was the one doing the protesting that the kids might come in and see them.

'Let them; I don't care,' Sally had lied recklessly.

'Oh, you don't, do you?' Joel had challenged her softly. 'Well, in that case...'

When he had started to lick his way slowly all over her body she had squirmed helplessly against him, torn between anxiety and delight.

Joel had laughed at her as she'd tried to wriggle away from him, but later, when she had given in, he had gathered up their scattered clothes and agreed that they would be far more comfortable in bed, and once there he had taken hold of her hands and asked her huskily, 'Make love to me, Sal—show me that I'm not the one doing all the wanting . . . all the needing . . . all the loving . . .'

Briefly she had hesitated, unsure if she really wanted what taking such a step would bring, half of her still wanting to cling to the passive safety of the familiar role she had created for herself; but then Joel had breathed out, his body pressing lightly against hers, and her skin had tingled where it touched his, and she'd given in to the lure of the deliciously wanton thoughts which had been tormenting her all evening.

Later she wasn't sure if it was shock or excitement that had brought that awed note of husky pleasure to Joel's voice as she'd touched him. Neither of them had ever been particularly vocal lovers, but suddenly, listening to him telling her how much she was arousing him, she'd discovered that she wanted to share with him her own excitement and need.

The extraordinary realisation that she was going to climax before he did, and that once she had she still wanted him, had been reflected in her eyes for Joel to see, and his pleasure in what she was feeling, the tears that had blurred his eyes as he'd kissed her and held her, had filled her with such a heady mixture of yielding sweetness and unfamiliar power that its strength had seemed physically to dissolve something inside her, some cold, hard, frightened barrier she had never known existed until she felt it melt away.

They had had other problems to adjust to. Joel still only worked part-time at the leisure centre and they had less money coming in now that she worked part-time as well, but somehow they managed and there were other compensations . . . like the time they spent together, like the fact that they could talk to one another . . . share their problems . . . air grievances.

Thoughtfully she looked towards Philippa, and then she saw the way she was smiling at the man with her and the small cloud lifted from her eyes.

'No, don't tell me,' she had said quietly to Joel. 'I don't want to know any more than I already know...except...do you love her?' she had asked him painfully.

'No,' he had told her, and she had known it was the truth.

She couldn't pretend that it didn't hurt, or that she would ever totally forget, but then neither could she deny that their marriage was stronger for what they had experienced, and Joel in his turn had never cross-questioned her about Kenneth.

But when Joel had explained through their counsellor what he felt was missing in their relationship she had not been able to stop herself wondering how much of the intimacy and sexual pleasure that was plainly so important to him, and which he said he did not get from her, he had found with that other woman. As he, perhaps, had wondered how much of the non-sexual attention and affection she had said she needed she had got from Kenneth.

What had happened in the past no longer held any threat or worry for her—she knew Joel loved her—but it still touched her heart with a cold finger of fear to know how close she had come to losing him.

She saw that he had finished his conversation and was walking back towards her.

'What did Neil want?' she asked him curiously.

There was an odd expression in his eyes, a mixture of elation and uncertainty. 'Colin has decided to retire early and Neil wanted to know how I felt about taking his job.'

'As assistant manager of the whole leisure centre complex?' Sally asked in surprise. Ten months ago, when Joel had passed his professional exams, the leisure centre had appointed him formally as a coach, but it hadn't been the small increase in his salary that had pleased Sally so much as their official recognition of all Joel's hard work.

They had had a small party to celebrate, and even though Joel had protested that there was no need for her to make such a fuss she had been able to tell that he was pleased.

Daphne, of course, had sniffed disdainfully, and Sally had refrained from reminding her how scathing she had been about Joel's ability to get any professional qualifications. Besides, Daphne had her own problems: Edward had apparently got in with a bad crowd at school and was not studying as hard as he should have been doing.

'Mmm...' Joel confirmed.

'What did you tell him?' Sally asked him.

'I said that I'd like some time to think about it and discuss it with you,' Joel told her.

'I'd have thought you'd jump at it... don't you want it?'

'Yes... It would be a bit of a challenge for me, but it would mean going back to full-time working... sometimes in the evening and at weekends.'

He reached for her hand and turned round slightly so that no one else could hear them as he told her softly, 'I don't want to lose what you and I have built up together, Sal... I don't want to go back to the way we were... I want the job, yes, but I want what I have with you more...'

Fiercely Sally blinked away her emotional tears, laughter dancing in her eyes in their place as she teased him, 'What you mean is you don't want to miss out on our afternoons in bed...'

'Who said I was going to miss out on them?' Joel teased back. 'There's always my lunch-hour... I like it when we have the house to ourselves and we don't have to worry about the kids overhearing us... I like it when you make those soft little noises when I touch you and I love it when...'

'You love it, full stop,' Sally told him forthrightly, giving him a little push, but she was still laughing and she didn't move away when he pulled her closer to him.

'I'll tell you what,' she murmured, teasing him provocatively. 'Get them to write a two-hour lunch-break into your contract and...'

'Two hours... Mmm... what a wonderful idea...'

'The second hour is so that you can catch up on the chores you won't have time to do if you're working full-time,' Sally told him severely.

Sharing their domestic responsibilities as well as their leisure time had become part of the new way they lived their lives, the new intimacy they had carefully and sometimes very painfully built for themselves.

'What will you do about coming here, though?' she asked him thoughtfully. Joel had become involved in the fundraising for the new children's ward and had agreed that he would help with the children's water therapy.

'Colin isn't retiring until the end of the year, which would give me time to sort something out.' She heard him groan as he told her, 'Here come Daphne and Clifford.'

As she glanced over his shoulder Sally could see her sister, resplendent in a far too fussy and frilly silk floral dress. Daphne had started to put on weight recently and the dress strained slightly at the seams.

Sally's own linen-mix chocolate-brown chainstore jacket, worn with a white T-shirt and a pair of tailored shorts, had been bought under Cathy's sternly critical eye. Sally had balked a little at first at the shorts, until she had seen the look in Joel's eyes when she'd modelled the outfit for him. 'You've got the figure for it, Mum,' Cathy had told her. 'Hasn't she, Dad?' The look in Joel's eyes had made Sally laugh and flush a little.

'She hasn't seen us yet... We've still got time to escape...' Joel whispered, grinning.

Sally looked over at Daphne, her face flushed with irritation and heat, and then she looked back at Joel. Daphne was her sister... but Joel was her husband.

'You're on,' she told him softly. 'Let's go...'

'Thanks.'

The photographer from the local paper grinned his appreciation as Stephanie and Deborah broke their pose. It would make a good front-cover print for their headline story: the local female businesswoman who had donated to the hospital the new children's water-therapy pool, standing side by side with her assistant, both of them attractive women...very attractive women. He turned his head to watch as they walked away from him, deep in conversation.

'That should get us some good free publicity,' Stephanie commented.

Deborah laughed. 'Which of course was why you decided to give Mark a fit and donate the money in the first place...'

Her boss grinned back at her. 'Well...'

'You could have bought full-page space in all the glossies for less,' Deborah pointed out to her, still smiling.

'Mmm...'

Both of them looked towards the pool.

'André says I'm getting soft in my old age,' Stephanie said.

She and her French supplier, much to everyone's surprise, but most especially to Stephanie's, had married the previous year.

'I don't want to get married,' she had wailed to Deborah on the morning of her wedding. 'Why am I doing this...why are you letting me do this...?'

'Because you love André and he's told you that unless you make an honest man out of him he's going to leave,' Deborah had told her forthrightly.

'You realise that Mark was threatening to get you to sack me for letting you do this, don't you?' Deborah pointed out severely to her now.

'Sack you? No way. Taking you on was the best decision I ever made...correction—the best decision Mark ever made... Where is he, by the way...?'

'The last time I saw him he was making eyes at another woman,' Deborah told her mock mournfully. 'And André was helping him,' she added mischievously. 'Babies,' she explained when Stephanie raised her eyebrows questioningly. 'A pair of them...twins...'

'Ah, yes, Blake Hamilton's children. Mark's still eager to become a father, then?' she asked Deborah.

'Very,' Deborah admitted, her smile dying away.

'But you don't want children?'

'Yes...yes, I do,' Deborah admitted, surprising herself a little by her admission. Seeing Mark enthusiastically if rather amateurishly clutching one or other of their friends' present crop of babies had given her a funny little feeling inside, a mixture of pain and pleasure, an odd, bittersweet twisting sensation which, although she had not told him so, had lent a new depth and intensity to her sexual responsiveness to him.

'But it's just not feasible, not at the moment, what with the way we're expanding and the fact that you and I are away so much...'

'Mmm. But Mark's at home and since you live right next door to his office...'

Deborah and Mark had bought the pretty stone town house next to Mark's office eighteen months ago, and, since Mark had been the one to urge its purchase, Deborah had remained firmly unsympathetic with his complaints that she had deliberately arranged for the builders to carry out the majority of their work while she was away...

The house was virtually finished now, its furnishings an eclectic mixture of things she had bought on her many trips abroad with Stephanie—silks and damasks from Florence, sturdy, simple cherrywood furniture from France which mingled easily with the antiques she and Mark had bargained for together at antique fairs and country markets...

'Yes, I know. Mark has said the same thing, but...'

'But you don't feel you'd want to leave him in sole charge...'

'Oh, it's not that. Mark will make a far better parent than I shall. But my career means so much to me. I do want children as well but I'm not sure if I'm ready yet, if it would be fair to the company, the baby or myself...'

'Mmm, that's a pity... I was thinking only the other night what a good thing it would be if we could manage things so that we were both pregnant at the same time…give or take a month or two, of course…'

'Both pregnant?' Deborah stared at her. 'You're not…?'

'Not yet,' Stephanie told her. 'But soon, I hope. What's wrong? I'm forty-four now, and if André and I are going to have children it will have to be soon…or don't you approve?'

'Of course I approve; it's just that I never imagined…' Deborah paused, struggling for the right words. It had been hard enough getting Stephanie to admit how much she loved André and how little she wanted to lose him, so to hear her say now that they were planning to have a child…

'I've warned André that we'll have to time things so that he or she arrives during our quiet season,' she added. 'And I thought that if things worked out that way and if we could find the right kind of nanny, she and the babies could travel with us… If they don't, I suspect we're going to have two over-besotted fathers on our hands.'

'You're really serious about this, aren't you?' Deborah asked the older woman incredulously.

'Uh-huh… Think how good it will look in our PR handouts,' Stephanie told her mischievously, 'the two of us heavily pregnant, photographed in a field full of flowers…us and them blooming!'

'There is no way that I'm going…' Deborah began, and then stopped and laughed. 'OK, I know when I'm being wound up. You said we'd time it so that we had these babies out of season…'

'Mamma Nature sometimes chooses her own season for these things,' Stephanie told her slyly.

'Not if I have anything to say about it, she doesn't,' Deborah objected. 'You really think it would work…?'

'Yes, if we wanted it to. I'm not going to pretend I'm an advocate of anyone, man or woman, being able to have it all—that's a PR myth that reality has well and truly exploded. I told myself I'd never marry again, that I was too old and too cynical to be foolish enough to fall in love, and yet I've done both and been happier for having done so than I've ever been or imagined being. I can't pretend, though, that the business doesn't mean one hell of a lot to me, or that I'd ever want to give it up, for anyone or anything. But I'm not going to pretend either that I don't want André's child, that some tiny idealistic, idiotic part of me doesn't want that very specific kind of female fulfilment.

'You've got plenty of time left to make those kind of decisions, Deborah. I haven't. Rightly or wrongly, I want to have a child.'

'Sorry...have you been waiting for me...?'

Smilingly Mark handed the baby back to Philippa.

She was a pretty little blonde with soft flaxen curls and dark blue eyes, and when she turned and looked roguishly at Deborah over her mother's shoulder Deborah looked hurriedly away, already dangerously aware of the far too strong hold those small, pudgy baby fingers could have on a vulnerable heart.

'They aren't all like that, you know,' she told Mark as she took his arm. 'Some of them are quite ugly; they cry a lot and smell...and they're sick...'

'What makes you so sure it's going to take after you?' Mark teased her.

Deborah glared at him.

'They could be like me...calm, placid...good-looking...'

'Big-headed...' Deborah added for him.

She waited a few minutes, drawing his attention to the murals on the walls of the new ward, and then said thoughtfully, 'We don't even know if I can conceive yet, anyway...'

She felt the responsive jerk of Mark's arm.

'We could give it a try, I suppose,' she added semi-musingly. 'But...'

'Deborah...'

She forced herself to look vague and innocent as Mark swung her round to face him, but her own laughter defeated her.

'Just you wait until I get you home,' Mark threatened her.

'I certainly shall,' Deborah told him mock primly. 'I don't want our child to have the embarrassment of being conceived ... Mark!' she protested as he took hold of her and started to kiss her. 'Mark ...'

'Have you heard the news about David Howarth?' Brian asked jovially as he came over to join Richard and Elizabeth. 'Apparently he's been head-hunted by one of the international industrial concerns and he's already handed in his notice... That's the official version of events; the buzz all round Area is that the Minister was so keen to see him go that they actually paid the head-hunters to find somewhere for him ...'

'Well, the truth probably lies somewhere between the two,' Richard responded judiciously.

David had ceased to bother him a long time ago ... from the date it had become official that the General was to get the new Fast Response Accident Unit, in fact.

Richard was as enthusiastic about the future of the new children's ward as Blake, but the Accident Unit continued to be his own special project ... It had opened officially the previous year, and the results they had achieved so far had far outweighed even Richard's most optimistic private hopes.

On the strength of their success Richard had been asked for advice and help by several other hospitals wanting to run a similar scheme, and Brian was beginning to become afraid that they could very easily lose their senior surgeon.

The mayor came up to claim Brian's attention. They had deliberately kept the launch of the new children's ward very low-key.

'People won't want to see the money they have donated being wasted on expensive entertainment for local dignitaries,' Blake had claimed, and Richard had fully agreed.

As Richard turned away to speak to Blake, Elizabeth watched him affectionately. It was typical of him that he bore David no malice, and typical as well that the issue of his ultimate retirement still remained.

Richard was proud of the results the Fast Response Accident Unit had achieved, and with good reason. Even David had been forced to back down and admit that the money had been well spent and, far from detracting from the service they were able to provide their other patients, had actually improved them.

'I was thinking, you know,' Richard told Elizabeth, breaking into her thoughts. 'Patrick Stowe got in touch with me the other day. He's thinking of setting up a unit similar to ours at Peterborough. He wants me to go down there and talk things over with him. I was thinking... if I did decide to retire next year it would give me more time to concentrate on that sort of thing. And I can always keep my hand in on the surgical side of things by working at Ian's practice on a part-time basis...'

'Mmm...' Elizabeth agreed. Richard would be sixty within a couple of years... young enough to build up a part-time secondary career which would give him a sense of purpose and self-worth. She smiled warmly at him. 'It's certainly worth thinking about...'

'I know what you're thinking, Liz,' Richard told her quietly. 'That all I'm doing is delaying the inevitable. But I am trying to come to terms with what lies ahead, to accept...' He paused, shaking his head. 'All human beings need their sense of self-worth; for us... for *men*, that self-worth is by tradition tied in with our work.'

'But men need to learn what women have always known... that there is pleasure in travelling slowly along life's byways, enjoying the journey and all its new discoveries, much more than racing through life on a motorway, blind to everything but overtaking the driver in front, oblivious to the misery and danger you're causing your passengers, their fear of the way you're controlling and risking their lives.'

'It is beginning to happen,' Richard told her. 'Look at the way Blake's reorganised the shifts in the new ward; his insistence on crèche facilities for both male and female staff... the way he himself scheduled his work to fit round his family, not the other way round. Look around you and see how men's attitudes have changed towards their children, how much more physically affectionate they are with them, how much more involved in their lives...

'We might not be wholly converted to your byways of life yet, but at least we're beginning to accept that we have to allow you your turn at the wheel and your choice of journey...'

'You, *allow* us...?' Elizabeth shook her head and laughed. 'Yes, you're right,' she agreed softly. 'It *is* happening...' She paused and then added, 'If you do decide to retire next year, I might start working part-time myself,' she told him.

'But you're in the early stages of getting your career off the ground,' Richard protested.

'My career can still progress, but at a pace of my choosing,' Elizabeth told him.

Richard looked at her for a moment and then told her softly, 'You don't have to do that, you know. You've already made more than enough sacrifices for me... for us over the years...'

'It isn't a sacrifice,' Elizabeth told him. 'You're my husband, Richard. I want to be with you... And I want to work as well, and in my world—a *woman's* world—there's room for both.'

'Mmm...seems like a very good world to live in to me...a very good world indeed,' Richard told her as he reached for her hand.

FULFILMENT
Barbara Delinsky

Diandra Casey and Greg York had been
rivals for years. Now, forced to work
together, they are in competition once
more—for control of the legacy founded by
their grandfathers. The Caseys and the
Yorks share a history laced with bitterness,
but also with love. As Diandra and Greg
work together to untangle their past, the
hostile atmosphere suddenly becomes
charged with something quite different—
something hot and blazing, passionate and
eternal.

The discovery of a priceless family
heirloom, with a history all of its own,
awakens a 300-year-old legend that they're
both powerless to deny…

> "One of this generation's most
> gifted writers of contemporary
> women's fiction"
> Romantic Times (USA)

MIRA

FIRE AND ICE
Diana Palmer

Like the heroine of one of her novels, bestselling author Margie Silver was willing to rise to Cal Van Dyne's challenge. The arrogant tycoon vowed that Margie's sister would never marry his brother; Margie was just as determined that the wedding would take place. Margie expected the worst from Cal—but not the cynical game of love he played with her on his lavish Florida estate. Suddenly Margie was gambling with her sister's future—and her own—with a dangerous adversary who made his own rules…until he met his match.

With over ten million copies of her books in print, Diana Palmer's readers treasure her emotional style. A gift for telling the most sensuous tales with charm and humour is Ms Palmer's trademark.

MIRA

TEST OF TIME
Jayne Ann Krentz

HE MARRIED FOR THE BEST
REASON…
They had a lot in common and would be
great together in business—and in bed.
Marriage to Katy Randall would also help
make people forget just how rough Garrett
Coltrane's past had been.

SHE MARRIED FOR THE ONLY
REASON…
Love. But the growing fear that shook her
during the ceremony exploded into
heartbreak when she discovered that love
was the only thing Garrett didn't want.

DID THEY STAND A CHANCE AT
MAKING THE ONLY REASON THE
REAL REASON TO SHARE A
LIFETIME?

*"A master of the genre…nobody does it
better!"*

Romantic Times (USA)

PRIVATE SINS
Janice Kaiser

BRETT—the stunning, brilliant attorney tested and tempted beyond reason when she falls in love with her husband's son.

AMORY—the new supreme court justice who will put his heart on the line to keep his young wife—and his life on the line to defend his beliefs.

ELLIOT—a political attaché trapped by his contempt for one woman and his forbidden love for his father's new wife.

HARRISON—a senator whose scandalous private life may cost him much more than his career.

Only by exposing the private sins and secret passions of this very public family can they fulfil a destiny that is theirs for the taking. Janice Kaiser delivers a red-hot novel of a powerful family—and the ambitions and desires that rule their lives…

"A bold, powerful novel."

Affair de Coeur (USA)

MIRA

LOVE CHILD
Patricia Coughlin

It was no more than a stone's throw from
the million-dollar mansions of Newport's
privileged few to their servants' weathered
frame houses, but they were worlds apart.
And yet, the cold and elegant facade of
Newport society concealed a bitter secret
that linked two proud, troubled families
from those different worlds—and two
lovers too young to understand their shared
destiny. Their love was a decades-long
drama of desire and betrayal, played out
against the glittering backdrop of America's
most exclusive—and most heartless—
playground.

*"A talent of surpassing excellence,
Ms Coughlin is one of the truly unique
voices in the romance genre today."*

Romantic Times (USA)

MIRA

FEVER
Elizabeth Lowell

Lisa Johansen, world traveller, had tasted the exotic and seen the extraordinary. But when a rancher called Rye came into her life, he ignited a feverish desire foreign to her mind, her body—and her soul.

Rye was certain Lisa was like the gold-digging women in his past. He'd been burned before, and he vowed he would make no more mistakes. Still, the sweet sting of her kisses tempted him to madness, and he knew he'd gotten dangerously close to the flame. But it was too late—he was addicted to the fire.

"For smouldering sensuality and exceptional storytelling Elizabeth Lowell is incomparable."

Romantic Times (USA)

MIRA